To Hedy —
search for truth

Amy Deardon

What Others are Saying:

"Who wouldn't want to time-travel back to first century Jerusalem to see if the Resurrection really happened? Amy Deardon has given me the next best thing with her novel bringing old Jerusalem to life. I raced through the book at lighspeed and enjoyed it immensely. Strong characters and an unpredictable plot made this a book I'll want to read again."

—**Randy Ingermanson**, Christy Award-Winning Author of
Transgression and *Oxygen*

"Amy Deardon's debut novel is compelling, intriguing and explosive! Fans of Michael Crichton, Mark Mynheir, and Creston Mapes will love the fast-paced, character-driven and suspense-filled plot. I cannot wait to see what else Deardon has in store for her fans!"

—**Thomas Phillips**, Author of *The Molech Prophecy*

"If you could go back to Christ's crucifixion, would you do it? What if the only way you could was by time-traveling with skeptics bent on proving Christianity is based on a lie? Author Amy Deardon tackles these provocative questions in her phenomenal debut novel: *A Lever Long Enough*. Readers will find themselves enveloped in the scope and import of this adventurous tale where love, loyalty, and faith will be tested in the crucible of first century Jerusalem."   —**Wayne Thomas Batson**, Bestselling author of
The Door Within trilogy, *Isle Of Swords*, and *Isle Of Fire*

"Did Jesus rise from the dead? Deardon wrestles with this question in an exhilarating adventure full of high technology, romance, and treachery that excites the imagination. There are no easy answers, only compelling arguments that will challenge your beliefs—whatever they may be."

—**Ralph Hamilton MD**, Professor of Surgery, Emeritus,
University of Pennsylvania

"In *A Lever Long Enough*, Deardon expertly weaves science, technology, fact, and fiction into a riveting tale. Deardon's ability to take the reader from within a top-secret military lock-down facility to a realistically depicted 1st Century Jerusalem makes this science fiction thriller a stunning and captivating read from start to finish."

—**A.K. Arenz**, author of *The Case of the Bouncing Grandma*

"This is a book packing multiple big pleasures within its pages—clever time-travel adventure, political intrigue, fascinating historical settings, philosophical/religious challenges, and a captivating mix of imagination and technological authenticity. Deardon's exhaustive and meticulous research and her deft writing skills set this book well apart from the crowd."

—**Donna W. Payne**, PhD, Biomedical researcher, co-author of
The Handel's Messiah Family Advent Reader

"Whiz-bang twists in a never-ending series of surprises and subterfuge drag the reader right inside all the thrills. Breathless shocks, sweaty fingertips, romantic suspense, forbidden faith, a trail of corpses—yes, this one is definitely hard-hitting...Ten out of ten! I hope to see more work soon from this brilliant author."

—**Grace Bridges**, author of
Faith Awakened and *Legendary Space Pilgrims*

"A fiction strong enough—To borrow a phrase from Archimedes, this "Lever" might just move your world. Smart, action-packed, and meticulously researched, this thriller is thoroughly believable. So buckle up and get ready for your own 'time throw'—once you open this book, you will immediately find yourself transported five hours into the future. Be sure to clear your schedule!"

—**Amy Fogelstrom Chai**, MD, MS,
author, columnist, educator

"A Lever Long Enough is a fascinating story of faith and action. Ms. Deardon's use of technology keeps the adventure high, and Biblical accuracy makes the story factual and believable. I could barely put the book down, and am eagerly anticipating the next part of the adventure."

—**Michael Saunders**, Biblical Teacher,
The Holy Land Experience

"Fascinating and intriguing...unpredictable and provocative... I look forward to the sequel."

—**T.H. Shumpert**, Ph.D., P.E., Professor Emeritus
Electrical and Computer Engineering,
Auburn University

A LEVER LONG ENOUGH

A Novel

Amy Deardon

 Taegais Publishing, LLC
Glenwood, Maryland

ISBN 978-0-9818997-2-5

Scripture taken from the Holy Bible, New International Version.
Copyright 1973, 1978, 1984 by International Bible Society.
Used by permission of Zondervan Publishing House. All rights reserved.

Cover Design and Cover Image by Archer Ellison, Inc. (www.Bookcovers.com)
Interior Book Design by Chris Yavelow (www.ChrisYavelow.com)
Author photograph by Kathleen Tully (www.kathleentully.com)

Published by:

Taegais Publishing, LLC
Glenwood, Maryland

Taegais books may be purchased in bulk for educational,
business, fund-raising, or sales promotional use.
For information, please contact Sales@taegais.com
Visit our website: www.Taegais.com
To contact the author: AmyDeardon@yahoo.com

Publisher's Cataloging-in-Publication data

Deardon, Amy.
    A lever long enough / Amy Deardon.
    p. cm.
    ISBN 978-0-9818997-2-5
    1. Jesus Christ -- Fiction. 2. Time travel -- Fiction. 3. Space and
time -- Fiction. 4. Israel -- Fiction. I. Title.

PZ4.D2849 Le 2009
813.54--dc22   2008933453

1 3 5 7 9 10 8 6 4 2

Printed in the United States of America
Printed on Recycled Paper
Published January 2009

To my family and dear friends.

Acknowledgments

I'd like to especially thank the following gentlemen for their extraordinary expertise:

Rev. G. Michael Saunders, Sr. M.Div., a researcher and teacher at the Holy Land Experience in Orlando, Florida, with impressive knowledge of first century Jerusalem. Any errors persisting in this book are surely not his fault! I was overwhelmed by his generous gifts of time and knowledge for this project.

Gary Habermas, Ph.D., Distinguished Research Professor and Chair, Department of Philosophy and Theology, Liberty University, Lynchburg VA, who kindly let me borrow for this novel a tool from his scholarship.

Mike Licona, Ph.D., debater extraordinaire, who patiently answered my questions throughout the development of this book.

Every book says at the front: "This couldn't have been written without the help and support of many people…" Well, it's true. While I'm the one who sweated over putting the words down, there were many friends who encouraged me, listened to the story, and critiqued what I had to make it better. You were with me in the trenches. Thanks, guys!

Mom and *Dad* who thought I could do it, and
who contributed greatly to this project

Lex who had creative ideas

Emily who also understands the story template

Grant who was always cheerful

Sarah who was with this book every step of the way

Marcel who encouraged

Susan M. who gave such good counsel

Jim who found interesting facts for my research

Donna, *Fran*, and *Bev*, my fellow "Weaklings,"
who believed in me

Christina who walked with me through a dark place

Jane who gave the best, and hardest, critique

Chandra who had gentle words

Susan F. who listened

Cheri who was enthusiastic

Amy C. who refined what was already there to make it better

Jean P. who gave excellent strategic advice

Chris who copyedited the manuscript with eagle eyes

Terry who was kind to a first-time author

"Give me a lever long enough, and a place to stand, and single-handed I can move the world."

—*Archimedes of Syracuse*
287-212 B.C.E.

1

THE ANCIENT QUMRAN MOUNTAINS were hard and dusty, fists of rock pushing upwards to strike the face of the sky. As the helicopter trailing the two paragliders banked to the left, Benjamin watched the lead figure closely. Sara soared between two peaks, smooth, so smooth, as she dodged a cliff and spun another turn in her ascent.

Benjamin shook his head. "She flies that thing like it was a part of her." He saw his pilot, Caleb Mendel, glance over at him.

"They're looking good," Mendel said. The earphone in Benjamin's helmet crackled, the voice tinny and mechanical from the transmitter.

"I'm pleased."

The two paragliders dangled about twenty feet below the arched cloth wings, the fanned lines passing in a spread to their hands, but Sara flew far ahead—silhouetted against the next cliff now, too close to it. Even as he watched, she executed another sharp turn and dove down, circling out of it and up again as the giant fan strapped to her back pushed the wing's edge forward. Benjamin let out his breath.

"She sure likes to cut it fine," Mendel said. "That gust of wind almost knocked her against the rock."

"She's all right," Benjamin replied.

There were three and a half days until FlashBack.

The pilot touched the controls, and Benjamin felt the slight dip as the helicopter rolled to the right on a longer trajectory to keep from staying ahead of the gliders. *Thumpa thumpa thumpa...*he felt the vibration as the rotors of the helicopter shook the pod. They were going around the turn now and the waters of the Dead Sea spread out before them, glinting red in the late sun. Several small boats floated near a trawler—Benjamin knew they were searching for the weak signal of a nuclear battery.

He was thinking of FlashBack, and the time machine.

Mendel glanced over at the trawler. "It doesn't look like they're wrapping up yet. Can they continue to search in the dark?"

"Not as well, but they will. If they find the data now, it will let some pressure off."

He shifted in his seat. The men on the boats were searching for the data capsule that he wouldn't deposit in the Dead Sea for another week, yet it may have been there since before the Roman conquest of Jerusalem. It was unclear how the time strands worked.

"If it's there, it could have corroded through," the pilot said.

Benjamin shook his head. "Unlikely." The titanium capsule was sixteen inches in diameter with extraordinarily tight seals. More probable that it was masked from detection by a two-thousand-year-old coating of deposited salt.

He turned his attention back to the soldiers riding on the air currents. How different would it be when they went back?

"Let's finish up," he said. The sky was bruising dark as the sun fell, and the gliders still had a good ten minutes to go before they landed.

Rebecca Sharett, behind Sara, was having trouble keeping to a smooth course. Benjamin knew that she wasn't confident in the air, but really, it wasn't critical, since they would use the paraglider only as a desperate measure to deliver the information capsule so that it could be carbon-dated. It was treacherous, that was for sure.

Sara cornered another turn, and Benjamin smiled despite himself. She was so smooth. Not just this, but everything to which she touched her hand, or her mind. Lately she seemed to be in his awareness more and more—

Don't think about her.

The helicopter turned course, following the gliders through the hard range. There were long shadows over the terrain.

"One more line of mountains," Mendel said.

"Excellent time," Benjamin replied. "Sara would be running under three and a half hours if she weren't turning back all the time to wait for Rebecca."

From the top of his helmet, the pilot pulled down infrared goggles against the growing dark. Full sunset now, deep shadows merged to black on the ground. Benjamin reached for his own set.

They flew on.

To the west the city lights of Jerusalem scattered the infrared image to a green shadow on the periphery of his vision. As they topped the last ring of mountains, he watched Sara glide several hundred feet farther, turn off the fan's engine on her back, and begin her landing cone of intention. He shook his head. Despite the darkness, Sara barely slowed. She was going to get herself killed.

The new Israeli military complex loomed ahead: multiple buildings guarded by a wickedly sharp perimeter fence and towers. It had been locked down for the past week in preparation for FlashBack. He watched the pilot flip on the microphone to receive clearance for landing in the restricted airspace.

"We're set," Mendel said after a moment. "They're putting on the lights now."

The helicopter jostled in the air current, and Mendel pulled up on the controls. "Wind's picking up."

Benjamin glanced at the lights of the complex, then back at his soldiers. Sara touched down, the cloth wing collapsing behind her like a giant blanket. The two men on the transport vehicle ran forward and began pulling out the wing before she'd even unclipped the harness. Rebecca began to circle. The helicopter whipped through one last circuit as Mendel began their own landing sequence.

Then the pilot made a sudden move.

Benjamin looked over. "What is it?"

The pilot stared hard at the residential building through his infrared goggles, as if trying to see the afterimage of something fleeting. Benjamin hadn't seen anything himself.

"I'm not sure," Mendel said slowly.

2

GENERAL SHIMON GIDEON, second-in-command of the complex guarding the time machine, shut off the palm-sized transmitter and threw it down on his bed. That was it, then. He was committed. It would go ahead in a few hours.

He stood by the window and looked out six floors below to the wired-in concrete courtyard. The lights of a helicopter moved distant toward the docking bay on the other side of the complex, and beyond that he could see the desert range of the Qumran Mountains, now barely visible, shaded purple and grey in the last rays of sunlight. With an impatient snap he pulled the drapery string. The curtains whipped dark across the window.

The transmitter was state-of-the-art, a communication device that used an infrared laser to pulse compressed messages to a geosynchronous satellite. The signals would be received by Marc Raseac, half a world away. Gideon had made his contact at 18:15 hours—a quarter after six in the evening—giving Raseac the timetable and a message to be relayed to the other operative inside the complex: check the dead drop in one hour. There was no return message for him, nor had he expected any. It was his show now.

He took a deep breath.

Gideon's directive from Raseac was clear: no use of the time machine until after the treaty had been signed, since Raseac didn't want the time machine to be considered functional until he could seize control.

On Gideon's advice, Raseac had advanced the date for the signing with Israel to less than one month from now, assuming Israel would abandon FlashBack in favor of a more certain contingency plan to deal with the followers. The time machine was extraordinary, certainly, but it was still a prototype where its inventors had only just started to achieve safe jumps to the past. Without further testing, a leap of two thousand years was unprecedented.

Alas, it hadn't mattered to the prime minister and the Knesset hard-liners—not after they'd considered the alternatives. FlashBack, the jump back in time, was going ahead. And, as Raseac's man, Gideon alone had to stop it now, no excuses.

Sabotage.

Blast his own ambitions.

Per Gideon's request, Raseac had notified his operative that the action was tonight. The operative should have retrieved the explosives and janitor's uniform by now, and just needed to learn the exact time and review the schematics. In a few minutes, Gideon would make the run to deposit final instructions at the dead drop.

The inner sanctum of the time machine was guarded by armed checkpoints, cameras, and locked doors keyed to biometric scans. Two nights ago, Gideon had been able to sneak through a "back path" that he'd planted into the computer's program long ago. That code had allowed him to substitute the operative's retinal data-points for those of the janitor scheduled for duty tonight. Gideon didn't want to know what would happen, or already had happened, to that man.

But a dozen things could still go wrong. Gideon simply had to have faith that the operative was well trained and capable. Raseac would permit nothing less.

Gideon picked up the optical disc for the dead drop. Time to go now. It wouldn't do for the operative to see him leaving the area.

3

SARA STOOD in the doorway of the hangar, and Benjamin hid his smile as she stepped back.

"All set?" he asked.

A loose braid kept falling over her shoulder; her dark hair was disheveled from wearing the helmet for so long. Her face was smudgy and sweaty, and her fatigues were covered with gritty Qumran sand. Even so, Benjamin thought she seemed softer right now—nothing like what some of the other soldiers called her: the ice princess.

But she distracted him. Not good.

"Where's Captain Sharett?" he asked.

Sara rolled her eyes. "Rebecca didn't want to wait. Said something about needing to put her feet up for the evening."

"Didn't you tell her I wanted to see you both after the ride?"

Sara shrugged. "After we waited a few minutes, she didn't think you were coming."

He shook his head. Maybe Rebecca wasn't the best choice for linguist on this mission, despite the fact that she had an extraordinary ear. It was many little actions like this one. Perhaps being nonmilitary, she wasn't used to the necessary discipline.

"I'll talk to her tomorrow," he said. "Meanwhile, how do you feel about the mission? Is everything on schedule?"

"I think so. They installed the telescopic mirror in the pod today, and I still need to check that."

"When?"

She nodded. "I'm scheduled for tomorrow morning but I want to get there early, before things get crazy. They're opening up the area for countdown preparations when? 05:00 hours?"

"05:30, I think."

"Plenty of time. I'm sure it's fine."

Benjamin nodded. "Anything else?"

"No."

"Let's walk back then."

The hangar was empty as they passed through, only long shadows, minimal lights, echoing footsteps. The seal over the complex had been placed last week, and would remain until FlashBack was completed. Benjamin was disturbed about Mendel's observation of infrared flashes, but knew the pilot would take care of reporting it right after his post-flight check. Benjamin would check tomorrow morning.

Sara half-stumbled, and he caught her instantly under her forearm.

"Sorry," she said. "Thanks. The heel of my boot is wobbly." She moved, rested her hand on his a moment longer than was necessary.

He forced himself to move away.

"You and Rebecca looked good out there. You made remarkable time."

"It clicked today."

"I was worried about you," he said, but softly so she wouldn't hear him.

She glanced over at him and smiled. "Let's eat."

They parted at the entrance to the residential section. Benjamin watched her until she turned the corner toward her apartment, and then headed to the mess to bring back dinner.

The mission would start in a little more than three days.

Israel had been torn apart by civil unrest ever since the reconstruction of the third Temple and the recommencement of the sacrifice three years ago. A barbaric custom—the sacrifice—but inexplicably popular, and it had awakened a new religious fervor. The people had elected so many splinter religious groups into the Knesset Parliament that not a single government coalition could be maintained. Although the moderates nominally controlled the Knesset, the Jewish Orthodox attached steel strings to their support of any measure under vote. As more people attended the daily sacrifices, the priests grew more vocal as a political force.

Arising close on the heels of the Orthodox revival had been a groundswell of the followers of the Way, named for the term used by the first century followers of Yeshua. Benjamin didn't understand what had precipitated it. Was it just a slingshot reaction, the other pole of religious extremism? The conversions seemed dramatic enough, though. These followers accepted Yeshua—Jesus—as their Messiah, and never missed an opportunity to challenge the nation to listen to their claims.

Because the Orthodox held the political power, the followers were stigmatized and prevented from working in most responsible positions or serving in the Israeli Defense Forces. Yet, they continued to multiply. The civil unrest between the followers and the Orthodox was explosive; even the moderates feared that the Jewish identity, kept intact for thousands of years, might be engulfed.

The situation might have been manageable—just barely—except for the threat from without, and the fact that the followers could scuttle the treaty with Marc Raseac and thereby plunge the country into open war with neighboring countries if they weren't stopped. Now.

From the officers' mess Benjamin brought back falafels, salads, two oranges, coffee, and cake. When he knocked on Sara's door half an hour later, she was showered and dressed in clean fatigues.

"It smells great," she said. "I'm famished."

Sara's apartment was small, with slate blue carpeting. The door from the hallway entered into a twelve-by-fifteen-foot living room with a low-slung couch and wooden padded chair. The walls were spare and efficient, no pictures or photographs, and a utilitarian metal bookshelf stacked with optical discs and a few print textbooks. Benjamin had read the titles before: subjects on astrophysics, computer science, and the like. It was as if Sara were afraid to reveal herself, even here in her own quarters.

Considering the trauma she'd gone through he almost understood this. But thirty-two, he thought, was too young for her to bury herself like this.

Sara had been an American astronaut on the space station *Eagle's Nest* during its spectacular demise four years ago. Although NASA had cleared her, the only other surviving astronaut had blamed her for initiating the events that led to the space station's destruction and the deaths of the rest of the crewmembers, including Sara's twin brother. The American press made her a national pariah. That was when she'd left the USA to become an Israeli citizen.

In a covert exchange with American intelligence, Israel verified that she'd done nothing wrong, and Sara was tapped into the pool of twelve candidates training for FlashBack. Last week during the final selection, she had been chosen—as Benjamin's second in command. Some people still didn't trust Sara, but Benjamin had worked with her enough over the past eighteen months to have confidence in her abilities, judgments, and loyalties.

In the narrow ribbon of her kitchen, the lights reflected brightly as they sat to eat. Sara's hair was damp from her shower. As she pushed her hair back, one strand fell over her eyes, and Benjamin smiled at her.

"Three days."

She nodded. "It'll be here quick."

Benjamin sighed. He and Tamar had experienced dinners like this before each of his missions in General Gideon's ReachDeep Special Forces unit; all they could do was speak trite phrases while their emotions percolated beneath the surface. He felt that rusty stab of anger and guilt again—his wife was dead, and he was not guarding his thoughts…

He was an island. And Sara was not Tamar.

She was peeling an orange across from him, precisely cutting the skin into strips and removing them without a break in the membrane beneath. Concentrate. He could smell the orange oils of the peel; see them squirt over her hands in translucent droplets. Sara wiped her fingers on a paper napkin, and then separated the sections one by one, pulling the white pith and string away and lining them onto a plate. He took a deep breath. It would be all right.

She offered the plate to him. "Want some?"

He took just a moment to focus.

"Benjamin?" She smiled at him. He glanced at her, then the orange sections.

"Oh. Thanks."

The fruit stung his tongue, and Sara seemed to relax. She was one of the most competent soldiers he'd ever known, smart and cool under pressure. It would be all right.

The reality of the time machine, actually going back in time—*dear God, this was real.*

4

DEEP IN THE COMPLEX'S SECURITY COORDINATION AREA,
Colonel Aaron jabbed a forefinger at the computer screen
showing an image from section C-17b of the complex.
Aaron's second, Etan Gold, leaned over his shoulder.

"Drenger's late," Aaron said. "He has a presentation in
five minutes with Historics."

The shadowed figure clutched a binder as he jogged down
the hall, and Aaron gave a punctuated laugh.

"He'll just make it," Etan said.

Aaron moved to the next camera view in the sequence.

The hidden cameras were so ubiquitous throughout the
complex that only a handful of people at the senior level had
any idea how closely everything was tracked. Computers used
data from badge RFID chips to collect movements of
hundreds of people, compare them with updated schedules,
and flag any inconsistencies. Even though Aaron's team of
twelve security officers reviewed these data twice a day, Aaron
also made a point of spot-checking the raw information.

Several years earlier, a worldwide depression had pulled
most countries beneath the umbrella organization of the New
World Order, initiated and held together by the charismatic
United Nations leader Marc Raseac. With the surrounding
countries unified and threatening overwhelming war against
Israel, Raseac had also promised peace for Israel. His promise
was as close to an ironclad guarantee as was possible, Aaron
thought. Raseac had completed amazing negotiations between
the individual warring nations of Africa and in Eastern

Europe. The moderates and most Orthodox were eager—panting—for his help.

Just one problem remained: the followers of the Way in Israel, those who claimed Yeshua's name, provoked so much turmoil through their resistance to Raseac that they threatened to scuttle Israel's signing of the seven-year treaty.

Controlling the followers seemed impossible. There were too many to arrest or deport, and sanctions had proved ineffective. One option remained, initiated more than two years ago as a desperate measure to regain unity in the country: FlashBack. Now FlashBack was three and a half days away, and if it couldn't stop the followers, the treaty would not be signed.

"Looks reasonable." Aaron scanned the computer readout of activities for the past twenty-four hours. "Have you found anything?"

Etan shook his head. "It's all good. We're safe."

But it took more than the machines and the technology to protect the time machine, Aaron thought. There was the human element.

"We're not safe until the mission's over," he replied.

Etan flushed, and Aaron studied his second for a moment. Etan was smart, curious, and exemplary in security work. He was twenty-eight years old, and hopefully recognized that he had his whole life in front of him if the country could survive to sign Raseac's treaty.

Aaron turned back to the computer display. Nothing was out of place, yet he couldn't push away the feeling of disquiet. Was it just edginess, since the mission was so close now? Well, he wouldn't let down his guard.

He and Etan finished the routine check, then left for dinner. It was almost 19:00 hours, seven in the evening, and FlashBack was set to go. Things would be crazy tomorrow morning when they opened the most secure area of the time machine to the many engineers and technicians needed to make final preparations for the transport pod that would carry the soldiers back in time.

HE WAS GETTING TOO OLD for this cloak-and-dagger stuff.

Gideon had just completed the dead drop at the designated restroom, hiding the encrypted optical memory disc in a high chamber of the toilet paper receptacle. He'd been back in his office for less than five minutes and had just activated the camera blackout sequence near the time machine when he heard a knock at his office door.

Not now. His thoughts were churning with the sabotage that would be accomplished in a few hours; there were so many variables.

The knock came again—sharp—and he cleared his throat. "One moment." He checked his office for anything incriminating. Clear.

"Who is it?" He thought it might be General Landau, the commander of the base and his only superior. The time was 19:13 hours, almost a quarter after seven in the evening.

Another knock, and he opened the door.

It wasn't Landau, but for a moment, he didn't recognize the man facing away from the door wearing fatigues. When the man turned, Gideon saw who it was.

"Caleb Mendel."

"Shalom, General. I'm sorry to bother you."

Gideon waved his hand. "My door is always open. What can I do for you?"

The pilot looked behind him, not sneakily but as if checking the area. The large common room of the suite was empty. "Sir, I need to talk to you. Make a report."

What was this about?

"Of course, of course. Come in, please."

Mendel was one of the chopper pilots who had worked for him in ReachDeep, the Special Forces unit for hostage rescue and impossible missions. Along with Gideon's star Benjamin Feinan, and a half-dozen others, the pilot had come along when Gideon took the job as second in command of the time machine complex.

Now Gideon feigned a caring tone as he reached behind him and closed the door. "What can I do for you, son?"

Mendel sat in the straight-backed chair facing Gideon so that his face was in semi-profile. The older man moved behind his desk and sat down.

"Sir," Mendel said, "I need to make a security report. I saw some unauthorized transmission signals an hour ago."

Gideon felt a thrill of panic, pushed it down.

"Have you told Colonel Aaron about this yet?"

Mendel shook his head. "He's not in his office. But I saw the light under your door."

The situation was retrievable, then. Gideon let out a deep breath.

"All right," he said. "Tell me everything that happened. From the beginning."

The pilot nodded. "Yes, sir. I was flying surveillance over the Qumran range, following Major Levenson and Captain Sharett in their paragliders. They returned to the compound right after sunset. The time was, I think, 18:15 hours."

That's about right, Gideon thought.

"I had put on my infrared goggles because it was getting dark and we were at a low altitude. I made one more circuit to check the complex perimeter. Everything was clear. But sir," he paused, "as I was flying in to dock, I saw pulsed infrared flashes coming from the complex, like those from a narrow communication beacon."

"Where was the beacon?" Gideon asked him carefully.

Mendel shook his head. "I'm not sure. This side of the building, but they were over before I could see more than a flash or two."

Thank goodness for that.

"Don't you think you might have been mistaken about them being communication flashes? Perhaps you saw some kind of localization signal."

The pilot sat back. "No, sir," he said. "They were coming from the residential area, a part of the building that no signals have a right to come from. I'm sure they were some kind of unauthorized communication."

It was an amazing fluke that the infrared signal had been seen at all. The compressed transmission lasted no more than eight or nine seconds. But he could handle this.

Gideon frowned. "Son, this is a serious accusation. Do you know what you're saying?"

Mendel shifted in the chair. "Of course, sir. That's why I want to file a report immediately."

"You're saying there may be a mole in the complex."

"Yes, sir."

Gideon thought for a moment. He knew Mendel would stick on these communication flashes until their origin was solved. There was little time to defuse this.

"All right then," Gideon said. "I need to make a few inquiries. This should be kept quiet for now."

"Sir, respectfully, I want to report the incident to Colonel Aaron."

Gideon held his hand out and lowered it, a calming gesture.

"Yes, Mendel, of course. I meant quiet from the general population. You're right, Colonel Aaron needs to know. I'll go now to tell him what you told me. He's in the security coordination area."

"If that's where he is, I'd like to save time and go with you. If that's all right, sir."

The boy's fate couldn't be helped then. Gideon sighed. "Of course. Just a moment."

He unlocked the secure drawer in the bottom of his desk, pulled it out, and unlatched the metal shield covering the top of the drawer.

The pilot looked at him questioningly.

"I need to lock up these secure files before we go," Gideon lied. "I was reviewing them when you came in."

Mendel stood up.

"Let's go," Gideon said.

The pilot had his hand on the doorknob when Gideon sidled behind him. He depressed the top of the plastic vial directly in Mendel's face, and then again.

The drug wasn't working. Mendel was fighting him now, reaching out to grab his wrists, leaning into him.

Gideon felt a flash of fear, steeled himself. Mendel would be able to easily defeat him if he wasn't subdued quickly. *Blast!* What other weapons were at hand? Nothing good...

Just hold on. Gideon shook the vial and sprayed more drug at Mendel. Come on.

The pilot was forcing him back now. He was strong, fit from training, and half Gideon's age. Gideon had to step back.

Then Mendel's eyes did a slow double blink.

Gideon sprayed him again.

The drug, niadezolam, was a newly-developed quick-acting inhalational agent that induced profound memory loss for two or three hours before administration—not perfectly, but it was the best there was. The niadezolam vials had been formulated for FlashBack as a way to erase inappropriate memories in natives without inducing lasting harm. Gideon had retained a few vials for his own purposes.

Mendel's hands dropped to his side and he seemed disoriented. Then he stiffened and toppled forward. Gideon was barely able to catch him on the way down.

The boy had begun seizing.

Oh blast it, he'd given him an overdose, and that complicated things a hundredfold. Anyone else in the office suite would hear Mendel's feet thumping on the floor. Gideon would have to explain Mendel's presence.

The pilot was having a hard time of it: his back arching, his head hitting the floor. Gideon watched Mendel dispassionately. Just another minute or two, enough time to remove traces of the drug from Mendel's system. That's all he needed: one more minute.

Gideon heard running feet outside, as he had feared. He picked up the empty drug vial, threw it back into the drawer, and locked it. There was no other evidence in the room.

He heard pounding on the door.

"Call medical!" he barked.

6

THE DOOR TO THE DOCTOR'S PRIVATE OFFICE WAS cracked. Good. Major David Baum knocked.

"Leah?"

The doctor was behind her desk underlining a paper with a ruler and red pen, and David laughed when he saw her. "You're the most fastidious person with articles that I've ever seen. I can't believe you still print them out."

Leah Rosen looked up at him and smiled. "David. What a nice surprise."

He shook his head. "You're hopeless."

She was, really, he thought as he looked around the small office. It was one of his minor goals in life to catch it just one time in a state of disrepair. The desktop by the window was clear except for a computer and a small stack of articles on top of a manila folder, and the bookshelves nearby were aligned as if with a straightedge: medical books and reference optical discs. She was boarded in both internal and emergency medicine, the only physician on duty now that the complex had been locked down in preparation for FlashBack.

She held up one hand. "Let me finish this paragraph." He smiled; it was always so with Leah. She was fit and in her early forties, short black hair holding just a tinge of softness, and the glasses that she pushed up onto the bridge of her nose were thin-lensed with round wire frames. Today, she wore civilian khakis and an open-collared shirt under her white jacket.

"What are you reading?"

"Mmm," she said, not looking up. "Lassiter's group from the University of California. They're working with nanotherapeutics for a new drug delivery system, but I don't know why they're bothering to write it up. They weren't too successful. It's an interesting protocol, though."

David had given up both lab research and the practice of medicine—neurology—six years ago, when he'd turned thirty, in order to pursue a Ph.D. in archaeology. Now he went to one meeting a year to keep up his continuing medical education credits and maintain an active license.

"Done." Leah closed the article and brushed the edges flush with the rest of the stack. "Now, what can I do for you?"

All business, as usual.

"I was going over the meds and equipment in the first aid kit for the pod, and I didn't have the ciprofloxacin."

"Oh," she said. "Sure. I'm sorry you came all this way yourself. I could have sent Yossi to bring you some."

"No trouble."

The doctor stood up. "How much do you need?"

"Ten doses—five hundred mgs."

"Just a sec."

As she left the room, David leaned over the desk to scan the article. It was an exciting time for the advancement of medicine, but he didn't miss it. His passion was first-century Jerusalem—the buildings, the manners, and the customs—and he was grateful he'd switched fields to archaeology while he was still young enough to do so. He'd whipped through the Ph.D. in little more than four years, been recruited into the FlashBack program, and now—

The doctor pushed the door open, holding a foil sheet bulging with white pills. "You must be excited about being selected for the mission."

"It's a dream. Ten days I've known now, and I still wake up thinking it can't be true. I'll actually be going back to that time."

"Brutal time," she said. "Those Romans were not to be trifled with. I hope you can find what you need."

"We'll do our best. It's a good team."

For the past eighteen months, ten soldiers and two civilians had been training for FlashBack—three in each of the four categories of commander, archaeologist, mechanical specialist, and linguist. The complicated mission had required training in both the classroom and the field, evaluation in nineteen separate classifications, and finally, the selection of the FlashBack team a week and a half earlier.

"A good team," he repeated.

"Hmmph."

"What's that supposed to mean?"

The doctor smiled. "Oh, I didn't mean you. Or Benjamin Feinan or Sara Levenson. She really is standoffish, though, isn't she? I was thinking of your linguist. I don't understand why they didn't choose Yedaiah instead of that woman from the university. She doesn't seem quite—"

"—Military?"

The doctor shrugged.

"Rebecca will be all right." David put his hands in his pockets. "Linguistically she's far and away the best of the candidates. She has an incredible ear, and we need that edge. Benjamin will keep her in line. Believe me." He wasn't worried. He was convinced Benjamin could do anything.

"Are you ready for the mission?"

He nodded. "As much as I can be. Whether I am or not, the time will come soon enough."

"Do you have any more training before you go?"

"Some loose ends, but not too much. They're letting us rest before the big day."

"Makes sense."

An awkward silence stretched between them. David felt a twinge of urgency, the most important thing he had to do before he left.

"Leah," he said.

The doctor looked up.

"I have a favor to ask you." He went on in a rush. "It's about...Keren."

Her face softened. "Yes. Anything."

He found himself speechless, overcome again with that strange mix of excitement and worry, and the feeling of being a pawn in the impending series of great events. It was close now. He took a deep breath.

"Keren," he said again.

Leah waited.

He twisted the wedding band on his finger, and then pulled it off. "I don't know if I'll see you again before we go. I wanted to ask if you would keep my ring safe for Keren in case… well, in case I don't return."

Her face was serious. "Don't you want to keep it in your room?"

He reached into his pants pocket for the envelope, slid his ring inside. "I have a letter for her too. I was hoping you could hold onto this, talk to her if, well…"

She took the envelope. "I'll give it back to you when you return."

Her beeper shrilled.

He smiled. "Never stops, does it?"

She reached down to read the tiny screen. David watched her frame become charged with energy.

"Someone's unconscious in the main office suite. I'm sorry. I've got to go."

She opened her desk drawer, put the envelope inside. "You'll be all right on the mission. You'll see."

The beeper went off again.

"I'm sorry, I really have to go."

"Do you need help?"

She shook her head. "Yossi's on duty with me, but thanks. You can find your way out—"

He watched as she ran from the room.

7

BENJAMIN RESTED his chin on the little ledge and stared straight at the dot. A horizontal beam of light slid down his forehead and deep into his pupils.

"Access Accepted" appeared on the small screen beside the retinal scanner.

"This won't take long," Sara said to the corporal seated at the station. "Maybe an hour or two at the most."

They stood at the entrance to the restricted area where the time machine was kept. It was 20:33 hours, just after eight-thirty at night.

The corporal shifted uncomfortably. "Your visit isn't on the schedule."

Benjamin smiled. "It is for tomorrow morning. We shifted up to tonight."

The guard looked skeptical.

"It's all right, corporal," Sara said. "We need to make sure a certain piece of equipment was correctly installed. We're on the FlashBack team."

"Of course, I recognize you, ma'am. It's just—"

Benjamin stepped forward. "Why don't you call Colonel Aaron? He'll give you clearance."

The corporal nodded. "Yes, sir. I was just about to suggest that."

On the telephone, Aaron asked to speak to Benjamin. Five minutes later Benjamin and Sara were in the far room housing the pod that would be the team's base of operations once they were back in the past. The room was crowded along three of its walls with the boxes of supplies still to be loaded.

The pod looked like a great grey-white marble, five meters across and four meters high. The surface was covered with a layer of dried polymeric coating, spongy-looking with glossy cracks and dips. The coating would shield the pod during the time throw; by the time the pod arrived in the past the coating would be compressed by time forces into a substance that would resemble granite.

Sara laid her hand on Benjamin's arm. "Would you help me with this ladder, please?"

The pod's hatch was located at the top; a small catwalk emerged for easy entrance. Sara climbed inside first.

"They've done a lot here today," he said.

The interior of the pod was about the size of a cargo van with just enough clearance for him to stand. The walls sloped inward; the computer ledge encircled the lot. Sara shook her head. "It still doesn't seem real. Two thousand years back. How can that be possible?"

Benjamin smiled. "That's what they said about the moon."

He caught a slight twitch of Sara's mouth, and mentally kicked himself. He didn't like to bring up anything to do with space around her; even four years later, she was guarded about the space station disaster.

He touched her shoulder, drew back. She paused, motionless.

"Let's get to work," he said.

The parabolic mirror had been installed in the center of the floor, and he pulled up on the floor panel to reveal a cavity in which a fluid black cloth was draped over a circular object. Sara pushed it aside, then gave a small nod.

"Perfect."

"It's good?"

She folded the cloth as she glanced at him. "It looks like they were able to accommodate the larger parabolic mirror, the one that's a full meter across. I'll be able to pick up stars with at least magnitude of seventeen. This is great."

The mirror was made of multiple reflective segments each about a centimeter in size, the adaptive optics, he knew. Still, as he studied the mirror he was able to evaluate it in only the most cursory fashion. This was Sara's realm of expertise.

He watched her power up the computer while he sat on the floor resting his back against the wall. The edges of the mirrored surface rose and changed conformation. She didn't need him for this, but he just enjoyed being with her. To be with her, it was the reason he'd pushed to go tonight instead of tomorrow, although as he'd said, he also wanted to know immediately if there were any problems.

About forty-five minutes into calibrating the system, his phone sounded. Out of the corner of his eye he saw Sara start, smiled at her as he flipped open the case.

"Feinan here."

"This is General Gideon." Gideon's voice was loud, and Benjamin pulled the phone a little away from his ear.

"Yes, sir."

"I understand you're in the limited access area."

"Yes, sir. I'm here with Major Levenson. We're calibrating the parabolic mirror in the pod."

"I want you to save that for tomorrow morning, and come over to my office now. I need to meet with you both."

Benjamin, knowing Sara could hear the conversation, shot her a questioning glance. She shrugged.

"Now?"

She held her hands palms out with fingers raised, once, twice. He nodded.

"Sara needs twenty minutes to finish."

"No. Please come now. I want to see you both in five."

The connection terminated.

"That was strange," she said. "I wonder what he wants."

Benjamin shook his head. "I hope the mission is intact. It sounds like there might be a problem."

"It'll take me a few minutes. I can't leave the mirror out like this."

He stood for a moment, thinking. "I should go over there now. Can you follow?"

She was typing a command at the keyboard. "Sure. I'll be right along."

As he climbed out of the pod, he had a sudden thought: How had Gideon known he was in the restricted area? Had Gideon talked to Aaron? What was the emergency?

He broke into a jog down the hall and into the maze of hallways leading out of the restricted area. However, as he turned into the last hallway leading out, he stopped short. One of the doors was cracked open.

He felt a strange fluttering inside his chest; the same feeling that had saved him more than once on the rescue missions he'd commanded. Something was wrong—terribly wrong. Right here.

Benjamin's steps slowed. Then he turned back.

8

THE SCENT OF ANTISEPTIC STRUCK Aaron as he walked through the sliding doors of the medical infirmary into the small waiting area. His assistant Etan was right behind him. The clock over the desk read 21:15 hours, nine-fifteen at night, as Dr. Leah Rosen entered from the inner door.

"I'm here, Colonel. I have the soldier in one of the back rooms if you want to question him now."

Aaron held up his hand. "I want to talk to you first. Is there a private room we could go to?"

"Of course, my office." She turned and led him and Etan through the door into the medical suite. "What can I tell you?" she asked as she waved the men to two padded metal chairs and closed the door.

Aaron approved of her attitude: all business. "Dr. Rosen, would you please review your interactions with Mendel, why he came here, why you became suspicious? Anything that might be relevant."

She didn't speak right away, and he waited. Then she nodded.

"This evening we received a call from General Gideon that a soldier was having a seizure in his office."

He sat up. "General Gideon?"

"Yes, sir."

He shot a look at Etan, who lifted his eyebrows.

"Go on," Aaron said.

The doctor tapped on the desk, thinking. "It was 19:20 hours or thereabouts," she said. "Two hours ago. My technician Yossi paged me, and we retrieved him on a stretcher. Mendel had finished seizing by that time so I didn't observe the attack, but General Gideon said it had lasted for a minute. Mendel was beginning to wake up but he was in a postictal state: disoriented and groggy. He doesn't have any history of seizures. I put him under observation and he was doing fine, but then my other technician, Shoshana, found the bead on his dog tags."

He raised his hand. "Let's go back over your bringing him here."

"All right."

"You said he doesn't have a history of seizures. What might trigger one?"

She shrugged. "Drugs, alcohol. Mendel had no traces of either on the limited scan I ran, although I did put a blood sample into storage. Head trauma. Brain tumor or other disease. And sometimes there doesn't seem to be any reason at all."

"Is that unusual?"

"Sure," Rosen said. "But it happens."

Etan frowned. "So you don't know why he had the seizure?"

"No. To work it up properly would require facilities that I don't have here. Mendel needs to be examined once the seal is lifted, especially if he continues flying."

Not likely, Aaron thought, not if he was indeed guilty.

"All right," he said. "Can you tell me why Mendel was visiting General Gideon?"

"I don't know, Colonel."

"Neither General Gideon nor Mendel mentioned anything."

"No, sir. Of course, Mendel doesn't remember anything for several hours prior to waking up. A seizure can do that. And I haven't talked to General Gideon."

Aaron crossed his arms. He found it strange that Shimon Gideon would want to speak privately to a junior officer at seven o'clock at night, even if they had worked together before.

"Very well," he said. "So I assume that Mendel has been quiet and you felt comfortable that he was recovering."

The doctor sat back. "I was comfortable enough. I was planning to discharge him in the morning."

"He hasn't done anything suspicious?"

"Absolutely not. In fact, I'm still not convinced that he is a—"

He held up his hand. "We're going to give him a fair test. Either he's not, or he will condemn himself. You know how it works."

She grimaced. "Yes, well. I imagine you want to see the bead now?"

"Please."

Etan cleared his throat. "You've told Mendel nothing of this?"

"Nothing, Captain."

"That makes it easier," Etan said.

The doctor stared at him thoughtfully for a moment, then reached behind her to pull open the top drawer of the desk. She withdrew a set of dog tags on a ball chain that wound around her fingers. "Here they are," she said.

Aaron reached for the tags. He pulled the chain through his thumb and forefinger, feeling for the bead that was larger than the others.

"It's next to the latch," she said.

"This one," he said after a moment, spinning it between his two fingers.

The doctor leaned over. "Yes, that's it," she said. "Now, let me show you the engraving." She switched on the desk lamp and pulled it so the light shone square over his hand, then reached into her lab coat pocket for the magnifying glass.

"See?" she said. "You take this, Colonel. See if you can make it out."

Aaron held the bead under the glass, turning it until he could see the fine line drawing.

It was the fish. The Icthus.

He passed the magnifying glass and the chain to Etan.

The symbol of the follower. Mendel carried the Icthus with him on his dog tags.

"How did your technician know to look for this bead in the first place?" Aaron asked. "It's not common knowledge."

For the first time the doctor looked uncomfortable. "Well, ah…" She glanced at them. "Does it matter?"

Aaron sat back expansively, but inwards he was honed tight. This was a major security breach to find a follower of the Way working inside the time machine complex. "You can tell me," he said casually.

She shot him a suspicious look.

Etan put the tags and magnifying glass back on the desk.

She shook her head. "All right. But Shoshana is a good technician, and she's done nothing wrong herself. She's not connected with the movement."

Aaron waited.

"Shoshana's—ah—cousin was discovered last year to be a follower. Before the cousin was caught, for some reason he thought Shoshana was a kindred spirit. He mentioned to her that some soldiers carried the bead as a secret identifier."

"Did she turn him in?"

The doctor was flustered. "I don't know the whole story. But there are no questions about her own loyalty. She raised the alarm about Mendel, didn't she?"

He nodded. He'd have to check out the technician, but she was probably all right.

He too had heard of some of the military followers carrying a bead on their dog tags, but this was the first time he'd seen it. Frankly, he hadn't thought anyone would be that stupid. It posed a tremendous risk.

He supposed the followers justified wearing such symbols because the beads were virtually undetectable, unless one knew what to look for. Perhaps they were used as a secret identifier for other followers. Perhaps they were an emotional touchstone for those who wanted a tangible symbol of their faith, but still…

The emotional, non-rational part of people could be quite useful in his job as security chief.

"Mendel," Aaron said. "Has he recovered?"

She nodded. "I think so. He doesn't seem to have any residual effects from the seizure except a bit of grogginess. This is normal."

He turned to Etan. "We need to set up Mendel for the *Danan* now. Will you do that?"

The *Danan* was a simple test designed to ferret out followers of the Way. It had been named for the professor who had discovered a unique weakness in followers that made them self-incriminate with little effort.

Dr. Rosen stood up. She was all business again. "Captain, let me take you to him."

Etan followed her out.

For a valid test, government rules required the person to be warned before undergoing the test, then put in comfortable isolation for at least half an hour, or preferably up to about six hours. The person would presumably think carefully about his response.

Aaron would know soon enough, but now he needed Shimon here. He needed to straighten out this mess.

He walked out of the doctor's office, through the short corridor into the front room, and picked up the telephone.

"Connect me to General Gideon's office," he stated into the receiver.

9

BENJAMIN NUDGED open the door into a small alcove leading to the equipment powering the time machine itself, and he wrinkled his nose at the odor of machine oil. The room was bare, only a bulkhead on the floor that lifted to access parts of the giant superconductors that bent the superfine threads of energy to unfold and disassemble time. During his training, he and the other soldiers had overviewed the time machine's mechanism of operation, but really, he knew little about this aspect of the mission. He hadn't needed to.

He crossed through the second door that also was notched open as the first one had been. It also should have been locked.

Benjamin saw the second chamber was fifty feet wide with a labyrinth of pipes and conduits crossing at all levels, a ten-foot path down the center. Above him, the fluorescent lights suspended from a high ceiling were bright, diffuse, and at his feet, the floor was an open grillwork. Vibrating noise was not loud but penetrating, filled with a constant hum as the capacitors oscillated at the primary frequency and its harmonics, and the sound pulsed the air so that it was difficult to think.

He skulked forward. For a moment, he felt a sense of vertigo as he looked through the floor at the superconductor's edge, but the hairs on the back of his neck still bristled. Doors left open were too suspicious. It might be nothing, but as soon as he left, he would notify the guard.

Benjamin peered around the next grouping of conduits. He saw nothing. There were too many places to hide.

He circumvented another tank.

And suddenly, he was caught from behind by an arm that wrapped around his neck like an iron wedge. The pressure cut his air, darkened his vision, yanked him backward and off balance.

Benjamin's reflexes kicked in. He turned his head to breathe, then set his stance and ducked low. He used the rush of adrenaline before it brought him trembling, grabbed the arm and pulled the attacker forward. Then he slammed the man off his feet, rolled him over and across his shoulder.

The grating shook as Benjamin flung the man down. He kicked toward the man's neck, but the man rolled a half-turn and Benjamin's boot just grazed his shoulder. The man hooked an elbow behind Benjamin's knee to pull him over. Benjamin twisted out of the hold in time, and then landed a solid contact with his heel into the man's ribcage. The man grunted and rolled away. Benjamin was determined not to let him regain his footing.

The man kicked at Benjamin's groin. Benjamin rotated in time so the man's foot glanced off his hip, but still it knocked him so that he staggered. The man hooked his foot around one of Benjamin's knees. Benjamin stumbled, and the man launched another strong kick to his knee.

Benjamin just spun away, but in that split second, the man attempted to stand. Benjamin turned on him savagely, raining three hard kicks into the solar plexus. He shifted to kick his throat. *Blocked.* Kick to the face, again the solar plexus. The man was tiring. Benjamin aimed his boot at the man's groin. The man was warding the blows, scooting back, trying to get away. Benjamin saw that the side of the man's neck was unguarded; the man was reaching for something on the floor—

Benjamin dropped down with all of his weight; his knee aimed toward the throat, ready to destroy him—

The man flipped over, and with a great burst of energy, swung his legs around. He caught Benjamin and slammed him to the floor.

Just in a glance, Benjamin saw a broad wrench as long as his forearm, lying underneath a conduit pipe just beyond his reach. If he could get there first—

The man spiraled away, knocked him with an elbow. In the split second during which Benjamin was distracted he sensed rather than saw the man rolling toward him again, squirting something at him—some liquid in a pump spray bottle—as he shoved Benjamin. The last thing Benjamin saw before his vision exploded into agony was the man's face twisted with hate.

10

GIDEON WALKED into the medical infirmary where Aaron awaited him.

"What's this about, Reuven?" Gideon tempered his voice to a false affability—as if he could afford any more problems right now. While he put out this fire, his man was carrying out sabotage in the restricted area around the time machine with Benjamin and Sara nearby. Before they'd been able to arrive at his office, Gideon had been called here with no excuse for delaying. He'd left a note on his door for Benjamin and Sara to follow him here to the infirmary.

There would be only one opportunity to pull off his plan.

Aaron nodded. "Shimon. We have a bit of a situation here."

Gideon's chest tightened as he saw Aaron check his watch. "Two minutes more," Aaron said.

Gideon speared him with his gaze, but Aaron was looking behind him at the door that led deeper into the medical suite.

Gideon cleared his throat. "What is the situation? Something serious?"

Aaron turned casually. Gideon wasn't fooled; he could see Aaron's eyes were shrewdly evaluating him. He willed his heart to still. Surely, Aaron would hear it.

"What is the situation?"

Aaron snapped back. "I have some questions," he said. "About Caleb Mendel."

"Mendel?"

"We think he's a follower of the Way."

Whatever Gideon had been expecting, it wasn't that. He stood silent, processing this new piece of information.

"You think—" he said after a moment.

"I can tell you for sure in a few minutes. Mendel's about to take the test—the *Danan*."

"The *Danan?*" It was absurd, like something out of a bad dream. This could also be dangerous for him.

"I'm trying to straighten this out," Aaron said. "After the *Danan*, I'll need you to answer a few questions."

Gideon put on his best expression of concern: furrowed brows, drawn mouth. "Yes, of course."

Aaron turned around as his assistant, Etan, entered through the inner door. "We're ready." Then he noticed Gideon. "Shalom, General."

Gideon nodded. "Captain, Colonel Aaron has just informed me of the circumstances." He saw Etan shoot a glance at Aaron. "My congratulations on security's discovery of this dangerous breach inside the base."

"We haven't gotten to the bottom of the breach yet."

"Is it time?" Aaron asked.

Etan nodded. "Yes, sir, just about. Mendel looks pretty nervous."

"Has the guard arrived?"

"He's waiting outside. We're ready."

Gideon clenched his hands. Mendel's being a follower called attention to things that were not helpful. He wondered how Aaron had fingered him.

"Let's go." Aaron pushed open the door.

When they walked in, Mendel was kneeling at the hospital bed, and Gideon winced as if he'd been struck. He could see, even before the *Danan*, that Mendel was indeed a follower. He'd observed that resolution before on a hundred faces.

As Etan closed the door behind them, Mendel scrambled up. He was dressed in clean fatigues, as if this was a normal event and afterward he would go back to his duties. The only unusual thing was Mendel's breathing—fast, deep—hyperventilating.

Aaron nodded to him. "We're here to administer the *Danan* now."

Mendel closed his eyes tight for a moment, then opened them. "Yes, sir," he said.

"Think about your answer to my question. If you answer well, you will be taken at your word and nothing more will be done. If you cannot answer this question satisfactorily, you will be court-martialed and dishonorably discharged from the military. Do you understand?"

"I understand, sir."

"Refusing to answer the question will represent a failure. Do you understand?"

"I understand, sir."

Gideon watched the pilot clench his fists.

"Lieutenant, do you deny Yeshua as Lord?"

Gideon flinched as Mendel glanced at the ground. Then he looked up, his gaze steady as it reached Aaron's eyes.

"No, sir. No. I do not deny him. Yeshua Ha'Maschiach is my Lord."

Sara turned from the guard's station and raced back down the corridor. Fifteen minutes had elapsed since General Gideon called to request that she and Benjamin come to his office. She'd stored the parabolic mirror in the pod so quickly that she thought that surely she'd be able to catch up with Benjamin, yet he hadn't even left the restricted area.

Where was he?

Could he be in the equipment room? When she arrived there, though, it was dark. The pod room was also empty. He might be in the restroom, but there was no answer to her knock and again, the lights were out.

She shook her head.

Her footsteps echoed as she started to retrace her steps. She hadn't seen the janitor who the guard claimed had entered a few minutes ago, nor his cart. That was strange. This section wasn't that big.

As Sara turned down another hallway, she noticed the door that led to the machinery powering the time machine was open.

Open...

She began to run, through the door and past the bulkhead of the anteroom. The inner door had also been left propped.

Where was Benjamin?

The vibration of the machinery was like cotton in her ears; it was still possible to hear but not well. The air—cool, with a scent of machine oil—drifted over her face. Sara inched her way around protruding metal, exposed wires, balanced tubes. The floor's open metal grid shook under her feet. She heard a soft asynchronous clang ring out to her right and ahead, within the forest of pipes and machinery and cylinders, but she still saw nothing.

She kept going.

Now Sara sensed a movement: two men savagely fighting twenty feet ahead of her, hidden behind equipment. As they moved to a clear position she saw that one was dressed in a janitor's jumpsuit with a jacket flapping, and the other was Benjamin.

The janitor was heavily built—all muscle—but apparently, Benjamin was holding his own. A wrench lay just beyond Benjamin, but he couldn't get over to grab it.

The man in the janitor's suit moved back as Benjamin advanced, and then something happened so quickly she barely saw it. Even as Benjamin's fingers brushed the wrench, the man squirted a cloud of mist in his face. Benjamin covered his eyes with his hands, still trying to kick the man even as he drew his upper body together to shield his face and chest.

"Benjamin!"

The janitor was scrabbling for the wrench fifteen feet from her.

She felt time and place contract as she contemplated her approach: every motion and reaction in crystal-clear clarity— movement so slow she could easily track it.

She leaped over a knee-high pipe, a clear route to the wrench. Her boot made contact with it a fraction of a second earlier than the man's hand; she kicked it out of his reach.

The man knocked her down over the wrench and threw himself across her upper legs, preventing her from turning over. She whipped sideways, trying to gain access, still trapped.

An enormous pulse of energy passed through her. In a single clear motion, she brought the wrench up, and as the man blocked her forearm, she swung it at his head.

The wrench smashed against his temple, and he dropped.

As his coat flew open, she saw something small—a button? —clatter through the grill. No, not a button. She tried to follow its path through the shadows, but it fell deep near one of the superconductors, irretrievable.

She slid out from beneath the man and pushed him over. "Benjamin?"

He didn't answer.

The man took in a deep breath. His eyelids twitched.

"Benjamin!" she called again. Her voice was swallowed up by the machine.

Benjamin groaned. "Sara, where are you?"

He had rolled to the side and caged himself behind a maze of pipes near one of the storage tanks. "I'm here," he said. Benjamin was rigid, his hands covering his eyes.

She felt a sense of panic as she stood and took a step toward him. "Can you move?"

"Where's the man?"

"He's unconscious."

"Call security."

Sara gripped the wrench tightly in one hand as she made the call.

Who was he? His jacket had fallen back, revealing a weapons belt from which hung several small packages. Sara saw wires trailing, and recognized the conformation instantly—explosives.

What had fallen from the man's jacket?

"Sara," Benjamin said, so softly she almost didn't hear him. "He sprayed something into my eyes. Everything's black."

"Let me look." She crawled beneath the pipes to get to him, and then brushed away his hands. His eyes were tearing copiously, and he immediately covered them with his hands again.

"Come with me." She hoped that her voice didn't sound too panicked.

"Sara."

"It's all right."

"I'm blind."

"It's all right. I'll guide you."

It took security less than one minute to arrive: a team of four MPs.

GIDEON PUSHED open the door to the main room of the medical suite. So Mendel was a follower of the Way…

They were like termites, devouring the security of the country. The followers had even infiltrated the time machine, the strongest foundation of Israel's defense. If nothing else, this event proved, once more, that FlashBack wouldn't succeed. The only way to deal with the followers was to remove them from the country, no matter how brutal, how disruptive it might be. The infestation had to be exterminated.

Gideon shook his head. After Raseac's treaty was signed, he would step into control as Raseac's direct subordinate, promote Raseac's policies, rule more excellently than anyone else might…

"Shimon," Aaron said, "Dr. Rosen has graciously offered the use of her office. Would you please follow me?"

Showdown was now. Gideon's heart skipped a beat, but he pressed to remain calm. They had nothing on him. If they even suspected what was going on in the time machine right now, Aaron surely wouldn't be here.

Suddenly he was blind with anger at Mendel for focusing all of this attention. Why couldn't the interfering boy just have been what he appeared to be: a pilot without a political agenda?

When Aaron closed the door, Gideon unclenched his hands. "What can I help you with?"

Aaron crossed the room and sat on the chair next to him, adjusting it so they were facing each other. "I'm sorry to drag you into the middle of this," he said.

Again, Gideon noticed the sharp eyes. Aaron would do whatever it took to get to the truth. He must never forget that.

"I was interviewing Dr. Rosen tonight," Aaron went on. "She said Mendel collapsed in your office. Tell me about that."

Gideon looked at him carefully. "I'm not sure how much I can help you. Out of the blue, the boy knocked at my door. He said he had something to tell me, he walked in, and then he started convulsing on the floor. That's it."

"Just like that."

"I'm as mystified as you are."

Aaron sat back and templed his fingers. "It sounds—too abrupt. Do you have any idea what he wanted to discuss with you?"

It was best to keep things as simple as possible. "No, no idea at all."

"I find it strange that a junior officer would jump multiple ranks to talk to you, the second in command of the base. It must have been important."

"Did you ask him?" Gideon waited anxiously for an answer.

Aaron shook his head. "Mendel doesn't remember anything. He remembers changing in the locker room, and the next thing he knew, he was waking up in the medical ward. We know that after the locker room, he flew the surveillance helicopter behind two of the mission soldiers while they paraglided over the Qumran range, and then he signed out on the post-flight check. Other than that—"

Gideon began to relax.

"He seems to have an impression of a hand in his face—"

Gideon tried not to start. Aaron would see. "A hand in his face? That seems strange." He thought quickly. "Could it have been a hallucination?"

Aaron was watching him. "Who knows? The doctor seems to think anything is possible. I was just wondering if you could think of anything that might help explain it."

"I have no idea."

"Do you know why Mendel would choose that particular moment to have a seizure, when he's never had one before?"

"I told you already, I don't. He just collapsed."

Aaron looked like he was moving in for the kill.

"Did I tell you how we first suspected Mendel was a follower?" He was changing subjects now, trying to knock him off balance.

Gideon shook his head.

"A bead on his dog tags. Do you know anything about that?"

"No. How—what kind of bead?"

Aaron shifted forward and waited.

Gideon was truly confused now. "I don't understand."

There was silence.

"Mendel is a follower of the Way," Aaron finally said. "For whatever reasons, you and he were meeting, after hours, in your office. You must appreciate that this raises certain questions."

Gideon suddenly understood. It couldn't really be this simple for him, could it? He could derail Aaron right now, throw him completely off track and definitively close this incident with Mendel.

"You think I'm in league with him!"

Aaron sat back.

"Let me make this simple for you." Gideon felt his eyes flashing. "I deny Yeshua as Lord. I deny him categorically. I deny him absolutely. Yeshua is nothing to me, and I deny him."

Aaron raised his hand.

"How could you suspect me of something so treasonous? How dare you jump to conclusions and point your finger at me?"

Aaron held his gaze. "Did you know he was a follower?"

"Of course not!" Gideon snapped. "I would have turned him in instantly. Now, if you'll excuse me—"

Aaron didn't move, but his voice was silky. "I still have a few questions, if you don't mind."

Gideon heard a large bang in the corridor, a door slamming, and Aaron broke off. There were voices outside in the hallway, excited voices coming closer. A moment later, he heard a frantic knocking on the door.

"Come!" Aaron called.

Etan slammed open the door. "They've just caught a saboteur in the time machine."

"What?" Aaron jumped out of the chair and crossed to the door. "Explain."

"Feinan and Levenson. They found someone trying to plant a bomb in the time machine."

Gideon sucked in his breath.

"The man's unconscious, knocked in the head with a wrench. I've sent a team to secure the scene, but we need to go over there right now."

Gideon clenched his fists. "How did they find him?"

Etan looked over. "I'm not sure, sir. But Feinan's been blinded."

"Let's get over there," Aaron said.

They left Gideon in the small office, alone.

13

EXCITED VOICES SWIRLED around Benjamin as he was wrested from Sara and pulled inside, into the scent of carbolic and antiseptic.

He couldn't see. His eyes were on fire.

Commanding voices, but he couldn't focus his attention to understand. His mind was a kaleidoscope of noise and pain interwoven with fear, and the best he could do was to follow, unresisting, the arms propelling him forward.

Where was Sara?

"Colonel Feinan," a woman's voice pierced the darkness. She was the dominant force leading him now, her arm around his shoulders, pressing ahead. He felt a swish next to his face as if he'd just been pushed through a doorway. "This is Dr. Leah Rosen. I need to know what that man did to your eyes."

Her voice was a focus in the kaleidoscope.

"Can you tell me? What did he do to you?"

Benjamin concentrated. "A spray bottle." He was surprised at the weakness of his voice. "A liquid. Burning—"

"Can you tell me more?"

His eyes were on fire.

He felt the doctor turn to talk to someone behind him. "Quick!" she said. "Someone radio down and find out what it might have been."

His elbow brushed against a sharp angle. The doctor's hand was unrelenting.

"Colonel," she said. "I need to irrigate your eyes."

He was lifted onto a padded table, and several pairs of hands held him down, forced his hands away from his face.

"Let's go," the doctor said.

Gloved hands pried his eyelids open and he felt a great relief inside as he realized he could still see—there was a bright light over his head. But the pain stabbed through his eyes as a living thing, and he twisted on the table. Hands pressed on his shoulders.

He saw wavering light as lukewarm water poured over his vision. It tasted like salt. The steady stream went on and on, and he gritted his teeth against the ripping in his eyes. He felt as if they were being torn away, yet he lay straight and unmoving.

"How are you doing?" the doctor asked after what seemed an eternity. Benjamin moved his lips to say "fine," but wasn't sure if anyone could hear him over the flowing water.

"The man sprayed you with a three percent solution of hydrogen peroxide. The people who work in the time room use it to clean some of the equipment. You probably won't have any permanent damage to your vision, even though it feels like that now."

Hands held him still as the water poured over his sight. He cleared his throat, moved his lips.

"What was that?" the doctor asked.

"The mission," Benjamin croaked. "Will I still lead the mission?"

But the doctor was silent.

14

HOURS LATER, SARA CAME to his hospital room. She was the only person he'd been waiting for.

"It's me." She hesitated in the doorway. "May I come in?"

Benjamin couldn't see—the doctor had covered his vision with eye shields to allow his corneas to heal. He rested on the hard mattress of the hospital bed; he was in a small room that smelled of disinfectant. The room was full of little sounds—a fan oscillating, the occasional soft step of someone outside the door—but deep in its real silence. He turned to Sara's voice.

"What took you so long?"

She sounded nervous. "I've been waiting half the night to come. They've just now given me permission to see you." She spoke from the door.

"Come closer," he said. "Why don't you sit down?"

He heard her move, hesitant footsteps, and swung his legs around over the edge of the bed. He sensed her standing near to him, and pulled on the starched sheets to straighten them.

"Sit," he said. "You must be exhausted."

"It's almost four."

He listened to her breathe. She paused, and then sat next to him on the mattress. He dipped toward her, barely touching.

They sat uneasily in the silence. Finally, Benjamin asked, "Have Aaron's people been asking you a lot of questions?"

He felt her fidgeting. "That's all they're able to do. All I know is, they think we were very good, and they don't want to say it."

Benjamin laughed.

Silence again.

"Sara," he said. "There wasn't any permanent damage to my eyes. My vision is back, and the light sensitivity will disappear in another day or two."

"Dr. Rosen told me. I'm glad."

He didn't understand the sudden awkwardness between them.

"What's wrong?" He reached over to take her hand, groping for a moment until he found it. "You saved my life tonight. Thank you."

Her arm stiffened, and he dropped her hand.

"I'm just glad I was there," she said after a pause. "When I saw that man reaching for that wrench to kill you, and you couldn't see him—"

Sara stood up. "I should go now."

He was desperate to have her stay.

"No." He reached out and touched her waist by mistake. Then he raised his hand to her forearm. "Don't go."

She hesitated. He felt her lean close to him, and then she encircled her arms about his shoulders, lightly, as she buried her head in the hollow between his neck and shoulder. He reached around awkwardly to pat her back. A moment later, she pulled away. He almost could feel the shutter bang in her mind, closing off again, protecting herself and he wanted to tell her no, don't run away from me. Stay.

She said nothing.

Clumsily Benjamin found her elbow and drew her forward so that she sat down again next to him. He took both of her hands in his. "It's all right."

She didn't pull her hands away, but she didn't move them toward him either. Her hands simply rested in his.

"It's all right," he repeated.

"I know. I was afraid—"

She stopped.

"I was afraid, replaying it all in my mind."

"What were you afraid of?"

She pulled away again. "That you'd be killed because you couldn't see. You couldn't know which way to move."

He moved forward, one hand on her arm.

"It's all right," he said. "It's over. You stopped him."

Sara was trembling, and he leaned toward her.

Slowly, without quite knowing what he was doing, Benjamin reached over and pulled her closer on the bed. She felt stiff in his arms, but he couldn't see her, and that made it a little easier. Gently he raised his hand to find her face. His fingers touched her ear, then her cheek, her eyelashes. He was surprised as he wiped away a tear. He pushed her hair back from her face, tangling his hand through it around her shoulders.

He tasted the air she breathed, so close, as he leaned forward to kiss her. *Soft.*

She seemed to melt against him—so gentle—and her hand rested on his shoulder as he pulled her tight to him.

He breathed the air she breathed.

She moved toward him, opening her arms to him and he felt, suddenly, that things were going to work out. A burden lifted from his shoulders. Difficult, but they would work out.

"Benjamin," she murmured, and he kissed her again. He felt he could have stayed blind and it would have been all right, as long as she was there with him.

"You do care, don't you," he whispered as he held her close.

Close...

The door clicked. Benjamin heard the sound before Sara, and even as he looked up reflexively, he tried to grasp the moment that he knew was about to vanish. With the opening of the door, he felt that heaviness fall on him as quickly as it had been lifted before, unable to overcome. Then in his arms, Sara froze.

"General Gideon," she whispered.

Benjamin heard him stride into the room.

Sara slipped through Benjamin's arms and away from him. He wanted to call her back but it was too late, and he felt exposed as he imagined Gideon observing her retreat through the doorway. The door closed.

"She's not Tamar," Gideon said blandly.

The room seemed suddenly suffocating, dark walls closing in, and Benjamin fought desperately for control. It was the coldest time of night and he felt as if he'd been in hand-to-hand combat for hours. His eyes ached. He longed for Sara to return.

There was a long wall of silence.

Gideon finally spoke in a low voice. "I'd stay away from her, if I were you. I'd stay far away. Don't let yourself become vulnerable."

"Sir, I—"

Gideon's shoes tapped towards him; Benjamin sensed him standing next to the bed.

"I don't want to know," Gideon said. "It's all right, son. I'm not going to say anything to anyone. I've known you long enough to know you'll do the right thing."

Benjamin nodded, but he was too confused right now to even think how he was going to handle Sara. All he could think of was how she'd molded to him in his arms just now, how close they'd grown despite their restraint over the past months of training, how he longed for her already...

He felt another stab to his eyes like fire, and he stiffened and covered his face with his hand. His palm brushed the eye patches, smooth and firmly seated. "Sir, if it's all right with you, I need some sleep."

"Wait a moment" Gideon said. "I came to give you some bad news before you heard it from another source."

Benjamin's heart sank, but it was subdued too. He couldn't call up any deeper emotions tonight.

"I won't run the mission."

Gideon paused. "Not necessarily. We've notified Eli, and he's prepared to lead the mission if necessary, but it won't be decided until later in the day."

"The doctor said medically I would be ready."

"It's out of your hands. You may still do it. As I just said, the decision hasn't been made yet. I want to discuss something else with you."

Benjamin sank back. "Yes, sir."

"This is about the spies that were caught tonight."

With a tremendous effort, he focused on what Gideon was saying.

"Spies? Plural?"

"Yes."

"During the debriefing they asked a number of times if I'd seen anyone else in the hangar with the saboteur, but I said no."

Gideon sighed. "No, son. The second spy was located here, in the infirmary, while the explosive was being planted. We know he wasn't there with you. However, he's been discovered to be a follower of the Way. I wanted you to know his identity."

"Who is it?" Benjamin asked slowly, almost reluctantly. He was suspended in dread.

"Someone we worked with in ReachDeep before we came here."

"Who?"

"One of the pilots who flew the rescue missions. Caleb Mendel."

"But no," Benjamin said. "That couldn't be..."

15

SARA STILL FELT Benjamin's touch as she left the infirmary, and as she headed across the shadowy courtyard, and as she let herself into her apartment. She felt it even after she had taken a shower and lain down on the narrow bed, and it comforted her as she wrapped it around her mind, a small stay against the uncertainty, and the fear.

She fell asleep thinking of Benjamin, but in her unconscious he soon gave way to uncertainty again.

Sara woke as if swimming upwards from a deep black pool, the heavy drops of sleep that clung to her mind falling away. She wasn't sure, she wasn't sure, and it was only three days until the mission.

It had seemed so straightforward in the beginning. What could be simpler? And so she had begun to dig, and the more she found, the more she couldn't explain.

The impressions from her dream hung heavily although she couldn't remember what had happened. Someone calling, who loved her? No one loved her. She was afraid to come to that voice.

Her research was now haunting her dreams.

She had begun to dig into the myths. They were so simple, so easy to refute, so destructive to this country. The followers were stirring up everyone and everything, requiring the government to suppress all free expression just to stem the riots. Yet, the followers of the Way stood firm.

She shook her head, trying to shake off this feeling of oppression. She saw it all so clearly: the religious demonstrations, the chaos, and the crackdowns, Marc Raseac and his treaty. *Please*, she thought, *just let the mission work to crush these religious demonstrations before things get worse.*

The lights guarding the borders around the time machine complex lit her tiny room with grey shadows. She was wide-awake.

She turned on the lamp by her bed, and reached over for a notepad and pencil. It was so simple, really—just prove that a man hadn't risen from the dead. Rip the evidence apart; it was child's play. Her brow furrowed.

The questions had been coming at her furiously over the last few months. They haunted her dreams, and dangled before her eyes. She was a scientist, trained to follow the trail of truth no matter where it led. She must answer the questions.

But what was truth? Wasn't that what Pontius Pilate had asked Yeshua at his trial?

She wrote a single name on the pad: "Paul." Then she put a box around the name. She put arrows around the box, pointing inwards, a dozen arrows along the border.

What had possessed this one man? In some ways, he was the crux of the mystery, the defecting Pharisee who had been privy to all of the arguments, explanations, and resources of the Jewish authorities. Yet he had turned. How had it happened?

She drew another box to hold in the arrows. Another question.

She was afraid where answering the questions might lead.

She was afraid she was starting to believe something that was impossible, absurd. It was subversive, tearing up the country.

Why had Paul turned?

She was a scientist and a soldier. She wished she had never begun to look. The questions haunted her dreams, dangled before her eyes constantly. So many questions.

Sara was torn: afraid to go on, but unable to turn back.

So many questions.

IT WAS 10:02 HOURS, just past ten o'clock in the morning, and less than three days before FlashBack would go. Gideon sighed. Here the three of them were again, inside the plush windowless conference room with him staring across at Aaron, Landau between them at the head of the polished wooden table. Again, they were formulating a decision that could in its broadest reach impact Israel's future.

Gideon banged his fist upon the table. "We've been infiltrated at two points that we know of. I want to know where else we might have a security breach."

Now that his sabotage of the time machine had failed, Gideon's only hope was to dissuade the head of the complex, Landau, from allowing FlashBack to proceed—although this was unlikely without alternatives on the table. He was furious that Raseac's operative had been caught. With the man under observation in the lockdown, Gideon didn't have a prayer of eliminating him.

Aaron looked over. "We're inspecting everything in minute detail, and so far there seems to have been no tampering. Barring something unexpected, FlashBack can go ahead on schedule."

Gideon snorted. "What if you miss something?"

"The saboteur was in the restricted area for less than twenty minutes before Feinan found him."

The commander sat forward. "Let's take it one point at a time. Reuven, update us first, please."

It was always so with Landau, blast him. Landau sat like a judge listening to arguments from two opposing advocates, and then issuing his ruling, moving ahead, alone. One would never know until he stood with his crutches that his gait was crooked. Nothing else about him was.

Gideon fidgeted as Aaron spoke. "We've learned a lot since last night. We discovered two spies, in two separate incidents that were nearly simultaneous. The first spy, Caleb Mendel, is a pilot who worked for General Gideon in the ReachDeep Special Forces unit. He failed the *Danan* last night and is in the brig. Twenty months ago he passed the screening *Danan* for clearance to work here, so we know he converted within that time."

"Who got to him?" Gideon asked.

"Not necessarily anyone inside the complex. Most of us know someone who knows a follower somewhere."

This was probably true. Studies estimated that from two to seven percent of the Jewish population had converted, although many kept it secret. Still, Gideon thought, the threat of having followers in the heart of the time machine was staggering.

"Is that all about Mendel?" Landau asked.

Aaron stared at Gideon for a moment too long, making him uncomfortable. "All I'll say right now. I'm still working on a few questions."

Landau leaned forward. "What about the other one?"

"Uri Seidel," Aaron said. "A low-level technician—aircraft maintenance. He's under guard in the medical unit, but we expect to move him to the brig shortly. He's recovering from a concussion. Levenson hit him with a wrench."

"How did he get into the restricted area?" Landau asked.

"We'll find out."

"He had to have had help," Landau said.

Aaron nodded. "Yes, sir. He did."

Gideon was suddenly grateful for Raseac's prudence in not revealing Gideon's identity to Seidel. Still, Seidel could lead them to some uncomfortable places.

Aaron cleared his throat. "Gentlemen. We have to accept the fact that we have a mole in the complex."

The silence stretched long. Gideon stared hard at the table.

"SO, WHO'S THE MOLE?" Landau asked.

Aaron noticed Landau was walking relatively well today, gliding with his crutches.

"I don't know, sir," Aaron said. "I have a few ideas of my own, but nothing substantial."

"Let's hurry. I want to see this."

Etan caught his eye. "I notice General Gideon's not here," he murmured so only Aaron could hear. Nodding, Aaron raised his finger to touch his lips: keep these thoughts quiet.

They were almost there. Aaron watched Landau bobble on one step, and slowed his pace as he turned a corner in the hall. Another corner, and they were at the entrance of the restroom. Etan pulled open the door.

The empty bathroom remained under observation by his security even though the initial investigation was finished. Aaron knew there would be more questions once the saboteur began to talk.

Landau walked past a partition. "Now tell me the details."

Aaron followed, and then Etan as the door closed behind them.

The bathroom was unremarkable: green tile, two urinals against the far wall, a long mirror over a bank of three sinks. It was close to the main entrance of the complex, meaning any male could access it without raising questions. Aaron walked to the last stall and pushed open the swinging door. The toilet paper dispenser had been swept of the white gritty fingerprint powder. His men had found no residual prints or other evidence.

"Here," Aaron said. "We discovered this about eight hours ago while we were pulling people out of bed for questioning. The janitor mentioned that he'd removed a thread wrapped around this rivet—" he pointed to a silver-colored disk on the black dispenser, being careful not to touch it "—two or three times in the last six months. He thought it must be from someone's dress shirt, but it seemed strange that it kept happening."

"The janitor didn't keep the threads?"

Aaron shook his head. "He had no reason to. They were unremarkable."

Landau straightened. "Hmm."

"This receptacle seems to be the dead drop as well as signaling area," Aaron said. "We found small scratch marks around the latch that opens the receptacle."

Aaron glanced at Landau, and then signaled to Etan who pulled on a pair of latex gloves and moved toward the box. With a small metal key, Etan manipulated the simple lock.

Aaron stepped forward and shone a light into the cover. "There's a shallow false pocket that blends deep in the well, here," he said. "Encrypted optical computer discs, maybe. It would be unlikely that anyone not aware of its existence would notice it, even if they opened the receptacle."

Landau knitted his eyebrows. "Fingerprints? Identifying marks?"

Aaron shook his head.

"It doesn't seem that secure."

Aaron shrugged. "It's a better place than you might think. Easy access. Lots of traffic, but privacy right where the drop is."

Landau backed away from the crowded stall and leaned heavily against the sink counter. "And you say you've contained the damage to the time machine equipment?"

That was the question.

Aaron was silent a moment. "Yes, sir. I'm reasonably sure. The head engineer informs me that as far as he can determine, the time machine has not been tampered with; it's fully functional."

"Can he check that enormous machine in just a few hours?" Landau asked. "I don't want the time machine killing those soldiers. Or worse, blowing up the base."

"It's always a possibility. However, I'm confident this is the only incident within the restricted area, because the surveillance recordings and retinal scan data support that no one else has circumvented the system before now. In addition, we have a limited window for transport, of course. If we don't go ahead it's a disaster for the country."

Landau hmmphed. "I don't like it."

"It was a sophisticated, targeted attack. The explosion would have occurred when the time machine was powered on, ruining the main conduit circulating the coolant for one of the four superconductors. During transport, nothing would have happened: the pod would have just stayed put on the tarmac. The mangled conduit would have been found within an hour or two, according to the head engineer, and would have been relatively easy to repair. But," he held up his hand. "The time required to repair it would make us lose our Earth position and miss our margin for transport until sixty-eight days from now, well after Raseac's visit and the signing of the treaty. It implies that whoever planned this had precise information about how the time machine works, and didn't want it permanently damaged."

Landau pressed his lips together. "It's the kind of attack I might have planned myself."

Aaron moved so he stood right next to Landau. "The two prisoners I have in custody are not sufficiently knowledgeable to plan such an attack. Our mole is still hidden and active."

He felt Etan's eyes on him, and knew Etan had not forgotten about Gideon's evening visitor, Mendel, who had collapsed in his office. This was exactly the type of attack that would be planned by followers. Aaron kept returning to the fact that only this one mission would have been compromised. There would be no films of the body theft, no evidence that the resurrection was a hoax, no proof that the government could use to weaken the Messianic movement to a manageable point.

Gideon was no follower, though.

Landau furrowed his eyebrows. "Very few people have that kind of access. Maybe sixty. Who is it?"

Aaron shook his head. "Sir, I don't know."

GIDEON DRUMMED his fingers on his desk. Feinan would be here soon.

There were only sixty hours until the team went back into the past. Gideon had lost his one chance to prevent FlashBack, and no matter that circumstances out of his hands had converged, Raseac did not brook excuses, only results. Raseac had been adamant—the time machine must not be considered functional until after the treaty had been signed and Gideon had stepped into control, since a functional time machine could undo the treaty signing with Israel.

Gideon shook his head. "Feinan," he said with a grimace. He should have known.

Gideon hated him.

The hatred had grown over the years. As Benjamin accomplished one high-risk rescue after another in ReachDeep, he had garnered the reputation of being invincible. Gideon had overseen each mission, and while Benjamin was good, sure, Gideon had been struck by Benjamin's countless narrow escapes and lucky turns of events. It was almost as if he were being protected by the hand of God.

He narrowed his eyes.

The protection hadn't covered Benjamin's wife Tamar, though, in that car explosion.

The knock on the door echoed in the room. Finally.

"Come!" Gideon called.

Although Benjamin exhibited some obvious light sensitivity, he looked much better than he had sixteen hours ago in the infirmary, when Gideon had caught him with Sara Levenson. Maybe he could use Benjamin's obvious infatuation with her to some good. At this point, though, he didn't see how.

"Shalom." Gideon forced his voice into cordiality as he walked around his desk and reached out to warmly shake Benjamin's hand.

Benjamin nodded. "Shalom, General."

"I see you've lost the eye patches, son. You'll be ready to run the mission?" A few hours ago the committee had made the decision, after the doctor had assured everyone that Benjamin's corneal injuries would heal in time.

Benjamin's face took on a grim cast. "Yes sir, I will. This one's too important. I know you supported the decision to keep me on FlashBack, and I appreciate your confidence."

Actually, Gideon had been the strongest dissenter, but he'd been outvoted. After last night, he'd found a role for Benjamin to play here, as a counter target for himself against Aaron.

"Sit down, please."

He pulled his desk chair next to Benjamin's and sat so he faced him. He knew exactly how he wanted to approach this.

Benjamin leaned back, waiting.

"I wanted to give you an update on last night's events. I thought you should know, and I'm not sure how much Reuven—Colonel Aaron—had time to tell you."

Benjamin nodded. "I appreciate that, sir."

He knew how to wait silently, Gideon thought, although he noticed Benjamin's hands clenched on the arms of the chair. Gideon cleared his throat.

"I told you this morning about Caleb Mendel," he began.

"He's a follower."

"Yes."

"Here in the complex," Benjamin said.

"Yes."

Benjamin pounded his fist on the arm of the chair. "I worked with that man! I saw nothing. How did he infiltrate security?"

Gideon held up his hand. "He's a recent convert, after we moved here from ReachDeep, so you shouldn't blame yourself. He passed the routine *Danan* twenty months ago. Colonel Aaron is compiling a list of his contacts, but so far it's unclear who might have gotten to him to make him convert."

"What a waste. What will happen to Mendel now?"

Gideon shrugged. "I'm not sure, son. After the mission he'll stand for court-martial."

"I don't understand this. I like Mendel. He's a good man. Brave. A good pilot. Why would a seasoned soldier like him stoop to sabotaging the time machine?"

Benjamin left unasked the question, why did he convert?

"Isn't it obvious?" Gideon sneered. "He's afraid of what you'll find on the mission."

"A body. But the truth is what it is. If I were a follower, I wouldn't want to be afraid that my beliefs were based on a lie."

The silence stretched for a moment. Then Gideon cleared his throat.

"This brings me to my second point: the man you caught last night."

Benjamin sat forward, focused attention.

"I was wondering if you could describe to me what you saw last night, what you did?"

Benjamin stiffened and covered his eyes with his hand. After a moment, he relaxed.

His eyes still hurt him. Gideon observed him dispassionately.

"Sir, I must have gone over that at least thirty times."

"I know, I know," Gideon said. "But I need to hear from your own mouth exactly what happened." He didn't want to add that Aaron hadn't released the information he needed. It was a constant dance within these walls.

"There's not much to tell. Sara and I decided to go to the restricted area last night instead of this morning so Sara could check the installation of the parabolic mirror inside the pod."

"Why?"

Benjamin shrugged. "We thought it would work out."

Gideon sighed. Of such chance events kingdoms rose and fell.

"Go on," he said.

He listened as Benjamin described getting Gideon's call, then finding the opened door and investigating it. He had been jumped from behind, engaged Seidel, and been blinded by the hydrogen peroxide. Then, Sara had discovered them and subdued Seidel. It was a quick, sad story.

"And so that's it?"

Benjamin sat back. "That's all I know. We were lucky."

Luck. Benjamin had more than his fair share. With surprise and his size, Seidel should have easily been able to kill him.

"Where was the man when you found him?"

Benjamin sat back. "At the far end of the room, in the right-hand corner."

Seidel had been planting only the first of the four bombs then. Benjamin must have entered before Seidel had been in the target area five minutes.

Gideon clenched his fists, then followed Benjamin's glance to his hands and forced himself to relax. *Don't give yourself away.*

Now that he'd learned what he needed, he had no more energy for this. He stood up, signaling the end of the conference.

Benjamin cleared his throat. "Sir, do you know if they've found the missing trigger yet?"

"The trigger?"

"Yes, sir. Colonel Aaron mentioned that the man had been carrying four bombs and two trigger mechanisms, plus another trigger for the wire cable that he'd been setting. There's—well, he seemed to think a trigger mechanism might be missing."

Gideon pressed his hands together. "Ah—no, they haven't found it yet. I believe it was like the one used in that car bomb that killed your wife."

"Like the one in the car bomb—" Benjamin grimaced as he covered his eyes with his hand again. He held himself immobile.

Blast it. Distract him from that slip. Gideon jumped forward. "Feinan, do you need to see the doctor?"

Benjamin lowered his hand, shook his head. "I'm sorry, sir. My eyes have some stabbing pain still, but the doctor says that will stop in a few hours."

"You'd better rest them. The mission's just two and a half days off now."

"Yes, sir."

Gideon pushed him to the door. "Go. Go. Now."

After he had left, Gideon sank into the chair behind his desk. He pulled out the top drawer to his cigarettes.

His hands were shaking as he lit the match, and then he breathed in the burning smoke.

19

Transport Day.

Benjamin slammed the hatch in the ceiling of the transport pod. They were isolated now on the runway.

"Are we ready?" Rebecca's voice was pitched too high and tight, and Benjamin worried that she might be panicking. David reached over and patted her gloved hand.

The pod did provoke a feeling of claustrophobia, Benjamin thought, as he stepped off the ladder and snapped it forward. He smiled at Sara. The ladder retracted underneath the cap of the hatch two feet above his head, a snick-snick-snick looping onto the spindle. It was definitely close quarters. The internal circular space was three meters across, and with the four padded seats unfolded, there was no room to move. Compartments behind almost every centimeter of wall and floor space stored equipment to prevent loose projectiles.

Benjamin glanced over at Rebecca. She was taking deep breaths, striving for calm, perhaps not even thinking of how easily this hollow space could implode during time transport, the exterior crushing them like coal into diamonds. Well, collapse hadn't happened in more than a year...

The floor rumbled as the pod fans clicked on to circulate the air through the carbon dioxide scrubbers. The air pulsed against his cheek, cool and dry with a slight scent of machine oil.

Benjamin picked up the radio transmitter. "Control. This is Feinan. My team is intact inside the pod; all systems online."

The responding voice was distorted. "Copy that. You have about ten minutes before countdown to launch."

His team was seated in place, waiting for him to finish up and join them. They all wore padded fireproof black uniforms, boots, and gloves. Helmets were beneath the seats.

Sara cleared her throat. "The waiting is the worst part. Once we go, we won't have time to think."

Rebecca laughed nervously.

Benjamin shook his head, and then pulled on heavy gloves, rocking each finger in to fit. He snapped the wrists onto the sleeves of the padded jacket, folding the long flaps over to cover the seam. But these clothes were not going to protect any of them, he thought. Problems during a time throw would be relentless and overwhelming.

During the time throw, temperatures on the surface of the pod dropped close to absolute zero, -273 degrees Celsius. Surrounding its hollow center, the pod had been fitted with a nuclear-powered heater that produced hundreds of degrees of heat almost instantaneously. This heater had to be faultlessly coordinated with the insertion of the pod into the time-space solid. If it powered on too early, the soldiers would be burned to ash, and if it switched on too late, they would be frozen solid.

Benjamin had faced death before. The trick was not to think about it.

The voice came over the microphone again. "Transport team."

Benjamin flipped the VOX toggle. "Feinan here."

"We're tracking the satellite. Countdown begins in five minutes."

"Copy that."

He imagined the Israeli satellite spinning into position along its orbital trajectory high above the Earth. Below him, below the frictionless floor of the Transport Room on which the pod sat, a series of linear accelerators rumbled in preparation for the time throw. When the controls on the time machine were activated, the fusion reactions would generate a focused particle stream called a graviton beam that would reach into space.

Sara had told him how, when she was on the space station *Eagle's Nest* four years earlier, she had seen the Israeli satellite drop far to Earth as it slammed into the graviton beam. Repeatedly, she'd watched this phenomenon as the time machine was tested and refined. It had been a great mystery and, in a sense, the start of the troubles on the station. However, all that was past now.

Even as the massive satellite slammed against the invisible graviton beam and drove against this long lever of the machine, the time machine would spin the fulcrum: the cosmic string, a minute strand of infinitely dense energy with the gravity of a small sun. Both lever and fulcrum would break up within another fraction of a second, and the satellite would make a powered rebound into its original orbit. The localized transient change in gravity caused by the cosmic string twisted the connections welding time and space together. The scientists had discovered that while the cosmic string was folding and distorting time-space, an unrestrained object resting on a frictionless platform could be hurled inside from the present or extracted from the past, accelerated by the massive gravitational pull of the cosmic string. The object would slingshot through time-space, traveling past seconds and years instead of distance.

So it would be. Two thousand years.

Benjamin slid into the padded seat that would hold him until the time was the past. He was ready for it to be finished.

"Helmets on," he ordered. The radio squawked again, and the voice sounded garbled through the power surges.

"Transport team, we estimate four minutes," the mission commander said.

"Copy that."

Sara was buckling the heavy harnesses crosswise over her chest and waist, legs. He reached for his own helmet.

The voices babbled over the intercom, final preparations before countdown.

There was another burst of static, and then Control's voice came online.

"Transport team, are you ready?"

Benjamin glanced around to check. "We're ready for transport."

"Copy that. We're beginning final systems check now."

There was a pause, and then Control's voice crackled, "Satellite position."

"Maneuvering. It will be three minutes until the last checkpoint on my mark." There was a pause. "Three, two, one, mark."

Benjamin saw the clock over the computer flash green numbers indicating three minutes, and then start its countdown.

More static. Benjamin pushed his head back against the chair, closed his eyes. It would be over soon, one way or the other. The voices of the people coordinating the time machine's launch filtered through the chamber.

"Final systems check," Control was saying. "Leaders, listen up. Give me a final Go-No Go for transport. Energy stream?"

"Go."

"Network?"

"Go."

"Guidance?"

"Go, Control."

"Recovery?"

"Go."

"Emergency Shutdown?"

"Go."

One and a half minutes left on the clock. The controller's voice paused. "All systems are Go," he said, his voice distorted over the radio signal in the pod. "We are ready for transport."

The signal began breaking up as the time machine wakened. Benjamin heard a burst of static.

"Thank you, Control," Landau's voice came back over the thin channel. "Go for transport. Good luck, transport team."

"Copy that," Control's voice replied. "Countdown is T minus sixty seconds on my mark. Start emission sequence. Three, two, one, mark!"

The mechanical timer to the right of Benjamin's seat displayed the seconds. Fifty-eight. Fifty-seven. Fifty-six.

Benjamin saw Sara take a deep breath. Her hands gripped the armrests so tightly he was sure her fingers were white underneath the gloves.

He noticed he was gripping the armrests also.

Forty seconds.

If the magnetic containment fields around the energy strings generated by the electromagnets were even slightly out of phase, it could open a rift in the time-space solid big enough for the Earth to fall through. The emergency containment would close such a rift in time, but annihilate the pod in the process.

Thirty seconds.

Benjamin double-checked his harness. The roar of the engines was overpowering, even through the insulated pod. The seats were vibrating in the eye of a tornado of energy.

Twenty seconds.

Liquid carbon dioxide circulated around the shaping superconductors nearby. Beneath the storage vats, high voltage cables also ran to these superconductors. The saboteur's dropped detonator was cradled between the cables like a cigarette where it had fallen and wedged itself.

The powerful current through the cables heated them, and thus, heated the detonator as well.

Ten seconds.

The detonator exploded, the noise drowned out by the surrounding cacophony.

Eight seconds.

The explosion was almost nothing—the detonator had been designed only to ignite the main charge. Not much of a spark. But it did interfere with an adjacent cable, and the current of energy was altered just enough to cause a fluctuation of electricity powering the electromagnet. Only a fraction, not enough to be noticed, except in a summary table with small print that briefly flashed on computer screens and then was gone.

Five seconds.

A change, an intensifying tear in the space surrounded the pod in Transport Room.

One second.

Zero.

The clock moved past zero. With infinitely dense energy and immeasurable charge, the linear accelerators spun the superfine cosmic thread that acted like ultra-dense matter. The pod stretched time-wise against the edge of the time-space solid. In orbit around the Earth, the satellite strained against the graviton lever. Unlike prior transports, the string wavered following the power surge, too small and too fast for anyone to see, but even as the string dissipated it shot the pod toward the time-space solid. Benjamin felt himself thrown into a void where he seemed to be floating; then the gravity was terrific, pushing him down, down against the seat.

Space turned on its side to become time.

20

THE ACCELERATION FORCES PINNED Benjamin to his seat. The platform base holding the chairs rotated toward the shift of energies along the path of least resistance. After the first roar, the pod was swallowed into a solid silence that was cold, chillingly cold and black, and then the pod slid forward into the time solid. The bitter smell of ozone rested on the air. From what seemed like a distance, Benjamin heard the nuclear heater fire on, opposing the sudden profound chill inside the pod. It was still so cold, though.

Further inside the time solid.

As the pod moved past the barrier, Benjamin noticed a change in his awareness. It wasn't so much a disconnection with what was normal and real, as it was a dissolving into a supradimensional reality—he was simultaneously trapped within the three-dimensional filter of his body, yet roaming a frame of space or time—what?—something that stretched far beyond him. His eyes were unable to interpret the true nature of the change; they relayed the information the only way they could, and so the air seemed to glow.

Time had ceased to exist. He simply was.

And in that place between space and time he felt cracks begin to form, already formed, in the seams between the panels of the pod as if the pod were a part of himself, the metallic atoms stretching below, pulling apart yet pulled apart already. He sensed the small bolts straining to hold together the sides of the pod, and shining through was an unbearable light that seemed palpable. Time was solid but there was no protection as it penetrated into the pod.

The hairline cracks disappeared into the light that was impossibly strong and unimaginably faceted. So beautiful. He saw nothing else. The light moved forward, engulfing everything in its path, but when it came to him it only lapped against him, touching him without penetrating although he sensed it could lay him open utterly if it wanted. He wanted it to. This was something different, something dynamic, something living.

The light stretched taut and flowed around the four of them, completely present in the compartment. Then he directed his consciousness to Sara, and was frightened.

As if part of himself, he felt a different throbbing trying to engulf Sara's mind, darkness pushing her down, further down...

Already knowing.

No.

Helpless. But even as he was aware he felt the light blunting the force, turning it away harmlessly even as the darkness continued to press on Sara.

Had he thought the light harmless? He couldn't trust...

He sensed Sara slump into her seat.

Trust me.

The light receded from the pod. Free fall ending.

So cold.

The connectedness retreated.

Like the snap of a rubber band they were back in a normal reality, but it was too late.

BENJAMIN THREW off the seat restraints and knelt beside Sara. She was unconscious, and he pulled her from the chair and laid her flat on the narrow floor.

She sank boneless against him. He held her tighter.

Sara.

She seemed barely conscious, so still. He reached down and took her hand. His Sara.

Her lips were moving, and he could barely hear her as she whispered a name. He leaned further over her, his ear to her lips. The name, she said it again.

And then he drew back in horror.

She had called to Yeshua Ha'Maschiach. No. It couldn't be.

But he hadn't misheard her. His thoughts were paralyzed.

A spy, a follower of the Way, *Sara*, had infiltrated the mission.

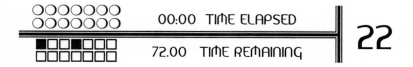

BENJAMIN'S THOUGHTS were as frozen as the pod. Sara was lying at his feet, and he hadn't known. No one had known—

It couldn't be true.

He saw David detach his harness and approach, then drop next to Sara. He nudged Benjamin out of the way, pulling off her helmet.

"Did she lose consciousness?" David asked.

"I'm not sure. I think—maybe just a few moments."

"I saw her go down. Like a bullet from a gun."

Rebecca was watching Sara, wide-eyed, from her chair. Benjamin glared at Rebecca, and when she noticed him, she started undoing her restraint as if only half-aware of what she was doing. He glanced at the thermometer on the console. Negative six degrees Celsius, about twenty degrees Fahrenheit, and the air was so dry it burned his lungs. The green display over the computer bank had begun the countdown: 71.58.18.

"Rebecca," Benjamin said. "David needs room to work. Help me put away these chairs." He folded the nearest one, then maneuvered it from its track into the storage space along the side of the pod. Rebecca started on the next chair.

David leaned close over Sara, his fingers pressing into her wrist. "Sara, can you hear me? What happened?"

Good question, Benjamin thought. Sara seemed groggy but rapidly recovering.

"Her pulse is strong and regular," David said.

"What happened?"

David reached in his pocket and pulled out a small flashlight, shone it in Sara's right eye, then the left. "Good. Rebecca, please hand me the blood pressure cuff and stethoscope."

Rebecca turned to get them. Sara moved as if she wanted to sit up. "I'm all right."

"No." David pushed her back. "Stay there for another moment, please."

Benjamin shoved the next chair into the wall's space. "Why did she black out?"

"Squeeze my hand," David said to Sara. "Good."

"David?" Benjamin said.

David looked over at him. "Not sure, sir. She doesn't seem to have a dysrhythmia. I'm thinking a vasovagal response."

"A what?"

Sara pushed up to sitting. "I need to get our time position." Her teeth were chattering.

David shook his head. "Wait a moment."

A follower—

Rebecca handed David the medical kit. "She looks pale. Are you all right, Sara?"

David waved Rebecca back. "Don't lean over her, please."

Benjamin watched David as he loosened Sara's jacket and wrapped the blood pressure cuff around her arm. He clipped the pulse oximeter to her finger.

Benjamin's thoughts were churning. He shoved the last chair away.

"Good," David said. He took the readings, then removed the medical equipment. "Stand up."

Sara tried to push him away. "Let me get to work, David. I feel fine. Really."

"Just stand." He helped her up. She was a little unsteady.

David turned to Benjamin. "She blacked out for a minute. I think it was probably vasovagal, which means her blood vessels dilated and she didn't have enough blood to her brain. It's not serious. It might have been a reaction to the time travel. The bottom line is, she seems fine now."

Benjamin watched all this through a sheet of ice.

"Sir?"

Benjamin looked up. "Yes," he said. "Thank you."

His thoughts were organizing furiously. *A follower.* How would he handle her?

David turned back to Sara. "Does everything feel normal? No numbness, no tingling?"

"Just a headache, and a little nausea."

"How bad?"

She shook her head. "Not terrible."

"Deep breaths," David said. "Sit down against the wall."

Benjamin edged toward her. He'd have to watch her constantly.

"That time throw was something else," Rebecca said.

David shook his head. "It was cold. But I'm not sure if it took seconds or hours."

Benjamin clenched his fists. He would confront Sara soon.

"David, help me open the hatch," he ordered.

The hatch in the ceiling of the pod was sealed on the outside by the melted compound that had protected the pod during the time throw. He and David squeezed together side by side, and threw their weight hard against the hatch mechanism in the ceiling. After a few tries it came loose.

"Got it," Benjamin said. "Sara, get going." They had to determine their position in time.

David stepped down and turned toward Sara. "How do you feel now?"

"I'm ready." She was sitting up straight.

Benjamin would have to monitor her as she performed her sequenced tasks. Although he knew the mission's operations like the back of his hand, he also knew Sara had a creative facility with the computers and equipment, and she had had months to plan a strategy to sabotage the mission if she so desired. She was brilliant. With so many variables, he wasn't sure that he'd be able to detect a change until it was too late.

"Let's go," he said.

Sara pulled out the folding seat next to the computer and sat. He was on her immediately, standing behind her as she launched the first program.

Sara said, "I'm deploying the camera now." She glanced up at him from her seat, confused. He didn't back off.

The camera at the top of the hatch whirled full circle in less than a second. Sara's screen glowed with the camera data. They were in a valley with a few gnarled olive trees, devoid of people.

"It's nighttime," Sara said. "By the position of the moon I'd say around three in the morning. It's nearly a full moon with early spring constellations. I've turned up the infrared spectrum so we can see better."

Sara examined the image. "We're at the base of the southern end of the Mount of Olives on the eastern side of the Kidron Valley. King David's portion of the city is farther up this hill, to our west. We're looking at the city's wall. And see, north of David's city, here—" she pointed—"northwest of us, is Herod's Temple Mount. This is the third tier and roof of the Royal Stoa inside the southern wall of the Temple Mount. You can just see the edge of the Eastern or Shushan Gate leading up to the Temple Mount, here."

"Where?" David said as he and Rebecca moved behind her. "Unbelievable."

Benjamin stared at the image. They were looking at fires on the southeast and southwest corners of the enormous wall surrounding the Temple Mount, the image smeared even after Sara had adjusted the contrast.

"Scan the area around us," Benjamin ordered, and Sara scrolled the 360-degree image across the screen.

He noted the campfires in the distance. "Lots of pilgrims. Good. It looks like we've hit the beginning of the Passover."

If Sara had been able to deceive him, whom could he trust?

No one but himself.

Sara looked up. "I need to get the telescope out to check star positions now."

He looked over. "Rebecca, David. Put the equipment away. Let's go."

Benjamin helped Sara lift the floor panel, revealing the draped primary mirror one meter in diameter. The pod itself served as part of the powerful telescope, the darkened living compartment acting as the bottom portion of the telescope within the focal length. Starlight was gathered into the pod through the hatch opening and then was reflected by the parabolic mirror up into the image enhancer at the primary focus just below the ceiling. The image was interpreted and resolved by the image enhancer at this focal point, translated, and digitized into binary data.

Sara was typing commands into her computer. "I need everyone to stay at the edge of the pod now. And don't move! I don't want any vibration. The parabolic mirror is going to be shifting on the floor as I guide the telescope."

They needed to determine their location in time.

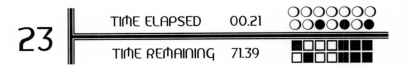

23

TIME ELAPSED   00.21

TIME REMAINING   71.39

BENJAMIN SANK onto the floor, back sliding against the wall
so he was sitting with his knees pulled up and his arms
encircled about them. A narrow floor rim about eighteen
inches wide jutted out between the base of the primary
parabolic mirror and the wall of the pod. David squeezed next
to him on the right, Rebecca on his left, as Sara pulled the
black drape over her head to seal herself and the computer
against the rest of the pod.

Benjamin heard Sara mutter "Let's do it," as she adjusted
the hooded drape to reach the floor. She spoke louder. "I'm
turning off lights—now."

The pod was plunged into darkness.

"Opening the hatch, and deploying telescope." Her voice
was muffled underneath the hood.

The metal floor vibrated, and Benjamin could hear soft
clicks and shifts. He knew what was happening: Sara was
adjusting the parabolic platform ranging in the floor base.
The clicks moved to the hatch as she fine-tuned the position
of the image enhancer at the ceiling. Benjamin listened to the
rumbling of the telescope as the parabolic platform glided on
the base. The room was warming: the air inside the pod
exchanged with the outside, but it was still below freezing and
he was grateful for the heavy clothing. His thoughts
consumed him. *Why, Sara?*

"Fantastic," he heard her murmur through the curtain.
"Just—fantastic." The parabolic mirror thudded next to him.

Benjamin knew there was nothing she could do to alter
the telescopic data. The pod's computer archives stored the

images in real time and transmitted them to Sara's computer screen. Analysis was, however, another story.

After twenty minutes Sara called out, "Done. I've got it."

"How does it look?" Benjamin asked.

He heard the smile in her voice. "Incredible. I'm closing the hatch and turning on lights. Now."

A dim overhead light went on in the pod, and it took Benjamin a few moments to adjust to sight again. The light gradually brightened.

He jumped up to help Sara. She covered the mirror with the protective drape, and then they both replaced the floor panel over it.

Sara sat back down in front of the computer screen, and Benjamin stood behind her. The telescopic images of stars glistened as simple points of light on dark under a superimposed grid. He watched Sara scroll through the stars, orienting them to the positional lines.

She nodded. "It looks good so far. Planetary positions aren't predictable over this long a period, but the stars look like they're where they should be. Let me just run the program."

The computer hummed as it measured the stars' orientation. Sara turned to the next computer and compared lists of numbers with star names.

"We may have a problem," she said.

Deep breath. *Stay calm.*

"I need to run another program first. I can't be sure, but it looks like we're about ten years too late." She snapped off the computer grid before Benjamin could see it, and the default image of the countryside she had taken when they first landed reappeared.

"Show me."

She looked up, surprised. "All right." She pulled up the star images again. "This is the picture of the star positions I just took. The constellations indicate we've landed in springtime, late March or early April." She paused, and then pulled up a grid.

"These are the star positions from our own time." Blue dots appeared on the screen, superimposed over the white ones. "Two thousand years is a small period of time to measure movement of stars so I have to look at the closest ones. I'm monitoring the positions of ten stars, then averaging the predicted time elapsed based on their amount of movement.

"The closest stars move about two arc-seconds a year, compared to the diameter of the moon which is about 1800 arc-seconds. So you can see Alpha Centauri, and Beta Hydri over here," Sara's finger stabbed the screen twice, "have moved approximately two widths of the moon from their positions in our time. Maybe slightly more. Arcturus, Sirius, and Veta Tucanae over here, have also moved."

She typed another command into the computer. Red dots mingled with the blue dots and the white stars photographed from the telescope. She looked up at Benjamin. "These red lights are the predicted positions for the stars on Thursday, April 6, 30 C.E. Although the stars look right, the positions given by the computer indicate that there's a discrepancy."

"Show me," he repeated.

Her fingers flew over the keyboard of the second computer. "This is the computer's raw positional data on this second screen. I'm starting the calculation program now. I need to input the conditions." He leaned closer to watch her, but Sara went through the computer's promptings too quickly for him to follow.

"There," she said. "Calculated date: 39 to 45 C.E. We're with Caligula or Claudius. We've missed it."

Benjamin wondered if she had just fed in wrong data.

"Recommendation?"

"We'll have to try. However, according to these data there's no way we can film the body being stolen. Christianity is starting to be exported throughout the Roman Empire via Caesarea and the other trade routes, and the Romans won't be able to stop it."

His thoughts ran furiously.

"Major Baum," he said. "What corroborating archaeological information might there be for the date Major Levenson has just given?"

He saw Sara shoot a glance at him but ignored her.

"That's easy," David replied. "Along the eastern edge of the city, a little north of here, they built another protective wall for the city in about 40 or 41. It was called the Third Wall."

That would do. "Rebecca, David. I want you to scout the countryside now. Thirty minutes or less, just to the edge of the city to find this wall. Get changed."

"Yes, sir."

"But—" Sara began.

Benjamin turned on her. "You heard me!"

Rebecca was removing the tunics and overcoats from the panel in the wall. David pulled the privacy curtain and stepped inside. A minute later, Rebecca changed.

Benjamin held out their transponders to snap onto their wrists. Each transponder also had a flat countdown clock along the underside of a leather band, not conspicuous but accessible while they were out of the pod.

Both David and Rebecca secreted small video cameras inside their wide, sash-like belts.

"Check surroundings once more," Benjamin ordered, and Sara deployed the camera. He watched as she scrolled the image over the screen. "All clear," she said.

Benjamin nodded. "Go."

David pushed open the hatch, and he and Rebecca climbed to the top of the pod. Then Benjamin climbed up, too, half out of the pod into the first century.

"The surface melted well." He knocked the exterior of the pod. "Looks and feels authentic."

They were three meters off the ground. Benjamin pulled out the knotted rope and threw it over the side, watching until David and Rebecca were on the ground. He slammed the hatch shut.

"I was supposed to lead any away team," Sara said, her back to him. "I'm the second in command." She was sitting on the floor. In that brief period, she had retrieved the drone and spread it open in front of her. The drone was a miniature airplane with a one-meter wingspan; at the end of the mission, it would be guided remotely to deposit the information they had gathered into the Dead Sea.

"What are you doing with that drone?"

She turned. "It was on its side under the floor panel. I saw it when Rebecca got the costumes. I thought it might have been shaken up during the transport, and I wanted to check it."

"Remove your hands from that drone immediately."

A shadow of doubt passed over her face but resolved in just a moment. Ice. "Benjamin, I have bad news. The photo multiplier cells of the guidance system in the drone are cracked. It's inoperable."

The ice princess had returned.

Benjamin felt a flush of anger wash through him in a great wave.

"Major." He bit down on the word, but then stopped. Control. "We have to talk. Now."

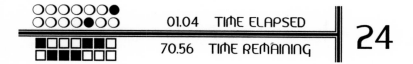

01.04   TIME ELAPSED

70.56   TIME REMAINING

24

DAVID JUMPED onto the ground before Rebecca. He'd known this hill all his life, and yet it felt different.

"Do you think we're in the wrong time?" Rebecca asked.

David was worried about that too, but he shrugged. "Hard to tell looking at the city from where we are. Ten years isn't much for star movement. Easy to make a mistake."

The tilt of the bare hill was much steeper than the built-up one it would be two thousand years from now, and his ankle wobbled on a loose stone.

"Benjamin didn't seem to think Sara was telling him the truth."

He laughed. "Why do you say that? She wouldn't lie."

"I don't know. Just an impression."

The pod had landed near the upper slopes of the Kidron Valley to the east of the southern part of Jerusalem. There were campfires in the distance, but none too close.

The Kidron Valley ran along the eastern wall of the city, separating the Temple Mount from the Mount of Olives, then continued east through the Judean Desert towards the Dead Sea. During the rainy winter months, an occasional flash flood might flow through, but now there was only a faint stream of water. By summer, it would be dry.

They couldn't see much of the city from where they were, since it was above them on a hill. Ancient Jerusalem was surrounded by a great stone wall fifty feet tall and five feet thick, built to defend the city from attack. People entered and exited the city through large guarded gates that stood open all night during times like the Passover when there were many visitors. Roman guards stood equally spaced at intervals along the wall, silhouetted against barrels of fire and the considerable light of the almost-full moon now setting on the horizon. About three o'clock in the morning, David thought.

Jerusalem's main water supply, the Spring of Gihon, was on the western slope of the Kidron Valley, northeast of King David's original city. Before King David conquered the city in about 1000 B.C.E., Jebusite natives had settled it, bragging that the city was so secure that the blind and the lame could defend it. King David had told his men to climb the water shaft into the city to, as he sarcastically put it, defeat those blind and lame.

Water was a central concern for life in this arid land. Three hundred years after King David, King Hezekiah had carved a deeper tunnel through the limestone underneath Jerusalem to channel the water from the Spring of Gihon almost 1800 feet away into the Pool of Siloam, at the bottom of a hill outside the original western wall, also near the southern tip of the Lower City. By Yeshua's time the city had added other water sources such as the Pool of Bethesda in the northeast portion of the city and multiple cisterns that collected rainwater, used for washing since it wasn't considered as clean.

The city of Jerusalem at the time of Yeshua was laid out into five sections. The center of the city, literally and figuratively, was the magnificent Temple at the eastern edge that Herod the Great had begun reconstructing in about 19 B.C.E. according to the Jewish historian Josephus. Although the sanctuary was finished in 13 years, work on the entire surrounding courtyard areas was not finished until about 63 C.E., and seven years later, the Temple was razed by the Romans. A punctuated stone railing surrounding the Temple, called the balustrade, reminded all visitors that only Jews could enter the Temple itself. Inside the Court of the Priests, the priests performed daily animal sacrifices for the atonement of sin.

The Temple was centered in a massive courtyard called the Temple Mount, 985 feet wide and 1576 feet long, which was more than twice as large as the largest contemporary temple enclosure in Rome. Herod had used massive stones, called ashlars—the largest weighing almost 628 tons—to build up the retaining walls of the Temple Mount from the bedrock of Mt. Moriah. The stones were brought from a quarry a mile away and fitted to form the amazing platform.

Surrounding the inside edge of the Temple Mount, stone colonnades held up a shaded porch. At the southern edge on top of this porch was the three-tiered building known as the Royal Stoa, with 162 columns, each more than fifty feet high and so wide that, again according to Josephus, three men with outstretched arms could barely touch fingers around. The Sanhedrin or Jewish ruling body met on the eastern end of the Stoa, in a building called the "House of the Sanhedrin" or "House of Hewn Stone."

Where David and Rebecca were walking, inside the city wall and to the west of the Kidron Valley, was the second of five sections of Jerusalem in Yeshua's time. This was the ancient portion of the city settled on a narrow nine-acre strip of land south of the Temple, known as King David's city.

A narrow commerce area started outside the southwestern wall at the tip of the city, from the Pool of Siloam, and stretched upwards through the Tyropean Valley, and continued all the way up from the Western wall of the Temple to the Damascus Gate. The Tyropean Street was nicknamed the "Valley of Cheese Makers" because the Hebrews could not pronounce the Canaanite word for this valley—Tyropean, or "Cheese Maker," was as close as they could come. The thoroughfare was crammed with merchants and artisans displaying their goods, and was exceptionally crowded during the Feast Days.

A wide courtyard just off the Tyropean Valley led to the magnificent southern entrance of the Temple Mount. The stairs—ascending to what Jews believed to be God's throne on earth—were wide stone, grooved with the passage of millions of feet, bringing people to the pilgrims' entrance of the Huldah Gates. A stone building housing the *mikveh*, or ritual bath, situated at the base of the broad staircase, allowed Jews to ritually wash before entering the Temple Mount.

To the west of the Tyropean Valley, the ground rose up
again into the Western Hill. The slope of the Western Hill
along the southern portion of Jerusalem was called the Lower
City, the third of the five sections and the one where the
common people lived in box-like houses crammed together.
The Western Hill or Upper City, the fourth section, was west
of the Temple Mount, and above and west of the Lower City.
It was the highest area of Jerusalem literally and figuratively.
Here the wealthy people, including the priestly families and
Jewish and Gentile nobility, had mansions decorated with
frescoes and elaborate mosaic floors. Herod's Palace, the
Hasmonean palace, and the theater were located here as well.

The Valley of the Cheese Makers continued past the
Temple Mount to the northern and fifth section of the city.
Here, overlooking the Temple Mount was Herod's grand
Antonia fortress. Additional Roman troops were stationed at
the Antonia during festival times. The high priest's sacred
robes were also kept here and only released during the
festivals so that the Jews remembered that the Romans were
in charge. Many shops and markets were located near the
fortress in this northern section. At the time of Yeshua the
Damascus Gate, the dominant northern portal of the city,
opened into an expanding housing area beyond the city walls,
called "Beth Chesda" or "House of Mercy."

David shivered outside the city wall. It was too wonderful
and magnificent, and yet he couldn't rid himself of the
haunting feeling that they didn't belong. This wasn't their
time. He almost sensed a disturbance of something deep and
profound in the universe. David shook off a heavy sense of
foreboding as Rebecca smiled at him. It wasn't right,
somehow.

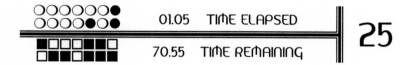

IN TWO STEPS, BENJAMIN CROSSED the pod and snatched the drone from Sara's hands. That quickly she had removed the panels covering the nose of the airplane-like device, exposing the delicate photoamplifier cells like little black buttons in rows. Half the cells had been smashed. As he tilted the drone, slivers of glass fell from the nose into his opened palm.

Sara stood. "I think the insulation around the drone wasn't sufficient, and the cells must have gotten cold. These cells are extraordinarily delicate."

Benjamin bent to put the drone back in its storage space in the cabinet. As he stood, he turned away from her. He didn't even want to see her. "Did you break that drone?" he said to her through clenched teeth.

Sara was silent, and he turned back to look at her. Her jaw tightened.

"What do you mean?" she finally asked.

"Don't give me that! I heard you. I know who you are. I know."

She stood, coolly watching him, but her fists clenched, nails biting into her palms.

"A spy."

But then he saw the muscle in her cheek twitch. She glanced away and back, only a split second, but he'd seen that look before when the person was hiding something. After a moment she said in a low voice, "Benjamin? I'm the one who was hit on the head. What are you talking about?"

He turned on her, his hands pressing on her upper arms pulling her close to him. His face was next to hers. "I heard you, right after the time throw. You called to Yeshua Ha'Maschiach. You're a follower, aren't you?"

She held his gaze for a moment, but then her eyes dropped. "How can you think that?" she murmured.

He closed his eyes for a moment, trying to close out the truth. The mission was in jeopardy.

She twisted between his hands to step away from him, and he watched her begin to move away.

"Look at me, Sara."

She did, slowly.

He had it now. Control.

"You're not indispensable on this mission. It wouldn't be so hard for me to take you out of commission. Tie you up, maybe, like a common prisoner."

"Benjamin, I—"

"Save it for the court-martial," he snapped. "You could even be the mole, as far as I can see. You have the security clearance, and you could easily come up with a dozen ways to sabotage the time machine. This isn't anything new for you. After all, no one really knows what precipitated the disaster on the space station either."

She looked as if he'd slapped her. Good.

"I don't know. I don't care. I'm only concerned that FlashBack is completed successfully."

"But I've done nothing!"

He held up his hand. "I don't want to hear it. I simply don't want to have any more problems on this mission. No equipment breakdowns or computer failures, no tapes that are mysteriously erased, nothing that doesn't work the way it should. If something does happen, I'll know who to blame. And I will take action."

It was as if a mask covered her face as she held his gaze. "If you think I'm a spy, why don't you just kill me?"

"Don't think I won't if I have to," he replied, but was dismayed to feel a twisting inside at the thought of it. He would never kill anyone in cold blood. She knew that.

Sara stepped toward him, angry now. "If I were the mole, why would I help capture that saboteur, my own man, instead of letting him kill you the other night? I could have prevented this whole mission. That would have been a whole lot easier than my tampering with equipment once we'd arrived."

It was a point he'd been turning over in his mind, but right now, he didn't have enough information to understand. Who was she working with? What were her goals?

He'd turn her over for questioning when they returned. Now he held her gaze. "Did you break those photoamplifier cells?"

She stared back at him. "No."

"Can the drone be repaired?"

She was silent for a moment. "Yes."

"How?"

"We need the light cells from the suspension camera. I can adapt the wiring to make them work."

Benjamin evaluated the statement. That camera would be suspended under a weather balloon at night to take pictures of the surrounding countryside, and they wouldn't deploy it until tonight at the earliest. She wouldn't be able to start work on the drone for twenty-four hours at least. Convenient for her.

"Aren't those cells too heavy to go into the nose of the drone?"

She nodded. "Yes. But I can modify the backing, lighten them up."

She began to walk away again. Benjamin growled, "Sara." She froze. "Yes."

"I'm going to be watching you. I'm your shadow now."

"Fine."

"Will you deny Yeshua as Lord?"

She moved to face him directly. "I refuse to play these games. I'm not a spy. I want to find the truth, just like you, I swear. I've done nothing, nor will I, to undermine this mission."

How had the followers gotten to her to convert her during the intensive training? She'd been protected; they all had. Why had she listened? Sara, of all people.

The air circulation produced a dry low thrum that vibrated the floor, and his hands moved only a little unsteadily as he straightened the storage panel covering the drone. It was still cold in the pod, but he felt perfectly warm.

They needed to find the tomb. Now.

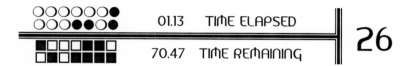

THE THIRD WALL WASN'T THERE. They hadn't even begun construction.

David breathed a sigh of relief as he finished panning the area with his night vision goggles. He and Rebecca had climbed the hill to the packed dirt road surrounding the city, and now stood near the northeastern corner of the wall. The warm spring breeze blew past the sparse grasses and the rustling olive trees, and he loosened the folds of his overcoat. The stars were like crystal fire in the dark sky. It was the deadest part of night.

"I want to get a bit closer," he whispered to Rebecca.

"Do we have time?"

"I need to get a better angle. I want to film it for our archives."

He left the road and walked closer to the wall over the wisping grass that tickled his calves. "Come on."

He didn't even glance back, just listened for the gentle swish of grasses as Rebecca followed him. His night vision goggles were set to amplify the ambient star- and moonlight, but as his path angled toward the corner of the Temple, the fire on the wall ten meters above played havoc with the image, smearing it to green. He pulled off the goggles and shoved them into the *scrip*, the leather purse that he carried on a strap over his shoulder.

"Now look at this," he breathed.

Rebecca also pulled off her night vision goggles as she drew beside him. "What?"

David put his hand on the cornerstone of the northern

Temple Mount. The surface was not too rough; it had been smoothed with a hand-held chisel. "Amazing. The Romans won't leave one stone upon another when they sack the city in 70 C.E. Yet it's here now, whole—"

He'd left his career in medicine to study archaeology, to learn more about his faith. He was overwhelmed with the thought of being so near to the Temple, the throne of God on Earth.

"Isn't that what we're looking for?" She pointed to the stone wall that joined the Temple wall ten meters back. "It's going north."

"No, no. That wall is old. If we followed it around, we'd come to the northern Damascus Gate into Jerusalem where the Romans will crucify Yeshua. The Third Wall was built later to surround the northern territory where they had begun to build more houses. But there's no evidence of it yet."

"How can you tell it's not the Third Wall?"

He was withdrawing the small video camera from the *scrip* as he talked. "Easy. The Third Wall is much closer to the junction of the Temple Mount, and the angle is different. There isn't even any construction begun. We're doing well."

"So we're in the right time? Sara was wrong?"

David looked up. "She said 39 to 45. The Third Wall was built about 41 C.E. She still could just be right, but it's unlikely."

Rebecca nodded. "Benjamin didn't believe Sara."

"He just wanted to confirm her estimate. Good thing too."

"It was more than that. He was looking daggers at her when we left."

He sighed and debated whether it was worth arguing. No, it wasn't. He turned to film the angle between the two walls, narrating as he panned the digital camera over the area. "This is the junction between the northern Temple wall and the original northern wall. The rock is limestone, carved into rectangular blocks several meters in length, each block with the peculiar raised Herodian border framing the exterior portion of the block."

Rebecca harrumphed, but didn't speak until he'd turned off the camera.

"Are you ready to go back now?" she asked.

"Yes. What's the countdown?"

He saw her shut her eyes a moment. "I'm guessing—70:38."

She had an incredible sense of the passage of time, but he glanced at his own watchband anyway. Correct, and he laughed. "How do you do that?"

She shrugged. "It can be a curse. I hear the music in language, in numbers, and in the flow of time. It clutters my mind."

"Well, let's turn back."

David watched Rebecca as she put on her night vision goggles, then reached for his own. He led the way back to the road.

He wondered if Sara was recalculating an accurate estimate of their position within the short period that he and Rebecca were scouting the northern wall. The lack of construction strongly suggested they were in the right time.

David shook his head. By all accounts, Yeshua had been a good, even extraordinary, person in life, but it was ironic that he'd been lifted up as the rallying point for the radical belief system of Messianism. He didn't think Yeshua would approve. Messianism had a good foundation, the Law and the Prophets, but the followers had built on it what they should not have. The *Shema* whispered in his head:

Shema Yisrael. Adonai Elohenu, Adonai Echad.

The followers claimed Yeshua was God as well as man. It was blasphemy.

Even with the bright moonlight, he was grateful for the night vision goggles. The road was lined with stones, and the thick leather soles of his open sandals were inflexible. He had to concentrate on his footing. The wind rustled the sinuous branches of the scattered olive trees next to the road, and on the top of the Temple wall to his right, the dark shapes of men, the Levites and Temple guards, crossed in front of the light as they tended the fires.

They were in front of the Eastern Gate at the center of the Temple Mount now. The construction of the gate was magnificent, tall and arched; it was from here that the scapegoat was led into the wilderness and pushed over a cliff every year on Yom Kippur, symbolically carrying with it the sins of the people. He checked his transponder again. It would take another ten minutes to get back to the pod. From the looks of the sky, there were just a few hours until sunrise, and once the dawn came, they wouldn't be able to move into or out of the pod for fear of detection.

Rebecca rested her hand on his arm. "Do you see that?"

"What?"

She pointed behind them.

"I see," he breathed. In the distance were several torches moving close to the top of the slope of the Mount of Olives. His heart beat quicker.

"Are you thinking the same thing I am?"

Rebecca's voice came back low. "It's later at night than it was thought to have occurred, and Sara did say we were too late. But it's suggestive."

He nodded. "Yes, indeed."

Could it be they were watching the arrest party made up of the Temple guards as they went to arrest Yeshua? If so, Yeshua was even now praying in the Garden of the Olive Press, the Garden of Gethsemane, waiting for Judas Iscariot to return. Yeshua would be tried and found guilty of blasphemy and sorcery tonight. He would be crucified tomorrow at noon.

A great surge of hope leaped inside him. They would film everything about Yeshua's death and the body theft, from beginning to end. They would control the followers, secure their country from attack—

He jumped as his eyes fell back on the road. No more than twenty meters in front of them were two young men, their over-robes wound tightly despite the fact that the night was warm. They looked to be in their late teens or early twenties. Both men were standing in the road with their backs to David and Rebecca, looking down the hill toward the pod in the distance that reflected like a white pebble in the moonlight.

"Quick," he hissed to Rebecca, at the same time holding his arm out to back her off the road with him. There wasn't much place to hide in the sparse shelter. They moved into the shadow of the city wall.

"Who are they?"

He shrugged. "Maybe a lookout for the group that went into the hills. I don't like how they're facing the pod, though." If the two men were familiar with the terrain, they might be noticing that a big boulder had appeared where none had been before.

Rebecca yanked off her goggles and started rooting through her own *scrip*. "I want to hear what they're saying." She pulled out the small directional microphone.

Holding the palm of one hand flat over her eyes, she listened, adjusting the microphone once or twice to improve directional focus on the conversation.

"Excellent transmission. The two men are speaking Aramaic. They're Jews. I'm not sure what they're up to, though. They're not talking as much as I'd like."

"What are they saying?"

"They're surprised to see the pod."

David grimaced. "That's not good."

She lifted her hand from her eyes. "They sound casual. Their accent is not what I expected, strange turns of the vowels. I'm going to need to hear some more speech to get it right."

He studied the two men.

She shook her head as if to return her attention to where she was standing. "We need to stay away from them. They have several friends, the ones we saw going up the Mount of Olives, who will then be going straight into Jerusalem."

"I don't like how they're studying the pod. We need to chase them off."

The bright moon provided excellent lighting for any observer to see the team moving around the pod.

He activated the range-finding laser on his goggles and switched to visible. A bright red dot appeared on the rocks down the hill.

"Thirty-eight meters," he murmured, then trained the dot in front of the two men's feet. One made a startled exclamation and backed off. The other seemed slower, calmer. As he turned around he seemed to see David in the shadows but then he looked past him and jogged after his friend who was running toward the Southern Gate.

"I hope I'm not changing history by chasing those two men away. We have to get Benjamin and Sara out of that pod now. The arrest party will be coming down the mountain any moment."

"Do you think that's what it is?"

David looked up. "It could be."

But inside he was sure.

He turned on the transponder and opened a communication to the pod. They had little time to move forward.

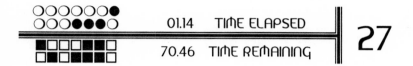

SARA'S HEART WAS THUMPING in her ears.

She looked down at her hands as she turned away from Benjamin in the pod. They were trembling.

Benjamin's eyes had been dead as he'd confronted her, cold and lifeless, merciless. She'd never seen him with that look before. It was something he must have developed dealing with the terrorists during his time in Special Forces. And in his eyes now, she too threatened him.

Now that the immediate stress of the confrontation was over, Sara began to tremble, and then she turned her back to him and crossed her arms over her chest so he wouldn't see. Something had ripped deep inside her.

His eyes were so cold.

She heard Benjamin's steps behind her, and then the sound of computer keys tapping—he was reviewing her calculations of their time position. The computer beeped, again, then silence. Her breath hung as a cloud in the frigid air, and she sank into a small ball resting her head on her knees.

So cold.

She despised herself for being so weak.

The image flashed in her mind of how Benjamin had kissed her the other night, so soft, how he had held her in his arms and smiled when his eyes caught hers. The warm feel of his breath against her cheek. The rise and fall of his chest brushing against her, his hand in her hair. She'd almost melted against him that night, so close.

No. It had been an illusion. She'd fallen in love with him from afar over the last year, had hidden it well until that night in the small infirmary room. She'd been a fool to open her heart like that.

She was shivering uncontrollably from the cold and the stress now as her thoughts lumbered, frozen in their long dance.

Hold on.

She had to gain control, pull a cover of ice over her emotions. She had to be able to function.

Benjamin, she thought again, and she felt utterly weak.

Sara searched for something to do, anything so that he wouldn't be right on top of her. After a moment, she moved to the wall panel at her right and began unpacking the costumes. The low hum of machinery in the pod plugged her ears with white noise, contributing to her feeling of heaviness.

Benjamin stood with his back to her. As she watched, he leaned over the computer again, the keys clicking as he continued to verify her calculations from the star positions. Or maybe he was recording his suspicions.

David would be radioing in with his report any minute now, and she had to be ready. Her whirling emotions coalesced and focused into stone-hard logic. Benjamin had accused her of being a follower.

Her breath came in little gasps. He'd said she had called out to Yeshua Ha'Maschiach as she regained consciousness.

She laid the first overcoat straight on the floor in front of her, adjusted the edge, and put the second on top of the first. She couldn't remember anything from right after they'd arrived in this time, just that she'd woken lying on the capsule floor.

He had heard her say something. She shivered.

She'd blacked out in the transport. Furthermore, the scientists had said the soldiers would not remember the time travel clearly since they would be moving through a distorted time-space that didn't allow the normal, time-based chemical storage of events in the brain. The images of what had happened could only dance around the edge of her brain, unclear.

She pulled the tunic from the storage space in the wall and shook it out as Benjamin turned around to face her. "Major. We're going out as soon as they return."

He couldn't have confirmed her calculations yet, not even close.

"Get changed."

"Yes, sir." But she moved slowly.

Sara paused, then reached up to pull the privacy curtain around her. The heavy curtain fluttered like a bird's wing against her face as she closed it. There was barely enough space to stand, but it felt good to be out of sight. She shook out the inner, linen tunic she would wear next to her skin and slipped the loose garment over her head. The weavers had used finely hand-spun linen threads, a mark of at least moderate wealth, to make strips of cloth that had been sewn together lengthwise with sleeves that came to her mid-forearm. She tied the tunic around her waist with the woven belt, or girdle, that was as wide as her hand.

The pod seemed to have been shushed into stunned silence inside the curtain; only the soft murmur of the computer remained. She tried to smile as she flung back the curtain and stepped out into the main room.

She wrapped about her the rough-woven woolen overcoat, or *haluk*; it was heavy enough to keep her warm in the cool spring weather. The fabric felt scratchy through the tunic. She placed another covering over her head. Her sandals had thick leather soles with a strap passing between her toes and another around her ankle, binding them to her feet. Like the other soldiers, she'd been wearing them for a month so the blisters were past and the calluses formed.

Sara picked up the weapons belt, a small pocket of leather with a flap folded over the top that contained several concussion bombs, a starburst bomb, and a taser. She tied it inside the girdle, hidden, yet she could reach inside to remove something from it instantly.

The speaker on the console beeped. There it was: David's transmission. She took a deep breath.

Benjamin glared at her as he picked up the microphone. "Go ahead."

David's voice came back tinny through the speaker. "There's no evidence of the Third Wall."

Sara looked away.

"We've landed well before 41 C.E. Furthermore, Rebecca and I observed a small party moving up Mount Olivet maybe five minutes ago. It's suggestive."

Benjamin's jaw was set. "You mean you think it's Yeshua's arrest party?"

"Maybe."

She shook her head. "No, it couldn't be. We're too late."

"Quiet!" Benjamin snapped.

"We've chased off two men in the vicinity, but there are bound to be more people soon."

"Acknowledged," Benjamin said. His eyes passed over her. Then he turned away.

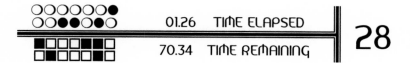

01.26 TIME ELAPSED

70.34 TIME REMAINING

28

"I KNOW WHERE another dead drop is," Etan said as he looked up from the desk.

Aaron tensed. "Where?"

They were alone in the glassed-in security control center, cross-referencing data. Beyond the clear walls of the cell he could see three more of his officers hunched over their own computers, trying to find something, anything, that would help in this investigation. Searches of the saboteur Uri Seidel's quarters and personal effects had revealed nothing, as had multiple interrogations even using scopolamine, a so-called truth serum. Once the seal over the complex was broken after FlashBack, Seidel could be transferred to a professional facility that had the tools to handle the job. However, by then it might be too late, so for now Aaron was focused on combing what data they had, trying to find something that might help them unearth the mole.

He got up and walked over to Etan. "Where is the drop?"

"If I'm right, it's clever. Really clever. Really bold."

He waited.

"This complex is not an easy place to hide anything. The public areas are completely monitored with cameras."

"Yes."

"But," Etan said. He jabbed his finger at the computer screen. "There's a blind spot surrounding each camera, you know."

Aaron nodded. "Of course. Directly underneath the camera, but the adjacent camera picks it up."

"Yes, usually, unless—"

He was looking at the location of two cameras, AC-21 and AC-20, that Etan had highlighted on the schematic displayed on the computer screen. Recognition dawned.

"Unless there's a right angle in the corridor between the cameras."

Etan smiled. "There might be a few feet of unmonitored space that the adjacent camera doesn't pick up."

"Continue." He saw where this was going, and Etan was brilliant to have worked it out.

"I think we may have a drop here. Look. I've been going over the computer records of Seidel over the past year, all of the places he's been localized to by the RFID readers. I eliminated all of the places cross-referenced with his duty schedule in Mechanics. Then I sorted for the locations where almost anyone—Seidel as well as the officers and command staff—could appear without raising suspicions, since we know our mole is high up. And I found something interesting."

Aaron leaned forward.

"Let me show you this." Etan typed a command on the keyboard. The schematic changed to a data table. "These two columns show the times of Seidel's localization at cameras AC-21, then AC-20. You can see over the past year he's gone past this particular intersection twenty-nine times, or on average slightly more than once every other week, although there are gaps of more than a month in some of these visits. This third column shows the amount of time he took to get from one camera to the other. His average is just over nine seconds.

"I've also taken a random sampling of the time it takes other people to get around this corner. With twelve hundred entries the average is 7.9 seconds with a standard deviation of 1.5 seconds."

"So Seidel's time is on the money."

"Yes, but wait a moment. If you look at the individual entries you can see that either he was very quick, or very slow."

Etan reached for a sheet of paper beside him with a bar graph printed from the computer. The vertical axis showed number of seconds, the horizontal showed individual occurrences. Aaron saw a clear bimodal distribution, nothing in the middle.

Etan cleared his throat. "Twenty-two times it took him under seven seconds to go around the corner. Seven times it took him sixteen seconds." He leaned back in the chair with a satisfied air.

"Was he talking to someone? Maybe he tripped?"

"I've checked the visual records. Nothing."

He pressed his lips together, thinking. Brilliant.

"Sir?"

Aaron focused on his protégé. "Let's go find it."

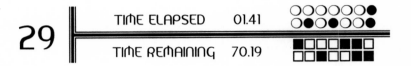

29

TIME ELAPSED   01.41

TIME REMAINING   70.19

AT ITS BEGINNING, THE CORRIDOR BRANCHED from the main thoroughfare toward the Physics complex. Aaron nodded, impressed. This was a devious location for a dead drop if the users had some courage. Like all of the corridors communicating between buildings, this hallway was made of white-painted cinderblock with bright fluorescent lighting. Despite its easy accessibility, it was narrow, six feet across, and meandered a long way through the building before ending at one of the equipment hangars. Consequently, it was not heavily traveled.

Aaron and Etan walked five minutes before Etan cleared his throat. "There's the AC-21 camera."

The corridor had several right angles from which a few hallways branched off, a few office doors set along its path, but there were also long sections of uninterrupted white wall. It was through one of these sections that they were passing now.

Aaron saw a wall ahead as the corridor made another right turn. The camera, AC-21, was mounted just beneath the ceiling. As he walked around the bend, he could see the second camera, AC-20, recessed about twelve feet after the turn.

"The drop must be in this area." Aaron stood in the corner and checked both passageways. The hallway was clear of people. "Where might it be hidden?"

Etan scuffed his boot against the polished white linoleum floor. "Smooth wall. No fire extinguisher. Not so much as a crack in the paint."

Aaron studied the two cameras' fields of view, and then turned back the way they had come. "The area we're interested in extends from about here—" he slapped the wall, then turned and walked back and around the corner, Etan following him— "to about here. About twelve feet total. Not much."

Etan scanned the area from the corner. "If I were hiding a drop I'd put it in the corner, as far away as possible from the arc of the camera. It would also be easier to locate. Too bad we didn't put a camera to watch here."

Aaron shrugged. "Hard to anticipate everything."

The area was unremarkable. How would someone hide a dead drop here?

"It's more likely to be low to the ground," Aaron said. "Someone could pretend to drop something and lean over to pick it up. His body would shield the opening. Check the toe molding."

Etan nodded, reaching into his pocket and pulling on thin latex gloves to avoid destroying any evidence. He dropped to his knees to examine the blocks near the floor, starting at the corner of the hallway and moving back the way they had come. Aaron snapped on his own gloves and started in the other direction. The floor was hard and uncomfortable against his knees; he was getting too old for this.

They worked in silence.

"Nothing's here," Etan said, but it was just then that Aaron saw something.

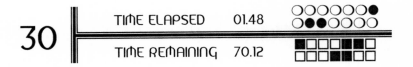

30 TIME ELAPSED   01.48

TIME REMAINING   70.12

BENJAMIN FOUND himself thinking of Tamar while his team walked along the road toward the tomb. They'd passed the junction of the northern wall with the Temple, as far as David and Rebecca had scouted. The sky was lightening, midnight blue, and the stars pierced the darkness.

A blue-tinged memory, like a surprising scent of flowers crossing his face. Maybe because this had always been Tamar's favorite time of day: the pre-symphonic hush before the dawn. She'd wake in the small hours of the morning, and sometimes Benjamin would open his eyes to find her pacing around their apartment or on the terrace, night robe tangled around her legs and her hair soft, and then he'd murmur to her to come back to bed—

He'd rescued tens of hostages and foiled a handful of terrorist plots, but he hadn't been able to prevent the car bomb that had killed his wife. None of that had happened yet, it was two thousand years before it would occur, and yet he couldn't stop it. Why hadn't he been told when they'd discovered the type of trigger device that had killed her? Gideon had mentioned it like it was an afterthought. Tamar shouldn't be an afterthought.

Stop it. His heart closed painfully inside his chest.

They had to find Yeshua's tomb.

He hadn't investigated the perimeter around the pod before they'd left, and he wondered if that decision would come back to haunt him. He had wanted to hurry to observe the arrest party from Mount Olivet. Even though the party had disappeared, Benjamin was optimistic that the time machine had brought them to the early Friday morning of Yeshua's crucifixion, exactly as planned.

"Countdown?"

Rebecca blurted out, "69.59," without checking her wristband. Benjamin knew she had an incredible sense of the passage of time, but they had no room for error or showing off on this mission. "Data, not guesses!" he snapped.

David said, "Sir, countdown is 69.57."

Benjamin yanked Sara's sleeve as she moved ahead with David and Rebecca. "You stay with me." She glanced at him with hooded eyes before pulling her head covering forward so it shielded her face from his view. He released the rough cloth of her overcoat.

"We're about halfway around to the Northern Gate," David said. "The arrest party almost certainly went south, the opposite direction, and up the stairs of the Pool of Siloam to access the Upper City. But we'll be in time to enter the city and film the trial in front of Pontius Pilate."

Sara sighed. "We won't film a thing. You didn't see the arrest party. It's too late."

Her words fell dead on the group.

"The arrest party was later at night than I thought it would be," David said after a moment. "But it's consistent with what we know historically."

"At four in the morning? You didn't see the group of men with torches, what they wore, what they were saying. Did you? How do you even know it was an arrest party?"

David held up his hand, palm up. "You're right, they were too far away. The timing is merely suggestive."

"Who else might it have been?" Rebecca asked.

"There are many pilgrims camping outside the city walls. Or maybe someone important was arriving for the Passover."

Rebecca shrugged.

Sara's chin jutted forward. "It wasn't the arrest party. It's too late."

David glanced back. "Too late at night, or too late year-wise?"

"Both."

"Drop it, Major," Benjamin said.

They walked on in silence.

The sky was lighter now, and the trees and grasses were beginning to draw outlines against the hills. Benjamin frowned as he walked with Sara by his side. The city wall to their left towered over them, and even as he moved forward, the thin, eerie cry of the *shofar* blew from the Temple behind. It was the ram's horn signaling the appearance of the sun's edge on the horizon.

"Daybreak," he heard Sara whisper.

Tamar flickered again in his mind, but he pushed her away for good. She was gone.

Sara's hands were buried in her overcoat, the edge of the head covering shielding her face from his view.

Rebecca looked back at Sara. "How can you be so sure we're not in the correct time? It doesn't make sense that we'd be years too late. The time machine has always been accurate to fractions of a second before now, and you've said yourself that star positions are impossible to predict."

"No. Planet positions."

Rebecca waved her hand. "Planet positions. Whatever. But just because—"

"I didn't measure planetary positions. I measured the positions of the nearest stars. I measured the arc of their movement over two thousand years. The computer estimated that the amount of their movement corresponded to the years 39 to 45 C.E."

Benjamin crossed his arms. "I'm still not convinced that's accurate." He hadn't had enough time to verify Sara's calculations, but even if he had, he wouldn't have trusted them. She had had ample time before the transport to alter the computer program. Who knew what she might have done?

David looked over. "There's no evidence of the Third Wall. That puts us well before 41."

Sara was maintaining her statement that they had arrived too late. She wasn't stupid, must know they'd discover soon enough where they were. Was there any chance she was telling the truth?

No. She was a follower of the Way, with a perfect motive for lying. She wanted to prevent the team from filming Yeshua's body being stolen from the tomb, prevent them from disproving Messianism. It wouldn't be long now until they did just that.

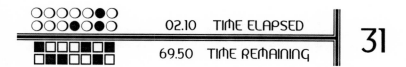

SARA TIGHTENED HER JAW. As she glanced over at Benjamin walking beside her, a great surge of anger washed over her. A spy, was she? A traitor? Well, she'd been called worse.

She had to hang on a little longer.

Benjamin grabbed her sleeve. "Slow down," he ordered, his eyes dead as they swept over her. "Stay with me."

Up ahead, beyond David and Rebecca, Sara saw her first group of natives walking south towards them. The six men and four women had just passed around the bend about forty yards ahead, two of the women carrying infants. Several little children darted between their feet. Sara was surprised at how young yet worn the group looked. They looked poor; probably they had traveled from some distance to make a sacrifice at the Temple for the Passover.

At least their own team's clothing seemed to blend. David, several yards in front of her, nodded his head in response to the pilgrims' greeting, and then they passed by. Dust from the well-packed dirt road covered Sara's feet.

"Good so far," she heard Benjamin say, and she could tell he was pleased.

The sun was rising up on their right, blinding now as it skimmed the hilltops. She thought again of the time. David and Rebecca were dreaming if they thought they'd seen Yeshua's arrest party a mere two hours ago, so close to dawn.

The sequence of events of the last week of Yeshua's life was clear. He had entered the city of Jerusalem on Sunday April 2, 30 C.E., riding a donkey's colt that some said was the deliberate fulfillment of a messianic prophecy from the ninth chapter of the prophet Zechariah:

Rejoice greatly, O Daughter of Zion!
Shout, Daughter of Jerusalem!
See, your king comes to you, righteous and having salvation,
Gentle and riding on a donkey, on a colt, the foal of a donkey.

At Yeshua's entrance into the city, the crowds had waved palm branches and shouted "Hosanna!" The palm branches were a national symbol for Israel, much like a modern country's flag, and "Hosanna" was a political term meaning "Deliver us." In other words, the crowds were looking for a national leader who would rise up and throw off the yoke of Rome. They thought Yeshua would be the one. Ultimately, he disappointed them.

Soon afterwards, Yeshua went to the Temple Mount, and found many sellers of sacrificial animals and money changers doing brisk business, as usual. Since the outer Court was the only place that Gentiles were permitted to worship, he was so angered by the commerce that he turned over the merchants' tables and drove out the buyers and sellers. Yeshua preached openly in the Temple Courts and on the Mount of Olives every day from Monday through Thursday about how God is accessible to everyone. The Jewish authorities, at the top of their own spiritual hierarchy, felt threatened. Not only had Yeshua damaged a major source of revenue for them, but he also had called them hypocrites and vipers in front of the people. He jeopardized their power and position; they wanted to eliminate this troublemaker, but didn't know how to do it.

That was when Judas Iscariot, one of Yeshua's twelve followers, approached these men and offered to betray Yeshua. For this, the authorities paid him thirty pieces of silver.

David slowed down ahead. "This is the Northern Gate. The tomb isn't far from here."

"It's magnificent," Rebecca exclaimed. The three entrances of the gate stretched thirty meters above them, the tall arch flanked by two smaller ones.

"Yeshua will be crucified outside these gates at noon, while the people walk past. It's an agonizing death."

"Where is the tomb?" Benjamin asked.

"Back this way. Behind the fields here."

Sara shook her head. It was too late.

To celebrate the Passover on Thursday night, April 6, Yeshua took his band of apostles to a house within the Upper City to eat the *Seder* meal after sundown. During the meal, Judas Iscariot bolted to inform the Jewish authorities of Yeshua's whereabouts. Yeshua finished the dinner, and then led his band of men outside the city and up the Mount of Olives into the Garden of Gethsemane—the Garden of the Olive Press—to wait.

Working on Judas' information, the priests sent an arrest party to bring Yeshua in for trial that night by the ruling body of the Jews, the Sanhedrin. He was taken first to the House of Annas, the former High Priest and father-in-law of the current High Priest, where he was tried in an illegal, secret nighttime trial and found guilty of blasphemy. Then Yeshua was taken to the house of Caiaphas, the current High Priest, where he was forced to endure another illegal, secret nighttime trial and again found guilty of blasphemy. The records indicated that Caiaphas—the High Priest—called many witnesses whose testimonies had to be discarded. Then he found two witnesses who both testified that Yeshua had stated he could restore a destroyed Temple in three days. Their testimonies should have been legally discarded also because they didn't agree well enough, but Caiaphas allowed the weak and disputable testimonies. Caiaphas then illegally invoked the Oath of the Testimony to force Yeshua to incriminate himself.

Sara thought there were some curious points about Yeshua's arrest and trial. For instance, why had the Jewish authorities not arrested Yeshua sometime during the week when he preached every day at the Temple, and returned every night to quiet Bethany to stay with Mary, Martha, and Lazarus? At the last moment, when the difficulties were multiplied, the Sanhedrin decided to go through with arrest. Failure at that late hour to secure conviction, an additional conviction from Rome, and a completed execution by sunset the next day when the week-long Feast of Unleavened Bread began would have had potentially disastrous consequences. If they had failed even by a whisker, the authorities would have had to hold Yeshua throughout that entire week while Rome stood poised to crush the demonstrations that would surely result.

What information had Judas brought? Was it just Yeshua's location and an offer to identify him? Sara thought it likely that Judas also reported Yeshua's apparent resignation to die as portrayed in the account by the eyewitness John. Maybe that detail had emboldened the Sanhedrin to go ahead. Had the authorities believed Yeshua could do miracles?

The sun was higher in the sky now, and Sara could see the day would be clear and cloudless. It was cold, mid-spring weather. She wrapped her overcoat tighter about her.

David slowed along the path. "There."

He was looking out over the fields, past several campsites, to the rocky hills about half a mile away.

"Let's go," Benjamin said, and David led the way as they cut across the field. The dewy grass wrapped around Sara's calves like fingers.

After the Sanhedrin convicted Yeshua, they brought him to Pontius Pilate, the Roman procurator who kept order in the city. Pilate heard the case quickly enough, but tried to dismiss it, first by declaring Yeshua innocent, then by offering to release him instead of the hardened criminal Barabbas, then by sending him to Herod Antipas to be judged. When Herod sent Yeshua back to Pilate, Pilate tried to appease the Jewish authorities by flogging Yeshua; they were not satisfied, and incited the mob to cry out that Pilate was not a friend of Caesar's if he did not crucify this man. Pilate took a bowl of water and washed his hands in front of the crowd, saying that Yeshua's blood would not rest on him. Then he ordered him crucified.

Again, Sara was intrigued. Although it was not stated in the historical records, she was almost certain that the Jewish authorities had visited with Pontius Pilate before Yeshua's arrest to ensure they would be able to carry out their plans for

Yeshua's execution in a timely manner. Not only was this prudent and common sense, but there was also an intriguing reference in the text of Matthew to Pilate's wife recounting how she had suffered many things in a dream because of Yeshua, and therefore had sent an urgent message to her husband to have nothing to do with him. How would she have known about Yeshua if it hadn't been discussed prior to her dream? It made sense that the Jewish authorities would not have initiated the arrest if Pilate hadn't assured them that he would confirm the findings of their court proceeding. The authorities no doubt panicked the next morning when Pilate seemed so determined to release him.

Ultimately, though, Pilate hadn't released Yeshua. After the flogging, where sharp bones and great strips of metal on leather straps tore the skin of his back into bloody strips and stripped the muscle, the executioners forced Yeshua to carry the heavy crossbeam of the cross through the city of Jerusalem. A bystander was forced by the Romans to carry the cross partway through the street because the flogging had so weakened Yeshua. Outside the gate, the Roman soldiers hammered great spikes between the bones of Yeshua's wrists and ankles, transecting the great nerve bands that supplied the hands and feet, and then hung up Yeshua to die.

Death by crucifixion is caused by partial asphyxiation: The person can breathe in, but can't exhale without lifting himself up through excruciating pain. Often the executioners broke the legs of the prisoner after a few hours to expedite death, but in Yeshua's case, no bones needed to be broken since he was already dead. One of the Roman soldiers thrust his sword between Yeshua's ribs and into his chest cavity to confirm this fact.

Then, Yosef of Arimathea and Nicodemus, secret followers of Yeshua and the only two of seventy members of the Sanhedrin who had voted not to convict Yeshua the night before, went to Pilate to ask for the body for burial. Pilate was surprised that Yeshua had died after just three hours on the cross, but when death was confirmed he released the body to them. They took Yeshua's body to Yosef's new tomb right outside the city, washed it, and wrapped it in long linen cloths. Nicodemus brought about 100 pounds of expensive spices to help with the preservation of the body.

They were almost to the tomb now, Sara thought.

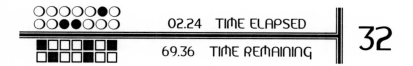

BENJAMIN GLANCED BACK, and he frowned as he saw the young man following at a distance behind them over the grass. Maybe he was going to one of the campsites they'd passed on the way over, not close enough to be a problem at this point, but the team would have to remain inconspicuous.

They were half a mile out from the road, right at the limestone hills. A cave nearby had been carved out.

"Is this it?" Benjamin asked.

David shrugged. "Hard to say. The tomb could be anywhere along here, but this is certainly much like Yeshua's. We'll be able to follow the progression of the body once it's taken from the cross, of course, so I wouldn't worry too much about finding the exact tomb right now."

Benjamin nodded. "I want to take a look inside."

The white limestone of the tomb followed the lines of the hillside. The squared entrance to the tomb was about one meter wide by two meters high. It yawned into the dark interior, and a musty odor wafted from inside.

Sara placed her hand on a massive disc-shaped rock standing on its edge about twenty feet away from the tomb entrance up a small hill. A small rock wedged it in front to keep it from rolling downhill.

"Is this the *golel*?" she asked. Benjamin narrowed his eyes.

David nodded. "Yes. That's the boulder that covers the tomb entrance."

The boulder looked immoveable. He watched Sara push against it. She asked, "Is this *golel* typical for this time period?"

Next to Benjamin, David was studying the entrance to the tomb, and he turned, distracted, by Sara's question. "Oh yes. It weighs several tons at least. Quite typical."

"How did they get the boulder to cover the tomb in the first place?" Rebecca asked.

"Easy," David replied. "They rolled it from the hill above. Two or three people could move the *golel*, with a lever system, you know, to start the stone rolling. It was guided by this trench here, along the hill."

"Really," Rebecca said.

"Of course, once it's in place in front of a tomb, it's much harder to move away."

Benjamin moved next to Sara to study the *golel*. The boulder was as tall as she was and two meters or more wide, formidable.

"What are you thinking?"

She shook her head.

"What?"

"Imagine the apostles sneaking up to the tomb guarded by a Roman contingent and pushing this great stone away so they could steal the body, without being noticed."

He shot her a dirty look. "We're here to film the tomb, not hatch theories. Leave it alone, Sara."

David touched the rock of the tomb. "It's something, isn't it? A new tomb like this was worth as much as an entire house in our culture. Very expensive. Once someone was interred in it, no one other than that person's relatives could be buried here. Yosef of Arimathea made a great sacrifice to donate this."

He brushed his fingers over the stone, tracing a darkened series of slashes in the soft limestone. "Here is the owner's mark. In first century burial customs, after they rolled the *golel* across the entrance of the tomb they wedged a smaller stone against it, the *dopheg*. In Yeshua's case, the Romans also sealed the tomb, a cord stretching between the two rocks with clay holding the ends and imprinted with signet rings. The slightest bit of tampering would have broken it. And it was death to break the Roman seal."

Rebecca walked over to touch the outside of the tomb. "It's interesting."

Benjamin wanted to finish with the tomb so they could see the trial of Yeshua in front of Pontius Pilate.

"Let's film the tomb" Benjamin said. "This may be our only opportunity while it's empty. Rebecca, you stand guard at the entrance. David, Sara, come inside now please."

David took his camera out. "I'll film."

As Benjamin entered the cool chamber, the musty smell of heavy dirt enveloped him. The air seemed almost reddish in the dim light. The three of them stood together, but there wasn't much more room. A black archway to a further chamber yawned opposite the entrance, and David panned his camera around the room.

"This is the antechamber of a first century tomb," David narrated. "The tomb was dug from the limestone rock of the hill. The antechamber is about three meters wide by three deep, and two meters or a little more high. This chamber is for preparing the body for burial, and it is also where people came to mourn the dead before interring the body in the far chamber." He shut off the camera. "I'm going to film the interior. I need someone to hold a flashlight for me."

Benjamin nodded to Sara. "Go on."

He moved inside the archway of the back chamber to watch. Sara's light reflected long and distorted shadows.

David continued his narration. "The burial chamber is somewhat larger, five meters deep, with trenches dug in the walls for the laying out of bodies. Also space for ossuary boxes in the corner.

"Ossuary boxes were a new burial custom in the first century. After a year, the skeleton was removed from the trench and placed inside the stone box. The bones of family members were intermingled. This tomb, though," he added, "is new. It's empty."

Benjamin watched David pan the camera in a complete circle, then checked his leather wristband. Countdown was 69.25.

"Finished?"

"Almost," David said. Benjamin watched him finish the circle, then aim the camera down to pan the floor.

Benjamin glanced at Sara. She held the light pointing to the low, carved ceiling to reflect an even illumination for the camera. Her face was in the shadows. Again, he wondered what had caused her to turn.

From the corner of his eye he saw a shape pass over the lit doorway of the antechamber. Rebecca stood in the entrance. "He's coming in. I couldn't stop him."

"Off," he commanded David and Sara. "Lights off, now!" Then he stepped into the antechamber. "Who?"

Another shadow passed over the entrance. Benjamin glanced back to the inner burial chamber, making sure it was dark inside. He heard soft rustling as David and Sara hid the camera and flashlight within their robes.

"Let's go." Benjamin stepped toward the entrance of the tomb. Sara and David appeared in the archway.

A figure straddled the opening. He'd edged Rebecca forward into the cave.

The man was young; maybe eighteen or nineteen, with a scrappy beard and a questioning look on his face. He wore the *tsitsit* or fringes on his overcoat indicating he was a Jew, but his clothing was worn and knobby. Clearly, the man was not of great means. He moved to block Benjamin from the exit.

Benjamin assessed the situation. Rebecca by stepping forward into the tomb, not back, had allowed the entire team to be boxed into the enclosed space. The situation needed to be reversed.

"Rebecca, at your first opportunity when he steps away from the door, get outside. How many are there?"

"Just him."

The man said something. The shape of the words was familiar, but Benjamin was too distracted to understand them. He glanced at Rebecca.

"Aramaic. He wants to know what we're doing here."

Benjamin shook his head. "Let's get out of here first."

The young man said something else.

Calm down. He knew these words.

"Are you seeking something here?" he had said. Or something like that.

Benjamin called up the words with difficulty. "We're leaving," he said to the young man, and held up his hands palms forward in the universal gesture of appeasement.

The man shook his head and said something else. Benjamin glanced back at Sara and David. "Come on! We have to get out of here."

"He wants to know who we are," Rebecca said.

The man stepped forwards another half-step, just enough room now, and Benjamin motioned Rebecca to exit. "Go."

She started, then slid past to the outside.

Now he had to get the rest of his team out.

"We're leaving," Benjamin said in Aramaic. He motioned David to come up next to him. "I wonder if we're trespassing on his family's property?"

"He doesn't look wealthy enough."

Benjamin again stepped forward, again the young man moved to block him. Benjamin didn't want to get into a shoving match with him.

"Who are you?" He would have liked Rebecca to handle the conversation, but even if she had remained inside, he wasn't sure whether this culture permitted a woman to address a strange man.

"Eleazar bar Simeon," the man said. "And you?"

The Aramaic was falling easier on Benjamin's ears.

"My name is Benjamin…bar Manaen."

"And your friend?"

Benjamin glanced around the dark tomb. "This is David bar Yonatan. May we come out?"

Eleazar shook his head. "I saw something in here but it's gone now. It looked like a torch."

Sara's flashlight.

Benjamin spread his arms out. "There is nothing here."

David stepped forward. "Sir, does this tomb belong to your family?"

The words fell on absolute silence. Eleazar stared at them for a moment, looking at them strangely. "What is it you seek?"

Benjamin shook his head.

"This tomb," Eleazar said, motioning with his arm. "Yeshua is not here. He is risen."

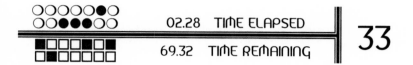

AARON KNELT as he passed his latex-gloved hand again over the painted cinder block in the corridor wall. It was low, in the row that was second from the bottom, with a faint but unmistakable circle about the size of his palm cut into its center. His heart beat faster.

"Etan, come here."

The hairline, almost invisible, rimmed the circle. He ran his finger around the edge of it, trying to feel for any loosening. Nothing. It was solid.

His second, Etan, came from around the corner. "Yes, sir."

"Look at this."

Etan whistled as he sank down and put his gloved hand on the block.

"You were right," Aaron said. "The dead drop."

His mind was churning. Had it been ready-made in the cinder block when placed during the construction of this corridor over three years before, or had it been drilled out later? Either way it spoke of a great deal of ingenuity and high-quality contacts of the mole.

"Let's open it."

Etan pressed around the edges of the circle, much as Aaron had done a moment before, but then he shook his head. "It's solid. It won't move."

"There's got to be a trick. Only nine extra seconds, remember? Not much time to open and close it."

Etan brushed his fingertips over the block, back and forth. "There's no finger hold, no indentation, nothing."

Why would there be? This cinder block had to look just like all of the others in the corridor. A dead drop situated so blatantly in the open was in profound danger of discovery, and its sealing and unsealing had to be sure and fast. It needed a handle, some locking device. Not pressure points on an unmarked surface. It had to be something simpler.

Aaron half-closed his eyes. There was no handle, no hold, at least not on the outside.

If he were designing this drop, how would he do it? He'd need a tool easily concealed, yet easily explained if found.

Not a chisel, not when it could mar the exterior of the cinder block and make it noticeable. No—

"A magnet," he murmured.

Etan looked up. "Sir?"

"A magnet. They could use one to release a latch inside and open the cavity."

Etan stared at the circle. "Yes. It could be."

Aaron stood up. "Etan, I need you to analyze the data over the past year. Find who else has delayed over this intersection."

Etan grimaced. "Sir, that may take some time. It's a painstaking process to pull out the raw data from the software, and then to graph it for each individual."

"There are only sixty-two persons who could be our mole."

"Yes, sir."

"Let's get this drop opened first."

They had to go back. At one of the labs, they found a set of standardized magnets. Aaron grabbed one, a block three inches long by half an inch by half an inch.

"This would be about the right size."

"Yes, sir. Let's hurry."

They returned to the dead drop in less than ten minutes.

The trick would be to fit the magnet in the correct orientation. Aaron doubted that the trapdoor would use an overly sophisticated system though, since speed was essential. He leaned down by the dead drop.

"Let's do it." Etan was ready.

Aaron pressed the magnet block to the circle, rotated it counterclockwise, and felt a snick under his fingers. The panel popped out of the cinder block and fell into his outstretched hand, the bar magnet still attached.

"Clever. This caulking rimming the entrance keeps the line of demarcation almost invisible."

"Is there anything in it?"

Aaron grabbed for the tiny flashlight in his pocket and shone its light as he peeked inside. The interior of the block had been hollowed out into a circular shelf about four inches deep and four inches high. He reached in and pulled out a metal circle, an inch in diameter.

An optical computer disc.

34

TIME ELAPSED   11.53

TIME REMAINING   60.07

BENJAMIN DIDN'T LIKE THE WAY THE MAN WAS LOOKING at
them as they stood on the northern end of the Temple
Mount platform.

It was approximately three o'clock in the afternoon;
they'd known they were in the wrong time period for ten
hours. The team stood with Eleazar, the young man who had
appeared in the entrance of the tomb to tell them that Yeshua
had risen. Even after wrestling with the information,
Benjamin still didn't know how they had missed the correct
time. The scientists had assured him the time throw, based on
trial calibrations, would be dead on even for this large a jump.
Had the scientists been wrong? Or maybe Sara had been able
to tamper with the machine before they'd left?

Eleazar stepped forward. "This way," he commanded in
his ancient Aramaic.

Benjamin kept his team close to the five stone steps
leading up to the shaded area under the portico, facing the
tall Temple building in the distance—a brilliant shining box
in the sunlight. People preparing for the evening sacrifice in a
little more than an hour crowded the paved flagstones of the
platform. Not so many people that he couldn't move freely,
but enough so that keeping a clear line of sight more than
four or five yards ahead was impossible. The babble of voices
and bleating of sacrificial sheep wove together over the area.

The Temple Mount was enormous. Benjamin had
studied the archaeological descriptions during the eighteen
months of preparation for this mission, but still he hadn't
realized how awesome this place would be. Great colonnades

around the perimeter rose ten times the height of a man and supported the graceful wooden porches—like huge balconies—surrounding the monstrous platform. It was hard to believe this area would be leveled in thirty years.

He studied the blocked grey granite of the Antonia fortress behind him and to the right; it merged with the northwest corner of the Temple Mount and was higher than the portico, with opened high windows. From where he stood, he could see an exit from the fortress onto the portico above, short stone stairs upon which four soldiers were descending in formation to join their comrades below. On top of the portico, spaced every ten yards or so along the perimeter, a Roman soldier stood guard overlooking the platform. Each soldier wore a breastplate and an iron helmet, and carried a shield and spear.

The people on the Mount seemed familiar to him despite the flowing clothing and babble of unfamiliar languages: the way the two men on the stairs were arguing with wide hand gestures; the way the young woman next to her husband leaned over to comfort their young son and kiss his hair. Many of the men and older boys wore small black boxes that were tied onto their foreheads with leather straps and around their fingers and wrists leather bands wrapped seven times, the *tvillin* or phylacteries, fulfilling the commandment to keep God's words always on their minds and in their wills. He was relieved to observe that his team's garb seemed to blend in without noticeable problems.

"Hurry!" Eleazar led them forward.

Benjamin nodded for his team to follow, then pulled up his prayer shawl to cover his head as many of the men had done. The marketplace rumbled like a low thunderstorm, the shouts and hundreds of conversations seeming to muffle clear thought or worship. For a moment, the scent of sacrificial roasted lamb wafted by from the Temple building then disappeared in the brisk wind. As he watched, an old woman scurried in front of him, her wrinkled face peeking out from under her head covering. She looked ancient but was probably only in her fifties, and that made his mind twist uncomfortably for a moment. Life here was too short and harsh. The woman carried a small wicker box by a rope handle, no doubt bought from under the portico. It held two pigeons, a poor person's sacrifice.

Benjamin shifted his gaze. The man who had been watching his team was still there, still observing. He was tall, with sharp eyes, mouth compressed and twisted at the corners in concentration. He looked to be in his early twenties. His robes were made of fine white linen and were beautiful: draped with the purple Roman citizen's stripe although he also wore the *tsitsit*, the Jewish fringes, on his shawl. When Benjamin caught his gaze, he looked away.

The man stood not far away in a little cleared circle. He had not moved since Benjamin first spotted him, disturbing his trained soldier's sense. Somehow, he knew that this man was trouble.

Benjamin nudged David. "Who's that?"

David glanced over. "Publican, probably," he replied. "A tax collector. He's not too popular with these folk. Do you see how they're giving him a wide berth, even in this crowd?"

"I don't like it."

Sara looked over. "What is it? Is there a problem?"

Benjamin gave a minor shrug of his shoulders. "That man. He's watching us, I think. We need to go—quickly and unobtrusively."

Eleazar glanced back at them. "Follow me." He was heading toward the far section of the portico underneath the Antonia. Benjamin wondered how safe they were trusting Eleazar. But if they wanted to gather any data—

"That publican is watching us?" David asked.

Benjamin jerked his head. "Come on."

He felt as if he could trace the edge of each cobblestone through his sandals as he led his team forward, moving through the people. Although he and his team were all average height or less in the twenty-first century, they were tall for this time. Even Sara was as tall as some of the men, and he hoped that fact wouldn't mark them as they moved through the crowd. After they'd gone about twenty meters, he turned to glance back at the man. The publican was keeping abreast of them on the portico.

Eleazar looked back. "What's wrong?"

Benjamin glanced over at the publican, then back to Eleazar. Grasping for the language. "We need to go this way."

"What? Don't you want to meet—"

He shook his head. "I want to see—" he gestured in front of him.

"The Temple?"

Benjamin nodded.

Eleazar turned but Benjamin pushed past him, turning left, parallel to the Temple Mount wall. Eleazar wasn't moving fast enough to lose the publican. Benjamin ducked behind a donkey laden with wicker panniers of wheat kernels, causing the farmer leading the donkey to glare at him.

His team was strung in a tight line behind him, and he stepped up the pace as he veered into the thicker crowds heading toward the Temple, touching his hand on Eleazar's arm to keep him with them.

"Are we going into the Temple?" Rebecca asked. Benjamin glanced back at her.

"No. He's Jewish, he could follow us in there. And we couldn't get out so easily."

He saw Sara scan the crowd for a moment, and then she said, "I don't see him. I think we're clear."

"Not too hard, in this crowd," David added.

"Keep moving," Benjamin said.

Eleazar's brow wrinkled at their unfamiliar language.

They were approaching the bottleneck about ten yards wide between the western portico and the back wall of the Temple. Now that they were up close, he could see that even the back portion of Herod's Temple was magnificent, more beautiful than the third Temple from his own time. Deep shadows fell over them as his eyes followed the golden columns and white marble walls to the squared roof edge of the Temple. On the other side of this wall stood the Holy of Holies where the high priest entered but once a year on Yom Kippur, the Day of Atonement, to burn incense. Ahead was the balustrade, the railing marking the limits where only Jews could pass further inside into the Temple building. He brushed his hand over the polished marble as they walked past.

"We need to get films from inside the Temple," David said. Benjamin knew the archaeologist had probably thought about little else for the past eighteen months. David was right, of course. Aside from filming the theft of Yeshua's body, filming the inside of the Temple was the top priority given to him for the mission, but now wasn't the time.

He shook his head. "We have to make sure we're clear first."

Eleazar slowed. "Do you have the Temple tax? We can't go in without it."

Benjamin scanned the portico to his right once more. There was no sign of the publican. "No," he replied in Aramaic. "We need to trade money for it."

Everyone who entered the Temple was expected to tithe an offering of money, collected in great boxes inside the entrance. The people could only use Temple currency, the silver Jewish coins from Tyre and Sidon available from the moneychangers under the porticos of the Temple Mount. It was exchanged at the extraordinary rate of twelve percent— one more tax to gouge the everyday people.

Eleazar pointed. "The southern portico is where we change money. Come on." He walked ahead, but Benjamin stepped back and scanned the area. He didn't see the publican now.

"It's cold with the wind here," Rebecca said as she adjusted her outer robe.

David barked, "Cover your tunic!"

Benjamin looked back. "What's the problem?"

"We need to exhibit the proper decorum," David said. "We don't want to call attention to ourselves. These people are sticklers for modesty."

Eleazar paused. "Don't fall back so far."

"Oh, all right." Rebecca tightened her cloak. "I didn't do anything wrong, you know."

Benjamin shook his head. "Keep up."

The five steps climbing to the area underneath the southern portico were wide, hewn from stone that was worn from many feet. Well-made wooden tables were set up along the entire long covered area. The moneychangers behind the tables were allied with the Sadducees, involved in Temple commerce that brought great quantities of silver into the coffers. Benjamin approached; the moneychanger he stood in front of nodded peremptorily, then turned back to counting a pile of coins.

The moneychanger had greying hair but smooth skin. Perhaps because he spent his days here, Benjamin thought, underneath the shade of the portico. The man's eyes passed over Eleazar, then Benjamin and his team as he said, "Yes?"

Benjamin stepped forward. "We need change for the Temple," he said in Aramaic.

The man looked puzzled. "Yes?" he repeated.

"Change?"

The man shook his head.

Rebecca sidled up next to him. "Try 'trade.' "

"We need to trade for the Temple," Benjamin said.

The man nodded, and Benjamin reached into his moneybag hidden in a folded flap of his tunic to withdraw a silver Roman denarius, worth a soldier's wages for a day. Eleazar's eyes bulged as he caught a glimpse of the rest of the silver in the leather sack before Benjamin closed the top. But he didn't realize, Benjamin thought, that these coins were merely manufactured counterfeits that had been aged in a salted rotational tank to look slightly worn.

The moneychanger counted the coins then pushed a small pile of the Jewish Temple money toward him. Benjamin nodded as he pretended to count it then poured the coins into another small leather purse tied around his waist. He motioned his team to step back as they moved again into the crowd.

Benjamin scanned the portico again. He didn't see the publican. He hoped that would be the end of it, but he didn't understand why they had been so closely observed in the first place.

TIME ELAPSED   12.20

TIME REMAINING   59.40

GIDEON GRIMACED. Aaron had found the second dead drop.

Every step felt as if it would launch him from the floor, but he covered the release of tension as he raced back from his office to his living quarters in the next building. He needed to destroy the other optical discs before they were found.

He wasn't a suspect, not yet anyway, or Landau wouldn't have told him about the developments. The operative, Seidel, must have talked. There was no other way Aaron could have found the dead drop in the corridor, not with it so well hidden.

Even so, he was safe for the present since Raseac had shielded Gideon's identity from Seidel. On the other hand, Raseac might not be safe.

He went around the corner, then opened the stairwell door and bounded up the steps.

It would be all right, he thought. It would be all right. Seidel knew nothing. Still, Gideon was not looking forward to apprising Raseac of this latest development.

There had been an optical computer disc in the drop, Landau had told Gideon. Blast it. Seidel hadn't picked it up before he'd been caught. The disc had schematics of part of the complex, nothing incriminating, but Aaron would naturally wonder who would be able to procure such plans.

He bounded onto another landing and began the next flight. Five floors? Six? Too much nervous energy.

At least he'd taken extra precautions to protect his identity.

Each computer in the complex was not only hooked to the Ethernet network, but had a unique electronic signature that could not be tampered with or duplicated. With his typical foresight, Gideon—over a year ago—had managed to format five discs on a different computer during a "friendly" visit. Aaron had found one of those discs in the drop. As soon as Aaron ran the analysis, he'd have a promising suspect.

Think positive. Gideon grimaced, the closest approximation of a smile he could manage right now. Aaron's sights would be trained directly on Benjamin Feinan.

"I THINK YOU'RE OVERREACTING to that publican," Rebecca said.

"Out," David said to Benjamin, then snapped off the transmitter on his wristband. He turned around to glare at her. "What do you mean?"

Rebecca shrugged, that dismissive half-movement of her shoulders that so much annoyed him.

They stood at the southern end of the Temple area in moving crowds, near an entry covering of the Huldah gate leading off the Mount. Benjamin had split the team half an hour ago so that David and Rebecca could film the evening Temple sacrifice, while Benjamin and Sara would stay with Eleazar to make contact with a group of followers near the southern porch. But with the reappearance of the publican, David's and Rebecca's filming would have to wait.

They had been standing in the shadow of the Temple, about to pass through the balustrade, when David caught a sudden movement out of the tail of his eyesight. He'd turned around. The publican had looked triumphant somehow, David remembered thinking, gliding stealthily up to them. Fortunately, the man had still been ten meters away, and David had just enough time to duck and pull Rebecca with him away through the crowd. She hadn't even seen the publican and had been annoyed, listening to a promising conversation nearby that might have provided another link to the stories surrounding Yeshua.

Now they had to go through the Huldah gate to get off the Temple Mount. The tunnel didn't look dangerous, and it was the quickest way off, but he couldn't push away his unease.

Rebecca shook her head. "It was a coincidence we saw that publican again. What else could it be? Why would he be interested in us?"

He glanced at the handful of Roman soldiers standing at the entrance of the gate. "It's not chance. There are thousands of people here on the Mount, and we're too far from our original position. He followed us. We were lucky we could slip away."

She gave another half-shrug, unconvinced, and he struggled to contain his irritation.

David knew a publican following them could be quite dangerous, since the publican's favor with Rome gave him the power to have any of the team to be incarcerated while being brought up on charges. There would be no protection.

Rebecca, he thought, took things all too casually, not savvy of how the world worked. She wasn't regular military, of course, and maybe that was it. Rebecca's knowledge of linguistics was essential on this mission, but she seemed to live in a bubble where nothing could go wrong, and life didn't work that way. David had first learned that lesson as a new physician working with a teenager who had a fatal brain tumor, and later as an archaeologist finding the bones of hundreds of babies at a massacre site. There was no safe bubble. He wished Rebecca would not act as if this mission were an academic exercise.

"Rebecca," he said. "We're getting off the Mount now."

She was silent.

"Do you see those soldiers over there?"

"They're not going to do anything to us. We have to listen for some leads. This is the best place to find them."

"It doesn't matter, because we have orders to move off the Mount immediately. You heard Colonel Feinan."

She tossed her head and started walking ahead of him. Great. Women in this culture did not act like this; he stepped forward and grabbed her by the arm. "Stay with me. Be discreet. We're going to stay in the center of the crowd and walk through that gate."

"Fine."

David could tell she was irritated. He turned in a full circle, checking the perimeter around them again.

Nothing.

He didn't see anything alarming, but straightened uneasily because the publican had managed to follow their team earlier even after they'd taken evasive action. He could do nothing about it, though. Just keep moving. The gate was close, on a diagonal about fifty feet away, and he grasped Rebecca's elbow to guide her forward.

Most of the people around them were moving in the opposite direction, toward the Temple, but people ahead of them parted enough to move forward at a good pace. The scent of burnt sacrificial lamb mingling with sweet incense was strong again here, air flow trapped from the Temple, and for a moment he wished he could be like Rebecca. He wanted to be free of worry and able to go now to the altar inside the Temple that, in his own time, had been destroyed for two thousand years. He had thought of little else since he had started training, praying that he would be the archaeologist selected for this mission.

Get off the Mount as quickly as possible. The moment to visit the Temple would come soon.

He pushed toward the gate, past the tables laden with silver and bronze coins, the sharp voices of trading, the bleating of sheep pulling against their rope tethers. He struggled past the people, so many people now, near the gate. Their head coverings were pulled low over their faces, their coats rasped against his shoulders as he walked by. These were Jewish pilgrims from all over the ancient world. Egypt, Rome, Asia, polyglot babble and skills and traditions long ago lost.

It was magnificent.

He tilted his head to check the camera hidden beneath his overcoat. It was still recording.

As they approached the entrance to the main gate, David stopped. Rebecca pulled her elbow away from his palm. "Let's go," she said.

He shook his head. "Wait a moment." He peered inside the tunnel leading underneath the Mount's supporting southern wall, guarded heavily by Roman soldiers. It was long, easily three hundred feet, and full of shadows.

"What's the problem? Or are we just waiting for Benjamin and Sara here?"

"No, we should go through." He was evaluating their strategy. If they were pursued inside it would be virtually impossible to escape in such a narrow area, but no one seemed to be watching them. It was the quickest way.

The breath of air from the mouth of the alcoves was moist, cool and pleasant.

It looked all right. There were fewer people in the tunnels than he would have liked, harder to hide, but they could go through swiftly. Beyond the tunnel to the right would be the white glimmer of the Hippodrome, Herod's oval chariot-racing track, and below the outer platform, the cobbled Tyropean Street through King David's city. He wanted to see it.

"We'll go now." He turned to check the Mount one last time. His eyes took a moment to adjust from the cool dimness of the tunnel to the bright platform beyond the portico, but even dazzled he saw a flash of motion on the stairs behind him. He froze.

"Rebecca," he whispered, and it was then he realized she was no longer next to him.

The publican came into view at the top of the stairs, his eyes scanning the crowd but David didn't think he'd been spotted.

Rebecca—

He glimpsed her a few meters away, going down inside the left tunnel. He glanced back. The publican was moving toward the Romans nearby.

In a split second, he made his decision. If they could get through the gate, they might be able to hide at the base of the southern stairs inside the *mikveh*, the ritual bath where only Jews were allowed to enter. Alternatively, they could lose themselves in the marketplace of the great plaza beyond the foot of the Temple entrance.

"Rebecca!" He ran toward her and pushed her ahead. "Go!"

She looked a question but moved with him. His heart beat like a drum inside his chest.

None of the Roman soldiers was giving them a second glance. She started to say something to him, but the tunnel amplified the echoes of the crowd and he couldn't hear her.

Keep moving.

He heard a sharp laugh from behind, and even as he turned, he knew. Suddenly he noticed there were fewer people than there had been even a moment before. Rebecca shook his hand off her elbow as he heard a shout and running feet from behind. He pushed her ahead of him then glanced back.

It was the publican.

"Quick!" He ducked through the people. Rebecca was separated from him as he dove toward the center of a small group of seven or eight people. The two Roman guards standing along the wall were shifting, alert for the conflict, and he forced himself to slow down to appear calm, calm even as his heart threatened to burst from his chest.

Where was she?

He took a deep breath. Calm. Everyone was turning away toward the noise ahead, not watching him, and he breathed again.

Where was she?

The soldiers moved into the crowd.

People scattering, and that was when he saw her, held by the publican who was shouting something. Time seemed to gel. In slow motion, he ran toward her, crashed down on the publican's grip, and he heard the publican gasp. David pushed Rebecca away. *Run away.* He ran too, two steps, three, four, through the tunnel.

She was ahead of him, dodging through the people and he found the crowd parting magically in front of him as he ran. The publican behind him was shouting, grasping at his robes just out of reach as he moved ahead.

Then he was at the edge of the arch, blinding sun but he kept running. The top of the steps, then the *mikveh*, wasn't too far.

He felt a tug on his jacket.

No.

The Roman soldier who grabbed him by the shoulder was immovable, stone cold, but he struggled even as the soldier imprisoned him in a strong grip. The publican came up to them, face red and beaded with sweat.

"What is this?" the soldier demanded.

The publican said something garbled. The accent was hard to think through.

The soldier hauled him back towards the tunnel. David saw two others running and knew he had but a moment. He twisted into the soldier's grip, broke his grasp and almost ducked out from under his hold, almost twisted away, so close, and he had to get away, he had to get away—

David turned beneath the soldier's arm, and for a moment, he saw a clear path. Then the crack of a Roman sword hilt came down on his head. He fell hard. The exquisite lines of Herod's arched stone gate swam before his eyes.

| TIME ELAPSED | 13.26 |
| TIME REMAINING | 58.34 |

SARA UNSUCCESSFULLY TRIED TO PUSH back the stab of alarm as she saw Benjamin next to her pull up. "They're in trouble," he said.

Benjamin, she knew, had an uncanny ability to sense danger. It had saved his life more than once.

He glanced back at her as he raised his wrist to his mouth, preparing to talk into the transmitter. Distract Eleazar, his glance said. She heard his voice double, next to her and in the earpiece, as he tried again to raise David.

"Major, please respond."

He paused.

"Major."

She balanced her left hand on Eleazar's sleeve beside her, making sure their one link to the past stayed nearby, and he caught her eye.

"Sara," Eleazar said. He must have seen the anxiety in her face. It was weakness.

She bit her lip and looked away.

They were standing to the right side of the double gate called Huldah, and her other hand was on one of the monstrous limestone blocks of the Southern retaining wall. Soon, she knew, every one of these blocks in the wall would be dismantled and thrown down on the ground. Only a few would be left in the foundation along the western edge. The Western Wall, they had called it in her own century.

"Major, please respond," Benjamin repeated.

The gate entrance was blocked by three Romans stretching spears out to form a barrier, and a river of people on the Mount flowed past the entrance, trying to look inside.

She had such a dark feeling about David and Rebecca.

Benjamin paused in his transmissions. Sara said, "Can you see what's going on in the tunnel?"

"Not yet. Someone's down, though."

She heard the murmur of many conversations from the passing people, different languages but from what she could decipher most reflecting curiosity or worry or outright rebellion at the Roman actions.

Eleazar nodded at the crowd. "They might start a riot."

The snare was tightening. Would they now change the past?

Benjamin moved forward two steps into the corner of the gate, inches from the outstretched spear. The soldier holding it glanced over. Benjamin motioned at his waist for Sara to come forward next to him.

"There are four more soldiers at the center, and at least three blocking the other end," he murmured in her ear. "I can't see everything. But I do see a man on the ground in the tunnel, stirring."

"Is it—"

He slashed his hand down, silence. Sara stepped toward the opening and then she heard Rebecca's voice.

"Colonel," Rebecca was saying. "Please answer. Respond."

He stepped back next to the wall. Sara moved near Eleazar as Benjamin began the transmission.

"Captain. Tell me your situation."

"Colonel?" Rebecca's voice was high with relief. "Thank goodness. I don't know where David is." There was a long pause. Sara glanced inside the tunnel again. It was in semi-gloom, but she could still see a figure in the center supine on the cobbles.

It had to be David, surrounded by soldiers. Dear God.

Benjamin said, "Captain, we're on the northern side of the Huldah gate, on the Mount. There is a Roman prisoner inside the left tunnel. Is this David?"

She heard Rebecca's edged panic. "That's where I saw him last, sir. We were being chased, the publican was chasing us, and the Romans joined in. They were guarding the entrance and David pushed me away. He didn't follow. I'm at the *mikveh* at the bottom of the grand staircase now." There was silence for a moment and then Rebecca asked, "Is David all right?"

Benjamin's jaw was tight. "We've got to get him out now."

Sara studied the unbreachable soldiers guarding the gate. A single Roman soldier was trained to defend a square of ground five feet on an edge from four enemies at once without giving way.

He paused for a moment, transmitter poised near his mouth. "Captain, where is the publican now?"

Rebecca's voice came back on line. "I have no idea why he followed us. He must have been keeping us in sight all along. I don't understand why he was there."

"Captain, focus! Tell me where the publican is now."

"Sir, I don't know. He was with David last I saw him."

"Great," Benjamin said. "He can identify us."

"We have to assume he's nearby," Sara said.

"In the tunnel."

"Unless he's looking for us."

He shook his head. "We need to get David out."

Rebecca's voice broke in. "Sir, what is the plan?"

He paused for a moment, studying the tunnel. "Stand by." He did a circuit to gauge the crowds and the distances involved, and then eyed the three Roman soldiers at the entrance.

He turned to Sara. "Don't lose Eleazar in the melee."

She nodded.

Benjamin brought the transmitter up. "Captain. Keep an eye out for the publican, but get as close as you can to the entrance of the tunnel. You need to be clear, right next to the soldiers. Alert me when you're in position."

"Yes, sir."

He grimaced. "It's going to be close. Get out your taser and a starburst bomb. You'll back me up."

"Yes, sir."

She pressed against the stone wall and dropped her hand

to the sack-like holster belted over her left hip underneath her coat. The holster looked like something from this period, made from leather with gross sutures, but it had an internal metal catch that could only be opened by a practiced hand. It was an extra precaution against bystanders having access to anachronistic technology. She fitted the cool metal taser inside her left hand to keep it secure, then pulled a short waxed paper tube as wide as two fingers out of the sack, and palmed it in her right hand as she turned to find Eleazar.

He seemed ready to walk away. She caught his arm and tried to guide him closer to the wall, but he resisted. "This is too close," he said. "I don't want to be caught up in this."

"In what?"

Eleazar shook his head. "I don't know. It doesn't feel right for me to be here."

She wondered for a moment if he was sensing the echo of the events that should have been, sensing the flow of time trying to right itself. How strange.

They couldn't wait, though. Even now, Benjamin was moving like a cat in front of the soldiers toward the open center of the tunnel, his right hand hiding another bomb beneath the folds of his outer coat. It would be close. She pulled Eleazar forward toward the cleft in the rock. "You have to come." She was desperate.

"I don't understand."

Rebecca's voice came on. "Colonel, I'm in position."

Sara moved where Benjamin had been, at the junction of the gate next to the soldier's spear.

Benjamin's voice. "Captain, get a starburst bomb. At the count of three I want you to fling it into the center of the tunnel, then get away."

"But sir, I'm right next to the Romans. They'll see me."

"I don't care! We have no options. Get the bomb out."

She tensed.

"Countdown." With his left hand at his shoulder, he signaled her silently from fifteen feet away. Wait two seconds after Rebecca throws her bomb, and then throw yours. She signaled back, two seconds, acknowledged.

"What is it?" Eleazar asked, looking between her and

Benjamin. "What are you saying with your hands? Who are you?"

"Get ready," she said between gritted teeth as Benjamin began the countdown.

"Go—Go—Go!"

The hiss of Rebecca's magnesium bomb reverberated as she counted one, two, then in a fluid motion pulled the tab from the top of the waxed paper tube. She threw the bomb in an arc a third of the way inside the tunnel, between the two closest groups of soldiers. "Watch out!" she cried as she ducked behind the stone wall and plugged her ears with her fingers. Her eyes were shut tight.

Eleazar didn't move.

A moment later, there was a shaking BOOM—BOOM BOOM, sounding as though the wall were being shaken apart. Sara felt the vibration deep in her chest. Light as bright as sunlight exploded inside the tunnel. The starburst bombs were meant to disorient without inflicting permanent damage.

"Now!" She pushed Eleazar through the tunnel. He was stunned, blind under her guidance as she darted past the three soldiers and into the darkened tunnel.

Benjamin raced two paces ahead of her. At the center of the tunnel, he bent down to sling David over his shoulder. David was conscious but disoriented, and it didn't look as if it were just from the starburst bombs. She didn't like how David's eyes rolled backwards in their sockets as he slumped over Benjamin's shoulder. Benjamin staggered under the extra weight as he ran ahead.

"Keep going!" he shouted to her.

Almost in passing, she noticed the publican opposite her near the wall. He still seemed unreactive, temporarily blinded and deafened, and she smiled bitterly. It served him right. He'd been the cause of all this trouble. David—

She saw one of the Roman soldiers get up and begin to run for Benjamin who was five or six paces ahead. The soldier was reaching out for him.

Sara rushed around Eleazar and pressed the taser against the side of the man's neck, in the small gap between his chest armor and helmet flap. The soldier slumped forward headlong into the cobblestones. Benjamin picked up speed despite his heavy burden. She saw him exit the tunnel and begin down the steps.

She caught Eleazar's arm and guided him forward again. He didn't resist. One soldier at the other end of the tunnel, but there was no time to worry about where the other two had gone as she slipped past him and down the broad stairs leading to King David's city.

Eleazar shook loose from her hold even as they were leaping over the stairs. "Who—are you?"

She shook her head. "David's hurt."

"We've got to get out of here," Benjamin said. "Eleazar, can you help us?"

"Who are you? Are you—"

Sara glanced over and saw Eleazar was afraid, an otherworldly fear. She would have been afraid too.

They needed to go to ground, now. Benjamin couldn't keep this pace for long.

They leaped off the last step and onto the plaza, past the Hippodrome, down the staircase and the hill of the Tyropean Street straight toward the Pool of Siloam at the bottom of the city.

"Hide us!" She was desperate. "We don't know where to go."

Eleazar stared hard at them even as they were running. "Are you from…Are you from Yeshua?"

"Yes!" Benjamin said. "We are. We need you to hide us."

Eleazar seemed to think a moment, then nodded. "Follow me." He veered off to the right, out of the valley they were in toward the Lower City. Benjamin slowed to a fast walk up the hill.

She touched Benjamin's arm. "Rebecca. I have to—separate. Find her. Two soldiers missing—" she took a breath, "—from the tunnel."

Distrust shadowed his face, but she shook her head. "There's no choice! She'll be caught. They'll kill her!"

"This way," Eleazar said. "Hurry!"

Benjamin struggled up the rest of the hill.

"Get her," he said.

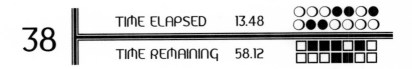

TIME ELAPSED	13.48
TIME REMAINING	58.12

BENJAMIN STAGGERED up the hill behind Eleazar.

He'd calculated they had five minutes to find a hiding place before the Roman soldiers organized a search. A minute of that was gone. They'd be easy to identify with him carrying a wounded man over his shoulders, but Benjamin couldn't put him down. David seemed on the verge of unconsciousness.

He saw Eleazar glance back at him, then slow his pace.

"No," Benjamin said. "Keep going."

They were in a small marketplace along the street of a residential area, common in this era. On the right was a man planing a board that rested on a wooden frame, a little boy holding a chisel-like tool as he looked on. Fallen sweet-smelling wood shavings between the cobbles swirled as Benjamin staggered past. On the left, two bearded men conversed in a doorway surrounded by clay pots and woven baskets. They gave him only fleeting glances. The houses along the narrow cobbled street were boxlike with whitewashed clay walls, most one level but all crowded together with low entrances like open mouths. Wooden doors on leather hinges were pulled open, allowing glimpses of a dark main room or, once or twice, a small common courtyard. Over many of the doors and the second-story windows were awnings of coarse-woven beige-striped cloth supported by wooden rods leaning upwards at an angle from the walls, providing shade.

He wiped the sweat off his forehead with the sleeve of his mantle. A woman carrying a basket on top of her head, moving in the opposite direction, was alarmed at the sight of David and made a motion as if he should put him down. Benjamin shook his head and continued behind Eleazar.

The street was difficult to navigate, the cobblestones uneven, and he slowed his pace behind Eleazar. Walk now. Eleazar led steadily through the cramped street.

He wondered if Sara would find Rebecca quickly.

Eleazar turned the corner onto a quieter passage. An old man sitting on a blanket leaned against the doorway of a house, asleep, and up ahead three boys of about eight ran near the end of the street. On the rooftops maybe ten feet above, Benjamin heard low conversation, and occasionally saw the white flicker of a face looking down into the street. Eleazar looked back once. "Don't worry about them," he said, jutting his chin to the rooftops. Benjamin wasn't so sure.

"Where are we going?"

"My uncle's house. It's not far."

"On this street?"

Eleazar shook his head.

Benjamin wanted to ask how far, then, but bit his tongue. Eleazar was already leading as quickly as he could manage, and when they turned another corner he pointed ahead.

This street was empty, so narrow that Benjamin could have touched the houses on each side if he hadn't been balancing David. David groaned as Benjamin half-stumbled over a loose rock. *Hold on.* It was after four o'clock in this time, he estimated, which meant the people living in these houses would soon return for the evening meal. Many of them, especially the women and children, seemed to already be in their homes, and he could smell muted smoke from the cooking fires. He was hungry. Not surprising, since he'd eaten nothing since the time throw.

David shifted on his shoulders, and Benjamin leaned forward to rebalance him. "Almost there," he murmured, clasping his arm.

Benjamin was close to the end of his own reserves as he stooped under the low doorway into the common room behind Eleazar. Eleazar took one of four rolled-up rush mats from against the wall and spread it out on the dirt floor. Benjamin put David down.

"My uncle will be here soon," Eleazar said. "I saw him this morning in the marketplace."

Benjamin heard him distantly as he turned to David.

The room was three meters by four, but didn't seem small because there was so little in it. A pungent odor of dried coriander and bay leaves permeated the room; the scent mixed with garlic, a hint of bread, and darker overtones. As his eyes adjusted to the low light he saw a raised platform against the back wall of the room with a large pot and small coal brazier. Dried onions braided together hung from the ceiling. A hanging loom stood at the near corner of the room, a half-finished piece of cloth on it with the vertical threads tied with clay weights. Benjamin peeked at the door.

"We need to hide. The Romans may be here soon."

Eleazar closed the wooden door. The door didn't have hinges, just two circular shafts at the top and bottom that fitted into sockets in the wall. Benjamin eyed it skeptically. That door would keep no one out.

David moaned as Benjamin leaned over him again, took his hand. "Hold on, Major," he murmured. Even in the poor light, he could see great bruises forming on the right side of David's face, under his eye, behind his ear. Battle's sign. He recognized it from the advanced trauma course he'd taken for this mission, and sucked in his breath. Very bad; much worse than the simple concussion he'd been thinking. Likely skull fracture with hemorrhaging under the skin, a possible meningeal tear—

"I need more light," he said to Eleazar.

Eleazar took the clay oil lamp from the platform and turned up the wick, then knelt next to David and examined him even as Benjamin did. Eleazar held the light low, a foot from David's face.

The lamp was not much help. The afternoon light coming in from the two slit-like windows was attenuated from the narrow street, but enough to give a cursory exam. He found a blood-matted area several inches in diameter near the base of David's head. He seemed to have no other contusions. Benjamin couldn't tell for sure if the area was depressed, but it seemed to be, with surface swelling around it. When David was captured, the soldiers must have hit him with something, hard, to keep him from getting away. A sword hilt, maybe.

David moaned and stirred, but not in any directed fashion. Benjamin leaned over him.

"David. Talk to me."

After a moment, his eyes opened, and with difficulty he focused on Benjamin's face. His lips moved, but there was no sound.

Eleazar's hand shook. Benjamin waved the lamp away, away, then shut his eyes for a moment. This was so bad. Eleazar stood up and moved back to the kitchen platform a few feet away.

"We're safe."

Eleazar was pouring water from a pitcher onto a short length of woven cloth. When he finished, he knelt down by David and reached forward as if to wash off the blood. Benjamin caught his arm. "Don't touch him."

"It's all right," Eleazar replied. "I might be able to help."

He was a teenager, knowing first century medicine. Sure, it was all right. Benjamin pushed down a twinge of panic.

"Don't touch him." He bent over David, circling his palm over the point of injury. Wisps of hair brushed his palm like the breaths of a ghost. There wasn't much blood on David's neck, just a trickle streaking up to his right cheek. More blood was in his hair.

Eleazar looked up. "Can't you just heal him? You've done some great miracles today."

Benjamin shook his head. "I need another cloth, please."

Eleazar stared at him a moment, then nodded and went to find something. David had closed his eyes again and Benjamin said, "Major!"

David didn't stir.

"Wake up! Wake up."

This was very bad.

After another moment, David opened his eyes and focused slowly. "I was...unconscious. Why can't I...stay awake?"

"Do you remember what happened?"

David started to shake his head, but groaned and stopped immediately. "Head hurts."

"Just lie still." Benjamin squeezed his hand. "You were caught by some Romans. You must have fought like a lion, because it took three soldiers to stop you. Do you remember any of it?"

"No."

"You have a bloody area at the back of your head. I'm not sure, but I think it's depressed. I'm holding your left hand. Squeeze my hand."

David was quiet for a moment.

"Squeeze it."

But he felt nothing. David's eyes slipped shut.

He was suddenly aware of Eleazar standing close, holding a dripping cloth. Eleazar was listening to the exchange with a puzzled expression, not understanding the language but understanding its critical nature.

He nodded and took the cloth. Eleazar shifted his weight. "Is there anything else I can do?"

Benjamin gave him the ghost of a smile.

David moaned and opened his eyes again. "Time," he whispered. "How much...time?"

Benjamin glanced at Eleazar, and then peeked under the leather band on his wrist. "We have fifty-eight hours."

David sighed and closed his eyes. After a few moments, his face went slack.

"Major! Stay with me."

David opened his eyes again. "Can't...stay awake."

"You've got to."

Benjamin felt a rush of panic. Without immediate surgery to stop the bleeding into the brain, he would die.

David was slipping again.

"Major! Look at me!"

David's eyelids slid open, and he focused again with an effort.

"Benjamin—"

He squeezed his hand. "I'm here."

"I'm a dead man." David's voice was far away, as he murmured gibberish.

Benjamin squeezed his hand. "Hold on."

David's eyes fluttered open. "Not...pod..."

"No," he whispered.

David's eyes closed again. Benjamin clenched his fist and turned around to find Eleazar watching him seated on the platform, five feet away. Eleazar shook his head.

"I'm sorry," he said, but his voice sounded harsh.

He nodded.

Eleazar pointed to the floor next to him. "You didn't use the cloth."

Benjamin picked up the wet cloth and leaned forward to lay it on matted blood in David's hair, staying well away from the injured area. Eleazar stood. He was suddenly commanding. "You need to tell me who you are. Now. My whole family is in danger because of you."

Benjamin suddenly recognized how far he'd pushed Eleazar, and just how vulnerable he and David were right now. But even as he framed a response, the front door flew open.

He turned to find an older man blocking the light, staring down at him and David behind him.

39

TIME ELAPSED	14.26
TIME REMAINING	57.34

FIND REBECCA.

Sara was knocked with each hard slap of the cobbles against the inflexible soles of her sandals as she ran uphill along the Tyropean Street, back toward the Temple Mount. She was thinking two simultaneous trains of thought: Benjamin carrying an injured David over his shoulders; Rebecca and how to find her.

Running. Past merchants selling dried fruits or pots or woven cloth, past people who must have turned to look after her. It didn't matter. Sara's overcoat wound about her legs as she raced up the steps to the plaza beneath the Temple Mount. Push it away. Push all thoughts, everything away.

She had to find Rebecca.

The stairs from the street to the plaza were stone, grooved with smooth depressions from constant use, and they were wide so she had to lengthen her stride to keep the rhythm. Quickly ascend.

The wide plaza was more Gentile than on the Temple Mount, but crowded nonetheless from the Passover week. She was surprised that there was no panic here less than half an hour after they'd exploded the bombs in the tunnel above. Perhaps the tunnel had muffled the explosions? Perhaps people would rather not admit something out of the ordinary had happened? She did see about twenty Roman soldiers conferring at the top of the stairs in front of the Huldah Gate leading to the Temple Mount, and a dozen more moving through the plaza in groups of two as though engaged in a search pattern. She wondered how many soldiers had moved further into the city.

She wondered if Benjamin and David had found safe shelter yet. And where was Rebecca?

Sara checked her position. No one was near nor showing any interest. She probed under the leather wristband, switching the transmitter to VOX, and then raised her wrist to her mouth.

"Captain, come in please."

She was facing the Temple. To her right beyond the plaza was the city wall, then desert wilderness. The pod was out there too, somewhere. The Lower City rose to her left, white boxes with dark windows and door slits, tiered row upon row. Closer by was the magnificent elongated Hippodrome where the Romans raced horses in the shadow of the entrance to the Temple Mount.

Sara raised her wrist again. "Captain, please respond."

"Major!" Rebecca's voice came back in the ear transmitter. "Where are you?"

"What is your position?" Sara asked.

"I'm not sure. Somewhere."

Sara rolled her eyes. "Are you being chased? Are you in danger?"

"Not that I know of. Someone might have been following me when I left the tunnel but I lost them in the marketplace. I kept going."

"Two soldiers."

"What's that?"

Sara gazed up at the gate from which they had rescued David. "Two Roman soldiers were missing from the tunnel when we ran through after the starburst bombs. They may have been the ones who were chasing you."

"I don't see anyone now."

"Good." Sara paused. "Captain, did you run out of the city? Or are you still inside?"

Four Roman soldiers passed near her now, scanning the crowd.

"I'm in the Tyropean Valley outside David's City, close to the city wall. Nothing but houses and the Pool of Siloam here."

Sara gazed down the slope of the wide street below the plaza as her thoughts ran. At the bottom, a quarter of a mile away, the falling sun cast shadows on the curved wall of the Pool of Siloam. It was a prominent landmark. Escape would be easy as it was right inside the Dung Gate that opened into the Hinnom Valley, although Sara didn't think either of them were in danger of pursuit at this point. Rebecca needed a visual reference. An academic recruited from the university for her expertise in languages, she wasn't used to thinking as a soldier. Pool of Siloam it was.

The sky faded with the iridescence of a tired sun. Sara noticed that only the top part of the stone wall surrounding the hill of the Temple Mount was now in sunlight; the fronts of the Lower City boxy white houses were in deep shadow. Sara talked spoke hurriedly into the microphone.

"I'm inside the City of David. I'll go out the South Gate, circle back in the Tyropean Valley, and meet you at the Pool of Siloam in about twenty minutes. We can leave through the Dung Gate. Can you find it?"

There was one hour or less until sunset. Darkness would make things easier in some ways, but also more difficult.

"I'll try."

"Just keep the city wall in sight on your left!" Sara snapped, and then took a deep breath. The way David's eyes had rolled back in their sockets—

She walked as quickly as she dared without calling attention to herself, down the plaza stairs to the route along the Valley of the Cheese Makers. Sara breathed narrowly through her mouth as she moved through the city. Both sides of the street were scattered with sellers, clay pots spread on the sidewalks, wares displayed and woven cloths hung, men clutching their head shawls tight under their chins as they haggled prices and walked away as often as not.

At least no one was noticing her.

Her sandals slipped against the wide cobbles as she tucked her overcoat about her body and pulled it tighter over her head. It was getting cold, a breeze coming up through the narrow walkway that had steeper hills on each side than in her own time. She wondered again how David and Benjamin were doing. Surely, they had found shelter with Eleazar by now.

Surely.

The Pool of Siloam was set in a clearing thirty yards across at the end of the Tyropean Valley against the outside southern wall of the City of David. As she approached, she noticed that the north side of the pillared entrance wasn't too crowded. The building was an oval about twenty-five feet wide and going back forty feet, colonnaded with pillars as tall as the city wall rising three stories behind it. Sara scanned the people but none was Rebecca. Her eyes searched the narrow staircase rising from the back of the building to the Upper City above.

The sun dazzled her eyes. Through it she saw a woman hesitate, then enter the clearing beyond the last row of houses. It was Rebecca.

Sara stepped forward in the street, loosening the shawl from her face so Rebecca could recognize her. She looked tense. Sara raised her wrist to talk into her transmitter.

"Captain. I'm across the clearing from you."

Rebecca's head jerked up, looking around. There, she saw her, and began moving toward her.

"Slow down. Don't draw attention to yourself. I'm not going anywhere."

Sara shook her head. Benjamin and David had been gone for almost three quarters of an hour, in strange territory, with an unfamiliar guide who had no reason to help them. She had an ominous feeling about David as she raised the transmitter to her mouth.

"Benjamin. I've found Rebecca. What is your situation?"

There was no response.

"We're at the Pool of Siloam, no problems. Answer please."

Nothing.

She and Rebecca needed to locate them as soon as possible, but they wouldn't be able to without verbal contact. She was so used to the geopositional satellite technology of her own time that was able to locate any person or object on the Earth within three meters. She suspected Benjamin wasn't receiving the signal because she was at the bottom of the valley. They needed to be higher, back on the plaza.

Sara nodded as Rebecca came next to her.

"That way is a direct route to the pod," Rebecca said breathlessly, pointing. "We can be outside the city in ten minutes."

Sara broke out of her thoughts. "What did you say?"

"That way is a direct route—"

"I heard you!" she snapped. "You're suggesting we leave our team to fend for themselves?"

Rebecca stepped back, suddenly wary. "No. I just thought—"

Sara glared at her, and Rebecca fell silent.

"Benjamin had to carry David out of the tunnel because he was unconscious!" Sara snapped.

Rebecca looked down at the ground. "It wasn't my fault."

"What happened?"

Rebecca shifted. "I'm not sure. We were leaving the Temple Mount when David saw the publican after us and pushed me out of the tunnel. I got away onto the plaza, but when I turned around David wasn't with me. I—"

She looked down, brushed her fingers underneath her eyes.

"I ran away. I looked back into the tunnel, but I—" she paused. "My legs felt so rubbery. I couldn't think. I ducked into a crowd on the plaza, and then I hid behind the *mikveh*. I got away. That's where I talked to Benjamin. But I didn't see what happened to David."

Sara shook her head.

"It was so quick," Rebecca whispered.

Sara glanced around the clearing. They were still safe, but she wanted to move on nonetheless.

"We're going back to the plaza now." She looked up at the sky; it was getting close to dark.

"We've got to find them."

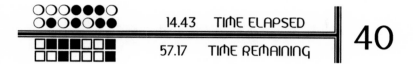

BENJAMIN LEANED protectively over the unconscious David as the door opened from the narrow street into the first century house. David lay in the shadow of the platform at the back of the room, and Benjamin didn't think he was immediately visible from the street. The man pushing open the door was tall and bearded, and he loomed as a dark shape blocking the light.

"What is this?" the man demanded, glaring at Eleazar.

"What is what, Uncle?"

Benjamin furrowed his brow as he glanced again at David's bruised face, streaked on the right side with dried blood from the head wound. He was wary of Eleazar too, an unknown who seemed to be choreographing events even as he watched everything from the back of the room.

"There is blood leading to my door," the older man said. "Not much, but enough. I followed it all along the street, and find you're here. What does it mean?"

"Blood." Benjamin felt himself turn pale. The man whipped around to him, and then he gasped as his gaze caught David in the shadows. He reached down and picked up one of the bloody cloths that had fallen to the floor.

A trail of blood. But the Romans would have found them by now if they were trying to. Wouldn't they have?

Desperate, he pressed the button on his wristband again, but there was only silence back. He still was unable to establish contact with Sara or Rebecca.

"What happened to him?" the man demanded of Benjamin. He pulled off his overcoat and flung it next to

Eleazar. "I am Matthias, as my nephew must have told you. Maybe I can help." He dropped to his knees beside David.

The room was semi-dark, the late sunlight streaming through both the door and the narrow window slits. After a moment, Matthias made a disgusted noise— "Tcha"—and pulled at the mat upon which David lay.

"Let's move him into the light. Help me."

Benjamin glanced at the open door. "The Romans. Keep him hidden."

"Romans?"

Eleazar jumped up. "The Romans, Uncle. They're after him."

Matthias scowled. "What, Eleazar? After this man?"

"Yes, Uncle."

"They won't come here. And hiding him in the shadows wouldn't stop them from finding him anyway."

That was true enough.

Matthias pulled David to the center of the room where a shaft of sunlight fell onto the floor. In the light, Benjamin could see more clearly the deep shadowed bruises along the right side of David's face and behind his ear. David had called himself a dead man.

Benjamin clenched his fists. Even with a time machine, he could do nothing.

Matthias reached forward to push David's hair aside near the wound, but Benjamin placed his hand on Matthias' arm to stop him. The older man paused a moment then withdrew.

"What happened to him?"

Benjamin leaned forward. "I'm not sure. He was hit on the head, I think with a sword hilt."

"He looks bad."

Benjamin pursed his lips. "David." He took his hand again. "Can you hear me?"

David didn't react. His eyes remained closed, unresponsive. A wave of despair washed over Benjamin.

"David," Matthias said. "Is that his name?"

Benjamin nodded, afraid to speak. He broke his gaze away.

"I would like to pray over him. May I?"

What difference would it make? Benjamin shrugged.

Matthias leaned forward and put his hands on David's shoulders, began to murmur and rock.

David was sinking deeper into unconsciousness. Benjamin thought about trying to rouse him again but didn't want to work over Matthias. No, that wasn't true. He was afraid he wouldn't be able to awaken him again.

He felt as if he could barely contain his sudden anger, and he jumped up and paced over to the open doorway, paced back. What did it mean—to die? Would David's soul be lifted up to heaven or to hell? Did he have a soul? What a cruel trick this brief existence was anyway.

It didn't matter: David, himself, this past, his own time in the future that was being torn apart by conflict. All of it was inconsequential. Death came to everyone. The earth would die too, a barren ball to be cremated by the sun. All of it was absurd.

Benjamin glared at the street outside the narrow window. The sun made a wide angle with the low buildings on the hill, pouring blinding light into the street. The light was moving away from inside the house though, would continue to withdraw until all was darkness. And then what?

Matthias continued to pray, the words too low and run together to be discerned. Benjamin turned his back.

"Sara," he whispered into his wristband. "Answer me." He pressed the relay button again.

Nothing.

He stood by the window for a long minute. An oil lamp burned in the corner of the room and he focused on it. The lamp wasn't much bigger than his hand, base terracotta earthenware that had a surprisingly elegant form. The wick sparked, then settled.

When he turned around again, Eleazar was kneeling with his hand on David's heavy hide bag that contained the twenty-first century technology. The strap was tangled hopelessly around David's waist.

"What are you doing?" Benjamin demanded, as he slapped Eleazar's hand back.

Eleazar leaned back on his heels with an expression of wide-eyed innocence while Matthias turned to watch the spectacle.

"Eleazar!" the older man said.

Eleazar scrambled to his uncle's side to whisper in Matthias' ear. Benjamin grimaced. He and David were so vulnerable. Matthias nodded and whispered back a few words.

"Go," Matthias said, and Eleazar jackrabbited out the door into the darkening street. The door banged shut behind him.

Had Matthias sent Eleazar after the Romans to arrest David?

Fear coursed through Benjamin. If so, he had just minutes to get away. How could he manage with David?

Again, he pushed the relay button to raise Sara or Rebecca. Again, nothing. He was alone, with few options. Matthias was looking at him, and as he caught his gaze, the older man nodded. "It's all right, son."

If he was going, it had to be now.

He would have to carry David on his shoulder and somehow find safe haven. The pod was over a mile away, too far to reach without rest or help. Where could he go? The closest place he could think of was the *mikveh* near the Temple Mount, but even that was a long way, and carrying a wounded man, he would be easily identifiable. Could he even find his way in the dark? He could use his compass to discover the general direction to the Valley of the Cheese Makers, but if some of the streets dead-ended—

Perhaps he could find a cart or an enclosure in which to hide David. But that wasn't likely.

And where was Sara? He was beginning to fear she had been captured or injured as well.

David moaned. Benjamin thought he might be coming out of the black unconsciousness, and he knelt next to him. But that quickly, David's face slackened again.

Benjamin looked up. "Where did Eleazar go?"

"To get a friend of mine."

"Soldiers?"

Matthias shook his head. "I have as little to do with Rome as possible. You must trust me."

Benjamin figured that Matthias wouldn't have told him the truth if he'd sent for the soldiers anyway.

As much as he didn't want to think so, he doubted David could even survive the rough transport slung over his shoulder, not with an internal head wound. Furthermore, if soldiers found them, they would certainly be captured, since there was no way he could outrun them carrying David.

An alien voice crossed his mind, whispering that he could strip David's technology and leave him here. David was dying anyway, and Benjamin could do nothing to save him. Benjamin's capture would serve no one. By himself, he could escape.

No. He would not leave an injured man behind. If he died with David, then so be it.

Matthias placed his hand on Benjamin's arm and repeated, "Trust me, friend."

Benjamin looked away.

"You're safe here."

Benjamin watched the oil lamp burn in the darkening room. No one came to the door.

The older man climbed onto the platform and stoked a small fire in the bronze brazier until the smoke flowed into the room. Small holes in the roof and the walls allowed some to escape, but the air still was heavy with its scent. Matthias suspended a rough clay pot above the stove. The scent of lentils mixed with spices, heavy and exotic and warm, entwined with the smoke.

It was twilight now. The room was in deep shadow.

Matthias talked while he sprinkled a handful of flour into another earthen bowl. He added a measure of oil from a crude decanter and mixed it into a lumpy dough. "I remember when my wife died," he said. "It was at the olive harvest four years ago. She lay on that mat, just like your friend. The illness brought her down quickly. She was at peace, unafraid. I will see her again someday."

Matthias shook his head. "I don't sense that peace in you. Eleazar tells me that you are a follower of Yeshua, that you even performed a great miracle to release your friend from the Romans. Tell me. What happened?"

"It wasn't a miracle. You wouldn't understand."

"I've been praying for you, just now. You seem troubled, but God is waiting for you."

Benjamin shook his head. "I don't believe that."

Where was God? Surely not here. The sky outside the window was dark, the landscape black. The mission was ruined, Sara and Rebecca were missing, and David was dying.

Lord, if you are here, reveal yourself to me.

Benjamin crossed his arms and faced away. "When will Eleazar return?"

Matthias didn't answer; he was shaping the dough into two round balls. He flattened them and placed them on the brazier. This was woman's work, but he did it without self-consciousness.

He had to get out of here. He couldn't let David die here.

His earpiece erupted into static, and for a moment, he was hopeful. But there was nothing.

David's breathing was labored behind him. The smoke mingled with the air, and Benjamin fought the great sinking feeling in his chest as he contemplated all he had—ashes. All of it was futile.

The static clarified. Then he heard a voice in his earpiece. He caught his breath.

"Benjamin, are you there?"

"Sara! Where are you?"

Matthias looked up as Benjamin spoke, but Benjamin didn't care.

There was another burst of static, and then she came on in mid-sentence. "—back at the pod. You must be in a pocket of bad transmission. We were unable to reach you without the pod's antenna."

"What is it?" Matthias asked. Benjamin stepped closer to the window.

"How is David?" she asked.

"Not good. He's comatose. Where's Rebecca?"

Silence.

"Major?"

Static again. "—here. She's fine. Where are you?"

"Lower City. One of the houses. I couldn't give you directions."

"Are you all right?"

No.

"Stable, for now. Marginally."

"I'll get you out." With her words, he suddenly felt a tiny lessening of his burden. Her voice cut away the dark images in his mind.

There was another burst of static, and then she came back. "Hold on," she said. "I'm coming to get you now."

41 | TIME ELAPSED   15.24
TIME REMAINING   56.36

THIS WAS FRIGHTENINGLY BRILLIANT.

Gideon hadn't known the respirospheres were anything but a molecular dream, years away from a practical application, yet Raseac had found a way.

He had uploaded Raseac's latest transmission onto his laptop, the secure one that neither his secretary nor anyone else knew anything about. The document had three dense pages of background and another of instruction.

He let out a low sigh as he reached the end and scrolled back to the beginning. Respirospheres. Astounding. He felt his skin prickle.

He had a new assignment.

Raseac was not happy that FlashBack had gone ahead and especially that the operative, Seidel, had been discovered. In his last communication, Gideon had explained that there was no way to eliminate Seidel under the surveillance of the lockdown. The best Raseac could hope for was that the man kept his mouth shut until Gideon could arrange to transfer him out once FlashBack was over.

In response, Raseac had sent this missive. Seidel, he said, was more vulnerable than anyone had dreamed.

More than a year ago, Seidel had gone to a bar he frequented and been given in his drink a quick-acting amnesiac called Rohypnol. While unconscious in the back room, Seidel had received an intravenous injection of three cc's of a turbid saline solution containing about five trillion respirospheres, the tool for his own destruction.

The respirospheres were tiny programmable nanomachines that now circulated inertly throughout Seidel's bloodstream. Each respirosphere was about one sixth the width of a red blood cell and made of carbon atoms arranged in a porous lattice spherical structure called a fullerene. Once they were in the body they were undetectable, and could only be removed by drawing out the blood, centrifuging it, and skimming off the layer where the respirospheres would collect. Then the "clean" blood would be returned, a process called plasmapheresis.

The respirospheres were like tiny pressure tanks capable of packing in so many molecules of a gas that a few trillion respirospheres filled with oxygen equaled the oxygen carrying capacity of the entire blood volume. The surface of each sphere was covered with thousands of molecular "pumps" that could be activated by an outside source. When activated, they would start releasing the gas into the bloodstream.

Here was where Raseac's sublime viciousness came into play. The respirospheres in Seidel's bloodstream were filled with carbon monoxide, not oxygen, enough to kill him in an hour or two once they started dumping it. To get rid of Seidel, Gideon simply had to walk into the lockdown and stay within six feet of him for about five minutes with a radio transmitter tuned to the correct frequency. The signal would be received by the pumps of these nanomachines. Soon after, Seidel would collapse and inexplicably die.

Gideon shook his head. His getting into the lockdown might raise some questions, but he could handle them. He was more worried about something else.

Had Raseac taken similar precautions with him?

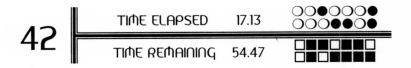

SARA DARTED into a narrow doorway on the main street, and stood still until the group of three men had passed by. Their murmured conversation dissolved into the clear night air.

Go quickly.

It was cold, the foul scent that hung over this part of the city somewhat dampened. She clutched her woven overcoat about her as she moved out again toward the Lower City.

"Captain," she murmured into the microphone at her wrist. "How is my position now?"

It took a few seconds for Rebecca to respond, an eternity.

"Hold on. I'm calculating."

Sara felt a sharp unease. It should not take Rebecca this long—not if she was following Sara's progress moment by moment, as she should be doing.

"Yes, Major," Rebecca said. "You need to head north-northwest from your position. I'm guessing about six hundred meters."

"Got it. Out."

Sara studied the compass on her wristband and confirmed her direction. The almost-full moon lit the stone city so she could see, even without the barrels of fire lighting the Temple Mount close ahead of her to the north. If she went forward to the staircase, then came back to the street across the gap and followed it along the ridge—

After she and Rebecca had returned to the pod, she'd reviewed with Rebecca the protocol of using the pod's sweeping antenna and a moving point—herself—to triangulate Benjamin's position in the Lower City. Weighing options with Benjamin, who seemed to be in a stable position for the moment, they'd decided she should wait for cover of full dark before coming out to find him and David. Benjamin had sounded desperate right before she'd left the pod. David had slipped into a deep unconsciousness, and Benjamin guarding him was unable to move him without help. He seemed to have shaken the Roman soldiers, but had picked up Eleazar's uncle whose potential actions were unknown. Eleazar had run off somewhere and he might bring others back at any time.

She just hoped Benjamin and David would be able to hang on.

She guessed it was about eight-thirty at night, and many people seemed to be preparing for sleep. There were a few Jewish men around, and five minutes ago, she'd passed a team of four Roman soldiers patrolling the area south of the Temple Mount. She'd seen no women.

Sara moved through the street of the Lower City, holding an infrared flashlight that pulsed invisibly, something only Benjamin could see with the night vision goggles. North-northwest, Rebecca had said. Up the street, turn, and Sara followed it along until it intersected in a tiny cobbled marketplace.

"Benjamin, do you read me?"

There was only static in her earpiece. She wasn't close enough, not yet.

Benjamin had said David might be dying, with bleeding into his brain. Sara shook her head and turned into the next street.

The houses were packed together around narrow streets, but she didn't feel trapped. There was some openness here, maybe because of the hill that kept the houses from visually piling together like blocks. The houses shone in the moonlight, an occasional glimmer from an oil lamp on the roofs. Many slept up there, she knew, even in the cold.

She brought her wrist to her mouth again. "Captain. How is my position?"

Rebecca's voice burst through the static in her earpiece. "I'm calculating."

Sara drew her coat close.

"You're almost there," Rebecca said. "Go straight northwest if you can. Your signals are practically on top of each other."

"Have you talked to Benjamin since I called you before?"

Static pulse.

"Captain?" She stepped away and turned, trying to find a clearer field.

"Yes, Major. He just called in. He's looking for your beacon."

"On the roof?"

The breeze through the streets whistled, lazily stirring dust.

"Yes, he's there now. David's inside the house."

Sara sighed. "Out."

Go northwest. She headed north along the street. In a minute, she turned left to head west. He couldn't be far; the signals were almost on top of each other.

She carried a rough blanket and two metal poles that appeared to be crude walking sticks; they could be attached to form a frame to carry David.

"Benjamin?"

Static back.

This street's two rows of houses were wider apart than the one she'd just come from. She was getting closer to the westerly side of the restraining wall surrounding the city, closer to the more elegant Upper City. They must be nearby.

"Benjamin," she repeated.

It was a clear night, anyway. That was good, and bad.

Her earpiece came on. "Sara!" Benjamin's voice sounded crumpled through the static. "Thank goodness. Where are you?"

She jumped. "I'm in one of the streets of the Lower City. I must be close to you if you can hear me. Can you see me?"

"Not yet."

"I'm carrying an infrared light. Look for it."

"I am. I don't see you yet."

She walked faster. "Can you give me some landmarks? Some indication of where you might be?"

Static again. She kept walking.

"—not sure," his voice returned. "The house is in the middle of the block. It's one story, pretty small, entrance facing west—"

"I'm looking. Anything else?"

He paused. "Look for a trail of blood on the street. Not too much. You may not be able to see the trail in the dark, but Matthias followed it to the house."

"David's blood? How is he doing?"

"I can't rouse him at all."

She shivered.

"Eleazar went to bring back someone. I won't let anyone touch him, of course. But hurry."

She turned left onto the next street running north-south and scanned the cobbles. Even with the bright moonlight she was unable to distinguish the shadows falling at her feet, unable to see if any blood was there. She sped past the houses, looking on her left—the westerly entrances.

"Do you see me?"

"Not yet."

She kept going, holding the infrared light in front of her like a candle over the woven robe and poles. Turn again. Turn again.

She was close. Rebecca had said their signals were almost on top of each other.

She turned onto the next street and stumbled as her toe caught an uneven rock. As she caught her balance, she saw two Jewish men twenty feet ahead, conversing under an archway. They turned as they heard her scuffle, and the well-dressed one seemed to melt back into the shadows, lost to sight.

She locked eyes with Eleazar before she could turn away.

He frowned as he advanced toward her.

43 TIME ELAPSED   17.25

TIME REMAINING   54.35

BENJAMIN SCANNED the street again with his night vision goggles, desperate to see the infrared flashing light that meant Sara was here. He could see about forty feet each way along the north-south corridor, but no farther. The night was clear, lit by the almost-full moon two days before the Passover.

Matthias was with David in the house, and Benjamin wasn't sure if that was better or not. He didn't want Matthias committing any acts of "medicine" on David, although Matthias had said he would only pray over him. On the other hand, if Matthias were here on the roof he might observe Benjamin using technology.

"Sara, how are you doing?"

"I'm still moving. Do you see the light I'm carrying yet?"

"Negative. Keep coming."

"I am, as fast as I can."

It was dangerous work for her alone inside the city at night. Even with the influx of the many people here for Passover, the streets in this area were quiet, and a single woman would be vulnerable. Matthias had said women did not often go around alone even in the daytime; it was unbecoming and unrespectable behavior. Women did not have many rights in this culture; they were almost treated as something owned instead of people.

Sara. He wished he knew if he could trust her.

He heard a shuffling below and behind him, along the outside of the house, and hid the binoculars underneath his coat. The night air was cold. In a moment, a dark shape appeared coming up the exterior stairs to the roof.

"Your friend is no better," Matthias said. "He doesn't move, and he doesn't hear anything. His breathing is troubled."

Benjamin nodded.

"I'll continue to pray over him. There's little else I can do. I'm still waiting for Hananiah."

Benjamin struggled to translate the quick words. "Hananiah?" This must be the man Eleazar had gone to fetch. "You must not touch my friend. I won't allow you to do anything to him."

He couldn't see Matthias' face in the shadow, but felt his frown of disagreement.

"We're leaving soon. We must get back to our camp."

Still Matthias was silent.

"Soon," he repeated. He fingered David's heavy sack carrying the technology that he'd cut from David's belt and tied to his own. Inside was the ear microphone and the leather wristband too, everything anachronistic that David had been carrying.

Matthias turned, his profile dark. "How will you get your friend back to your camp? You need to stay here." His voice was firm.

"No."

"I've been praying over him."

"Yes," Benjamin said.

"He's dying."

Benjamin felt a twisting inside. "I know."

"You weren't able to save him. I might be able to."

He felt another surge of anger, clamped it down. In this primitive world, what could work?

Matthias sighed, folded his hands together. Then he repeated the statement he had made earlier: "Eleazar told me you performed a great miracle to rescue your friend from the Roman soldiers in the tunnel."

"No," Benjamin said. "No miracle." He turned so his back shielded Matthias' view of the binoculars and scanned the street again.

Matthias crossed the roof to stand next to him and put his hand on Benjamin's shoulder. Benjamin again hid the goggles.

"Can you tell me what happened?" He looked square into Benjamin's face, uncommon in this culture. His gaze burned. "Tell me," he said, "tell me how you brought him out of the tunnel. I need to know."

Benjamin pressed his lips together, thinking how he could phrase the event. "I'm not sure."

Matthias waited.

"There was a loud—" he groped for the words— "a loud fire, nothing like I've heard ever before, and the light was blinding—"

His voice trailed.

Matthias nodded. "Go on."

"We ran inside the tunnel, Eleazar and I." Benjamin paused just a moment, considering how to refer to Sara in this culture. His sister?

"And my wife," he said.

"Yes."

"We found David, and I carried him out. Eleazar showed us the way to your house."

Matthias leaned on the edge of the guarding wall surrounding the roof. "Where is your wife now?"

"I'm not sure. She must have gone back to the camp."

"You follow Yeshua." It was a statement.

"No."

He turned away, but not before he saw Matthias' face tighten. He checked the street again but there was still nothing. "Does it matter? I won't turn you in. You've been more than kind to us."

Matthias was silent for almost a minute while he seemed to be deciding on a course of action. Finally, he stepped to the low wall edging the roof and looked down into the street. "I don't know what to think of you." He shook his head. "It's clear God has led you to us. Yet to me you're a cloaked—" something, Benjamin didn't know the word. He seemed to be saying he couldn't ascertain Benjamin's motives, and thought he might be dangerous. Benjamin waited.

Matthias turned to him. "Are you Jewish?"

"Of course."

"Yes, I believe that. A good Jew. I am, too."

Where was this leading?

Matthias sighed. "It's in Yeshua's hands now, anyway. You know enough. You've experienced extraordinary events. Tell me, Benjamin, what holds you back from him?"

As Benjamin looked up in surprise, he heard the familiar static in his earpiece. "Colonel!" Rebecca's voice came on. "Sara just called in. She's close to you."

He froze. Matthias had turned to lean against the wall, and Benjamin pressed the relay signal on the transmitter, acknowledging the contact.

Matthias stared at his hands. "I think I may be able to help your friend."

"You said that before."

"I will tell you my secret. For your friend's sake, and for your own, and your wife's. I am expecting a secret visitor for the Passover to arrive any day."

His earpiece exploded in static, then Sara's voice clarified. "Benjamin!" He winced.

Matthias stepped forward. "You must mention him to no one—"

"Benjamin, I've found Eleazar, here on the street—"

"He can heal your friend, so that you may believe—"

"I've had to hide the light under my robe." Sara's voice sounded tense. "Eleazar seems to be reluctant to take me to you. He's stalling me."

Benjamin grabbed the binoculars and looked through them, not caring suddenly if Matthias saw or not.

Matthias' voice was startled. "What is it?" He leaned over and looked where Benjamin was facing, so that Benjamin had to lower the binoculars into his coat.

"I thought I saw something. It was nothing."

He wanted to go out to help Sara, bring her in. "Which way did Eleazar go? Where is he now?"

Matthias lifted his hands, palms upward. "Listen to me!"

Benjamin turned with difficulty and focused on Matthias. This could be important. "Yes," he said, but his eyes still slid to the street.

"Benjamin! Do you read?"

He acknowledged with the relay signal.

Matthias was hesitating.

"I'm near the northwest corner of the Lower City, close to the Upper City. I'll need to take evasive action if I can't get past him. I don't know what he wants."

He felt the great pulse of adrenaline that he pushed into calm while focusing on Matthias. "Who is coming?"

Matthias brushed the wall with his hand. "My visitor can heal your friend. I know it. It is Yacov, the brother of Yeshua, who is coming here."

Benjamin drew in his breath. Yacov. This might save the mission.

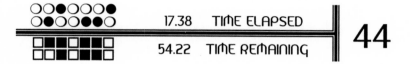

17.38   TIME ELAPSED

54.22   TIME REMAINING

44

"I FOLLOWED YOU today," Yohanan said.

Eleazar looked up, but he couldn't clearly see Yohanan's face through the shadows. They stood in an open area of the Lower City where craftsmen worked during the day. Now it was empty.

"I saw you," Eleazar replied. He was angry, but didn't want to show it—he suspected that Yohanan had had a hand in David's near-capture by the Romans.

Yohanan rocked back on his feet. "Who were they?"

"Visitors to the city. No one important."

Yohanan readjusted his robe so that the stripe showing his newly-purchased Roman citizenship fell just so. He was too proud, Eleazar thought, too secure in his fine clothes and the rich young woman he had betrothed and his expensive house in the fashionable Upper City. And yet—

He studied his friend with narrowed eyes.

Yohanan still wanted to use him as a touchstone to the past, no matter how he tried to act as if he didn't. He felt the familiar struggle inside him, attraction for Yohanan's power and money as a publican, yet distaste for his alliance with Rome and his job of collecting taxes from his own people. The only people Yohanan could socialize with now were other publicans or Gentiles, rich men but arrogant and shallow. No one else would touch him even if he lay bleeding in the street.

His uncle, he knew, would not approve of this continued friendship.

Yohanan put his hand on Eleazar's sleeve. "Those visitors weren't important? Why did you spend the entire afternoon with them on the Temple Mount?"

He shook his head.

"Are they, perhaps, people I should know about?"

"They don't have anything for you." He remembered Benjamin's full sack of money but pushed the thought away. The strangers possessed something much greater than money, although Yohanan couldn't understand it.

They had performed miracles.

Were they from Yeshua?

Yohanan shook his head. "Are you upset because the one man was injured?"

Eleazar shrugged.

"He must have been guilty because he was trying to escape from the soldiers. I saw all of it."

"Are you sure you weren't trying to take money from him?" he said, and then wished he could call back the words. He didn't want to give away his growing disdain for Yohanan. The man could hurt him and his family if he so chose.

His friend scowled. "You're not taking their side over mine, are you?"

Eleazar bowed his head to hide his flashing eyes. "I need to go now." After going to Hananiah's house and not finding him, it had been a mistake to search out Yohanan to confront him. He was too close to their great secret: Eleazar and his uncle, many of their circle, were followers of Yeshua.

He could destroy them.

What had happened to harden his boyhood friend?

At first Eleazar had thought if he continued to see him, he might be able to show him the way of salvation from hell after this brief life. Now, he knew, Yohanan would never convert, yet he continued to hold onto his old life through Eleazar. Eleazar was afraid to ever cross him. Yohanan might betray him if he became angry.

He shook his head. He might have to leave Jerusalem, leave his uncle who had raised him since his father's death when he was less than two years old.

"So, was there anything you came to tell me? Was it something about these strangers?"

Eleazar wished that he could tell him about the strangers, how the red eye of Satan had chased him away from them early this morning on the road outside Jerusalem. The eye had been as bright as the sun but very small, and it had moved over the ground as fast as a bird flew before it rested in front of his feet. His companion, Levi, had run in terror.

He wished he could tell Yohanan how he'd been afraid and had run, too, although he was waiting for the group to come down from Mount Olivet with Yacov, the brother of Yeshua, in tow. He wished he could tell him how, a few minutes later when he'd gathered his courage in his hands, he'd come back and followed the strangers straight to Yeshua's tomb where he saw them conjure light without fire before they knew he was there.

He wished he could ask Yohanan where he thought the thunder and lightning inside the Huldah tunnel had come from.

Eleazar turned away. "No, there isn't anything I can tell you about these strangers. They've disappeared, I know not where. One of them is dying."

He saw Yohanan look up, across the open area. A lone woman had appeared at the end of the street.

Eleazar drew in his breath. It was Sara.

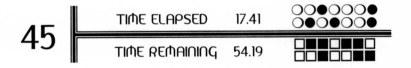

IN THE LOCKDOWN, TOBIAS STARED at the chess knight just put down by his fellow-guard for the night, Hirsch. It stood threatening his queen but also next to his king, free to take.

"You're asking me to take your knight." He was suspicious. "What are you trying to do?"

Hirsch shook his head. "You've got one course of action."

He stared at the board. Hirsch was setting him up with some luscious bait; that's how he played. He never made needless sacrifices. On the other hand, there were no other pieces nearby, and Tobias' king was well-defended.

Forget it. It was the middle of the night, and it was a stupid game. He took the knight.

Hirsch shook his head. "That's it. Checkmate in three." He moved his queen from the back to take the pawn cater-corner to his king.

"Check."

Tobias reached to take the queen.

Hirsch shook his head. "If you do that, I'll move my other knight and you'll be mated."

Tobias narrowed his eyes. He'd be trapped, by the knight or the bishop. He sighed and pushed his king forward, the only safe square open.

Hirsch moved a pawn forward.

Tobias brought his bishop forward, beginning to defend.

Hirsch shifted his knight to the board's edge and cleared his throat.

Tobias studied the board for a long moment. He shook his head and knocked his king over. "You got me."

Hirsch looked up from the board to meet his gaze, then swept the chess pieces off the board and stowed them in the hollowed area on its underside.

"You need to remember your ultimate goal," he said. "Don't grab an opportunity unless it suits your purpose. By taking my knight, you moved your king into the most vulnerable spot on the board. Plus, you lost your opportunity to loosen some of the pieces around your king and maybe even mount a counter-attack."

"Hmmph." Even though he liked Hirsch, sometimes he found him annoying.

Tobias glanced at the digital clock above the door leading to the prisoner quarters. "Almost two. Do you think we'll see any action?"

Hirsch shrugged. "Probably not."

Normally the lockdown interior was guarded by two enlisted MP soldiers. However, Colonel Aaron, the security chief, had changed the routine two days ago by placing twelve intelligence officers on rotation to guard the two prisoners. Furthermore, they were given enlisted insignia to wear instead of their regular uniforms, since Aaron hadn't wanted anyone but his intelligence officers to know there had been a change in the routine. A mole still was loose in the complex, a high-ranking officer who could be anyone.

Tobias stood and stretched. "Just a few more hours." He picked up his cola and took another swig. It was warm and flat. Yuck.

Hirsch pushed back his chair, stood up, and paced in the narrow room. Tobias watched him for a moment, and then sat again and put his feet upon the table, deliberately, one boot crossed over the other. As a lieutenant, it felt strange to be wearing only a corporal's stripes on his arm.

He sighed. His new wife Tali, an engineering technician for the time machine, had been disappointed when she'd learned he had been assigned to night duty tonight. At least he and Tali were able to stay together, since they both worked in the complex. The complex had been sealed for a week in preparation for FlashBack, and it would remain sealed for at least a few days after the pod returned. That was why the two prisoners remained here in the brig instead of being shuttled to a real prison outside the complex.

Tali had been one of the technicians involved with the time transport of the four FlashBack soldiers to first century Jerusalem. He didn't himself understand the time machine. To him it made sense that the time machine should be able to transport the pod back in time, then immediately bring it forward again, mission accomplished. Tali had explained that this was impossible, that the time machine linked the time past with time present. They flow together, she had said, so the countdown here was parallel to what the soldiers experienced in the past. Tobias shook his head. The idea of it was alarming. If the pod had been atomized in the void between time and space, no one would know for two more days.

It was too theoretical. Tobias preferred to work on concrete problems, such as finding the mole.

The buzzer echoed in the lockdown. He started to his feet and glanced at the monitor over the door leading to the outer hallway. The security guard stationed in the hallway outside was looking into the camera.

Hirsch looked back. "Yes, Private. What is it?"

The guard nodded on the monitor. "General Gideon is here. He wishes to interview one of the prisoners."

Tobias saw Hirsch raise his eyebrows. "Please show the general inside. Give us a moment." Hirsch punched the mike off. "I wonder if something else has happened."

"If it has, Colonel Aaron will tell us soon enough."

And as Tobias looked at Hirsch, he inexplicably felt an uneasy finger of doubt touch his spine.

General Gideon strode into the room. Tobias hadn't seen the second in command of the base close up before, and was surprised at how ordinary the man looked, down to the shallow stubble on his chin. Yet, the man projected a presence of well-channeled energy right below the surface, almost as if he'd deliver an electric shock if he was touched.

Gideon's gaze swept over the room. Hirsch had pushed the chairs underneath the table. It was set up as the interrogation room now.

"Corporal. I need to talk with the prisoner Seidel. Now."

Hirsch saluted him then stepped back. "Yes, sir. Please leave all your weapons on the table here first. My partner will put them away. I'll accompany you for the interview."

Gideon looked as if he were about to argue, but then clenched his jaw. His Field Dress uniform was still neat, Tobias thought, although he'd probably been up since well before the time throw eighteen hours ago.

"I have no weapons, Corporal."

Hirsch nodded. "Very well, sir. Please wait here while I get the prisoner." He tugged at the door leading to the prisoner cells and walked through, leaving Tobias alone with the general. Tobias crossed his arms.

Gideon glanced at him and then looked away as if he didn't think much of him.

Seidel in his bright orange jumpsuit came first into the front room, followed by Hirsch. Seidel did not look pleased to have been awakened, but remained quiet. Tobias pulled one of the chairs out and motioned the prisoner to sit down.

"I'm going," he said, and Hirsch nodded.

He slipped into the monitoring room, closing the door behind himself, and then he turned on the microphone and camera to film the front room through the observation mirror. Gideon was saying, "No, this shouldn't take long, Corporal," as he positioned the chair across the table from the prisoner while Hirsch stood at the edge of the table between them.

Tobias picked up the telephone and punched four numbers into the keypad.

"Aaron here."

"This is Lieutenant Tobias at the lockdown. General Gideon just arrived to interview Seidel. I'm notifying you as per your orders."

Aaron's voice sounded crisp. "Right. Wait until I arrive before you do anything."

"We just put the prisoner in the room. General Gideon has begun the interrogation."

Aaron made a deep noise in his throat.

"Sir, is there a problem?"

Aaron paused. "Did General Gideon say why he wanted to interview the prisoner?"

"No, sir."

There was silence on the phone.

"Sir?"

"Thank you, Lieutenant. I want you to observe and record the interview as we discussed. I'll be there shortly."

"Yes, sir."

"Carry on."

Tobias' gaze fell to the chessboard on the counter. He slid open a drawer and put it inside. Keep your mind on the goal, he thought.

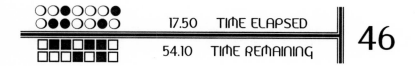

SARA PULLED her coat further over her face as Eleazar advanced towards her.

She couldn't see his companion clearly since he stood deep in a darkened archway. He was maybe twenty-three, and he wore good-quality clothing as far as she could tell under the moon's light. Sara knew he was Jewish since he wore the *tsitsit,* or fringes, on his coat, but he was also clean-shaven in the cosmopolitan Greek style. Secular, prosperous, contrasting with Eleazar who looked more like rabble. It did seem odd that they would meet like this at night, in secret on the streets.

When she'd first seen Eleazar, she'd thought to ask where David and Benjamin were, but he seemed so wrapped up in a secretive conversation that she had the impression he wouldn't be happy to be approached. He was also potentially dangerous. Her thought now was that it might be better to get past him and his friend as quickly as possible.

Then Eleazar stepped in front of her, and his eyes flickered in recognition. "Woman, where are you going in such a hurry?"

His tone wasn't threatening, not exactly, but he seemed eager to determine her business.

She looked down submissively and tried once more to move away, but he still blocked her. Her hand fell almost without her awareness to the bag at her waist. She had a small smoke bomb she could drop as she ran away—

No. No more tricks if at all possible. He'd already seen too much.

"Woman, what do you want?"

"Good evening." She cleared her throat. "I wish to pass, if you please."

She saw the other man five paces away start, as if he'd recognized something unusual. "Your accent is strange," Eleazar's friend said.

Sara glanced at him over Eleazar's shoulder. It seemed peculiar that he remained hidden in the shadows rather than coming out.

"Keep your voice down!" Eleazar whispered urgently. "Don't attract his attention."

She folded back the overhang of her cloak so he could better see her face. "I need to find my companions."

"You need to get out of here."

"I must find them."

"How did you even find me?" Eleazar moved in front of her, shielding her from his friend's view. "It's not safe."

The other man called out, "Who is she?"

"She's lost," Eleazar called back. Then he turned to her and said, "Woman, don't you know it's dangerous to be on the streets this late? And by yourself." He peered down at her. "What is your purpose?"

"Help me," she said, but softly, so his friend wouldn't hear.

The other man took a step forward, although Sara still couldn't see him well through the shadows. "Do you think she needs an escort?"

Eleazar held up his hand in a "halt" gesture. "She needs to go through the part of the city where you might not be welcome. I know who she is; her cousin lives near me. You can leave her alone, Yohanan. She has nothing for you." Still standing in front of her to block his friend's view, he reached over to pull Sara's cloak over her face again. It was an intimate gesture in this culture, and she jumped. "Don't let him see your face."

Eleazar walked back to speak a few additional words to his friend. His friend nodded, glanced at Sara, and then retreated into the darkness. Eleazar came back to her after a moment.

"Woman, let me help you," he said, but his eyes were still on his friend, as if to make sure the man wouldn't follow. Then, he touched her shoulder to guide her in the opposite direction.

She turned to glance back, and just caught the flash of emotion cross Eleazar's face as he saw her do so. The expression was gone as fast as it had appeared. What had it been? Anger? Fear?

Who was this man, Yohanan?

"Let's go," Eleazar said.

"Where are we going?"

His hand pressed her shoulder. "Trust me. I'll take you to your husband and his friend, but we need to get away first."

She started at the word "husband." He must mean Benjamin. She turned to him. "But your friend—"

He shook his head. "Let him be, Sara. Let him be."

She held the infrared light above her wrist, hiding all but the flashing end under the cloak and camouflaged poles she carried. He led her one more block, turned up a little alley into a wider street, then looked behind him.

"Yohanan's not following us," he said with evident satisfaction. "He'll go back to his home."

Sara glanced at him. "Who is he? I never even got a good look at him."

"Just as well. He's no one you want to know."

Was he telling her the truth about taking her back to Benjamin and David? Although she was not defenseless, following him, she had few options.

"Where are we going?"

He turned down another street. "My uncle's house."

"How is my friend?"

He looked outraged, and Sara wondered if, as a woman in this culture, she was asking too many questions. She bowed her head.

Suddenly she heard the familiar static in her earpiece. "Sara!" Benjamin's voice rang in her ear.

She wasn't able to answer. Eleazar was too close.

"I see your light," Benjamin said. "I'm coming out to you now."

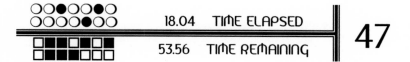

KEEP YOUR MIND on the goal, Gideon thought. He needed to eliminate the operative, Seidel, as quickly as possible.

The corporal, Hirsch, pushed the prisoner into the metal chair. "No problems," he warned, leaning against him.

Gideon hoped not. Seidel wasn't wearing handcuffs or other restraints, just a bright orange prison jumpsuit unzipped halfway down his chest. He was, no doubt, used to intimidating others with his size. Well, the man wasn't going anywhere tonight—not with the corporal here, the other corporal behind the mirror, and the private at his post in the hallway. There was nowhere to run.

Gideon sank into the other chair. The room was cool, or maybe it was merely the dull white of the block cement walls and linoleum floor with nothing but the one-way observation mirror behind his back. He wanted to finish this. He had turned on the electronic transmitter, and even now, it was signaling its deadly message for the respirospheres to dump carbon monoxide into Seidel's bloodstream.

The rush of air began in the overhead fans, and he waited a moment until it died down again. "This won't take long," he said to Seidel.

He watched the prisoner squirm in the hard chair, then turned his head to glance at the corporal to his left. The man stood near the edge of the table between Gideon and the prisoner. The corporal's name seemed familiar although he didn't recognize the face. He'd have to pay attention to him. Hirsch carried a sidearm in a holster on his right hip, standard procedure for all guards in the brig, but the gun made him nervous.

"Do you know who I am?"

Seidel turned a cold fish-eye on him. "I know who you are. You're one of the water buffalo in charge of this complex. But you don't know who I am."

Gideon took a deep breath. "Why don't you tell me then?"

The saboteur smiled, then looked away.

Gideon hated every bit of the man in front of him. He hated the man's sunken dark eyes and his narrow lips twisted in a sarcastic smile. He hated the man's arrogant attitude; he hated the way this man had bungled his assignment and put Raseac and the whole operation in danger. He hated him. The man caught Gideon's stare, then looked away. Contempt.

He suppressed his rage. "I can make this easy, or I can kill you."

Seidel laughed. "I doubt that."

"How did you get into the restricted area to plant an explosive?"

Out of the corner of his eye, he saw Hirsch shift as if he were uncomfortable with the question.

Seidel stared at him stonily.

"Who are you working with?"

Silence.

"Who sent you?"

Silence.

Gideon got up and walked around the table to the prisoner's side; he paced behind Seidel. "You're motivated by your ideals, aren't you?"

Hirsch shot him a questioning glance. He understood that he shouldn't be giving the prisoner any tactical advantage during questioning. *Sharp kid.*

Gideon wished he could remember why Hirsch's name sounded familiar.

Seidel laughed. "Don't patronize me."

"I know more than you think."

Gideon crossed over and sat down again. He placed both hands on top of the table and played with a single white thread lying against the dark cloth of his sleeve, the same kind of thread he'd used as a signal outside the dead drop in the toilet paper dispenser to indicate a message was waiting.

"For example, I know I have a great deal of control over your fate."

The saboteur continued to look away. Gideon unfolded his hands and tapped his left forefinger on top of the table, trying to get the man to look here—here—to look at his hands.

"Telling us what we want to know will keep you buried here, in this complex."

I'll bury you myself, he thought. You're jeopardizing things further, and I have to make sure you don't talk. It won't be much longer.

Seidel laughed. "What makes you think I'll tell you anything?"

Gideon hit the table with his open palm then. "Look at me."

Seidel turned to him, and then looked down at the table where Gideon had spread his fingers on the table. Gideon removed the thread and draped it over the man's sleeve. The man stiffened.

Gideon nodded.

"Do you understand?" he asked in measured tones. "This facility is not independent. They're all connected."

He clenched his hands into fists and drew them close.

"Talking will keep you here in this complex. If you won't talk, I'll have to transfer you. I'll transfer you to another facility."

The air rushing through the vents disturbed the silence.

Gideon studied him. He wanted to make sure he had been understood. Seidel met his eyes and promptly looked down, resting his gaze on the thread, so like the ones he'd retrieved at the bathroom's dead drop. The arrogance that had inflated him was gone.

It was the fabled carrot and stick. Seidel understood, all right. Even though Gideon had just handed him the single piece of information that the man could bargain with—his identity as the mole in the complex—Gideon had traded it for the assurance of an hour more of silence. The saboteur wouldn't talk in that time, hopeful for a transfer to safety. He was dying now, his cheeks beginning to flush with the carbon monoxide release.

He wanted this to be finished. The situation was too dicey even for the few remaining days until Raseac could move.

Even as he thought this, he felt a sudden shifting in the atmosphere, dangerous, intangible. It was a movement out of the corner of his eye.

As he turned his head, he saw Hirsch step back from the table. He stared at Gideon with sudden wariness, at the white thread that had fallen from Seidel's trembling fingers as if he recognized somehow that it had been a signal to the saboteur. Gideon slammed his left hand down on the table to cover it but was too late. The guard shook his head as he met Gideon's eyes, and then his hand dropped down to the gun on his hip.

"Corporal."

He knew.

No. It couldn't be. A lowly MP corporal wouldn't even know there was a mole loose in the complex, much less any details of the dead drop. Only the officers would have been told.

But as he studied him he was convinced.

Seidel was coiled too. Gideon could sense it; Seidel focused on the guard as well.

He drew in his breath. Of course. Now he understood: Hirsch wasn't a corporal even though he wore that uniform. Gideon suddenly recalled the name as belonging to one of Aaron's intelligence officers, one of his elite corps, who was guarding the prisoner like a spider—

Watch the gun.

Even as he lurched out of his seat, the saboteur lunged across the table toward Hirsch. The guard was watchful but hadn't anticipated Seidel's almost prescient response and thus lost his opportunity to gain control of the situation. There was nowhere for Hirsch to hide in the small room, he was backed against the wall, and as the saboteur tackled him,

Hirsch pulled the gun out of the holster and fired it point-blank into Seidel's chest.

The floor shook under Gideon's feet as the two hit the floor, Hirsch struggling to escape from beneath Seidel's two hundred pounds of dead weight. Hirsch still clutched the gun as he rolled the saboteur to the side and oriented toward Gideon, but the guard was off balance.

Gideon knew he had only seconds, but his thoughts were crystal clear. There was one way to prevent the guard from revealing his identity.

His anger was like a tidal wave, and this time he let it rise, let it hit and bury him and help carry him through as he kicked the gun out of Hirsch's hand. It skittered out of reach. The guard leaned after it, but Gideon had turned in a half circle off his chair and dropped to his knees over the guard. He drew back his elbow to knock the guard while he was on the floor. Hirsch grabbed his right arm, attempting to pull himself up, but he was still trapped under the saboteur's body. He didn't see the heel of Gideon's other hand as it smashed under his chin and pushed him back onto the floor. The angle of Gideon's body shielded the action from the observation mirror.

Maintaining his upward push on Hirsch's chin, Gideon drew back his other hand, his right hand, shaping his fingers and thumb into a cruel semicircle that he drove against the man's throat and upward just below the larynx. He clenched his fingers around Hirsch's throat to fit into the grooves between muscle and artery and vein, digging in until he found the ridged landmark of the trachea. He felt the palm of his hand move over the hard bump of the cricoid. When the position was correct he grasped hard, twisted his hand around, and felt the sudden mobility under his palm as he snapped the man's larynx like breaking a twig.

The guard looked at him in shock and began to gag, his hands clasping his throat. The airway had collapsed. Gideon looked dispassionately on him as the door to the room burst open.

He pulled the soldier out from under the saboteur and laid him supine on the floor. The guard fought him a little, kicked ineffectively, but he couldn't breathe and would lose consciousness in a minute. It was done.

The guard entering from the monitoring room behind the mirror ran over.

"Get a medic!" Gideon ordered. "He can't breathe!"

"The private is inside the lockdown. He's calling now."

The guard knelt and tried to straighten Hirsch's head, hyperextend it to clear the airway, but the man kept rolling away.

Gideon leaned over the saboteur and checked for a pulse in the neck. Seidel was dead from the bullet wound.

As he looked up, he gasped. A message—if the other soldier understood it—Hirsch was grasping the hand of the other soldier, and even as he kicked, he was pulling, pulling at the man's sleeve, trying to pull loose a thread.

48

18.12 TIME ELAPSED

53.48 TIME REMAINING

THE MEDICS ARRIVED too quickly.

Gideon held the unconscious soldier down on the floor at the far end of the room. It hadn't been long enough, not long enough at all.

The second guard, Sol Tobias, scurried on the other side of Hirsch, pushing up on his diaphragm to try to remove any obstruction, manipulating Hirsch's head back and forward to open the airway, trying to blow air into lungs that wouldn't inflate. Gideon grimaced. It wouldn't work. Gideon felt sure Tobias was from Aaron's group of elite security officers, just like Hirsch. If Hirsch hadn't been quite so observant, he never would have had to hurt him in the first place. Such a small thread.

Gideon pressed his fingers against Hirsch's wrist. Pulse was losing strength, soaring. It wouldn't be long now.

"This way," the private said from across the room as he held open the door. Two people rushed in, past the dead saboteur to the downed soldier beside whom Gideon and the other guard knelt.

Gideon recognized Leah Rosen and winced. The doctor was dressed in nonmilitary blue flannel pajamas and a red terrycloth robe flapping about her knees; her sneakers were loose, and she carried a bulky leather bag. She pushed her wire-rounded glasses up on her nose as she entered. The man behind her—the medic on call, Gideon guessed—was pushing a chest-high box on wheels ahead of him. The crash cart.

They crossed the small room in four steps, the physician skidding off balance for a moment on the saboteur's blood.

"Get back!" she ordered as she dropped to her knees. The medic bumped Gideon out of the way as he moved to the doctor's left, near Hirsch's shoulder.

"Yossi, my laryngoscope and an ETT. Move back, move back!" She slipped on latex gloves. Then, she repositioned Hirsch, pulled his chin up and forward, and placed her hand on his neck, checking his pulse.

The medic also put on gloves, then took a white cloth from the top of the bag, spread it on the floor, and laid the contents of the bag in a line on the cloth.

"How long has he not been breathing?"

The security guard, Tobias, answered. "Three minutes. The prisoner hit him in the throat as he went down."

The doctor grimaced. "We'll get him back." But Gideon knew that every tick of the clock took Hirsch further away.

The doctor manipulated a lighted silver blade within Hirsch's mouth, peering in as she attempted to push a plastic tube down his throat with the other hand. Hirsch gagged.

The doctor shifted the bladed instrument sideways and lifted up, pushed the plastic tube in again.

"Tube won't pass," she said, almost in an automated voice. She pulled out the laryngoscope. "I have to cut."

Gideon stepped back against the wall opposite the mirror.

The doctor ripped open Hirsch's shirt from top to bottom, buttons flying off like small missiles. The medic held out a hand-sized bottle. She grabbed it and poured a quantity of the brown iodine liquid low onto Hirsch's neck, wiping it over his skin. Then she snatched a cloth-wrapped package from the towel and ripped it open. Inside was a scalpel.

"Hold him." She moved to Hirsch's shoulder. The medic grabbed Hirsch's head and pulled it back.

A small line of black followed the scalpel's blade. Dark blood along Hirsch's throat, it turned red as soon as it appeared.

Hirsch lay motionless.

The medic held open a paper package containing a plastic airway tube. The doctor inserted the tube into the throat wound, taping it down.

It was three minutes since they'd started.

"Ambu bag," she said.

The medic was holding a black balloon. The doctor attached it to the tube and squeezed air into Hirsch's lungs. Hirsch's chest rose.

No.

For the first time Gideon felt dizzy with the thought that he might not be able to contain this. He looked up, and his eyes caught the saboteur's unblinking stare.

His own death.

Stop it.

"Take over respirations," the doctor said. The medic moved in, took back the ambu bag and squeezed again. The doctor pressed her hand to Hirsch's throat.

"No pulse. I have to shock." She pulled cables from the side of the EKG box, and then slapped a lead onto Hirsch's chest, another on his side.

Hirsch's skin was grey beneath the bright fluorescents.

The soldier's chest rose again. Another breath.

The machine buzzed.

"I am going to shock on three," the doctor announced. "Get back. One, two. Yossi, hands off. Three, everyone's clear. Now!"

A jolt of energy went through the leads, and Hirsch's body jumped.

"V-tach," the doctor said, looking at the monitor. "Yossi, start CPR. I'll ventilate."

Gideon could see a thin green trace across the screen— jagged triangles.

Yossi clamped his hands together, heel of one hand over the other, and pushed down on the chest. Again. The doctor gave a breath to Hirsch, and then threaded an I.V. into the inside portion of Hirsch's elbow. Another breath. She handed a bag of saline to Gideon.

"Epinephrine one mg. Time is...0243." She pushed in the syringe plunger.

Breath. The doctor looked at the screen. "Yossi, good perfusion. Let's do another shock."

"Yes doctor."

The EKG squealed, charge ready.

"Get clear. One, two. Yossi, back. Three. Now."

Like running a machine, Gideon thought. It was a smooth drill to bring someone back to life.

Hirsch's body jumped.

"Come on, soldier," the doctor murmured. "Still V-tach. Yossi, start CPR again."

"Yes, ma'am." Yossi knelt forward and again leaned into Hirsch's chest.

The doctor gave another breath. Gideon watched the trace on the screen jiggle with each compression.

Breath.

The buzzer on the EKG squealed.

"I'm going to shock again," the doctor said. "One, two. Yossi, hands off. Three. Clear."

Hirsch jumped again. The trace on the monitor was flat-lined, and then it started to move in what looked like a better rhythm. The line was stretched out more.

The doctor nodded. "That did it. Sinus."

She motioned to Gideon to elevate the saline bag, then turned. "He's holding sinus. Yossi, I need another line please."

Hirsch's chest rose again as the doctor gave another breath.

"Come on, come on," Gideon heard the doctor mutter. "You can do better, soldier."

The medic pushed a needle into the soldier's other inside elbow. The doctor gave another breath.

"I have that second line now," Yossi said. He was taping the tubing to the guard's forearm, the other guard Tobias holding another bag of saline aloft.

The doctor gave another breath. "Heart looks better. Still sinus. Pulse oximeter?"

"In the bag."

"Give a four mg Tocofel push, then another four in one minute. Now!"

"Yes, ma'am."

The doctor gave another breath.

"What's Tocofel?" Gideon asked.

The doctor was fixated on the EKG trace, and then she glanced up at him. "Yes, General. It's a new drug. Tocofel chemically combines with the free radicals generated during reperfusion after anoxia. In simple terms, the drug prevents brain damage."

"Will he be able to remember what happened?"

"Very likely. If we're in time."

The medic pushed in the syringe plunger. Translucent yellow fluid flowed into the cap of the second I.V. Gideon watched, immobile, as it marked out the I.V. line and disappeared into Hirsch's arm.

Gideon stared, fascinated, at the spectacle of his own demise.

Breath. The doctor rummaged in the bag and pulled out a box the size of a deck of cards. She extended the sensor from its side and pushed the clip onto Hirsch's finger.

"Sat's ninety," she said. "Come on, soldier."

Gideon wished he understood what was going on.

There was a commotion at the door. The private was out of sight, in the vestibule by the monitoring room, but Gideon could hear his voice talking to someone, and running steps. Then he saw Aaron standing at the entrance.

Who had notified the security chief?

Aaron's gaze was trained on him, and Gideon masked his face. Then Aaron broke away to survey the room. "Lieutenant! What happened?"

Lieutenant. He'd been right about the other guard, Tobias, being an officer.

Tobias looked up, juggling the second I.V. bag. It was obvious he hadn't been aware of Aaron's entrance. "Sir, it was so quick."

"What happened?"

"General Gideon was questioning Seidel. Seidel jumped Hirsch, no warning or reason. Hirsch shot him, but Seidel must have punched him in the throat on the way down."

"You saw Seidel punch him?"

Tobias shook his head. "It was too quick, sir. Seidel's dead. And Hirsch is—"

The doctor looked up. "He's stable now, Colonel. I don't know how much damage yet."

"Why did he need you?"

"Airway obstruction. He wasn't able to breathe."

"Colonel," Gideon said. "I feel responsible. I questioned Seidel. I had no idea he was so unpredictable."

Aaron walked across the room, all the while locking his gaze to Gideon's. When he stood next to him, he put his hand on Gideon's forearm.

"Don't worry," Aaron said. "I'll get to the bottom of this."

A warning? Did he even suspect him?

Gideon shook his head.

Aaron stood behind the EKG. "Doctor, what happened?"

She squeezed the ambu bag, and then looked up. "When the soldier was punched, his larynx was smashed. I had to do a trache, then resuscitate his heart."

"Do you know for sure that he was punched in the throat?"

The doctor shrugged. "The airway was completely obstructed."

Breath. She turned back to study the monitors. "Yossi, sat's up to ninety-five. We're almost ready to transport. Wake up Shoshana. Tell her to bring a stretcher on the double, and oxygen."

"Yes, ma'am." The medic stood stiffly. A large patch of Seidel's blood from the floor had dried on his fatigues from the knees down. The medic didn't seem to notice it as he walked through the door in search of a telephone.

Aaron turned his body to Tobias, but his gaze stayed on Gideon. "Lieutenant, is the camera still live?"

Gideon twitched his hand involuntarily but otherwise remained immobile. Had it all been filmed? Or was Aaron bluffing? Where was the camera, what angle? He longed to sweep the room with his eyes but pulled himself back. Aaron was watching.

Tobias shifted the bag of intravenous fluid. "Yes, sir, it is."

"I want to review the record in five minutes. Get it ready." Aaron's eyes were still on Gideon.

"Here, sir." Tobias handed his saline to Gideon.

Gideon stepped back.

The doctor looked up again. "This man needs a hospital. I can stabilize him, but I don't have the resources to keep him. We need to get him out now."

"Out of the question," Gideon said. "We can't break the seal over the base for another week."

"How soon would he need to be transported?" Aaron asked.

The doctor shrugged. "Within the next few hours at the latest. This is a critical time."

"I see," Aaron said.

The doctor gave another breath, then checked the monitors. "Heart seems stable. Sat's at ninety-eight."

"When will he wake up?" Aaron asked.

"Unclear. Depends how long he was anoxic, how much brain damage he may have sustained."

"I need to question him."

The doctor shook her head. "Your best bet is to get him out of here and to a specialized unit. That's all I can tell you."

The medic reappeared in the doorway. "Shoshana will be here in five minutes."

"Excellent."

Aaron glanced at Hirsch. "Doctor, you saved his life."

"Let's hope so."

"Bring him back."

He nodded curtly to the medic as he exited.

"How is he?" the medic asked.

"Stable."

Gideon watched the doctor. She was monitoring the EKG trace and her patient, and squeezing the ambu bag every five seconds. Blast it; she'd brought him back. Now, his only hope was that Hirsch wouldn't wake up in time.

"Let me take these, General." The medic reached for the bags of saline.

Gideon glanced at the monitoring mirror as he walked out. Once he was in the vestibule, he turned around, scanned the room for possible camera locations. If it was in the mirror, there was nothing to worry about. Light fixture, a problem if located there. Doorframe, possible.

Aaron's voice filtered through the vestibule. "Yes, General Landau. One hour, your office. Thank you, sir."

Aaron was going over his head to talk with the base commander.

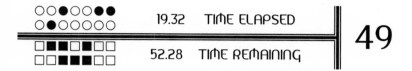

REBECCA PUSHED against the winch, trying to make it turn, trying again to lower the suspended camera into the pod.

She was finished taking infrared aerial photographs of Jerusalem and surrounding countryside; the camera dangled beneath a weather balloon, a hundred yards above the pod. The images displayed on the computer screen had looked good; yes, they were fine. Aside from boundary fires on the city and the Temple walls, it was dark within five hundred feet of the pod. The infrared showed up well.

Thousands of stars—jewel dust sprinkled on black velvet—peeked overhead through the hole in the top of the pod. She was unaccustomed to seeing so many stars, like sand, ones that Sara said hadn't been seen by the naked eye for more than five hundred years before their own time. The air was sweet but cold as it drifted inside.

But the winch was stuck. Grinding like stones.

Stay calm. Check the guide wire, but the wire didn't seem to be tangled. Was it? She tried the winch again. It still wouldn't turn.

Try again.

Then she heard singing. Two men, fifty yards away, were coming up the side of the hill. They hadn't seen anything yet, but it was just a matter of seconds.

The winch still wouldn't turn. In the spring breeze the suspended camera whipped over the pod.

AARON PEEPED in Gideon's office and saw him seated behind the desk, his cigarette glowing like a ruby eye in the darkened room.

"Reuven," Gideon said to Aaron. "Come in if you'd like."

The suite of offices was deserted at three-thirty in the morning, the big room leading to the individual doors off-lit with foot-level lights. Gideon's was the only door open, and Aaron smiled as he stepped inside. He'd catch this spider in its lair.

The tip of the cigarette grew bright red as Gideon inhaled.

"Cigarette?"

Aaron hesitated, took one, and Gideon slid his pocket lighter across the desk.

The smoke was sharp but not unpleasant in his lungs, hot, and as he breathed in again he drifted into the cold awareness of the chase.

"How's your man?" Gideon asked.

Aaron rolled the cigarette between his fingers for a moment before answering. "Stable. He's unconscious. The doctor says he needs an MRI and some specialized drugs we don't have here. He needs to be moved out."

"Mmm." Gideon breathed against his cigarette. "No one likes losing soldiers under their command, but these things happen."

"He's not lost. The doctor holds out good hope for him if he can be transported."

"One man isn't worth the mission. We can't lift the seal over the base."

Aaron bit back a retort, then tapped his cigarette against the ashtray on the desk. He'd broken the habit years ago but all the little motions of smoking came back so easily.

The base commander was due in ten minutes.

There was dark smoke in his lungs.

Gideon sat forward and ground the end of his cigarette into the ashtray. Ashes flickered and went black.

"I lost men in ReachDeep," Gideon went on, almost as though he were talking to himself. "Four years, thirteen operations, twenty-two men. It's never easy."

Aaron steepled his fingers together, and nodded.

Gideon went on. "Horrible deaths I've seen, and afterwards. The bodies of two of my soldiers were dragged through the street, spat on, torn apart. Another body was tripped with mines so we couldn't retrieve and bury it. He rotted in the open, with just a poor shelter we built over him to keep the wild animals away. After awhile—"

He shook his head.

Aaron snuffed his cigarette.

Gideon sighed. "I'll tell you who has nine lives."

"Who?"

"Feinan. Extraordinary. He went into situations that were nigh impossible; not only came out but always successful. Hostage rescue, mostly. I swear soldiers jumped in front of bullets for him. He was called the "Viper" by the Palestinians."

"I know."

Gideon leaned forward to reach for another cigarette. Aaron pushed the pack and the lighter toward him across the desk. His face was in shadow, he knew. Sometimes that helped people to talk.

For a moment, the bright orange flame illuminated Gideon's face. Dark shadows under his eyes. His cigarette glowed.

"He had a bounty on him," Gideon said. "A king's ransom. They almost got him too: that car bomb when his

wife died four years ago. He's never been the same. But still
dangerous. Very dangerous."

"How did they know where to plant the bomb?"

Gideon shook his head. "Someone close to him might
have leaked the information, but they never found who. All
that money."

Aaron wasn't sure, but he thought he saw Gideon smile.
Aaron shivered.

They sat in silence then, Aaron pressing back against the
chair. He felt sick. Maybe it was the early hour, or the
cigarette, or the mole in the complex. He was sure the mole
was Gideon. Now he was going to have to save his man over
Gideon's objections. The battle would be soon.

Gideon took another breath of smoke.

They sat almost companionably for a few minutes, no
conversation. Then the lights from the outer room flooded
through the doorway, and the shadows sank under the
furniture as low voices drifted without. Aaron stood up and
walked to Gideon's door.

Landau hadn't seen him yet. He stood with his crutches
fifteen feet away at the desk outside his office talking to his
secretary, an unshaved thirtyish sergeant who had obviously
just been summoned out of bed. The secretary flipped
through a stack of papers as he nodded. Landau was walking
better, Aaron noticed, and then Landau looked up and caught
Aaron's eye.

"Reuven," the base commander said. "Where's Shimon?"

Aaron gestured behind him. "Here. We're ready, sir."

"Right. Let's go. My office."

Aaron glanced around the base commander's office as
Landau waved them to two chairs near his desk. The room
was big as offices in the complex went, fifteen feet by twelve,
but with little ornamentation. Two detailed maps of
Jerusalem—modern and first century—were side by side on
one wall. Opposite was a three-by-five foot schematic of the
time machine complex. There was a wall safe behind the desk,
the high bookshelf next to it crammed with books on nuclear
physics, military tactics, ancient history, and governmental
documents. Optical discs lined an entire shelf. The private

bathroom door nearby was closed. The only unusual object was a reproduction of a first-century oil lamp, resting on top of the small refrigerator in the corner.

The secretary appeared in the doorway. "Sir, the doctor's on the line."

Landau looked up. "Thank you, Hod. Put her on speakerphone in here, then shut the door."

"Yes, sir."

The doctor reviewed the situation. The unconscious soldier, Hirsch, was stable but needed urgent medical care outside their facility, in Jerusalem.

"Do we break the seal over the base?" Landau asked after the doctor had hung up.

"Absolutely not," Gideon said. "The time machine is running. We can't risk its going out of phase with the past. And with a mole present we can't risk unknown personnel gaining access to the base."

Aaron shook his head. "That won't happen. The pilot and the doctor return immediately. No one else goes out or in."

"There's a seal for a reason!" Gideon snapped. "You're the chief of security. You should know this. We don't know what might happen, and FlashBack is critical."

"It's my considered opinion that we can do this safely."

Landau shifted in his chair.

Aaron sat forward. "There's a moratorium on outside communications, so they wouldn't know we're coming. The only people who might even know about the possibility of breaking the seal, General, are the doctor, two medics, two of my security people, your secretary, and us. It's early in the morning. We could be out and back before anyone knew it."

Gideon snorted. "So could a bomb planted on the underside of the helicopter, or an enemy if the security code were tracked. The point is, you can't guarantee anything."

Aaron locked eyes with Landau. "General, I need to question him. He was beginning to draw his gun before the saboteur jumped him."

"What?" Landau asked.

"Yes, sir. I have the visual right here."

Landau tapped his forefinger on the desk. "Shimon, what was going on in that interrogation?"

Gideon shifted in his chair. Aaron wasn't sure, but he thought Gideon gave Landau an almost imperceptible shake of his head.

Aaron sat up. "I suggest we view the recording now."

"Sir," Gideon said to Landau, "may I speak with you privately for a moment first?"

Aaron's ears burned.

Landau looked up. "Yes, of course, Shimon."

Aaron glanced at Gideon, who had the ghost of a smile on his lips.

"You don't mind, do you, Reuven? Why don't you set up the recording in Conference Room A, and we'll be right in."

Aaron flashed through his options. He had no choice. He gritted his teeth. "Of course."

He deliberately left the door to the office open. Keep watch, he thought as he passed the secretary behind the front desk. Surely, Gideon wouldn't be so bold as to try anything now.

He had a bad feeling as he stalked away.

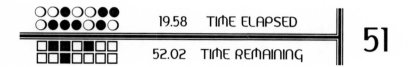

GIDEON CLOSED the office door and turned to Landau.

"Sir," Gideon said. "I didn't want to say in front of Reuven why I was with the prisoner this morning. The fact is—"

"What?"

He'd planned just how to say this. Pause, and then speak as if unloading a painful thought.

"I—sir, I was questioning the prisoner because I wanted to make sure I heard firsthand what he had to say, without interference."

"The prisoner has been questioned extensively."

"By Colonel Aaron, sir. Only under his direction."

"Well, he is the chief of security."

"Sir—" Gideon took a deep breath. "There is still an undiscovered mole in the complex, someone with a high security clearance. And now Reuven wants to break the seal over the base."

He fell silent.

Landau started to shake his head. "Shimon, tell me you're not saying what I think you're saying."

Gideon stared at him.

"Let's be clear. Are you saying that Reuven is the mole?"

"No, sir." He shifted as if he were uncomfortable—just enough hesitation to convey doubt. "There have been a few— I'll call them questionable—incidents, but I have no proof yet to suggest such a thing."

"What sorts of incidents?"

Gideon shook his head. "It's too complicated to explain right now. It breaks my heart, but sir, I could also be dead wrong."

He was balancing on a thin line here.

Landau studied him for a moment.

"Chaim. I am simply advising caution. Don't break the seal over the base. We don't know who the mole is."

Landau knit his eyebrows. He sank into his chair, tapping his fingers against the wood desktop. Finally, he nodded.

"Your concern is noted. Is there anything else?"

"No, sir."

"Then we need to see those camera records now."

Gideon knew Aaron had nothing on him from the interview with the saboteur, or he'd be in the brig right now. But the guard could nail him if he recovered—

Events were shaping poorly. He needed to take care of Landau, now. He needed to take command of the complex, and this might be the only opportunity he'd have.

It was too bad. He liked Chaim.

Gideon turned away from Landau as he spoke. "I need to get something from my office. Start the recording, and I'll be in the conference room in five minutes." He was eyeing the closed door to Landau's small private bathroom.

They moved toward the office door, and Gideon held back, hoping that Landau would exit first so that he could leave Landau's office door open. They stood in a stalemate for a few moments until it was uncomfortable, then Gideon had to walk through. Landau followed him out.

The secretary, Hod, was behind his desk in the outer room. Landau nodded to him as he locked his office. "Wait here till I come back. I have some calls to make."

"Yes, sir."

There was no time to lose.

Gideon's office was cleared of the odor from the cigarettes he and Aaron had smoked a half hour before. He heard the air rumbling through the circulation filters overhead as he shut the door behind him. What he needed was in the bottom locked drawer of his desk.

Gideon found the medical glass vial filled with clear liquid, provided by Raseac for just this type of problem. This was the ricin, one drop of which could incapacitate and kill within hours. Gideon pulled out a syringe, then removed the vial and popped the plastic cap off, revealing a rubberized guard beneath. He felt nervous even touching the vial although the liquid inside would harm only if it were breathed, injected, or eaten. It was scary stuff. He attached a needle and stuck it in the rubber cap, pushed the air in, and pulled the poison out, drawing up two milliliters. He capped the needle and twisted it off. Then he capped the syringe, dropped it in a rigid box to protect it from discharging, and put the box in his pocket.

In the main room, Hod looked up at him from the desk.

"Sergeant," Gideon said. "I need something from General Landau's office. Would you be good enough to let me in, please?"

Hod nodded. "Of course, General."

Gideon shuffled the file he'd brought in as cover as he glanced at the conference room door. It was closed. *Excellent.*

The sergeant stood in the doorway as Gideon went to Landau's desk and made a show of examining the files on top. He picked up a manila folder at random, opened it and thumbed through the papers as he turned his back to the door.

"Is there something I can help you find, sir?"

Gideon looked up. "No. No, thank you. I've got to just look through to find what I want."

The sergeant was still there, watching him.

Think.

"Sergeant, I need the work schedules for the time machine for the past four days. All personnel assigned to the control room itself. Would you make the copies?"

"Yes, sir. Now?"

Gideon nodded. "Immediately."

He continued to flip through the papers a few more seconds until the man was gone.

And then he held a tissue over his hand as he opened the bathroom door and entered. Landau's toothbrush was slung in a clear plastic cup, but as Gideon reached into his pocket for the syringe, he felt a mental twinge.

Ricin was perhaps the most potent poison known to mankind. Derived from castor seeds, once it was absorbed into the body it sliced through each cell it contacted and halted protein synthesis cold, causing the cell to explode within hours. When enough cells had died, the person died.

Gideon took out the syringe and squirted its contents onto the toothbrush, saturating the bristles. Even if the toothbrush were rinsed, enough of the ricin would remain to do its job. It would be a relatively quick death. Not painless, but not prolonged either.

As he walked into the office, the bathroom door closed behind him with a hollow sound. From the desk, he picked up the file folder that he had brought in, and shut the office door as well. The lock clicked under his hand.

"Sergeant. Just put the schedule in my box," he said as he headed away.

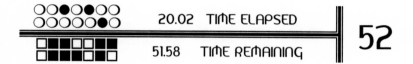

BENJAMIN SHIFTED his grip on the poles of the litter, flexing his wrists for a moment before moving back to the strong position. He and Sara, carrying David, had passed through the Southern Gate without problems, and now were more than halfway to the pod.

He heard Sara at the rear of the litter let out her breath. "That was tense."

"Not so bad."

"We're out of the city, anyway."

Benjamin glanced back at David on the makeshift stretcher. He was still unconscious.

He hesitated to use the word "coma," even in his mind.

"Let's go," he said.

He felt Sara push forward on the rods of the litter, moving toward the pod and safety. He was exhausted; Sara must be also. It was about eleven o'clock at night and they'd been awake for almost twenty-four hours, since before the transport into the past. But if they could hold on a little longer...

"Do you think Yacov will arrive in time?" Sara asked.

In her voice he heard a small catch of excitement or anxiety, he couldn't tell which. He glanced back at her. They were moving down a small incline onto the dirt road that encircled the city.

"Passover starts a few hours before we go back. Matthias said he'd be here before then. It'll be tight."

"I thought we'd never get out of that house."

He stumbled on a rock, caught himself. "Watch this section of road here. It's rough." He shifted the litter again, and as he did so, David moaned.

Maybe he was waking up. Benjamin whipped around, dipping down as he turned to study David's face. "Major." He tried to discern movement in the dim light, but there was no glimmer, no response, nothing.

He'd seen others die before, sure. Sara had too, but it was never easy. He pushed away the sinking feeling in his chest.

"It'll be all right," Sara said.

It wouldn't, though.

He picked his way over the stony road. It had been a little after this time yesterday when they had arrived and seen Matthias' party going up the Mount of Olives, hoping to find Yacov waiting for him. Matthias would do so again tonight.

Benjamin shook his head. "We meet Eleazar the day after tomorrow."

"Why not tomorrow?"

"He didn't want to meet with us before then. I gathered he had duties for tomorrow, but at least this will give Yacov another day to arrive. I arranged for us to meet inside the Temple at the first hour." The first hour was seven o'clock in the morning, give or take a few minutes since time was not so rigidly demarcated in this culture.

"Then we'll go to meet Yacov." He hoped. "He might be able to help us."

Sara was silent as they moved on. Finally, she sighed. "It's cold."

Cold.

Yes. He felt the night pressing on his heart.

Get David back to the pod.

Benjamin's conversation with Matthias, before Sara had arrived with Eleazar, had been surreal. Matthias seemed to believe that Yacov could heal David. Matthias claimed to have seen two similarly dramatic healings, miraculous healings done in the name of Yeshua. He'd been quite specific: time, place, and person.

Sara stumbled behind him and he glanced back at her. "Are you all right?"

"Yes." She looked as if she were about to say something else, but before she could his earphone sounded.

"What now?" He motioned to put the litter down. "Yes, Captain."

Rebecca's voice came on. "I have a situation. It's urgent."

He straightened. "What is it?" There were some thumps in the background before her voice came on again. Sara moved next to him.

"Sir, the camera is on the tether. I was taking the area photos."

"Why do you have the camera aloft right now?" Benjamin felt his pulse speed up in his temples. Pale fingers of moonlight swept everywhere.

"The winch!" Rebecca said. "I tried to get the camera down, but the winch is jammed. I've tried—"

"Well, put the handle on it and crank it in by hand. Someone will see the camera and balloon against the sky. Do it now! We can finish the photos later." Benjamin rubbed his forehead.

"I've tried the handle, sir. I'm standing on top of the pod, pulling the camera in by hand, but it's too slow. Two men are approaching."

Sara put her hand on his arm. It felt like ice. "I need that camera. I need the photomultiplier cells to repair the remote."

"How far away are the men? Do they see the camera?"

"Not yet."

"Thank goodness for small favors," Benjamin muttered. "How much of the tether is still aloft?"

There was silence on his earphone.

"Captain?"

"About a hundred feet. It's tangled."

Sara shook her head. "If it's as she says, the guards on the Temple wall might also see her standing on the pod. She needs to get down now."

"How far away are the two men?" Benjamin asked again.

Rebecca let out a squeal. "They're running toward me!"

"How far?"

"A hundred yards downhill and to the north."

"She's got to close the pod," Sara said. "They'll be inside of it."

Benjamin's thoughts churned. "Cut the cable with the clippers in the panel below the hatch, then lock the pod and get away. Do it now!"

Sara shouted into the microphone, "No! I need that camera to fix the remote!"

"Captain, do you hear?" Benjamin asked.

"Colonel?"

"Cut the cable!" He glared at Sara. "There's no choice. I'm sorry."

"I have the clippers," Rebecca said. "I'm cutting the cable now."

"Captain, where are the men?"

There was silence on the line, and then Rebecca's voice came back on.

"The camera's floating off now. It's been caught by the wind and going west, over Jerusalem. It's high up. The men have stopped, and they seem to be watching it."

"Close the pod!"

"I'm doing that." Benjamin waited a moment that stretched long. Finally, Rebecca came back on. "The pod's locked. It's—"

"Get off the pod now and get away. Go north and up on the pathway around the city, away from our position on the road. Get the men to follow you if you can. You have to get them away from the pod. We need to have it cleared so we can get David inside as soon as we arrive."

"Yes, sir."

"We're heading back directly."

Sara clenched her jaw. "What about the camera?"

He shook his head. "There wasn't anything I could do."

Emotion flamed her face.

"We've got to get back." He was furious and so tired. He wondered how much more he could bear.

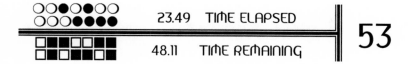

AARON TAPPED the optical disc containing the lockdown camera's data against his palm as Landau limped into the conference room. Aaron pulled a chair out for him, then sat down next to Landau at the head of the long table.

"Let's get started," Landau said.

"I'm ready." Aaron placed the disc in the player, then paused for a moment. Gideon still wasn't here. He glanced at the opened door to the office suite.

"Where's Shimon?"

"He'll be along. He wanted to get something from his office."

Aaron made a deep noise in his throat.

"What did he want to get?"

Landau shook his head. "He didn't say. Don't worry. He knows we need him."

Aaron felt crushed by the threats to the time machine from within the complex. They threatened his country's survival.

"Let me find General Gideon."

Landau laid his hand on Aaron's arm. "I want to hear this. Shimon will be right here."

Aaron paused, considering. Then he shut the door, came back and pushed the disc into the slot to start playback. The five-foot screen on the near wall brightened.

The camera showing the lockdown had been positioned high and to the left, recording from the top of the mirror. The voices filtered through the microphones, distorted but understandable.

"I haven't had time to run it through the computer yet to fine-tune the signal," Aaron said.

"That's fine. Just proceed."

On the screen, Gideon sat at the table with his back to the camera, his hands and face hidden. Aaron's officer, Hirsch, stood in profile to Gideon's left. On the other side of the table was Seidel, arrogant, leaning back in his chair.

Gideon's questions were straightforward as they watched five or six minutes of the recording. At one point, Gideon got up and walked around the table. Aaron strained to see if there was any physical exchange, some signal or item passed between him and the prisoner, but saw nothing.

On the screen, Gideon sat down again. Aaron pointed to the saboteur. "Watch this man now, sir. He's comfortable, secure. Now here's another question. Gideon asks the saboteur to betray his sources. It doesn't faze him."

Aaron watched the screen. "Now. Nothing else has been said. Seidel looks at Gideon, looks down. He seems suddenly afraid. The guard is looking at the table, no reaction. Nothing on the table."

Aaron reversed the disc. "Watch again."

He reduced the speed to half and ran the sequence forward again.

Landau leaned forward. "I see it."

"Another moment. The prisoner's eyes are glued to General Gideon. General Gideon catches eyes with the guard—see that?—and the guard steps back. His hand drops to the gun—"

"Again."

"Yes, sir." He brought the disc back to that point and switched playback speed to one quarter. "Even slower this time. Watch. Both the prisoner and the guard are looking at Gideon. Gideon meets eyes with the guard, there. Guard reaches for the gun—"

"How strange," Landau murmured.

"Yes, sir. It is. Half speed now. After the guard has reached for the gun, the prisoner gets up and jumps toward the guard. Did you see that? After."

Landau nodded. "I agree."

"All right," Aaron said. He stopped the disc. "Sir, you can see we need to question the guard. There was something there, something he saw that made him pull his gun. He didn't pull it because of the prisoner threatening him. It was something else."

Landau was nodding his head. "I see your point, Reuven. But the seal over the base—"

"Sir. This is critical. It is my firm opinion as chief of security of this base that we must break the seal to get this man to a hospital. We must get him out now. Now, sir."

"Can you guarantee no consequences?"

Aaron took a deep breath. "There's something else I want to show you on this disc."

"By all means, proceed."

Aaron knew the next part would be a hard sell, but essential.

He started the disc again. "All right. Still half speed. The guard pulls the gun out and shoots the prisoner—here—one shot to the chest. The bullet went through the heart. It was a quickly fatal shot, only enough oxygen available in the body for him to move for another twelve seconds or so. Watch the prisoner's hands. Nothing on the guard's throat as the two of them go down. Yet the guard had a complete airway obstruction that would have killed him if the doctor hadn't arrived when she did."

"Let's see it again."

"Yes, sir." Aaron reversed the disc, began it forward again, this time at one-quarter speed. "Guard reaches for gun. Prisoner jumps up. Gunshot." The sound from the bullet reverberated low on the screen, echoing in slow motion. "Prisoner continues to fall forward, falls on top of guard, and pushes him back as they go down beneath the table. No blow to the guard's throat during the fall."

"Yes," Landau said. "It's clear."

"It would be almost impossible for the saboteur to inflict such an injury on Hirsch once he was down," Aaron said, and he stopped the disc again. "Sir, I believe I know who the mole is."

"You told me. You suspect it may be Feinan."

Aaron sat back for a moment, framing his thoughts.

"Circumstantial evidence suggests Feinan might be guilty. His buried computer signature was found on the disc in the dead drop. Multiple identifying codes had been erased, but not those deeply hidden ones I had installed as an extra precaution."

"There's nothing we can do about him until he returns."

"Yes. However, Feinan may or may not be guilty. And even if he is, he may not be the only one."

Landau sat back and templed his fingers together. "Reuven, make this clear to me."

"Sir, this interview with Seidel was catastrophic. Coupled with certain other recent events, it makes me suspicious. I believe—"

Landau remained silent a moment, and then he leaned forward. "What do you believe?"

"Sir, the second prisoner, the pilot Mendel, worked with Feinan for a number of years in ReachDeep. He also worked with someone else."

Landau began to shake his head. "No, no. I can see where you're going with this."

"There's just a little more on this disc that I want you to see." Aaron turned it on again and adjusted the playback to half speed.

"The guard and the prisoner have fallen under the table. Now there goes General Gideon, out of sight. You can hear scuffling. There's the guard's foot, kicking." Aaron raised his hand. "Hold on, hold on. It's—now!"

A dark object skittered across the screen. He froze the image and pointed to it. "The gun, all the way to the far corner of the room. Let me show that to you again."

He brought the disc back to that point. "That was half speed. I'll speed it up to normal time."

Landau nodded. The screen showed the prisoner crashing into the guard, falling out of sight again.

"All right. Table. Table. Gun! See how fast it moves across the floor?"

"Yes," Landau said.

Aaron stopped the disc and turned to the base commander. "Sir, that gun was kicked or thrown. As in a fight. It was not dropped. And the prisoner had a bullet in his heart that would have killed him almost instantly."

Landau was still shaking his head.

"Sir. The mole. It's General Gideon."

54 | TIME ELAPSED   22.27
TIME REMAINING   49.33

BENJAMIN WOKE inside the pod, two hours after they'd gone to sleep. Grey shadows around him.

Sara next to him stirred again, and he realized she was awake. Had she awakened him? He didn't know.

"Sara," he whispered.

She rolled back. "Yes, I'm here."

Benjamin heard the even breathing of Rebecca on the other side of Sara, and next to him the strange respirations of David, deep breaths that gradually tapered to nothing, and then starting again. The sound of it spooked him.

"Why aren't you asleep?"

She sighed. "I've been awake for awhile. My mind won't slow down. I'm worried—"

"You need to sleep."

But he was awake now too, and troubled.

"Go to sleep," he said.

Sara moved against him again, and he couldn't help thinking that if this circumstance had occurred two nights ago he would have been tempted to take her in his arms and hold her until morning. Now, he just didn't know.

Was she a traitor?

He had so many questions for her, so many.

Sara sat up.

"What is it?" he asked.

"I need to think."

He studied her profile, then sat up next to her. "Who was it?"

He felt Sara flinch.

Rebecca was asleep. This was a good time, and he leaned toward her. "Who was it, Sara? Who got to you?"

She remained still.

"You won't deny Yeshua."

She turned away from him, and he could see that her hands were clenched.

"I don't want to talk about it."

In that moment, she seemed so unchanged from the person he'd known before, the person he'd fallen in love with. It was too confusing.

"Let me be your friend. Help me to understand. This is just between us, I promise."

She held still for a moment. Then she said in a small voice, "I haven't converted. I'm not a follower of the Way."

Draw her out. "I have great respect for you as a soldier, and what you've done on this mission." Yet, he felt a twisting inside. Would he have to turn her in when they got back? He was too tired to think.

"I'm afraid," she said.

Afraid.

"I'm being pulled in."

Benjamin felt a jolt of concern. Here was confirmation. "Who is it? Who's been talking to you? I'll help you fight."

He put his hand upon her shoulder, and was startled as she turned into his arms and buried her head on his shoulder.

"Sara," he said, and brushed her hair with his hand. He didn't want her this close to him now, though. It was too confusing, overpowering. "Tell me who's gotten to you."

She shook her head.

"I'll help you fight. Don't be afraid."

"You don't understand."

"Help me understand, then. Who is it?"

She straightened in his arms, pulled back. "No one. No one has talked to me."

"But—"

She was pulling that shutter over her thoughts again, slipping away from him.

"Tell me." He was desperate.

She backed away. Rebecca was still asleep in the corner, hadn't stirred.

"Tell me who it is," he said again. "I'll help you."

"No one has talked to me."

He waited.

"Help me," she whispered.

Silence. Her closeness was overpowering, but he held himself back. He needed to know where her mind was. *Hold back.* After almost a minute, she went on.

"I'm beginning to doubt what I've always known. I have a file on my computer with a list of facts, and I can't explain them."

"What facts?"

Her hand tightened on his shoulder.

"Yeshua's death," she said, so low he could barely hear her. "I can't say more."

"Sara, I'm with you. You can trust me."

She shook her head. "I can't."

"But—"

"No." Then she looked square into his eyes. "I promise you, I am not a follower."

But you will be soon, he thought. I see that you're falling now. He was engulfed by a great wave of despair.

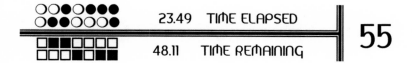

AARON SHOOK his head as he looked down at his man, Hirsch. It had been a little more than five hours since the guard had been attacked and lost consciousness, with his airway crushed. Hirsch's eyes were closed but his face didn't seem peaceful. His bare chest rose as the doctor standing next to his head squeezed the bag again, pushing air past the plastic tube in Hirsch's throat.

"He seems to be doing better, Colonel," the doctor said. "He has some independent respirations."

They'd had to take Hirsch off the ventilator for transport. He was so young, so bright, one of his best officers. Aaron pushed down a surge of anger.

"He has a good chance now that he's being moved to Jerusalem."

"He's still unconscious."

The doctor looked up at him. "He's moving spontaneously, grimacing. He's not deep. They'll bring him around."

She leaned close over Hirsch, listening to his chest with her stethoscope.

The female medic came to the door of the small observation room. "Dr. Rosen, they're ready to transport."

"Good, Shoshana. Let's get going."

Aaron stepped back. "I'll escort you. I want to make sure you get on the helicopter safely." He wasn't going to leave Hirsch unattended.

Gideon had been absent a long time during the meeting in which Aaron had shown the recording of the encounter in the lockdown to Landau. They'd waited fifteen minutes and then Landau had paged him; Gideon had opened the door a minute later. Aaron didn't like it. What had Gideon been doing?

Aaron had succeeded in getting Landau to lift the seal over the base, though. The recording showed Hirsch pulling his gun before the saboteur's attack, and it was essential that Hirsch recover so they could find out why.

Aaron had also succeeded in getting permission—however reluctantly—to place hidden electronic surveillance equipment in Gideon's living quarters and office, a bigger coup than he had anticipated. Landau was pragmatic about these things, Aaron thought, although Landau still didn't want to believe his second in command was guilty. However, he would be cautious now.

Aaron just hoped it wasn't too late.

The doctor gave another breath. "Come on, Shoshana. Get the patient ready, then let's go."

"Yes, ma'am." The medic adjusted the I.V. bags suspended over the wheeled stretcher, and then spread a waffled white blanket over Hirsch's chest. Aaron could hear the crunch of starch as it fell on top.

"Ready, Doctor."

The infirmary was located near the heliport, just two turns in the hallway and up the elevator to the roof. The sky had lightened to blue. It was almost eight in the morning, and the sunrise already an hour old. Etan met them at the elevator doors.

Aaron nodded to him. "Things squared?"

"Shouldn't be more than seventy minutes, round trip," Etan replied. "That includes fifteen minutes for transferring Hirsch. How is he, by the way?"

Aaron shook his head. "Still unconscious." He watched as the doctor and medic wheeled the patient to the helicopter, and transferred Hirsch inside.

"Real shame," Etan said. "He's a good man."

Aaron nodded. "He saw something."

Etan looked at him. He knew. He'd watched the recording too.

"It's cold up here," Aaron said.

The doctor reached back from inside the helicopter for her black leather medical bag. The medic stepped away from under the rotors, and then the helicopter door slammed and they took off.

"I've arranged for a twenty-four hour guard on Hirsch once he arrives at the hospital," Aaron said. "I don't want anything to happen to him."

"Prudent."

"I'm going to nail Gideon."

"You're sure it's him."

He gazed at Etan. "After the disaster this morning, who else could it be?"

The wind from the helicopter liftoff rushed across the top of the platform, and Aaron turned toward it. Etan jumped next to him. "General."

Aaron saw Gideon had just arrived on the heliport.

The helicopter retreated past the complex's air space, toward Jerusalem, as Gideon approached. "Reuven," he said. "It looks like you won this one."

Aaron stared ahead, not wanting to look at him. A few more minutes and his man would be safe. *Just let him come out of the coma.*

He faced Gideon then. "It's the only way. We need to know what he saw."

Gideon shrugged. "Saw what? You analyzed the recording. There's nothing there. It was just unfortunate that Seidel fell on him like that."

Etan shifted. "Why did he pull his gun, sir?"

Gideon was disdainful. "We have two days left in the mission. Let's try to keep things intact."

| TIME ELAPSED | 39.50 |
| TIME REMAINING | 32.10 |

IN THE POD, REBECCA LOOKED AWAY from the computer screen when her gaze fell on David. He looked just like he was asleep. She felt tears forming in her eyes again but angrily brushed them away. She knew it had been her fault.

"How do the images look?" Benjamin asked.

"I'm getting them," she muttered rebelliously. Sara was leaning too closely over her shoulder, as if she didn't trust her.

The pod's air was humid and heavy after a full day with the four soldiers trapped inside. The pod was designed to remain cool by using fuel cells powering Peltier thermovoltaic cells at night to chill a reservoir of water under the floor—like sitting on top of an iceberg. Encircling the pod were a series of circumventing fissures that provided an air exchange area of twenty square feet, barely adequate for ventilation. A slow bellows below the floor moved the air with a minimum of noise.

The local time now was about seven o'clock at night. Once it became fully dark, they would open the hatch to increase ventilation. An hour, it wouldn't be too soon for her. Rebecca couldn't breathe. She stretched, and then got up to use the tiny bathroom in the corner. They had another ten hours in here, Benjamin had said, because there was no further information to gather until daylight. It wouldn't be soon enough for her. She was spooked by being trapped so long in the pod with a living corpse—

As she emerged, she saw Sara and Benjamin leaning together, consulting over the data. It triggered in her the ghost of a memory. Rebecca furrowed her eyebrows. Hadn't she heard something last night?

She seemed to remember something disturbing and completely unexpected. Something to do with followers—

Rebecca studied Sara and Benjamin. Yes, she was almost sure. There had been something; if only she could remember what she'd heard while half-sleep.

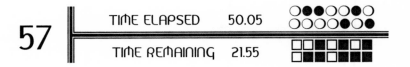

57 | TIME ELAPSED   50.05
        | TIME REMAINING 21.55

YOHANAN REMEMBERED this neighborhood.

He'd arrived while it was still dark because he didn't want to be seen in this area. *Not yet.* Not until his trap had been sprung, and he had returned in triumph.

It wouldn't be long.

The anger burned inside of him, crowding out all other thoughts. His old friend Eleazar was too proud to be seen with him anymore, although Yohanan had only been trying to share some of the benefits of his new position. So, Eleazar wanted nothing more to do with him? He would see about that. Eleazar had thought himself so coy, so subtle, so adept at hiding his identity as a follower of Yeshua, and yet it was common knowledge to those who paid attention to these things that Eleazar's uncle Matthias was one of the more influential followers of Yeshua in the city.

He would also see about those strangers who had visited Matthias. He'd already disposed of one. Heretics!

He spat on the street.

The moonlight reflected on the cobbled streets; it was low in the sky, but still high enough that he could see his way through the narrow passageway without a lantern. It would be dawn soon. He didn't want to be noticed as he made his way to Matthias' house.

Here was the street, and he picked up his pace as he passed the rough doors of the rough one-roomed houses. He was far above this now. He had a house with a courtyard, two servants, and he was betrothed to the daughter of a rich trader.

If the people here didn't appreciate how his status had risen, then that was their problem. People without two denarii to rub together walked by him proudly in the marketplace as though he was too low to even grace their vision. They didn't accept the fact that Rome was here to stay, and that the best way to keep life peaceful was to tolerate the Romans and pay their taxes. It was no shame to collect tax money. If he overcharged a little so that he could support himself, well, he had to live.

Eleazar was the worst because he knew what kind of person Yohanan really was, had grown up with him, and yet he still pushed him away. Well, Yohanan could push too. He could push hard.

He clenched his fist and pounded on the door.

Matthias was awake, Yohanan could see through a sliver between the wooden shutters, sitting on the mat by the fire. He startled when he heard the knock. When he cracked the door and saw Yohanan's face outside, he blanched.

Yohanan pulled back the fold of his cloak, uncovering his head. "Sir, I need to talk to you."

Matthias shook his head. "Be gone. There is nothing here for you."

The old man hadn't changed much in the six years or so since he'd seen him.

"Sir, may I come inside so no one sees me?"

"Yohanan, we have nothing here for you."

"Don't you even want to know what I have to—"

"No! There is nothing here."

Yohanan took a deep breath. He'd known this would be challenging.

"It's about Eleazar. About his visitors." He smiled as he saw Matthias catch his breath.

"I don't know about any visitors," Matthias said, but his face was white.

Yohanan shook his head. "Please let me in. Before anyone sees me."

Matthias stood straight. "No."

"I know who your visitors are. They're putting you in danger."

Matthias' hand on the doorframe trembled.

"The authorities are after them. They will take Eleazar
too."

Matthias pulled the door open. "Come in quickly. And
then, please leave!"

"I want to help Eleazar."

Yohanan walked through, and Matthias banged the door
behind him. "What is it?" Matthias asked, his eyes as hard as
flint but Yohanan saw a glint of fear in them too.

The room looked the same as it ever had. It was clean—
swept and neat, mats rolled up in the corner except for the
one Matthias had been sitting on, a skin bag cooking
something over the fire, nothing else. The weak light of the
oil lamp sputtered shadows over his face.

"Why do you want to help Eleazar?" Matthias demanded.
"You broke his heart after the way you left, and you haven't
even seen him for six years."

Yohanan shook his head. "That's not true."

"You haven't spoken to him."

"Not true."

"Tell me what you have to say."

He knew what Matthias was thinking: A publican here in
this house. Unclean. But Matthias might also be
remembering him as he had been growing up, days he'd spent
here playing with Eleazar. He would tap into that bond of
fond memories to destroy them both.

Yohanan's wrath had finally been raised. He would
destroy them quickly.

"Someone has been watching your visitors."

Matthias crossed his arms. "I have no visitors, as you can
see. I don't know what you're talking about."

Why then had the old man let him inside? But he let it
pass. It was too close to dawn.

"I need to speak to Eleazar."

Matthias shook his head. "He isn't here. Say what you
have to say to me."

"All right." Yohanan took a deep breath. "You have no
visitors. Fine. I see none. I just know that there are certain
men who have traveled to Jerusalem for the Passover tonight.
These are high-ranking men in the new cult that follows
Yeshua, including Yacov, brother of Yeshua. I also know that
some Jewish leaders are aware of their visit, and have been

watching for them." This was true; he had heard this from a friend who ran in the leaders' circle. However, he also knew that the ruling Jewish authorities had no idea where these men were or how they could capture them.

Yohanan, though, thought he knew how he might accomplish it.

"The authorities plan to raid the place where they are hiding. They have the cooperation of Rome in these matters. Anyone caught with them at this raid—" he looked at Matthias meaningfully— "will also be arrested. I know this does not concern you or Eleazar in the slightest, because I know you are innocent, but I thought these were interesting rumors."

Matthias stood pale and unmoving in the dim light.

"The raid is scheduled for this afternoon," Yohanan went on. "That way, there will be enough time to bring the followers of Yeshua in before the Passover begins at sunset. This is all I know."

Matthias stepped back, brushing against the raised platform of the kitchen area.

"Sir?"

"Thank you," Matthias whispered. "Why are you telling me this?"

Yohanan smiled. "I am not welcome here anymore, I know. But still—"

Matthias watched him.

"I remember."

Matthias was silent for a moment. "I pray for you," he finally said. "But I have thought—forgive me—that you were like a serpent, dangerous. Perhaps I was wrong."

Yohanan covered a smile with his hand.

"I thank you, friend, for bringing me these rumors. I will think on them."

"Do that."

Yes, there would be a raid—now. Matthias would lead him to where he needed to go, and he could bring in the big prize himself.

It was almost dawn. He had to leave, but the noose was set now, ready to be tightened. Perhaps Eleazar and his visitors would be drawn into it as well.

SARA BLINKED against the glare of the rising sun.

Benjamin glanced over at her. "Come on. We'll get this done." He started up the hill toward the city.

She stepped away from the pod, following him. It was the last day of the mission.

How could they have missed the correct time? She wanted to know beyond a doubt what had happened, but the events were lost to history—even lost to those with a time machine. Now there was only rational restructuring from the data of the events surrounding Yeshua's death, and she was afraid where that path was leading her.

The sun was shining in her eyes, too brightly.

Yeshua. She was on the verge of accepting it was true, with all of the implications that entailed.

No, no, don't think that.

Benjamin was ten paces above her on the hill, and she rushed to catch up. He nodded. "Sunset's in thirteen hours. That will leave us about seven hours at night to deliver whatever we have to the Dead Sea so that it can be dated. Will that be sufficient?"

"It should be."

"I don't want to have to use the powered paraglider."

"No, sir."

She took a deep breath. Dangling below the silk wings with a large fan on one's back was the last-ditch choice for transporting the information capsule with all of their data so that it could be carbon-dated and verified as authentic. She was pretty sure, though, that she'd been able to repair the remote last night.

Five paces to the road. She climbed the rough hill, raising her long overcoat and tunic over her feet so she wouldn't trip.

He smiled. "We're going to be successful today. I can feel it."

She nodded, smiled back, but her heart beat faster as he took her hand in his to help her onto the road.

The *shofar* call from the Temple that signified the sunrise still echoed in her ears. It was a clear day; the Passover to begin at sunset. They entered Jerusalem through the southern gates and walked straight up the road to the Temple.

"The Temple will be packed this morning, no doubt," he said. "We'll be less conspicuous."

The open marketplace at the south side of the Temple Mount entrance was crowded with people; vendors with booths lined up all along the edges of the courtyard. The smell was overpowering: burnt animals, body odors, some moldering substances, and everywhere people were talking, laughing, shouting, and gesturing so that they had to duck as they walked past different groups. She pressed into Benjamin.

He nodded toward the right, drawing her attention to the *mikveh* at the base of the stairs leading up to the Temple Mount. Jews ceremonially washed here before entering the Temple, but Sara and Benjamin had agreed that as interesting as the data recording might be, washing here was another task that could reveal their unfamiliarity with this time. It would separate them, it would delay them, and it wasn't worth the risk.

Ahead, she eyed the gates at the top of the wide stone stairs leading to the southern part of the Temple Courtyard. This was where David had been captured and injured.

"I hope we can find Eleazar," Benjamin said. She saw him glance at the great crowd of people entering the Mount through the left gate.

In the Temple Courtyard, the marble of the Temple glistened in the bright sun. The shining golden spikes on the roof of the building kept the birds of prey—the kites and ravens—from gaining a foothold to snatch up the sacrificed meat inside.

The Temple was magnificent, Sara thought. The first Temple had been built by Solomon almost a thousand years before this time, and had stood for about four hundred years before being destroyed by the Babylonian King Nebuchadnezzar. The Persian King, Cyrus the Great, allowed the Jews to return to their homeland to build the second Temple, seven decades after Solomon's Temple was destroyed. That second Temple stood for almost five hundred years, until King Herod the Great decided to replace it. The Temple building was begun in 19 B.C.E. and finished twelve years later, without a single day of sacrificial offerings being missed, but work would be continued on the Temple Mount area and the buildings and courtyards until 63 C.E. The entire area would then be destroyed by the Romans under Titus seven years after that. Thus would begin the second Diaspora.

But here and now, Herod's Temple stood. It was magnificent.

She saw Benjamin filming the area, the people, the Temple itself. He moved around to the eastern side of the Mount where the entrance lay to the Temple itself. She passed with him through the segmented stone wall, the balustrade called the *soreg* that separated the inner, Jewish territory from the rest of the world. Inscriptions carved along the top of the balustrade warned in both Greek and Latin that any non-Jew entering the area would bear the responsibility for his ensuing death. She knew that the ruling Romans respected this prohibition, and would allow even a Roman citizen to be executed if he disregarded the warning. She had seen some of these inscriptions in museums in Jerusalem and Jordan.

Sara shivered as she walked into the heart of her people's heritage.

He turned to her and smiled. "We're doing well so far."

She didn't trust her voice. The thought again flashed through her mind of how much David had desired to see this place.

Inside the balustrade, there was another low flight of stone steps stretching around the perimeter of the Temple. She followed Benjamin through the nearest of the three gates that opened onto the Court of the Women.

She could see at once that it was a joyful place, even under the heavy hand of Rome. Perhaps it was joyful because Rome could not reach inside here. The court was open on top, and in each corner, a small walled chamber served a specialized function: one chamber for inspecting lepers who believed they had been healed; one for inspecting the wood for the sacrifice; one for storing oil and wine for the services; and one for the Nazarites, men who were dedicated to God and could not drink wine or cut their hair.

Spaced around the court were thirteen chests to collect money for the Temple, with each chest shaped like the bell of a horn. Ahead, she could see, were the fifteen broad round steps, called the Stairs of Ascent, leading up to the next level of the Temple. But as a woman, she was forbidden from going further.

"Do you see him?" Benjamin asked. She shook her head.

The court was crowded—young families, men preaching in the corners surrounded by knots of listeners, women greeting each other—people everywhere. The polyglot of sound rose in her ears. Some of the men, and a very few women, held domesticated animals—a goat on a lead, or two birds in a cage—that she knew must be for personal sacrifices. The Paschal lambs would not be offered until the afternoon.

"Are you getting all this?" she asked. "It's fabulous."

"I want to go up to the next court," Benjamin said. "Just for a minute, to film a sacrifice. Will you be all right?"

"Of course."

He moved up the rounded stairs, through the Nicanor Gate and into the Court of the Israelites or Court of the Men, which stood in front of the altar. The court he entered was only for men—Sara could not follow, although she greatly desired to see what was there. She caught a glimpse of it through the entranceway, but not enough.

Benjamin would film it. She would have to be content.

More important was to find Eleazar.

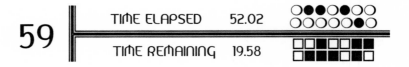

59 | TIME ELAPSED   52.02
| TIME REMAINING   19.58

BENJAMIN CLIMBED the rounded stone steps through the arched Nicanor Gate and into the next court, in which the Temple before him stretched high above.

He'd visited the third Temple that had been built two thousand years later, but as remarkable as that building was, it could not compare with this one. He stood now in the Court of the Israelites, a slim strip of pavement about twenty feet across surrounding the front and sides of the court of the priests. There, a balustrade separated the "Priest's Court," containing the Temple proper with its altar and appurtenances, from the place assigned to the lay people. This was as far as he, a non-consecrated Jewish male, could go. Many men crowded the strip, and the air was smoky with the sacrificial scents of incense, blood, and burned animal fat. He heard music, a choir singing a psalm, strange harmonies lost to time.

Ahead of him stood the altar used for animal sacrifices in the Court of the Priests. Two priests were pouring water from a ceremonial bucket down its sides to wash blood away, and as Benjamin watched, the reddish liquid flowed into a trench and drained through small openings below. The water came from the 17,000 gallon bronze laver, which stood beside the altar. It was considered living water and thus had to be drained and refilled every day. The altar was a tall structure 45 feet square and fifteen feet high made from unfinished stone that had never been touched by metal tools. A horn-shaped projection emerged from each of its four corners. A large ramp led to the top; the priests had to walk up the ramp and around the top of the altar to place the sacrifices on it in the prescribed ritual manner. Benjamin saw a number of other priests crossing the large court, busy in their jobs tending to the multiple sacrifices for the people. They were easy to distinguish: ankle-length white linen seamless tunics, with a long belt or girdle that almost touched their bare feet. On his head, each priest wore a simple white linen cap.

He filmed it all, the camera hidden beneath his robe.

At the back of the Court of the Priests, a magnificent curtain two stories high and thirty feet wide fell down over the entrance to the 180-foot tall porch leading into the Sanctuary. The porch had no spiritual significance, but because every other Temple in the Roman world had a porch, Herod was determined to make his the most impressive of all. The porch was fifteen feet deep; the curtain leading into it was dark blue with a multicolored design of stars and other shapes patterned to represent the universe. Behind the curtain, Benjamin knew, were double doors covered in gold, with relief of golden vines and clusters of golden grapes.

Inside the Sanctuary was an altar for incense, a seven-branched lamp stand called a *menorah*, and a table for the shewbread: twelve loaves of unleavened bread offered every Sabbath. At the back of the Sanctuary, covered by another double veil, was the innermost sacred chamber, the Holy of Holies, which the Jews believed was filled with God's physical presence. It was an empty, windowless room that the high priest entered only once a year on Yom Kippur, the Day of Atonement.

Benjamin watched the High Priest push the heavy curtains back and emerge from the Sanctuary of the Temple. He was regal as he descended to the Court of the Priests, wearing a blue and white headdress and an over-tunic of royal blue fringed at the bottom with tiny golden bells and pomegranates. The ephod he wore like a vest, with twelve gemstones over his chest set in four rows of three and representing the twelve tribes of Israel. Benjamin knew the Romans stored the high priest's vestments in the Antonia fortress all year except for the important Holy Day celebrations of Passover, Rosh Hashanah, and Yom Kippur.

A Levite approached the man standing next to Benjamin in the Court of Israelites, spoke with him a moment, then took the rope lead of a young goat over to one of the many priests at the altar for the next sacrifice. The priest slit the goat's throat with a stone knife. As the blood spurted out in time to the heartbeat, Benjamin slipped away, back through the Nicanor Gate to the Court of the Women. It was time to find Eleazar.

He was relieved to see Sara. "Any luck?"

"Not yet. It's crowded, isn't it?"

"He said he'd be here after the general morning sacrifice, around the first hour." Benjamin sighed in frustration. Time was dealt with differently in this culture: fluidly, where people marked the measurement in hours, not in minutes or seconds or microseconds as they did in his troubled present. The first hour corresponded to about seven o'clock in the morning. Eleazar might show up an hour, even ninety minutes, from now and still not consider himself late.

Benjamin shook his head. "It all depends on Yacov."

Sara touched his arm. "It's all right," she said, but she was wrong.

Benjamin was still torn about Sara. He wanted to know who had presented Yeshua to her so appealingly. Whomever she'd been talking to had done a good job. She wasn't yet a follower, he'd decided, but she was close to the edge and he wondered if she might even fail a formal *Danan* at this point. What weakness in her psyche was pushing her over? He'd never thought of Sara as weak.

He led her into the angle made between the wall and the Chamber of Oils so they wouldn't be crushed in the moving crowd, then scanned the Court of the Women again for Eleazar. Nothing, but the room was packed. He wished again that he'd been more specific about where in the room they would meet.

Benjamin grimaced. "I want to split up to check the court. Meet me here in ten minutes."

"Yes, sir."

He elbowed out into the heavy crowd.

If only Yacov—James, the brother of Yeshua—could provide some clue as to what had happened to Yeshua's body after it had been sealed in that great cave on Friday night. Yacov would soon be the leader of the Jerusalem church, and he was the greatest known converted skeptic except for the apostle Shaul, Saul—Paul. Something Yacov had seen or heard or been told he had misinterpreted, and that had changed the course of his life. If Benjamin could learn the kernel of that event, he felt sure he might be able to reinterpret it in light of two thousand years of knowledge. He might gain a hint of what had happened to Yeshua's body.

There were so many here for the Feast of Unleavened Bread. How would he ever find him? The crowds would only continue to increase as the sacrifice of the Paschal lambs began in a few hours.

He pushed his way through the streaming mass, concentrating on the areas near the three doorways through which people entered from the outside. He saw nothing. Nothing.

And they were losing time.

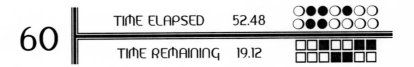

60   TIME ELAPSED   52.48
     TIME REMAINING   19.12

YOHANAN STEPPED BACK into a shadow, watching.

Matthias moved up the arched stairway to the second tier of the Royal Stoa, the colonnaded balcony on the Mount, where meetings and heated exchanges often took place.

Yohanan smiled. He would bring down Eleazar, and Matthias too, before the sun set tonight on the Passover.

He wished he could have stayed at Matthias' hole of a house to observe but, as a publican, would not have been able to wait in that neighborhood unnoticed. He'd decided instead to wait for Matthias at the upper portion of the Tyropean Valley, the lower court marketplace of the Temple.

And here Matthias was, he thought. It was confirmation that his suspicions had been correct.

Yohanan left a good distance behind him. It wasn't time for confrontation, not yet. Right now, he wanted to see what pieces were in place.

Matthias seemed worried as he climbed the stairs and crossed the polished flagstone of the porch. There were more people than usual at this time of day, but still the platform was much emptier than below. This was the "intellectual" area—Yohanan made a face—where the philosophers met, who liked to talk about air and nonsense. They felt they were closer to YHWH than others and wouldn't deign to even glance at one such as he, although as a tax collector he kept the wrath of Rome away from them better than their God did.

He watched Matthias join a small group in a corner. These were some of the followers of Yeshua his friends had been tracking, the disciples of a dead leader.

Yohanan had seen Yeshua seven years ago when Yeshua had come to Jerusalem for the Passover. His death hadn't seemed like a big deal—just another criminal, crucified by Rome. Later Yohanan had been surprised to learn that one of the Pharisees, Yosef of Arimathea, had claimed the body from Pontius Pilate and buried him in his own new tomb outside the city. Although Yohanan had not been involved in politics at that time, he had wondered what had been going on beneath the surface to trigger such a gift.

There had been near-riots once the tomb was found to have been opened, questions of who would dare defy the Roman seal. Yeshua's apostles had waited until six weeks later to start making public announcements that Yeshua had risen from the dead, but an empty tomb did not a risen man make. He shook his head.

Yohanan watched Matthias from fifty paces away. He was warning his follower friends. *Perfect.* No doubt, now Matthias would proceed before long to the camp itself. And then...

He smiled.

| TIME ELAPSED | 53.27 |
| TIME REMAINING | 18.33 |

BENJAMIN GLANCED again at Eleazar. He and Sara had finally found him, and were now heading north over the crowded Courtyard away from the Temple. Eleazar's face was set, inscrutable, as he pushed a way north through the people, off the Mount and out of the city.

"So Yacov has arrived?" Benjamin asked.

Eleazar turned and gave him a strange look.

Sara leaned forward. "Yes?"

The young man nodded. "Yes, he's here."

Benjamin didn't know why his eyes were so shielded, but it worried him.

It had taken the better part of an hour to find him inside the Temple. The sun had climbed higher in the sky; it was now nine in the morning, and there were only nine or ten hours left of daylight. Within that time, they'd have to travel to the camp, interview Yacov, and find their way back. After dark, they'd have the further problem of delivering the data. Time pressed in on his team.

"Is Yacov at the camp now?" Benjamin asked.

Eleazar pulled his cloak tighter. "When you arrive he'll be there."

He shook his head, frustrated.

As they reached the northern entrance of the Mount there was a disturbance, a Jewish man in a rough-woven overcoat shouting something that he couldn't understand. He glanced over at Sara, but she shrugged. Eleazar paid the man no heed.

The man didn't seem to be drawing much of a following nor attention from the Romans. Still, Benjamin picked up his pace, trying to rush Eleazar along. In this culture, "hurry" was not a word except perhaps in battle. Nevertheless, as they walked through the gate and into the street filled with vendors and milling crowds, the stream of people going out of the city picked up and many seemed angry, others afraid. The intensity of the crowd signaled caution. He tried to understand the polyglot of conversations but found the words without edges, running together. Sara caught his eye and shook her head.

"What is going on?" he asked Eleazar.

The young man glanced at the crowd. "*Talah.*" It sounded something like that. Benjamin furrowed his eyebrows.

Eleazar continued to lead them forward, and he wished, again, that he had Rebecca's ear to translate. There was no way he could contact her at the pod right now to have her listen remotely and find out what was going on.

Past the Antonia now, its polished stone walls gleaming in the sunshine. There were so many soldiers stationed in Jerusalem to keep the peace. The street narrowed further, and then they were through the northern gate that led outside the city.

This northern area was becoming settled as the city expanded, with a number of wealthy dwellings that he could see not far from the road. David had said the Third Wall to enclose them within the city would be built within a year or two.

Eleazar stopped. They were a hundred meters from the gate on the road.

"Where now?" Benjamin asked.

Eleazar stared at him for a few moments, then his gaze dropped to study the bag at Benjamin's waist. He pressed his lips together.

"How is your companion?" he finally said.

Benjamin felt that stab of pain again. "Not good. He's dying."

Eleazar nodded, but he seemed too still.

"Are we going to go?"

"What do you carry in your bag?"

Benjamin dropped his hand down protectively.

"Could you not heal him with what's in your bag?" Eleazar asked.

Sara broke in. "Eleazar, what is it?"

Eleazar stepped back. "I know who you are."

There was a commotion on the path behind them, toward the city. Four Roman soldiers dragged a stake about twelve feet long from the far end of the road and onto the hills overlooking the valley. The stake was pointed at one end but otherwise had been barely finished.

Benjamin caught his breath, suddenly understanding. He watched the crowd clear as the soldiers flung the stake down on the ground.

"They're preparing for a crucifixion," he said.

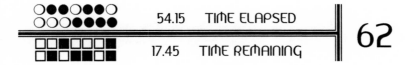

ELEAZAR'S FACE WAS SET, determined, and Benjamin wondered again what lay inside this young man's mind.

Next to Benjamin, Sara leaned close. "I'm not sure I want to watch this."

Benjamin wasn't sure he wanted to see a crucifixion either, but it would be important to document. Besides, right now Eleazar showed no signs that he wanted to go.

A roar sounded below them.

"Will we go to the camp soon?" he said to Eleazar.

"Soon."

More people streamed out of the gate now, surrounding something or someone. The crowd unfurled. Benjamin saw a shaggy man weighted down under a three meter beam emerge, limping, from beneath the city's gate, with Roman soldiers holding spears prodding the man to the side of the road thirty meters outside the entrance. The man left smears of blood behind him as he walked. His back was covered with a thin tunic, an undergarment, stained crimson. When he stopped and the soldiers stripped the tunic off, new streams of blood flowed from his back. The man was naked, and Benjamin felt a smack of revulsion so strong it was almost a physical blow. He'd never seen anything so ghastly. The man had been flogged, and wide strips of skin hung down the man's back and to his thighs. His back showed rippling muscles and even the grey glint of abdominal organs beneath the ribcage. The soldiers flung the man backwards down on the ground and spread his arms out.

Sara shook her head. "I can't watch this."

Benjamin took a deep breath. "It's already happened. Remember that this is the past and we can't change it. This man has been dead for two thousand years."

Eleazar looked at them curiously. "Have you not seen the *talah* before?"

Benjamin shook his head.

"This man is a murderer and a thief."

"It's horrible," Benjamin said.

Eleazar grimaced. "We will leave soon."

Sara took a step back as if to get away, but Benjamin drew her close to him. She stood still then, her head turned away but she was breathing hard. After a moment, she seemed to relax just a bit.

"I'm sorry," she said. "I just wasn't prepared for this."

He nodded.

"We should film this."

Benjamin indicated the camera under his overcoat. "I'm on it."

The man was screaming. Even from their position fifty yards away Benjamin could hear the dull thunk as the Roman mallet drove two long iron spikes through the man's wrists, between the bones, one arm and then the other. A soldier held the man's feet together while another drove a single spike through the instep of one foot, the heel of the foot underneath.

Eleazar seemed to have cast his face in stone, but as Benjamin watched a muscle in his cheek wavered and flinched.

The soldiers hoisted the man up, inserting the pointed base of the stake into a hole. The cross wobbled for a few moments, held steady by the soldiers until they could stabilize it. The man's screams grew more terribly pitched.

Benjamin shuddered.

The man silenced as the cross settled upright into the hole. The red strips of flesh hanging from his sides and back glinted in the sun. He raised himself, then collapsed in agony. No longer did he seem human.

It was unspeakable.

The sun was in Benjamin's eyes.

The man pushed up again on the ankle spike, raising himself for a moment before falling back. Benjamin knew this was so that he could exhale the burning carbon dioxide from his lungs. Crucifixion was a slow death by partial asphyxiation and eventual exhaustion.

Sara grimaced. "Those spikes pierce the great nerves of the hands and feet," she said. "Every time that man moves, it jolts unimaginable pain through him. Yet he has to move to breathe."

He didn't want to think about it anymore. It was time to go.

"Eleazar."

The young man's eyes were dark as he looked over. He seemed angry at the spectacle.

"Are we ready to go to the camp?"

Eleazar shook himself out of his stillness. "Yes, the camp. Let's go." Then Benjamin saw him glance again at the bag Benjamin carried, and he felt a cold chill go through him. Eleazar seemed too curious about the tools they had used to work the "miracle" to rescue David from the Romans. Did Eleazar understand that their power might come from their possessions, not from faith, not from something otherworldly? Had they changed the past, even this subtly, by destroying the faith of one young man?

It was too late to blur his memory. It had been almost two days since they had set off the stunning explosives in the tunnel.

Benjamin felt the chill rush of adrenaline. What was happening with Eleazar? What was he hiding behind those shielded eyes? He had seemed so much more open when they'd first met him two days ago.

But what could be done?

63 | TIME ELAPSED   57.08
   | TIME REMAINING   14.52

IT WASN'T A LONG WALK UP THE HILL to the garden, but Benjamin couldn't get away from the countdown. There were fewer than seven hours until dark, and then a handful more until the time throw back.

Eleazar led them around the city wall on the path toward Bethlehem. They were entering the Garden of Gethsemane— the Garden of the Olive Press.

Benjamin glanced at Sara walking a step behind him as women did in this culture. She had buried her arms within the overcoat so that she was hidden, her thoughts and motives kept to herself.

Eleazar motioned ahead of them. "We're going to the far side. We will meet Yacov there."

Benjamin nodded.

What was in the computer file that Sara had told him about last night, containing the list of facts about Yeshua that scared her? It was grit in his mind.

A number of olive trees grew in the garden, grand trees with spreading overhanging branches and gnarled trunks that two or three men would have to hold hands to reach around. They passed an olive press on a central hill, a well-worn clearing. The press was composed of a circular stone basin three meters in diameter, and a giant stone wheel lying upright in the trench. A bar extending from the wheel allowed oxen or people to walk the wheel around the basin to crush the olives that would be strewn beneath.

Benjamin caught Eleazar's sleeve. "Will Yacov be here soon?"

Eleazar still seemed guarded. "Yes, yes. He's coming here."

"In this garden?"

"Yes."

Benjamin didn't see anyone else.

After another minute, Eleazar turned to the right and walked off the path, among the ticklish grasses toward a small rock outcropping not far away. He looked over his shoulder once as if to make sure no one was observing, then ducked into a crevice and disappeared from sight.

Benjamin slid through beside him, Sara right behind.

They were in a hidden enclosed area open to the sky, about five meters in diameter.

"This is a place I used to play as a child," Eleazar said. "I don't think many people come here. My uncle should arrive shortly."

Benjamin looked around. They were hidden, but they wouldn't be able to see anyone approach either. It was not his choice for a meeting spot, but right now, he had to follow Eleazar's lead. He was anxious to talk to Yacov. Time pressed on him like that stone wheel.

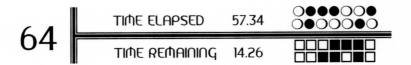

ELEAZAR STUDIED HIS VISITORS from under hooded eyes. He wished again that he had never met them. Both of them, the woman Sara and the man, confused him.

The *Pesach* was in a few hours; at the camp, they would celebrate Yeshua's deliverance as well as Moshe's from Egypt two thousand years ago. For the first time, though, his beliefs about Yeshua's miracles and message were suffused with doubts that he would chase from his mind if only he could.

He glanced again at the bag that the man who called himself Benjamin wore tied to the belt underneath his cloak. This man held his "miracles" in there.

"Will Yacov be here soon?" Benjamin asked in his strange accent. He seemed anxious, running his forefinger under the leather strap around his wrist. He was continuing to hide his identity, and Eleazar felt another flush of irritation. Didn't Benjamin know Eleazar saw right through him? However, he'd wait for his uncle to arrive first before confronting him.

It wouldn't be long now.

He reached for his satchel. "I have some bread. Here, eat."

They seemed reluctant, but he was starving. He untied the skin bag of water from around his belt and drank.

Benjamin murmured something to Sara, again in that strange language that he'd never heard, couldn't understand, and yet it sounded familiar. Sara nodded.

"What is it?" Eleazar asked. He was tired of this game.

His faith had been unshakable before he'd met these travelers. As a young boy, he'd gone with his uncle and heard

Yeshua speak—twice—although he'd never witnessed any healings or other miracles. Yeshua said strange things. He drew in and pushed away his listeners at the same time.

Eleazar remembered when Yeshua had hung on the cross, the *talah*, and when his tomb in Jerusalem was found to be open and empty a few days later. Still, no one thought much about it until Yeshua's apostles started preaching in the streets during *Shavuot* seven weeks later, saying that Yeshua had risen from the dead and had appeared to them.

What a strange thing for them to claim, Eleazar remembered thinking even then, even as a child. Yeshua was a martyr and would have been venerated regardless, but this story of Yeshua's coming back to life was bizarre, crazy. The stories became even more bizarre when Shaul—Paul—the zealous Pharisee who persecuted the followers of Yeshua, went on a journey to Damascus, and returned as the most outspoken proponent of Yeshua's resurrection after, as Shaul claimed, Yeshua had spoken directly to him from the clouds.

Yet, his uncle Matthias knew two people who claimed to have seen Yeshua alive after his execution, and Matthias was convinced. Eleazar had eventually put aside his skepticism and come to believe, as well.

Until he met these strangers who had caused the greatest, the only, miracles he'd ever seen, from tricks and tools in their bags.

There was a rustling beyond the tree. Eleazar saw a flash of brown cloth as someone walked past their hiding place, then pulled back the overhanging branches of the tree to peer inside. "Shalom," the voice said.

Eleazar didn't realize he was holding his breath until he let it out in a long stream. It was Matthias, not another surprise visit from Yohanan. Yohanan had a habit of following him, always with a nefarious purpose.

"Shalom, Uncle. Welcome."

He saw Benjamin straighten, then move back toward Sara.

"Eleazar," Matthias said. "And my good friends. You are safe, then."

His uncle's voice had an edge that he didn't like. "What do you mean?" he asked.

"Have you been to the camp yet today?"

Eleazar saw Benjamin glance at Sara.

"No-o. We stopped here first."

"Don't go there. As you value your freedom. I've warned the others."

Benjamin shifted, spoke in his strangely accented Aramaic. "Matthias. What do you mean?"

"I had a visitor this morning. Eleazar's old friend, Yohanan."

"Yohanan! What lies did he tell you?" Eleazar was furious.

He saw Sara sit straight up as she heard him say the name, then whisper something to Benjamin.

Matthias sat down next to him on the ground. "I'm not so sure they were lies. He told me some of his friends were planning on raiding the camp—"

"Excuse me," Benjamin broke in. "Who is this Yohanan?"

Matthias shook his head. "Someone who has sold out his heritage."

Benjamin and Sara looked confused, but then Benjamin's face blanched. "A tax collector? A publican?"

Eleazar wanted to hide his face. He was so ashamed to have the connection that couldn't be broken.

Matthias nodded. "He was a friend of Eleazar's when they were both boys. They haven't seen each other in six or seven years."

Eleazar glanced at Sara, willing her not to say anything to his uncle about their meeting the night before last.

"What did he say about the camp?" Benjamin asked.

Matthias frowned. "He said there would be arrests of the followers of Yeshua there this afternoon, before the Passover. He knew there would be an important visitor."

"Yacov," Benjamin breathed.

Eleazar shook his head.

"And you say you've warned the others?" Benjamin asked.

Matthias nodded. "This morning, on the Southern Porch. I found two men who will give the alarm."

"Don't trust him," Benjamin said. "I think this Yohanan is the one who followed us the other day and caused so many problems."

Eleazar saw Sara's fists clench, and it was then that his anger boiled over. "Well, at least we don't have to worry about him finding Yacov."

He saw Matthias look over. "And why not?"

"Because," Eleazar said, looking at Benjamin, "Yacov is here with us now, with his bag of tricks. No real miracles."

"Eleazar!" Matthias started. "What are you saying?"

Yohanan stepped into the clearing. "Yes, Eleazar. What do you mean?"

TIME ELAPSED   58.02

TIME REMAINING   13.58

LANDAU FELT as if a stampede of horses was running through his head, and he leaned back in his chair. His office door was locked. He'd given orders to his secretary Hod to keep him undisturbed while he finished a report, although he simply wanted to organize his thoughts.

The country couldn't hold on much longer. Palestine, Iran, Jordan, and Saudi Arabia—all were mobilizing again for war now that Israel's signing of Raseac's treaty had been cast into doubt. The followers of the Way in Israel were protesting Marc Raseac too furiously, calling him Antichrist and the seven-year treaty an agreement with the devil. Although Raseac had brought peace to most of the world, it had not yet come to Israel, and it wouldn't until the followers were quieted.

He didn't want to think the mole was Gideon, but as much as he wanted it not to be so, Aaron's accusation made a circuitous kind of sense.

Landau glanced at the near wall. The maps of Jerusalem were hung side by side, first century and modern—Benjamin Feinan was present in both of them. But he was a hero. Could Benjamin really be the mole?

Landau's stomach gave another twinge, and he groaned. He had a roaring headache too, both over the last few hours, and he wondered how he could be coming down with the flu when the base had been sealed for a week.

He'd go to see Dr. Rosen soon. First, though, he had to get an update from Aaron.

Fog permeated his brain, pressing. He suddenly realized he was battling for consciousness, and didn't understand why.

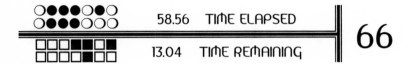

SARA STARED at Yohanan, speechless, as he stepped into the middle of the clearing. She'd seen this same man with Eleazar in the alley the other night. She could also see now that he was the one who'd followed them on the Mount and caused such grievous injury to David.

Benjamin jumped to his feet, and she followed. Matthias seemed to be frozen in surprise, but Eleazar looked angry as he too stood and took a step forward, crowding Yohanan and trying to force him back.

"Get out of here."

Yohanan laughed and pushed Eleazar's shoulder. "Calm down, friend. I just want to talk to you."

"No. I want you to leave, now. We have nothing for you. You're not welcome here."

"Eleazar," Matthias said. "Perhaps we should listen." He pushed up from where he was sitting like an old man, in stages, leaning forward, then using his hands to straighten.

"Yes, Eleazar," Yohanan said. "Why don't you listen?"

Sara saw Benjamin glance at her and then nodded. Yohanan was blocking the entrance, but at this point, they were still all right. It was four against one. Still, she didn't trust Yohanan.

She dropped her hand to the bag around her waist, making sure it was ready.

Yohanan took a step in, then turned to face Benjamin.

"So, this is he," Yohanan sneered. "Yacov, brother of Yeshua. Sir, you're making quite a name for yourself in the northern provinces."

"No. Eleazar is mistaken."

"Your accent betrays you."

"No," Benjamin said again, and Sara could see he was barely containing his anger. "We wish you to leave."

Eleazar jumped forward. "Leave us now! We don't want you here."

"I'm not ready to leave yet. Yacov. You're a better catch than I thought I'd get. I want to hear you preach, brother of Yeshua."

Sara caught Benjamin's eye, jerked her head to ask if they should exit. He opened his hand palm down, wait a bit. The situation was still manageable.

Matthias cleared his throat. "Yohanan, what do you want? Tell us quickly."

But Yohanan seemed in no hurry as he paced in front of the entrance, a wide smirk on his face. He turned again to face Benjamin.

"Yacov. You'll make a good presence when I bring you before the Sanhedrin."

Eleazar stood still. "What are you saying?"

"All of you. You're conspiring with one of the leaders of the movement. Don't you know this is against the law?"

"You wouldn't turn us in," Matthias said. "We were as close as your family when you were a boy."

Yohanan's face twisted. "Oh, was I that close? You don't want anything to do with me now, *Abba*, do you? So if I said 'No, I won't turn you in,' would you believe me?" Then he pulled back his cloak, revealing at his hip a metal blade as long as a forearm.

Sara turned as Benjamin reached over to place his hand on her arm. "We have to get them out of here, now. It's a trap. This will change their future."

She nodded.

"If I hold Yohanan back, can you get those two out of here?"

"The knife?" she asked.

"I can handle it."

She saw Eleazar was thinking of escape too, starting to slip around the publican. Yohanan took a step to block him from the entrance, and then he laughed.

Benjamin's grip tightened. "You get them out and signal me when you're clear. Then come back to help me tie him up. We'll catch up to Eleazar and Matthias on their way to the camp."

Their opportunity to do an interview was evaporating. Sara pressed her lips together. Maybe they still would have just enough time.

"Sara?"

"Yes, sir. I'm ready."

"I want you to walk in front of Matthias and toward Eleazar. Distract Yohanan. I'll get behind and pull him down."

She nodded. "Here goes."

She caught Eleazar's eye as she stepped toward him, jerked her head toward the opening. He nodded. She reached then for Matthias' hand and he started at her touch. She pulled him toward her.

"You must follow me now," she said.

She could see Benjamin edging around the opposite way. With a leap, he wrapped his arm around Yohanan's neck and pulled him off balance, flinging him to the ground. "Go!"

Sara pushed Eleazar and Matthias ahead of her. They ran through the entrance and out of the enclosure. The clearing was empty.

With a dizzying speed, she was grabbed from behind and thrown against the rock.

BENJAMIN SLAMMED Yohanan down to the ground, making him eat the bitter dirt as he twisted his arm high behind him. This one had caused too much trouble. Yohanan wriggled beneath him.

"You'll die for this," Yohanan spat, but Benjamin simply pressed his knee deeper into his back. He couldn't remove the knife trapped under the publican's body, but Yohanan couldn't draw it either. It wouldn't be much longer now. He and Sara might still be able to salvage something from this afternoon, although the countdown held them now without any margin for error.

"Yacov, brother of Yeshua, let me go," Yohanan whined, and Benjamin desired for a moment to break his arm, perhaps worse. This man had injured David, and through his own greed had destroyed lives and perhaps even the future. No, leave him untouched. Yohanan gave a great thrust then, trying to turn over but Benjamin blocked him. The publican was young and strong, but untrained.

Hurry Sara, he thought. She, along with Eleazar and Matthias, had been gone for over a minute. They must have reached the outskirts of the garden by now, heading for the camp, and he knew Sara would send a vibrating signal to his transponder at any moment indicating they were clear. He would just wait here until she came back, and then they would tie Yohanan with his own belt and leave him in this enclosed clearing to work his way out of the bonds.

The publican stopped squirming under him, but then he gave a bitter laugh. "This is death, you know. The *talah*. The

Romans will not stand for you to lay hands on one of their servants. When I'm free—"

Benjamin still hadn't felt Sara's signal.

"I will kill all of you. Eleazar, Matthias, your wife, all of your friends at the camp—"

"No."

"All of the followers of Yeshua in Judea—"

"No."

"I will destroy them."

He heard a scraping near the entrance, and as he glanced over Yohanan lurched again; he blocked. The shadows around the tree entrance darkened, and then he saw the glint of metal at Sara's throat. The man behind her with his arms around her neck was just as young and strong as Yohanan, and the knife he held was just as large. Sara's hands were tied behind her back.

Yohanan laughed. "You see, Yacov, I have friends too."

Friends, plural—

Another dark shape entered, holding a struggling Eleazar with bound hands.

How many?

Another man shoved Matthias in front of him. Also bound. The three men spaced themselves next to the rock wall with their hostages.

"Sara! How many?"

"Just these three, plus your friend there." The man holding her pulled up slightly on the knife to silence her.

"Let me go now, brother of Yeshua," Yohanan growled. "It will go easier for your friends if you do."

Benjamin could only gasp at Yohanan's treachery.

Sara was standing stock still in the man's arms, unable to work her bonds, and the point of her captor's knife dimpled her skin near the jugular. Benjamin shifted his hold on Yohanan so he could drop a free hand to the bag at his waist. Even as he toggled the clasp open, he saw Eleazar slip sideways and fling his weight back at the man holding him, trying to knock him off balance. The man shoved Eleazar to the ground and drew his blade close.

Yohanan bucked again. "Let me go now, brother of Yeshua. Do you see? You can't win."

Benjamin's fingers slipped around the palm-sized taser, shaped like a small gun. He pushed the button to charge its sting even as he withdrew it from the bag. Five seconds. An eternity.

"Give it up now," Yohanan said.

"No." He held him down, and then he pressed the taser tip to the side of the publican's neck. Yohanan's muscles contracted, wrenching his body into a fetal position under him. Benjamin pulled back and shoved the publican onto his side. *One down.*

He heard Sara call his name, and looked up to see the man who had been holding Matthias advancing on him. Matthias was on the ground next to Eleazar, watched over by the third man. Sara's captor held her upright, using her as a shield. Benjamin reached under Yohanan with his left hand to pull the knife from his belt, and then he stood up in a fluid motion.

"I thought followers of Yeshua didn't know how to fight," the man said as he approached Benjamin, knife drawn. "They only know how to die, like sheep."

"I'm not a follower," Benjamin said.

The guard was rushing him now. Five feet. Benjamin fired the taser.

Two metal prongs on thin wires flew from the barrel and landed in the man's abdomen four inches apart. The man was flung back, dropped to the ground. Benjamin ejected the first cartridge, then aimed at the third man guarding Eleazar and Matthias.

He dropped.

The taser was empty of cartridges now, a stun gun needing direct contact with skin. He wouldn't have been able to shoot through Sara, anyway.

One man left.

But even as he watched in horror, the man yanked Sara's head back, raising the knife as he prepared to stab her in the heart to avenge his fallen comrades.

THE POD WAS SWELTERING.

Rebecca wiped her forehead with the sleeve of her tunic, but it was futile, she thought. The air was too thick, like breathing inside a cloud. In the corner, David was as comatose as he'd been yesterday, the same heavy, strange breathing, and it spooked her to listen to him.

It was her fault. If only she hadn't gone into the tunnel. If only that publican hadn't followed them. If only the Roman soldiers hadn't been right there, or David had been a little quicker...

No. This was Sara's fault.

Two days ago, she should have been with Benjamin, not David, in the Courtyard. Sara had manipulated Benjamin to change the assignment. Sara continued to talk her down in front of him so that he avoided her, would never consider her. But she was better than they both thought.

Sara was outside right now doing the job that Rebecca had been chosen for, interviewing people with Benjamin, even though they both spoke the first century languages as though they had marbles in their mouths.

She wiped a tear from her eye and turned back to the screen. It was still copying the star data onto the optical disc that would be left here in the past, but it was going slowly, scads of numbers and terse technical terms that couldn't be interpreted without another computer.

It was so warm.

She thought about popping the lid of the pod for a few minutes to circulate some air inside. No. It was full daylight, a little after two o'clock in the afternoon.

Maybe she could open the pod just a bit?

Benjamin and Sara planned to return with about eight hours in reserve to copy the day's information and deliver the data to the Dead Sea by drone. That left almost five hours by herself in this pod.

She couldn't breathe. It would be all right. In a single movement she pulled the ladder down then stepped up, pushing the lid of the pod open about three inches. The cool air felt like heaven against her face, and she gulped it in deep breaths. Maybe she could prop the top open with something. She wished she could just open the pod completely, but that would be too obvious in a landscape that demanded strict anonymity.

Just for a few minutes. The hot air would rise and dissipate even through a small opening. She pushed a clamp into the gap.

As she descended, the sweltering air of the pod seemed to wrap around her again like a hand. She listened to the deep rasp of David's lungs. He was dying, and she shivered in the heat. Would he even survive until the time throw?

Her eyes narrowed. *Blast Sara.*

Rebecca shook her head. She'd never liked Sara, but something more had happened since they'd arrived in the past. Some change between Benjamin and Sara that Rebecca couldn't put her finger on.

She'd been turning over in her mind that strange memory or dream, something, from yesterday. It seemed to her that Sara had done something wrong and Benjamin was covering for her. Was that it? She couldn't quite grasp it yet, but it would come to her. These things always did.

Then she shook her head. Benjamin would never compromise himself by covering for someone. She was getting paranoid from being locked inside here. She had to keep her wits about her.

YOHANAN'S THUG SHOVED Eleazar onto the ground.

Eleazar was unable to break the fall with his hands tied behind his back, and his shoulder exploded in pain against the rock outcropping.

Matthias made a noise as if he would help him, but his uncle's own thug held him back. Sara on the other side had a knife to her throat, and the man who held her—Naphtali—would not hesitate to use it even without provocation. Eleazar knew his reputation well.

How quickly events had collapsed.

He stared at Benjamin five paces across the cavern, no longer sure if he was Yacov, brother of Yeshua, or not. It didn't matter though, not really. They would all die on the *talah* as soon as the Passover week was over. That was certain, now that Yohanan had been manhandled.

He shuddered.

Benjamin was leaning over Yohanan, holding him sprawled in the dirt with his arm held high on his back, and then he reached into the bag at his waist and pulled out something black, like a long polished stone hidden in his palm.

He moved in and gave Yohanan's neck just a touch.

Eleazar felt a finger of fear as Yohanan convulsed, his body forced inward. What powers did Benjamin possess?

The thug holding his uncle gave an angry grunt and shoved Matthias down next to him. "Watch them," he muttered to Eleazar's captor. "I'm going to kill this one now."

Eleazar heard Sara call "Benjamin!" to warn him.

Suddenly action became a blur. Benjamin pushed
Yohanan over and grabbed the knife from under him, then
stood, turned, and the next thing shining threads like spider
webs seemed to come out of his hand toward the man. The
man spun and fell with a jarring thud.

Benjamin turned and the spider webs flew out again. The
captor standing over him and his uncle slammed to the
ground.

What kind of man was this?

Just Naphtali next to him, holding Sara, stood standing.
He had turned his knife at her throat inward so that a point
of blood appeared deep within the angle of her neck.
Naphtali's eyes widened for a moment as he took in the
disaster, and then his face hardened, and Eleazar could almost
hear his thought as he gripped the knife and pulled it back
ready to stab Sara through the heart: *Your people for mine.*

A cloud passed over the sun.

"No!" He sprang up and knocked Sara away just as the
blade came down. The clouds seemed to blacken the
enclosure then, although he knew that wasn't possible.

He heard Matthias' voice from a great distance. Painlessly
he felt Naphtali's blade pass through his right thigh.

It was deep.

Dark as night.

Then the pain poured out with the blood, so much
blood, so much pain as he felt Benjamin's strong hands pull
him away and Naphtali collapsed behind him. He was filled
with weakness.

Benjamin leaned over him. "Open your eyes!" He
murmured something in that strange language to Sara, and
then he spoke again. "We need to get Eleazar out of here.
Yohanan and his men will be moving again soon."

Yohanan and his men were dead, though. He felt his
thoughts swimming in deep water, not touching a point for
more than a moment before they were gone.

He wasn't sorry he'd taken the knife for Sara.

"Eleazar!" Benjamin called. "Stay awake!"

He saw as clearly as in a crystal pond where plants swayed
in the water currents two depths below. Yes, he could see it.

The water was warm. He felt it running over his side.

Sara said something else in that strange language.

"We have to leave." Benjamin's voice drifted over him.

The thought floated to him, caught in his hands, strangely welcome, that he might be dying. It washed over him like a warm current and then it was gone.

Truth was suddenly so clear to him. It didn't matter if Benjamin's miracles came out of his bag or not. If someone claimed to be a follower, and was not, that didn't change the fundamental reality of what Yeshua had taught and, especially, who he was. Heaven beckoned.

The thought floated. He felt his uncle leaning over him. He heard him praying.

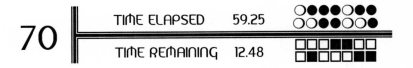

TIME ELAPSED   59.25

TIME REMAINING   12.48

SARA STARED down in horror at Eleazar.

The rich blood gushed from his thigh and soaked dark into the ground. His face was white.

Matthias knelt close by with tears streaming down his face. "My fault," he kept saying. "My fault. Yohanan followed me. I brought him here."

"Eleazar!" Benjamin said in Aramaic. "Stay awake!"

Eleazar's lips moved. "Cold," he whispered, and then his eyelids closed.

"He hit a vessel for sure," Benjamin said.

Sara ripped open the medical bag at her waist and took out a specialized bandage, coated with chitosan, that would stop the bleeding in seconds. She slapped it on. "There. We can't let him go into shock."

"We have to get him out of here. Those thugs will be able to move in about ten minutes. They'll kill us all. Sara—"

"Let me tie them up while you carry Eleazar out."

"Get the taser cartridges first." He looked up at her. "Quickly. Then tie them. They may start moving before you're finished."

She pressed her lips together. "If I have to I can stun them again."

The taser wires stretched over the ground, and she wound them around her hand, plucking the metal probes from the men's clothing. She shoved all of it in her bag. Then she leaned over her would-be slayer, unknotted his belt, and pushed him over with her foot to loosen it. The man lay as limp as a jellyfish.

The rope belt was about six feet long, but thick and coarse enough that it wouldn't knot easily. She did have some water in a skin bottle, though, and she could pour some on to make the knots swell.

She tied the knots, hands and feet, so tight her hands hurt pulling them. She'd left thin pads of cloth between each knot and the wrists and ankles. When she was finished, she pulled the cloths, leaving just enough slack that the blood could still circulate. The man below her groaned.

Sara saw Benjamin glance at the guard, and then he turned to Matthias. "Quietly," he whispered in Aramaic. "They may still be able to overhear. How far distant are your friends?"

Matthias looked up from where he was praying, leaning over Eleazar. "A Sabbath's walk."

About ten minutes away.

"I'll bring them now," Matthias said.

"And a donkey."

"Yes."

"I can't carry Eleazar far. Which direction?"

Matthias nodded. "Straight as you came. I'll find you." Then he placed his hand on Eleazar's head as if in blessing. His face was pained. "My son. You must live."

Sara knelt. "We'll take care of him."

Matthias stood, and a shadow fell over the enclosure as he went between the rocks to the outside.

Two minutes were gone.

She took the second guard's knife and belt, and began to work on him.

Benjamin rewrapped Eleazar in the cloak, and Sara could see he was trying to fold it so as little blood as possible would drip on the ground. The guards, when they were free, would be able to follow any trail left.

Benjamin hoisted Eleazar onto his shoulder and lurched toward the exit.

"Wait!" she called. "Your transponder is about to fall off." She ran over and put her hand around his wrist. Without resistance the leather band released and dropped into her palm.

"The clasp is damaged."

He looked pale, and she understood. Losing any technology in the past could cause grave repercussions.

"I can't fix this right now," she said.

He shifted Eleazar a bit. "Put it in the bag around my waist. It'll be safe there. Good observation."

She nodded and reached under Eleazar, dropped it inside.

It took her about ten minutes, an eternity, to finish tying the guards. They were beginning to stir. She debated whether to stun them again, but decided it was better not to. Double stunning could have physiological repercussions, and her knots were strong.

She gathered the knives, looked around the enclosure for anything else that might have been left behind, then slipped out to find Benjamin and Eleazar. With a shock, she realized she'd forgotten to give Benjamin the medical bag that rested on her hip. She wondered how badly they'd just changed history.

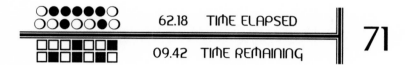

GIDEON COULDN'T SLEEP.

It was ten o'clock at night. He had only the next three hours to rest, but he turned on a light and threw back the covers anyway. His mind raced. What would be, had to be in place in the next few hours.

He lit a cigarette and savored the warm rush of nicotine like a calming blanket. It would work. Aaron would run out of time before he could put everything together.

If only he hadn't had to injure that soldier.

Gideon breathed in. Raseac would not risk a man to finish the job, not for him, not yet. Gideon's best hope was that the soldier would remain unconscious, or if he did wake up, that he wouldn't remember anything. It would be just a few days more.

He had played his last ace in the deck: Landau's demise. Landau had died two hours after he'd collapsed in his office. There had been some pain, but the death was fast and would remain untraceable. Now Gideon was in control of the complex, the time machine, and soon, the country.

He rotated the half-burned cigarette in the ashtray to staunch the fire, rolling it into a small point. The next few hours before the pod came back with the soldiers were critical.

Maybe a shower and shave now. It would calm his thoughts.

In the bathroom, he turned the water in the shower icy cold and stepped in without flinching. The shock was helpful for focusing his thoughts.

He shut his eyes. "Traitor" was such an ugly word. "Opportunity." That was more like it. Or "destiny."

This was preordained, his acquiring greatness by overseeing the Middle East for Raseac. Israel had held him back, not completely but enough to prevent him from having the leadership he desired and would fulfill more excellently than anyone else.

He withstood the icy shower for a full six minutes.

Attention in the complex was now focused on the information capsule that Benjamin would deposit in the Dead Sea at the end of the mission. The latest report through the encrypted channel described the newly discovered location of the same capsule.

Gideon wrapped the towel closer about his waist as he leaned over to skim the few pages of text and coordinates again.

It was too strange to think about. As best as Gideon could understand what the scientists said, the time machine linked the flow of time between the past and present so that the mission was going on with its outcome still uncertain, yet simultaneously it had taken place thousands of years before. Which strand would prevail in this current time?

Besides the tangled strings of theory, finding the information capsule in the Dead Sea posed practical difficulties as well. Anything situated there over a period of two thousand years would accumulate a great layer of salt that would make distinguishing the object from its surroundings a formidable task. The information capsule had a dye pack around the exterior that would release an infrared substance to incorporate into the salt, plus a nuclear battery that would emit a radio localization signal for thousands of years. However, the signal would be weak, and the high salinity of the Dead Sea would scatter the signal further, making it tricky to distinguish from background noise. The capsule was also fitted with a passive reflector system that could respond to a focused radio beam, but the target-to-area ratio was small, requiring someone with a great deal of patience to handle the search. It was very much like searching for a small needle in a haystack.

Yet, surprisingly, the information capsule had been located a few hours ago.

Major Horowitz's report was dull and thorough. Horowitz himself was a dull and thorough head of the team who—since the search began—had performed countless crossings of the northern part of the Dead Sea on a trawler boat, sending radio signals down to the Sea's floor and electronically listening for a response from the capsule. Now the information capsule was almost liberated. The divers would have it in their hands within the hour, and the team would return just after that.

Gideon shaved and dressed into a clean uniform. Maybe he'd still be able to rest for a bit, but first he wanted to review his personal plans.

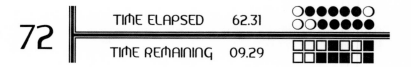

72 | TIME ELAPSED   62.31
TIME REMAINING   09.29

"COUNTDOWN?" BENJAMIN SAID to Sara.

They sat in front of Eleazar's tent in the camp of the followers of Yeshua. The sun cast deep shadows over the bowl-like terrain although there were still two hours until sunset. Once it was dark, they'd have to get back to the pod and deliver their data to the Dead Sea so that it could be carbon-dated and authenticated to come from this time period.

Sara lifted the leather band around her wrist and peeked underneath. "Nine twenty-nine. We may yet have time to see Yacov."

The time margin for their remaining tasks was razor thin. Benjamin's transponder was still in the bag around his waist so that he couldn't check it every minute, but perhaps that was for the best. His nerves were stretched too tight as it was.

Benjamin had carried Eleazar from the enclosure along the hidden grassy path leading away from the city, making poor time down the hill with its slippery coat of pebbles. Sara caught up with him from behind and then Matthias came from the camp ahead, accompanied by two other men and a donkey. They arrived at the camp a mile north and west outside of Jerusalem. Sara's bandage had worked—the blood flowing from Eleazar's leg had stopped, and he would probably survive—but the boy was still semiconscious and in pain.

To what extent had he and his team changed the future, their past, through this young man?

The camp was setting up for the evening. Benjamin watched an older woman flatten a roll of dough on a rock and place it over the fire to bake. She had a half dozen rounds of bread next to her, and the scent of sharp smoke drifted past him with the air currents. Several men walked the perimeter of the camp to secure it. They would need it secure, Benjamin thought. He hoped they had lost Yohanan and his friends, but one could never be sure. The camp was well-hidden, but it was a dangerous time considering that anyone could be arrested on a whim.

The twenty or so people in the camp were like Matthias: they had not seen Yeshua except at a distance and certainly didn't claim to having seen him alive after his crucifixion. No one had been close enough to the events to give the kind of details Benjamin needed: a body, a confession of theft, evidence of lying, or evidence of gullibility or mental imbalance on the part of the eyewitnesses. Perhaps it was too tall an order when there would be not a whisper of any of those charges throughout the two thousand years hence.

Benjamin felt a sinking in his chest along with the sinking of the sun. The mission would fail.

Sara put her hand on his wrist. "Courage," she whispered. Her hand was smooth and warm on his skin.

Someone from the periphery of the camp was walking toward them.

He hadn't heard anyone arrive. Still—

The man came up to him and Sara. "I am Yacov, brother of Yeshua."

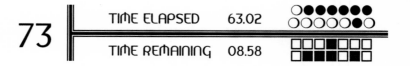

THE MAN TOWERED OVER BENJAMIN. His dark hair was twisted and long past his waist, tied back with what looked like a braided reed, and his beard flowed over his chest. His eyes were sharp. Benjamin crossed his arms.

Yacov nodded and lifted the flap of the tent. "Let me see Eleazar." Benjamin sprang up and signaled Sara to follow.

Yacov walked inside and murmured a few words to the three men praying over him. The men left. As Yacov lowered the open flap, though, he caught sight of Benjamin behind him and started.

"Who are you?" he said.

"We need to speak with you, sir."

Eleazar moaned. Yacov glanced at the young man on the ground, then back to Benjamin. He held his gaze, studying him. An expression of compassion passed over his face for a moment, and Benjamin felt uncomfortable that it was meant for him rather than Eleazar.

"I am Benjamin bar Manaen."

Yacov seemed to deliberate for a moment, and then stepped back. As he sat down on the ground, he moved his robes back, and Benjamin glimpsed Yacov's knees. They were dark brown, callused and hard.

Yacov cleared his throat. "Sit. Ask me what you need to know."

Benjamin hesitated, then sank onto the ground next to him and motioned Sara to get her camera ready. Yacov waited.

"I have questions for you, sir." His Aramaic was halting. "I wish to know what you believe about your brother Yeshua."

Yacov's mouth twitched. "Benjamin bar Manaen, what do you believe?"

"I'm not sure."

Eleazar groaned, and Yacov looked over at him. "I would like to pray over him soon. But I sense, strangely, that your need is greater."

Sara shifted behind him, and he saw Yacov look over at her and smile. In this patriarchal culture, Yacov still included her. Benjamin met his eyes again.

"Let me tell you my story," Yacov said.

Benjamin was anxious to hear this. He knew that Yacov had not converted until after his brother Yeshua's death, and would soon become the leader of the Jerusalem church before being executed in 62 C.E.

Yacov sat back. "In our family Yeshua was the eldest son. I am a year younger. We grew up together, five boys and two girls, in the northern regions of Nazareth. Surely you can hear my accent?"

Benjamin looked down for a moment. In fact, he couldn't, although he understood the words well enough. Rebecca could have heard it if she'd been here.

Yacov sat forward. "You have a strange accent, too, my friend."

Benjamin waited.

"My father died the year I took my place in the synagogue and became a man. A cut from an awl, and then he received a sickness inside his body from it. Yeshua was yet unmarried, and he and I supported our mother and our brothers and sisters. I did not yet know who he was."

"He didn't heal your father?"

Yacov fixed him with a look. "No. It was not my brother's time."

Benjamin pressed his lips together.

"Yeshua reached the age for marriage, but remained single. We didn't understand this at the time. And then he left and began his ministry."

"Yes," Benjamin said.

"He infuriated everyone. They said he performed miracles, but none of us in Nazareth believed. We'd all grown up with him! He taught from his own authority rather than falling back on what others had taught, and he told the strangest stories about the kingdom of God. He seemed to lift up the poor and sinful, and at the same time squash the rich and powerful.

"The Jewish authorities hated him, but couldn't do anything about it because of the talk of the people and the miracles Yeshua performed."

"Did you ever see a miracle?"

Yacov shook his head. "Not during his ministry. I didn't yet believe."

Benjamin pounced. "So, you're saying you had to believe in order to see a miracle?"

Yacov was silent a moment, uncomfortably so.

"In a sense," he said. "Yes."

Benjamin saw Yacov glance at Sara again. Then he turned to Benjamin. "Tell your wife to speak her question."

Benjamin nodded to her.

Sara spoke. "I don't understand what you're saying. Yeshua's ministry was not done in a corner, and the crowds followed him to see miracles, even the people who didn't believe Yeshua was who he said he was. Either he did wondrous deeds, or he didn't."

Yacov shook his head. "Miracles. Yeshua hid most of the ones he did."

Sara was silent. Benjamin glanced at her, and then he turned back to Yacov. "Can you tell us about some of these miracles?"

Yacov sat back, lost in thought.

"The miracles," Benjamin repeated.

"Miracles," Yacov echoed. "Yeshua did indeed do miracles, both physical and spiritual. Tell me, which do you think was more difficult for him?"

"Could he have healed Eleazar, here? That kind of miracle?"

Yacov remained quiet.

This was frustrating. Benjamin was getting no information.

Sara sat up. "Which is more difficult?"

Yacov had been waiting for this question. "There wasn't a physical ailment he couldn't heal if he wanted to. Blind, lame, deaf, leper, even dead. He laid his hands on the person, or simply prayed. Anyone who asked him, he healed. He would ask them not to speak of it, but the news got out.

"Still, he didn't heal all. Why would he choose only one person at the pool of Bethsaida when so many lay ill? Why did he pass by so many in the crowds?"

Benjamin shook his head.

"He came to Earth to give spiritual healing, not physical. He wanted to reconcile us with the holiness of God. He is the only means of redemption."

Benjamin shifted uncomfortably.

"Yeshua couldn't always spiritually heal. People turned away from him. Didn't the crowds call for Yeshua's blood in front of Pontius Pilate and Herod? They didn't want to answer the question of who he was."

Sara cleared her throat. "Who was he?"

Benjamin saw Yacov fix her with a piercing stare.

"I feel you are close to answering that."

Sara sank back as if she were frightened.

"Who was he?" Benjamin asked.

Yacov caught his gaze. "Messiah," he whispered. "*Christos.*"

Eleazar moaned again. Yacov glanced over at him, then back to Sara. "Many people saw the healings, of course. Believers and unbelievers both. Many miracles, but they didn't always inspire faith. Didn't the authorities question the man blind from birth, and charge him not to say anything to anyone? Didn't they try to kill Lazarus, the brother of Mary and Martha, after Yeshua raised him from the tomb?"

"Did you see any of these things yourself?" Benjamin asked. "How can you be sure they happened?"

Yacov furrowed his eyebrows. "Can so many who witnessed these things all be wrong?"

"You said yourself you didn't believe in Yeshua during his ministry. Why do you believe now?"

Yacov met his gaze. "I have seen my Master and my God, Yeshua Ha'Maschiach, risen from the dead, shining with the light of heaven. He is the Passover Lamb of God sacrificed for our own transgressions."

"No," Benjamin said. "I can't accept that."

Yacov stared at him. "God will reveal the truth to you if you ask him to. Whether Yeshua is or is not Messiah. Ask him."

Benjamin wrenched his gaze away.

Eleazar groaned again, almost awake. It would be a slow recovery for him, and he might never again walk without a limp.

Yacov stood and moved closer to Eleazar, then dropped to his knees. He closed his eyes as if in prayer, then slowly, slowly reached forward to place his hands on Eleazar's shoulders.

"Be healed," Yacov said. "By the will of Yeshua..."

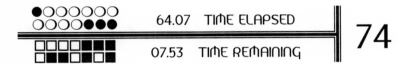

BENJAMIN AND SARA LEFT the camp and traveled along a back route to the pod. Benjamin couldn't brush off his growing sense of despair. The mission had been lost. There was no recourse before the time throw to the twenty-first century.

Yacov had not seemed in touch with reality, thinking he could heal Eleazar. Of course, nothing had happened. If everyone let Eleazar be, he would heal after some time, but that would be the only miracle—nature's miracle.

Sara was no better than the others. A follower of the Way herself, or close to it—what was there in this mishmash that appealed to so many? He dared Yeshua, if he was who the followers said he was, to convince him that he was indeed Lord.

Show me, he thought.

Sara walked along beside him. "Interesting people there."

"They're unbalanced. They believe in magic—someone rising from the dead."

"That belief overtook the Roman world."

Benjamin shook his head. "So did the idea that the sun revolved around the Earth. That doesn't make it true."

Sunset was in half an hour. They were free now, and he wanted to find his wrist band to contact Rebecca—he needed to make sure she would be ready with both the data and the drone when they arrived at the pod.

He pulled back the leather security flap from the bag at his waist. Inside his fingers passed over waxy paper cylinders of concussion bombs, the cool metal of his taser, sharp picks with covered ends, a small inner compartment with grainy bars of concentrated food. Another leather sack contained coins. He didn't feel the worn leather wrist strap of his transponder.

Sara didn't say anything. He stopped and removed the bag from his belt, opened it wider.

"What is it?" she asked.

He rooted through the bag. "It's not here," he said. "Not here."

"What isn't?"

"Hush!" He took out a few items, but still didn't see it.

"What's missing?" Sara asked.

Benjamin shook his head. "My transponder. It's not in my bag."

Their time was up.

He emptied the bag and then flung it to the ground. Next to him Sara leaned forward to pick it up.

She ran her hand inside it, even as he again sorted through the contents spread in the dust of the road at his feet. There was no leather band.

This was a catastrophe. The transponder was an anachronistic piece of equipment. It could not be left behind.

He sank down to his knees, thoughts churning.

"Where did you have it last?" Sara asked.

He closed his eyes. "I was carrying Eleazar. I stopped to rest twice, and each time I took a cloth out of the bag to wipe away some of the blood. I didn't notice whether or not the transponder was still there."

"I know I put it in your bag at the enclosure," Sara said. "I put it in deep. Also, I followed your trail as I left, and I think I would have seen it on the ground if it had fallen out."

"It might have fallen out one of the times I pulled out a cloth."

"Maybe," she said. "Probably."

He shook his head. "We don't have much time to find that transponder."

She peeked beneath her own leather strap. "Countdown's seven forty-two."

Shadows reached across the road now, the sun no longer visible above the hills in the distance.

"Call Rebecca," he said. "Tell her to locate the signal. Now!"

Sara was nodding even as she brought her wrist close to her mouth. "Captain."

Benjamin heard the response of static in his ear.

She spoke again. "Captain, please come in. Come in."

They waited.

"I can't get through," she said after five attempts.

"Why not? Are there too many hills between us and the pod?"

Sara looked up. "Maybe, although I'd have expected the transponder to work from here. I'll keep trying as we walk."

"Good. In the meantime, let's retrace my steps. It looks like we may have twenty minutes of daylight."

They went back toward the city. He furrowed his brow.

"This is where I met you and the men from the camp," he said after they'd gone about eight minutes.

Sara nodded. "Yes, I recognize that tree and the boulder over there."

"Let's keep going."

Back up the hill. He'd turned along the path here, stumbling with Eleazar over his shoulder.

The shadows were deep now, almost twilight.

"Here. I rested here."

It was a dirt patch next to the road. He recognized the configuration of boulders and pebbles.

"Captain. Come in, please," Sara said.

He heard static.

"I put Eleazar down here," Benjamin said, pointing to a circular area. "See, here's some of his blood on the ground, and one of the cloths I used. I was sitting over here," he said, trying to construct exactly where the bag might have been. "Near this boulder."

The shadows were now deep, twilight. Sara looked around at the road. "May I use a light?"

He nodded. "I think we have to. Shield it."

As soon as she'd put it on, he saw the glint of something wedged deep under the boulder. He shoved the rock with his shoulder. There was something reflective trapped beneath in the small crevice, but the rock wouldn't budge.

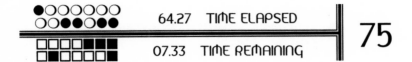

"I'LL NEED YOUR HELP to move this boulder," Benjamin said. It rested on the edge of a clump of similar rocks, each about two feet in diameter and easily weighing five hundred pounds. He remembered sitting here with Eleazar while he'd opened the bag around his waist.

"What do you see?"

Sara lowered her light. "There's something reflective wedged between these two rocks, fallen between the crack. I hope it's the transponder."

"Where is it?"

She pointed. The glint of reflection was far back, and he wouldn't be able to pass his arm through the crevice to reach it. The opening was no larger than two fingers.

"Can't we just leave it there?" Sara asked. "It's inaccessible."

He shook his head. He wished he could simply leave it, but he knew the crevice between these boulders would not be a permanent tomb for the transponder, not over a period of two thousand-plus years of erosion, earthquakes, and people. No, it wasn't an option to leave it here, as tempting as that might be.

"Not safe," he said, and he knew she understood.

He saw her glance again at the sky. It was almost dark, the sky painted with shadowed, dull colors. They would have to hurry. "Let's move this boulder," he said. "Ready." Sara nodded as she moved beside him, placing her hands near his on the boulder. He set his feet.

"Now."

His arms and legs ached with the stone's weight. It wobbled for a moment, then Sara's hand slipped and the rock dropped back. Benjamin stood straight. His forehead was moist.

"Let me get a better purchase on it," Sara said, as she reached forward to grab the opposite side. Benjamin positioned himself and bent his knees.

"Ready? Go."

They pulled it back again, not easily. The boulder was entrenched.

"Do you have it?"

He felt the stone creak up from its place but it refused to budge further, and after a moment, they dropped it.

Sara stood up. "I don't know if this will work. It's lying in a depression, as deep as the one in front of the tomb that we saw. We need to find another way."

"Let's try it again. We can do this."

He was still breathing heavily as he leaned against the boulder. "I'll pull it back. You reach in and grab the transponder. Are you ready?"

He glanced at Sara, and for just a moment felt a pang of something, he didn't know what. Was it a premonition that her time was short, maybe? Superstition from all that had gone before.

Her veil was slipping down past her shoulders. He reached over and pulled it up.

"Ready," she said.

"On three, then. One, two, three."

He pulled the boulder mightily. Again, he felt the rock move, but it was stubborn. His hands were on fire.

Sara pushed against the boulder with her legs, back braced upon the adjacent boulder, even as she leaned between the rocks to find the object.

"Watch out!" he called, a moment before the boulder slipped from his grasp and crashed down again. Sara jumped out of the way. "Did you get it?"

She shook her head.

This wasn't going to work, and he gritted his teeth. The lost transponder could change two thousand years of history. Yet for him to move this boulder—

Think.

Herod had done so. No trivial problem, but he had quarried and moved massive stones for the beautification of Jerusalem: the Temple, the palace, the Antonia. He'd used levers. Of course.

"Sara, where's your walking stick?"

His hands were bleeding. Wind breathed against his face. The full Passover moon was rising, although the daylight hadn't quite vanished.

She handed it to him, and he shoved it deep beneath the boulder, put a smaller rock nearby to act as a fulcrum.

"You push on this," he said. "When this moves the boulder, I'll try to roll it away. Ready?"

As he heaved the boulder, she leaned against the stick, forcing it to rotate against the area that would help turn the rock over. He felt his grip slipping again. "Going!" he called.

He dropped the rock, and took a deep breath. "We almost pushed it over that time. I felt it."

"Did it shift position at all?"

The crevice was still too small to reach inside.

Benjamin sat down to catch his breath, Sara next to him. She leaned toward him for a moment.

"Let's go," he said.

This would be the last time. Sara bore down against the stick, and with a great burst of strength, Benjamin pulled back on the boulder. This time it seemed to catch; he felt the power. The stone rocked into a new, stable position.

The crevice was open.

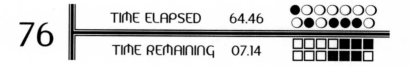

TIME ELAPSED	64.46
TIME REMAINING	07.14

AS THE STONE ROLLED AWAY, HE FELT a mental crash like a physical blow, the breach against a wall.

The stone lay at his feet, immovable.

"Benjamin," Sara said. "Are you all right? You're trembling."

No, an explanation existed for the problem he'd just seen, and he'd figure it out as soon as he could. Right now, he had to focus.

"The transponder," he said. "Let's get it."

"Yes, sir."

He watched her jump down into the moist sandy soil where the stone had just been. He moved behind her as she took out her light and shined it in the open space.

"Don't see it," she said. "The reflection was right about here."

"Sara," he said.

She turned and looked at him quizzically. "What's wrong?"

"Shifting that boulder. Yeshua's tomb..." he said, as if to himself.

On that early Sunday morning, how had the stone in front of the tomb been moved?

She was silent for a few seconds. Then she said, "Benjamin?"

Her voice called him back, and he shook his head to clear it.

"The transponder should be right about here," Sara said. "I think I see something." She reached forward into the shadow and put her hand on something, then pulled it back.

"Oh," she said, and her face fell.

"What is it?"

She opened her hand. Two first century pennies rested on her palm. "Someone must have dropped them. They could have reflected the light we saw."

"Let me check. The transponder might still be there."

Sara handed him her light and moved aside.

There was an angle between two of the remaining rocks, but it was shallow now that the crevice had been opened. He shined the light around the surface, but saw nothing.

He leaned forward and searched again.

As he sat back, his hand brushed against the boulder they had just moved. The transponder wasn't here.

"You're trembling," she said, putting her hand on his shoulder. "What is it?"

"I'm fine."

Before he could control it, though, the question assaulted his mind again. He narrowed his eyes as he looked at her.

The tomb.

It was an historical fact that the tomb had been closed Friday night, affixed with a Roman seal on Saturday night, and opened sometime between then and Sunday morning. Whether Yeshua's body had been stolen or never placed inside, whatever had happened, the tomb was opened and found to be empty. Otherwise the stories would have never started. People could walk inside and verify that the body was gone.

It was ludicrous to imagine that any of Yeshua's apostles had sneaked up at night, broken the seal of the tomb when to touch it meant torture and execution, and rolled the two-ton stone aside. Simon Peter two nights before had publicly denied Yeshua, and except for him and John, the rest of Yeshua's followers had run away. Although historically less established, Roman guards had probably been placed in front of the tomb on Saturday night, well-trained men like the ones who had injured David, and attentive to duty because failure meant their own deaths.

Yet the stone had been moved.

How?

No, no, there had to be a rational explanation. Maybe an earthquake? Israel was prone to them. It was exquisite timing, but such a scenario could explain why the guards had not kept their place in front of the tomb.

Sara put her arm on his shoulder. "Benjamin. We have to find your transponder."

He looked at the sky. It was night now; the only light that of the moon.

"What's our time?"

She shook her head. "Seven ten."

He wrestled his thoughts under control.

"We must get the drone going immediately to deliver the data so it can be dated," he said after a moment. "You go back to the pod and check Rebecca's progress, make sure everything's ready. I'll keep searching for the transponder."

"Where is it?"

He grimaced. "I walked up this road. I'll find it and follow you back."

"But—"

"No! Get the data ready. We don't have time to waste."

They'd stayed too long at the camp.

Sara stood still a moment, then unclasped her own wristband and tried to hand it to him. "Take this. When I get to the pod, I'll track both signals for you. You'll need to communicate."

"But you won't be able to until you're back at the pod. What if you have a problem?"

"I'll be at the pod directly. I'll call you in thirty minutes."

"No."

"It's the right decision," Sara said. "You know it."

"I won't endanger you."

She smiled. "I'm fine. You're going to be in the field longer than I am. Take it."

He shook his head. "No. Now go."

She turned and quickly went down the road. When he picked up his bag from the ground her wristband fell out of a fold, and he grimaced.

His hand brushed against the stone.

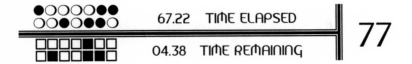

SARA HAD LEFT Benjamin and returned to the pod, but more than two hours later, he still hadn't returned. She hadn't been able to make radio contact with him, either. The low areas outside the city were full of static.

Sara had to implement her plan. There was no choice; there was barely enough time.

"I've got to leave now," she said.

Rebecca grasped her arm to hold her back, and Sara winced. Rebecca's hand squeezing her wrist felt like a vise. She shook her off.

They were outside the pod. It was quiet because of Passover; most of Jerusalem's visitors were inside the city celebrating the *Seder* meal. There would be ample time for her to launch without observation. She was already dressed in her return clothing: black jacket, black pants, black gloves, and boots. Around her wrist, she wore David's transponder to replace the one she'd given to Benjamin.

Sara saw Rebecca shake her head. "Shouldn't you wait for Colonel Feinan?" Her voice was high with fear, but Sara rolled her eyes. He would be angry, yes, but this was how it had to be, if they wanted their data verified by carbon dating.

She'd have to take the powered paraglider.

Her repairs on the miniature airplane hadn't held. Not a complete surprise, maybe, but she was still disappointed. The drone had broken during the test flight. With Rebecca's help, she'd copied the last bit of data and assembled the powered paraglider, but time was running out. The paraglider round trip would take up to four hours, and afterwards the harness and the bulky nylon wing would have to be folded and packed in the pod before the time throw. She'd be lucky to finish.

Rebecca seemed panicked. "What am I going to tell Colonel Feinan?"

"The truth. Help me strap the motor on."

She didn't understand why Rebecca was so afraid, although being shut alone with David had seemed to make her a little crazy. Sara had returned to find Rebecca in near hysterics.

Sara strapped on her helmet and pulled the infrared goggles over her eyes. The harness attaching the nearly transparent paraglider wing to her was tight, a five-point restraint, and that, plus the thirty pounds of engine on her back, inhibited her motions. Even so, quickly but carefully she laid out the cord-like risers so that the wing was ready for takeoff, spread in an arc behind her. She gathered the guiding cords of the wing in both hands, and then picked up the throttle of the engine in her right hand, the kill switch under her thumb. She'd forced some gas into the carburetor until it overflowed out the air filter, and now she gave the handle a good pull. The motor roared even through the muffler. She warmed it up for a minute, and then dropped it back to idle.

Sara raised her voice as she turned to Rebecca. "Captain, after I've launched, you monitor my progress from inside the pod. Tell Benjamin to call me as soon as he arrives. I should be well on my way to the Dead Sea by then."

"But shouldn't we let him know what you're doing—"

There was the puff of wind she'd been waiting for. Reasonable conditions, albeit dark with intermittent clouds over the moon. Sara ran into the wind, maneuvering the bulky paraglider wing upward until it spread out over her head. The giant fan on her back blew air underneath the wing, helping to inflate it, and after a few moments she felt her feet lift from the ground. She was off.

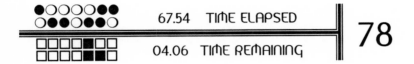

67.54   TIME ELAPSED

04.06   TIME REMAINING

78

BENJAMIN ROUNDED the wall of the city on his way back to the pod. With pure luck, he'd found his transponder in the dark, hidden in the dust on the side of the road near where he'd moved that boulder. The road was deserted. Heavy clouds now scudded across the sky, alternately diminishing and brightening the moon's soft glow. He wanted to get back to the pod.

The time throw was in a few hours.

Benjamin shook his head. FlashBack had been a complete failure, doomed from the moment they'd landed nine years too late. David was dying, Eleazar might be crippled, other lives in the past had also been changed, and for what? Although he had tried his best to salvage the mission, the events in his own present now would unfold however the cards fell. If the followers of the Way weren't stopped—if Raseac's treaty were prevented from being signed—full-scale war was imminent.

He saw a distant flash of lightning from the west. A storm was coming up from the Mediterranean. Just a few minutes more to get back to the pod.

He wondered if Sara had been able to get the drone working. He'd had a bad feeling over the past half hour.

If the drone wasn't working, they wouldn't be able to deliver the data for data verification purposes—the capsule would have to travel back with them in the pod. Really, though, that wouldn't be a tragedy, considering that they hadn't found anything. Still, it wouldn't sit well with Sara. She never liked to leave anything unfinished.

Suddenly a dreadful thought entered his mind.

The powered paraglider.

Sara knew darn well she was not to take it out without his explicit permission. It was to have been used only as a desperate resource to deliver the capsule to the Dead Sea, but now it didn't make sense to take the risk. Did she know that, though?

An icy finger passed down his spine. That feeling he'd had before, that Sara wouldn't return.

He brought his wrist up, turned on the transponder. "Sara," he said, but the static back in his ear told him the signal wasn't getting through. He'd have to go a little farther to get a clearer transmission.

Had she tried to call him for permission and been unable to get through? She might take it upon herself to go while there was still enough time.

He felt an ice shard pierce his heart.

No, surely she wouldn't use the paraglider, not with a storm coming up. Of course not.

He began to run.

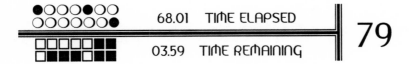

SARA THROTTLED DOWN the motor and floated on the stream of air. Her goal was to fly over the Qumran Mountains to the northwestern part of the Dead Sea, remove and drop the thirty-pound capsule currently suspended below the J bars of the motor, then return to the pod. Straightforward, about a forty-five mile round trip, three hours if everything went smoothly. She'd been in the air half an hour already.

She pulled back on the brake lines, rising another few feet as she coaxed more lift from the wing. The air was not as liquid as when she'd started out—some turbulence now. The breeze flowed cold against her face. Through her infrared goggles, she could see rough fists of rock and great canyons, streaming one hundred meters below. In the air, some heavy clouds came up to her left and behind her, but she was flying fast enough to outrun them.

Another sharp air current flowed diagonally up and across, and the mountain ridge dropped even further away under her feet. She weight-shifted in the harness and pulled the left brake line to turn into it, let up a bit on the right brake. The air was suddenly choppy. Her turn had been too abrupt, too fast, and she fell into a turbulent pocket. The left wing flapped as she sank; now almost at the level of the ridge she had just flown over but the paraglider kept turning. She let up on the left brake, hoping to pull the wing out of its flat spin.

The ruffling noise overhead sounded like an angry stampede bearing down on her. The lines bucked in her hands.

She was still turning, retracing the distance she'd just covered. She was fifty feet away from the ridge but the wind was driving her toward it, and the flapping paraglider wing was causing her to lose still more elevation. Sara wanted to increase the motor's rotation, but couldn't remove her grip from the brake lines until the paraglider wing righted itself. She let more of the left brake line slide through her fingers, feeling the sting of the friction through her gloves. Come on. Pull it around.

She felt a sudden smooth lift as the flat left wing curved into its normal position and the paraglider caught the current. She exhaled, but she was still not safe. The wind was at her back aiming to slam her straight into the cliff. If she couldn't rise quickly enough—

She reached behind to turn up the motor, and the noise roared in her ears. Gently, gently she pulled both brake lines even, tweaking the leading edge of the wing higher to catch more lift. As if in slow motion she rose, but the distance to the ridge was closing fast.

Up a little further.

She felt the shadow-touch of the ridge against her feet as she came over it. *Just a little more lift, come on.*

Barely enough clearance to get past but she made it. Dodged that bullet, she thought.

She turned the paramotor around, all the time rising further as the motor added wind pressure below the wing. The crosswinds now were strong as heavy clouds approached. A storm was coming, and she couldn't allow herself to forget the sheer unforgiveness of these rock cliffs should she lose control. She tilted the wing and rose further over the range, into another smooth current.

Her earphone came alive. "Sara!"

It was Benjamin. Carefully, because she was holding the wing lines, she drew her left hand across her chest to turn on the transponder and switch to VOX.

"Yes," she said. "I'm here."

She floated on the dark wind flowing past her.

"What are you doing?"

"I'm going to the Dead Sea to deliver the data. I'll be back as soon as I can."

She heard Benjamin sigh with frustration. "You shouldn't have made this trip! Our data is useless. We don't need to deliver it to be dated. You're needlessly endangering yourself."

"Is everything else ready for the time throw?"

She heard some rumblings in her ear as if he was asking Rebecca something, but she couldn't make it out. "Sara," he said again after a moment. "There's a storm coming up behind you. It's passing over us now. Turn back."

"What about the information capsule?"

She almost heard him shake his head. "Dating the data won't help our country. There's nothing there. We'll have to find another way once we return."

"But—"

"Turn back. That's an order."

There was another choppy current. Maybe he was right. She pulled on the lines, tipped the wing up again. The crosswind pushed her closer to another ridge.

"Do you read?"

"Sir, I'm running into rough air. I can't talk."

The cliff wasn't as far away as she'd like, but she managed to pull up to avoid it. The crosswinds were coming harder now, and she could see lightning in the distance.

She brought up her wristband again. "I may have to go ahead to outrun the storm. It's beginning to look ugly."

There was static in her earpiece. The reception was fading out.

"Sir?"

"I heard you. I want you back here as quickly as possible, but I'll have to trust your judgment."

The winds were violent and almost upon her. Still, she could hear the disapproval in his voice.

The wing bucked over her head, but she managed to keep flying forward. Soon, the storm would be past her, and then she'd return to the pod to await the time throw. The data wouldn't be delivered into the Dead Sea, but he was right—

the data showed nothing. They would still bring a copy back with them in the pod.

Sara needed more lift to get out of the basin and over the cliffs. The motor was helping, but even so, the crosswinds were fierce.

Up ahead she saw a flat platform about forty feet across. Could she do a landing to wait out the storm? She thought the platform was long enough to take off from after the storm if she started her run at the far edge.

Yes? No?

Another gust of wind, and she headed for it, fighting the air currents to stay overhead. The lines to the wing bucked in her grasp.

The rain began when she was about fifty feet above the platform. She began to spiral down into a cone of intention, preparing to land quickly.

The storm was relentless.

The wind beat against the wing, and suddenly she felt that great flapping again as the inner wing went flat.

Sara was pulled off balance. The wing puffed downwards, tangling her inside, and she plummeted the last ten feet. Her head cracked on an outlying rock, and she knew no more.

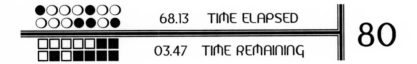

BENJAMIN HEARD the crash before he'd even closed the hatch of the pod, locking himself and Rebecca inside. It was an ugly scraping against his eardrum. He pressed his palm to his ear.

No, he thought.

"What's that?" Rebecca asked.

The sound went on and on, and in his imagination, he saw Sara tumbling over a cliff, dead.

"Sara!" he cried.

There was no response.

No more noise.

There were fewer than four hours left before the time throw as he punched up the telemetry program on the computer. *Please, let her be all right.* After a few moments, the screen light came on.

"Let's find her," he said.

"The transmission is intermittent," Rebecca replied. "She might just be in a bad pocket. She didn't necessarily crash."

He shook his head as he turned back to the screen. What else could that sound have been?

"She's right here." He touched the display. Sara's position was superimposed on the screen display of a map of the Qumran range taken from their readings before the suspended camera had been lost. Benjamin pointed to the bright red dot. Sara's position was not moving, and she was surrounded by a steep elevation.

He pulled out the handheld localizer and attached it to the computer, feeding it the data. "Sara's seven miles away," he said. "A little more. I'm going to get her."

Rebecca clung to his arm. "You don't have time."

He grabbed the black modern clothing he would wear for the time throw back. "Let me change!" he snarled. "I'm going." In the privacy area, he threw off his tunic, and dressed. Rebecca looked startled as he threw back the curtain less than a minute later.

"You stay here," he said. "Correlate my moving signal with hers."

"Benjamin! You can't get there and back in time. Not over that rough ground."

He pulled on his black jacket, grabbed the large compass, and shoved it into the equipment bag slung over his shoulder even as he ascended the ladder.

He needed to move west-northwest to find her. It was seven miles in a straight line, but more distance following the rough paths of the mountains. It looked like much more.

He felt panic. *Sara.*

Now that the storm had passed, the moonlight was so bright he barely needed the infrared goggles, but he kept them on anyway. It made sense to use every available scrap of technology to find Sara.

He jogged along the path leading west away from the city, breaking away to cross over rocky soil when the path veered north. Not much farther, his route headed downwards around a rocky cliff. He tried to raise her a few times on his transponder, but either she was in a bad pocket of reception, or else—

Just like Tamar.

The paths were quite different from what they had studied in the twenty-first century. It could not be expected to be otherwise, with two thousand years of earthquakes, rocks sliding, and human development. Nevertheless, he found the unexpected turnings frustrating, as they seemed to head more westerly than he wanted to go.

The mountains were foreboding with their dark hulking contours. The brush of pebbles underfoot and the occasional clump of his walking stick as he planted it along the loose shale sounded loudly in the silence of the night. Benjamin wished he had the equipment to get there quicker: a motorcycle, or maybe another paraglider. In his mind's eye, he saw Sara unconscious and bleeding, smashed against the rocks at the bottom of a twenty-foot cliff.

"Sara," he called again on the transmitter.

But there was silence.

He came to another fork and chose the right-handed one, heading northwest, even though it looked narrower and steeper along the sharp drop-off of the range. He hoped it would level out and take him where he wanted to go.

The rim of mountains behind him obscured the way he had just come. It would not be easy to find the pod again either.

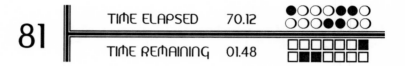

| TIME ELAPSED | 70.12 |
| TIME REMAINING | 01.48 |

BENJAMIN TRIED NOT TO THINK of the time slipping away, without any response from Sara.

His heel slid in the loose shale, almost tripping him and he leaned on his walking stick for balance. It was too far. Too far.

He drew up his wrist with Sara's transponder on it. "Rebecca," he snapped. "How close am I?"

There was another burst of static in his earpiece, and he almost threw his equipment bag down in frustration. Yet another bad cell. Wouldn't anything work on this mission?

He walked ahead a few steps. "Captain, do you read?"

It was after one o'clock in the morning, the sky clear and cold in the spring winds.

"Captain," he said again.

Rebecca's voice sounded in his ear. "Yes, sir."

"Has Sara's signal moved at all?"

There was a pause.

"No, sir. You need to come back to the pod. You've used up half your time."

"Don't tell me things I already know. How far away is she from my position?"

He heard Rebecca sigh. "It looks like five miles at least, and she's on top of a tall ridge. Sir, you can't make it. You have to come back now. You'll barely get back for the time throw as it is."

"I didn't ask for your opinion!"

Rebecca was right, though, as much as he didn't want to admit it.

Sara.

She hadn't answered. He didn't know what was wrong.

The mountain in front of him rose high and steep, and he studied it with a practiced eye. The flat ridge continued another ten or fifteen meters, it looked like, but after that he'd have to do more climbing that wouldn't be easy. Behind him, the way was smoother.

He knew he was endangering what was left of the mission. His first duty was to get back to the present and deliver the information they'd collected. There still might be something in their data or during the debriefing to disarm the followers so that Raseac's treaty could be signed.

Even if he found Sara now he wouldn't be able to bring her back, not in time. However, if he returned to the present, the time machine would still be calibrated to this precise moment in history and there would be about sixteen hours left in this period during which another time throw would be possible. If he convinced the mission leaders to let him come back and rescue Sara before the transport window closed—

It was possible.

Perhaps it was the only solution. If he stayed behind, Rebecca wouldn't be willing or able to complete a rescue mission. And would the others who hadn't been here before have the ability to find him and Sara?

He had to get back to the pod. *Sara*, he thought, *hold on.* Just for a few hours.

He wiped the image of the blown car with Tamar inside from his mind. No. Sara wouldn't die.

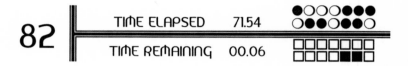

82 | TIME ELAPSED   71.54
   | TIME REMAINING 00.06

ALMOST TWO HOURS OF ROUGH TERRAIN LATER, BENJAMIN saw the pod on the horizon. Breathless, he felt a final burst of energy as he ran toward the pod. There were no first-century observers around. Even if there had been, he would have entered.

Rebecca was waiting for him outside, dressed in her black padded uniform. As soon as she saw him, she moved out of the shadows and pulled the ladder down, clambering inside. He wondered how much more time she would have given him. Another minute?

He closed the remaining twenty yards uphill at a run. Still time but barely. He grasped the ladder, climbed up to enter the hatch, and then pulled the ladder inside.

There were four minutes left on the clock.

The hatch was stuck as he reached up to seal it. With a great pulse of energy, he slammed his forearm against the lock. Turn again. The pins locked.

Ninety seconds lost.

"One-fifty seconds," Rebecca said, as if he couldn't see the green countdown digits over the computer bank. She was raising the transport seats out from the floor.

"We can just do this."

As Benjamin picked up David, he could feel the floppiness of his body. David won't survive the time throw, he thought. He lifted him up and buckled him into a chair.

"Sixty seconds," Rebecca said.

She buckled herself in. He sank into the chair while pushing on his helmet, struggled with the restraints tucked beneath the cushion.

Thirty seconds.

Benjamin took a deep breath to calm his shaking hands, clicked the last buckle across his chest.

The air was beginning to shimmer.

"We're going," Rebecca said.

Cold. So cold.

"Now," he murmured.

The pod slid into the time stream.

83 | TIME ELAPSED   72.00   ●○○○●○○○ ○○○○○○○
   | TIME REMAINING 00.00

BENJAMIN FELT THE PRESENCE in the pod again.

He shivered in the sudden cold. The light of the time solid penetrated the air, even as time seemed to gel into an enormous now where all events happened simultaneously and yet had always preexisted. How could he explain?

The presence approached.

He felt it touch him, lapping against him like a great ocean wave that didn't penetrate, although he sensed it could rip him utterly open if it wanted. He was afraid and yet not, powerless and yet not, and even though he was strapped down in the seat, he somehow knew that if he wanted to, he could push the presence away with a single thought.

He didn't want to. The solid was beyond all understanding, incomprehensible, but it drew him. It was unspeakably beautiful beyond anything he could possibly imagine.

"Sara," he asked it.

Even as he thought her name, the events that were connected with her touched his mind, flashing past him so fast that he couldn't grasp anything in detail, just knew that somehow...

Somehow...

It would be all right.

His thoughts floated like great pearls that he could touch and hold. David. His country. Strange they didn't matter in the ways that he thought, yet in the undercurrent of the time solid they mattered more than he could comprehend. He couldn't explain.

David was dying. That's all he knew. David had turned away from the solid again even in his coma and now he was slipping away...

He was dead.

Infinite loss. Benjamin felt it through the solid. *Crushing loss...*

Stay focused on the solid, now retreating.

The pod was coming out of the time throw into the present.

84

THE POD SMASHED onto the tarmac of Transport Room, and Benjamin felt as if he'd be ripped out of his restraints. A thin layer of frost covered him; he brushed it off. His lungs shuddered as he breathed the stinging air.

"Sara," he murmured.

Fifteen minutes later, he and Rebecca were out of the pod. Twenty minutes after that, the doctor had finished examining him, and he was whisked away to the conference room for debriefing. The conference room felt closed after the first century.

"David Baum is dead," Colonel Aaron told him as he led him to the head of the table. "Your data from the pod is being analyzed but we need your report, as detailed as possible."

Benjamin looked up. "Did you find the information capsule?" If they'd found it in the Dead Sea, that meant Sara had survived to launch it.

Aaron tightened his lips and shook his head. He seemed to be hiding something.

Benjamin looked over his right shoulder. General Gideon was entering the room now, followed by Colonel Schultz, the mission planner, and Colonel Gelfand, the historical consultant. Gideon moved around the polished wood table to sit at Benjamin's left, and Aaron stood to Benjamin's right. The other two sat farther down. From the other end of the room Benjamin could see that the camera had been activated and was recording his every move, every gesture.

"Where's General Landau?" he asked.

Aaron shut the conference room door and pulled his own chair out to Benjamin's right. "Dead."

"Dead?"

Gideon shook his head. "Later. You need to tell us what you know first."

"But—"

"Major Levenson is missing," Gideon snapped. "Where is she?"

"I need to go back and get her before the window closes."

Gideon shook his head. "Out of the question."

"But—"

Aaron sat forward and turned to him. "Colonel Feinan, we need to understand what's going on before we make any plans. We need your summary of the mission."

Benjamin glanced at his wristband, forgetting for a moment that it was not his regular watch but the leather-strapped transponder Sara had given him. The display was blank now that the countdown had expired. He looked up at the clock on the wall: ten after nine in the morning. The window for transport would remain open for at least fifteen hours. He had to rescue her.

"Colonel?"

He focused on Gideon. "Yes, sir." Thoughts of Sara passed through his mind, whether she had survived the paraglider crash, and he flinched. Concentrate. He closed his eyes for a moment, organizing his thoughts.

"We collected no data of value on the mission," he said. "There is nothing we brought back that can be used to disprove the Messianism in our country."

Gelfand burst out, "More evidence of his—"

Aaron slapped his hand down on the table. "Let Feinan talk!" Gelfand sank back in his chair but Gideon leaned forward aggressively.

Benjamin was shocked by the sudden blast of hostility. He glanced at Aaron but his eyes were hooded, no help. *What was going on?*

"We landed about three in the morning," he began again after a few moments. "Sara measured the star positions and determined we were seven to ten years too late. I wanted to confirm since the movement of stars over ten years is a subtle measurement. I sent David and Rebecca out to check the surrounding area for evidence of the Third Wall which was built about 41 C.E.—"

He continued for almost eighteen minutes, every detail he could think of as he went through the mission, everything except the small facts pertaining to Sara's doubts about the historical events.

Were they becoming his own doubts also? He thought again of the stone in front of the tomb, and how a band of humble, fearful fishermen could forge the enduring belief that a man had risen from the dead.

When Benjamin had finished his summary of the mission, there was silence in the room. Aaron's face was neutral, but Gideon and the other two nodded stonily to each other as if reaching some agreement, and he didn't understand what that might mean.

Gideon cleared his throat. "Colonel, when you sent your team to make a first pass over the terrain, why didn't you send Sara with David? Rebecca was not experienced military."

"That was how the team was supposed to be divided," Schultz added.

Benjamin sat up. Again, he felt that undercurrent of hostility.

"Yes Sir. I thought—ah—in the situation, that Rebecca would be helpful as an interpreter if they ran into anyone." He didn't want to mention his confrontation with Sara in the pod.

Gideon looked at him beadily. "And yet when you went on the Temple Mount a few hours later, you split the team the same way again. This, even though you were the one conversing with a native and could have better used an interpreter than David whom you'd sent to scout out the area. Do you care to explain?"

Benjamin held his gaze. "I was on the scene. In my judgment this was the best course of action."

Schultz the mission planner shook his head. "This makes no sense."

He remained silent.

"Let's continue," Aaron said.

There was a pause, and then Schultz sat forward. "Colonel, what were you trying to accomplish after you'd learned you were too late to film the body theft?"

"We were about nine years out," Benjamin said. "There were many people still around who might have had direct knowledge of what happened. I thought that if I could interview one or more of them, we might be able to disprove the resurrection story."

"You took it upon yourself to change the mission goal?"

"I had no choice. We weren't going to get another shot at this before Raseac's treaty. And as I mentioned before, I learned that Yacov, brother of Yeshua, was due to arrive at any time."

"Yes," Gideon said. "But why was he so blasted important that you would risk changing the past? Not to mention needlessly risking your own team."

Benjamin raised his chin. "Besides Shaul, Paul the apostle, there is no more famous convert than Yacov."

"Dov?" Gideon asked.

Gelfand the historian nodded. "Feinan's correct. According to the historical records, Yacov was a confirmed skeptic until after his brother was put to death. Paul repeats an ancient creed in his first letter to the Corinthians, chapter fifteen, verses three through seven, that states Yacov is one of the people to whom Yeshua supposedly appeared after his crucifixion. Eventually, Yacov led the Jerusalem council of followers of Yeshua until he was stoned by the high priest Ananus in 62 C.E. under Nero."

"All right," Gideon said. "But Yacov didn't tell you what happened to Yeshua's body, did he?"

"He truly believed Yeshua had risen. He thought he could heal Eleazar, as I told you."

Schultz shook his head. "He was not part of the conspiracy then, clearly."

"If he wasn't putting on an act for you," Gideon snapped.

Benjamin glared. "He wasn't."

There was a long silence. Finally, Gelfand cleared his throat. "I know you gathered no firm evidence. However, you

must have formulated some theories. Could you tell me..."
He paused. "How do you think this story of Yeshua's rising
from the dead came to be?"

Again, Benjamin saw a quick glance pass between
Gideon, Schultz, and Gelfand before they turned back to
him. Aaron kept his eyes averted, a neutral face.

"Lieutenant Colonel?" Gideon asked.

"Yes, sir."

"What happened?"

Benjamin shook his head. "I don't know."

85

BENJAMIN DREW in his breath as the silence stretched out. Not much time left to rescue Sara, but he had to get through this debriefing first. Colonel Gelfand shifted in his seat, then said, "We know some facts that are well established. For example, we know Yeshua really lived at this time. He was an itinerant rabbi who gathered a following and infuriated the Jewish authorities. They worried Yeshua might disturb their beneficial relationship with Rome, and they brought him to trial, first in their own court, then in the Roman court where he was sentenced to death and put up on the cross."

"Yes," Benjamin said. "That is consistent with our data."

"And then?"

Benjamin looked down at the table for a moment, thinking. He sat up straight.

"He was crucified."

"Did he die?"

"Crucifixion was brutally efficient. Sara and I observed one, as I mentioned." Sara. *Where was she?* "Before the cross, the man was flogged so severely that internal organs were visible. Then on the cross he could breathe only by pushing up with his legs. The soldiers eventually broke them to put the prisoner out of his misery. He suffocated."

"Yeshua's legs were not broken," Gelfand said.

"Because he was dead. The Roman soldiers stabbed him through the heart with a sword to confirm. They were not fools; neither were they inexperienced."

"Hmmph," Schultz said.

Gelfand nodded. "Good. So you believe Yeshua was dead. Then what happened?"

"He was buried."

"How?"

Benjamin shrugged. "I wasn't there, sir. I know what scholars accept. A member of the Sanhedrin, Yosef of Arimathea, claimed the body from the Roman governor of the region, Pontius Pilate. Yosef recruited a fellow Sanhedrin member, Nicodemus, to help him. To prepare a body at that time, they wrapped it in long strips of linen, and within the grave clothes they place spices, aloes, and myrrh: a sticky paste. The body was placed on a shelf in the tomb and the entrance sealed for a year or more until the bones could be placed in an ossuary."

Aaron looked up. "Ossuary?"

Gelfand said, "The stone box that held the bones of all of the family members."

Gideon sat forward. "Colonel, do you believe Yeshua was placed in the tomb?"

Benjamin gazed at him coolly. "I don't know, sir. Scholars accept that the tomb was found opened on Sunday morning. This was also consistent with our data. Either Yeshua hadn't been placed inside, or he escaped, or the body was stolen."

Schultz cleared his throat. "Body theft."

Benjamin shut his eyes. According to the records in John, supposedly an eyewitness, the grave clothes had been found on the shelf in the tomb when it was opened. Why would anyone stealing a corpse unwrap it first?

He took a deep breath. "Body theft was our working theory when we went back to film the entrance of the tomb."

"You mentioned Yeshua might have escaped," Gideon said. "What do you mean by that?"

"Sir, some people believe Yeshua was not dead when he came down from the cross. They believe he was able to unwrap the grave clothes and push away the rock in front of the tomb."

"Do you think this could be true?"

"No, sir. Even if he had survived the flogging and crucifixion—something I cannot imagine—he would have been barely alive. The wounds we saw in the other man were clearly mortal. For burial, Yeshua's hands and head, his chest, his entire body would have been bound and weighted down with seventy-five to a hundred pounds of spices and heavy grave clothes. He would never survive that after crucifixion."

"But what if he wasn't wrapped for burial?" Gelfand asked. "What if Yosef and Nicodemus attempted to revive him? He might never have been placed inside the tomb."

"You're saying he could have survived?" Gideon asked.

Gelfand shrugged. "In all of the documents Yeshua is noticeably absent after a short period. The disciples said he ascended into heaven. I think it's safe to say he survived the crucifixion to show himself, but died shortly afterwards."

Benjamin felt Gideon's sharp eyes on him. "Feinan?"

"Anything's possible," Benjamin replied, although he was sure it wasn't so.

Gelfand continued. "Josephus—" the first century Jewish historian—"describes how he revived a man taken down from a cross."

Benjamin shook his head. "Yes, but the man had only been up for a short time, and furthermore two other men taken down at the same time died."

"Nevertheless, it is possible."

"The Roman soldiers told Pontius Pilate that Yeshua was dead. They stabbed Yeshua through the heart to make sure. They knew how to execute someone; look at the film of the crucifixion victim we took."

Gelfand narrowed his eyes. "I think Yeshua survived."

"Even if he did survive, he allegedly started his appearances within two days. At that time, he would have been at death's doorstep. The apostles told stories that Yeshua had come back to life with power from God, made multiple appearances indoors and out, day and night, to one person or many at a time, had walked miles, broken bread, eaten fish, and so forth."

Schultz looked sour. "That just means the apostles were in on the scam. It was almost six weeks before the rumors publicly circulated. If Yeshua had died in that time, the body might not have been identifiable by then."

All of the apostles had forsaken their routine to endure persecution for the rest of their lives while they preached that Yeshua had risen, and all but one had died by torture for their faith. Surely, they had believed what they taught.

Benjamin shook his head before he'd realized it, and then caught Gideon watching him with an apprising look. *Careful.*

Gideon sat forward. "Feinan, what happened next?"

Aaron cleared his throat. "Shimon, does this line of questioning have a point?"

"Yes!" Gideon snapped. "Colonel, answer my question."

Benjamin drew a breath, met Gideon's eyes. Keep your thoughts clear.

"The tomb was closed Friday night. A day and a half later, it was found to be empty because the *golel*—the stone—had been rolled away. The *golel* was moved sometime on Saturday night, but it would have taken several people to push it away."

Gideon waved his hand. "So the apostles moved the stone."

"On the *golel* was a Roman seal that meant death to break."

"Or an earthquake opened the tomb," Gelfand said. "That's even suggested in the book of Matthew."

The room fell silent.

"I believe Yeshua was never placed inside that tomb," Gelfand said. "Yosef of Arimathea and Nicodemus closed the tomb to keep people away. Unfortunately for them that it was opened."

Benjamin sat up. "No. Why didn't they produce the body when the public rumors and strange talk began?"

"As Colonel Schultz has just observed," Gelfand said, "the body might not have been identifiable by then."

"But there are no records that they even protested!"

"Perhaps they left on a long journey," Schultz said.

The room fell silent.

"Even if all of that is true, it just explains an empty tomb, not the conversions of so many people. There were thousands of them in a few years despite horrible persecution, so many that the Roman Empire was overtaken. It doesn't touch the question of the persistent faith of the apostles, or why Yacov who had rejected his brother during his life suddenly believed in him, or why Paul converted on the road to Damascus. Not to mention—"

Benjamin shut his mouth. He suddenly realized just how strongly he was betraying his own doubts.

He shook his head. "I have no answers. We were too late."

Gideon smiled coldly. "Yes, you were, weren't you? If I may, Colonel Feinan, I'd like a quick private word with the others. Please wait outside for just one moment."

Benjamin felt the hairs on the back of his neck stand up. "Of course, sir."

He paced by the door for a full eight minutes before he was invited back inside to take his place at the head of the table. The hostility in the room was barely veiled now.

Gideon sat forward. "Please tell us again how you learned you were in the wrong time."

Benjamin passed his finger under Sara's transponder around his wrist. "We were filming the tomb. A native, Eleazar, entered and asked us why we were there, since Yeshua had risen."

He glanced at Aaron, who at least nodded to him before looking away. Gelfand tapped his finger on the table. "Did anyone else hear this native say Yeshua had risen?"

Benjamin thought back. "Yes, David and Sara. I had sent Rebecca outside again."

"How convenient," Gideon said darkly.

"I'm sorry?"

Aaron cleared his throat. "Colonel, do you have any of this recorded?"

Benjamin felt a cold finger run down his back. For some reason, they didn't trust him. They were asking for corroboration that he couldn't give, shouldn't have to.

Aaron held his gaze. "David died during the transport back, and Sara has been left in the past. This mission was a disaster. We're trying to understand what happened. Please answer the question."

Benjamin sighed. "We have recordings of the tomb itself. You'd be able to see that Rebecca wasn't present. But no, we didn't record what Eleazar said. We had to scatter to hide our technology when he walked into the entrance."

"Rebecca as sentry didn't warn you that the native— Eleazar—was approaching?" Schultz said.

"She gave us a second or two."

"Yet with her negligible military experience, you chose to put her out front as sentry instead of yourself or Sara?"

"I—"

"Did you have any other evidence that you were in the wrong time?" Schultz asked.

Benjamin's jaw dropped. "What more did we need, sir?"

"We've analyzed the star positions. They're inconclusive."

"You've analyzed them already?" They must have called for an update while he was out of the conference room.

Gideon frowned. "In fact, you guided the mission on the presupposition that you were in the wrong time based on a statement that only you can attest to, since David is dead and Sara is missing."

Gelfand shook his head. "Colonel, the only hard evidence we have from you so far is that the Third Wall around Jerusalem had not even been started, and that you landed during a spring full moon consistent with the Passover around the target time."

Silence.

"The time machine has proven accurate in all of our tests."

Benjamin shook his head. "I also interviewed Yacov, brother of Yeshua, who talked about Yeshua's having risen."

"Again, it's your word," Gideon said softly, dangerously. "It will take a day or so to get a transcript from your tapes."

"But I need to go back to get Sara now." He glanced at the clock. "The window closes in fifteen hours."

The moment seemed suddenly solid, as if he were in the time throw again.

Gideon sat up. "Enough!"

The three other questioners seemed to hold their breath, as if they had reached the crux of an issue of which he was unaware.

Gideon turned again to him. "Rebecca is being debriefed now, even as you are. She has stated that there seemed to be a subtext between you and Sara throughout the mission. I want to know what it was."

"Sir—"

Images of Sara flashed through his mind.

"I don't know what you're talking about."

Gideon sat back and templed his fingers together. "Are you sure?"

Benjamin caught his gaze and held it. "Yes, sir. I don't know what Rebecca could be talking about."

Gelfand cleared his throat in the sudden silence.

Gideon shook his head. "No."

Benjamin felt a great hammer about to fall. He watched Gideon slap his hand on a beige folder in front of him and draw it near. Inside was a single piece of paper.

"We extricated the information capsule from the Dead Sea about two hours before you returned," Gideon said.

Benjamin felt a leap inside, Sara had survived the crash to launch that capsule, but something was still horribly wrong.

"There was a letter from Sara inside," Gideon said. "Written on parchment, and this paper is a copy of it. I think you should read it now."

The letter read thus:

Two weeks ago, the paraglider crashed about 20 kilometers from the Dead Sea. I was knocked unconscious but unhurt. I salvaged the capsule and launch device and scuttled the paraglider, but was unable to return to the pod in time for transport. I am convinced—the word is "truth"—that there are no naturalistic theories that can explain the events after Yeshua's death. Yeshua is truly risen.

Benjamin felt his face flush, then drain and turn deathly cold. He looked up.

Gideon was watching him. "Sara by her own admission is a follower of the Way. Will you deny that you knew this during the mission?"

Silence.

"Will you deny that you are in love with her?"

Benjamin glanced at Aaron as if he could save him.

"Colonel Feinan," Gideon said. "I submit that you are a follower also, you knew you were in the correct time, and you purposefully sabotaged the mission."

86

BENJAMIN WAS REELING.

Finally he was alone in his apartment, away from the prying eyes of questioners who had been transformed into his accusers. He was scheduled to take the *Danan* in three hours, as if anyone in the world could question his devotion to his own country and the mission.

He clenched his fists as he sank onto the bed. The pulse of adrenaline that had flowed through his body had dissipated, leaving him weak and shaky.

Sara.

His strength was gone. He couldn't push her away from his mind.

Sara.

Sara's transponder was on his wrist. He brushed it with his finger, and then buried his face in his hands.

Sara had survived the crash, been able to launch the information capsule into the Dead Sea two weeks later. There were—

Benjamin looked at the clock on the dresser.

A little more than thirteen hours left in the transport window during which he could go back to rescue her, bring her back with him, follower or no. He couldn't lose her. Wouldn't. Not like Tamar.

What had impelled Sara to write that confession?

His bedroom was small and cold.

Don't let the circumstances paralyze you. He took a deep breath. Another, and his thoughts began to clarify.

It would be all right. He would be cleared of the *Danan* before long, cleared of throwing the mission. There would still be time for him to go back. Still, he could never erase Sara's confession.

He sat back and took a deep breath. Could he?

Separate timelines.

Benjamin heard the wind whistling past the window, and then die down again. Although light streamed in the window, to him it seemed like the darkest part of the night.

Sara's note had been written two weeks after the paraglider crashed, but in his timeline she had crashed a few hours ago. Benjamin knew that the time past and time present flowed together as long as the time machine settings were not altered. If he could somehow pull her back before she launched that capsule—

Was that right? That he might still be able to prevent her confession?

Benjamin jumped up and paced through his small apartment, two steps to the bedroom door, another five to cross the living room. He turned and walked back, then turned again.

Once he found Sara, he would first have to prevent her from converting, or turn her back if she had. He didn't know whom in the complex or outside had been talking to her, so he couldn't learn what the particular approach had been. Yet he thought he now understood some of her turmoil. He'd almost been convinced himself that Yeshua had risen while under the pressure of the debriefing. If he were there with her, she wouldn't feel so isolated and it might keep her from breaking.

He needed to understand why she was breaking.

Think. There had to be an answer.

Then it came to him. He remembered in the pod when Rebecca was asleep, Sara had mentioned she had a file on her computer. She had seemed almost frightened of it.

That was it.

87

BENJAMIN'S HANDS WERE SHAKING, and that was unusual for him. He had trouble typing the keys of his computer.

The answer must be here. Sara had said so.

Within the complex, all computers were networked, and all files were stored automatically on a remote server as well as on the individual's computer. Benjamin activated the encryption filter so no one else could read what was on his screen—as he and everyone else usually did—and he began the sequence that would access Sara's file.

The group of twelve elite soldiers from which he and his team had been selected for FlashBack had used a common password access the first tier of their own minidata pool. Benjamin typed in "BARAK"—"lightning." He highlighted Sara's name and typed in another password, "NASAEAGLESNEST," which he knew because they had so often exchanged files. The computer blinked, and then listed more than twenty folders. He selected the one marked "PERSONAL."

"PASSWORD?" the computer asked.

Sara had used his computer terminal twice over the past eighteen months. He pulled up the text capture feature, sorted by command, and scanned the list for anything unfamiliar. After a minute, he found it: the third-tier password that would open all of the folders in Sara's pool. He typed in the sequence "z7b4#f33c" at the computer's prompt.

The "PERSONAL" folder opened, giving a list of subfolders, and Benjamin sighed. He wouldn't be able to penetrate further without some luck, because fourth-tier passwords were unique for each subfolder, and Sara wouldn't have opened these particular subfolders on any but her own computer. Benjamin scanned the list. The most likely candidate was the one named "HISTORICAL." He hoped she hadn't used random alphanumeric combinations for this level. Most people didn't, but Sara was more cautious than most.

He clicked on "HISTORICAL," then typed in "PASSWORD CLUE." The computer came back with "HE FLEW," then asked again for the password.

Now what? As a former astronaut, Sara knew dozens of pilots. He had to be careful, because after three attempts the anti-hacker software would shut down the file. He knit his eyebrows, then typed in "DREW," the name of Sara's twin brother who had been killed in the space station disaster.

"PASSWORD INVALID," the computer responded.

He was thinking too linearly. Sara enjoyed word-play with a quick and creative mind. Flew.

It was a historical folder. He typed in "YESHUA," a historical person whose name had flown through time and the world.

"PASSWORD INVALID," the computer responded.

Flew. What could that mean? Fly in the air, or running on the ground or under the sea...

Wait. She had mentioned once that she had used the name of her pet greyhound for one of her passwords. Greyhounds were fast runners, so it would fit. What had been the dog's name? It was at the edge of his mind.

After a few moments, he came up with it. "FRODO," he typed.

The folder opened.

There was one file inside, and one more password to go.

Benjamin glanced at the clock. He'd been at it for twenty minutes, and he was so tired. He clicked on the file then typed in "PASSWORD CLUE," but this time nothing came back. She must keep this word close. The computer again prompted him for the password.

He sat back and closed his eyes, taking a deep breath. What could the final password be?

The word is "truth." The sentence echoed in his mind.

He stared at the computer.

Sara had written that in her note found in the information capsule. It had struck him as a nonsequitur at the time, but he'd been too shaken from the debriefing to pay much attention.

Could she have been sending him a message?

His hands were trembling, and he pressed them together.

"PASSWORD?" the computer asked.

"TRUTH," he typed.

The file opened.

Finally, he would learn what had been breaking her.

He checked the size of the file. Not long. He scrolled down the text that Sara had written.

> The following facts surrounding the death of Yeshua and the early growth of Christianity are accepted by the vast majority of New Testament historians, whether followers or not. Any naturalistic theory put forth must adequately explain each of these historical facts:
>
> Yeshua was a real person.
>
> Yeshua died from the rigors of crucifixion.
>
> Yeshua was buried.
>
> Yeshua's death caused the apostles to despair and lose hope.
>
> Yeshua's tomb was found to be empty a few days later. (Most New Testament historians accept this)
>
> The apostles thought they really saw Yeshua risen from the dead.
>
> Because of these experiences, the apostles were transformed from doubters who

were afraid to identify themselves with Yeshua to bold proclaimers of his death and resurrection, and were willing to die for this belief.

The doctrine of the resurrection was central in the early church preaching.

The resurrection was first proclaimed in Jerusalem, where Yeshua had died shortly before. The Jewish authorities, who had much power and motivation to disprove the resurrection, were also centered in Jerusalem.

As a result of this message of the resurrection, the church was born and grew.

The primary day of worship in the new church was changed to be celebrated on Sunday (the day that Yeshua had supposedly come alive) rather than Saturday.

Yacov, the brother of Yeshua and a skeptic, was converted to the faith when he believed he saw the physical resurrected Yeshua.

A few years later Shaul (Saul, Paul), the persecutor of Christians, was converted by what he, too, believed to be an appearance of the risen Yeshua.

Benjamin shook his head. That was all? This was what had broken her? There was nothing on this list that he didn't know or agree with. Their mission back in time had only confirmed what was already firmly established.

He continued reading. At the bottom, Sara had typed a brief summary:

These facts preclude the argument from
ignorance that we can't know what
happened two thousand years ago. We do
know the above. Furthermore, naturalistic
theories (such as body theft, people going
to a different tomb, apostolic
hallucinations, Yeshua's survival from
crucifixion), even in unlikely
combinations, don't work with these facts.

The greatest obstacle is the sudden,
inexplicable change in the character of the
apostles from frightened and generally
uneducated men into powerful orators
who preached unto torture and death that
Yeshua had risen from the dead. They
started their campaign in the very city
where Yeshua's tomb (and the Jewish-
religious and Roman strongholds) resided,
yet multitudes of their contemporaries
converted, to the point that the Roman
Empire was overwhelmed.

What will you do with these facts?

Benjamin pulled his hands back from the keyboard as if it
were burning him.

He could see where Sara had ensnared herself. She was
rigorously analyzing the events as the scientist that she was,
testing and rejecting hypotheses, not recognizing that
historical events were not repeatable or subject to explanation.
They simply were, like the immoveable stone in front of the
tomb.

Immoveable.

What will you do with these facts?

88

As HE OPENED his office door, Aaron thought Feinan looked terrible.

Benjamin nodded. "I need to talk to you."

"Of course," Aaron said. "Come in. I'm surprised you're not resting."

Benjamin walked in, and Aaron shut the door. He blinked sympathetically at Benjamin's obvious agitation; he didn't like to see anyone railroaded.

"Now, what can I do for you?"

Benjamin stared at him. "Sir, there are twelve hours before the transport window closes. I need to go back to get Sara. I don't understand why you're preventing me from going."

Aaron pressed his lips together.

Benjamin shook his head. "She can't be left in the past. I'm the only one who can get her out of there in time."

Aaron held up his hand. "Feinan."

"Sir, the window is closing."

"Feinan, I know. Listen to me a moment."

Gideon had tied Aaron's hands by convincing the other mission leaders that Feinan was disloyal. If Feinan were innocent, though, as Aaron suspected, then his being here might be the break he needed to expose Gideon as the mole.

Benjamin took a deep breath, calmer. Aaron pulled out two chairs from the corner and motioned to one. After a moment, Benjamin lowered himself warily, balanced on the edge.

"Good," Aaron said as he sat. "I've given the orders to have a pod prepared for another transport. It should be ready within the hour, but at this point I cannot authorize a rescue attempt by myself."

He calculated. Yes, it might work. First, though, he had to make sure Feinan could do it. He'd have to determine this quickly.

"You've got to let me go back."

Aaron shook his head. "Feinan, listen to me. I am unable to authorize the transport when the—ah—commander of the complex is dead set against using the time machine again."

"But—"

"Stop. I'm on your side. I have an idea that might be able to get you back, but you've got to cooperate with me."

Benjamin shook his head. "What are you talking about?"

"We don't have much time. You must trust me if you want to get Sara."

Aaron's thoughts were running furiously. He had to make sure Benjamin was innocent before he could do anything.

"Will you trust me?"

Benjamin studied him. Finally, he nodded. "I've always known you as a man of honor, sir. Yes, I will trust you."

"Good. I need to ask you some questions."

"If you say the pod is being prepared, can't I just get ready to go now—"

Aaron held up his hand. "You need to trust me."

Benjamin sat back.

"I need you to answer these questions as candidly as you can. First, during the mission, did you know Sara was a follower of the Way?"

Benjamin fidgeted.

"You've got to help me understand this entire situation. I will keep as much confidential as I can."

Benjamin seemed to ponder this for a moment, and then he nodded. "I'm trusting you, sir. Yes, I knew. She was hit on the head during the initial transport and as she was coming to, she called out 'Yeshua Ha'Maschiach.' I sent David and Rebecca out of the pod so I could question her more closely. She was—unable to give me satisfactory answers."

"So that's why you kept splitting the team the way you did."

"Yes, sir. I wanted to keep her close so that she wouldn't be able to interfere with the mission."

"Why did you protect her during the debriefing, then? Why are you so anxious to retrieve her now?"

He'd hit a soft spot, he could see.

Benjamin looked down at the floor.

"Feinan? Was General Gideon right? You're in love with her?"

Benjamin caught his gaze then and nodded, leaning forward. "Yes, sir. But it's not like it sounds. Sara wasn't a follower during the mission, just tottering toward the edge. She broke since I last saw her. I don't understand why, but she can't have gone far with a conversion."

Aaron held up his hand. "I just wanted a 'yes' or 'no.' We need to get to the bottom of this, but not now. I have to ask you another question.

"Did you sabotage the mission?"

Benjamin sprang forward on the seat, and his eyes blazed. "No, sir! Never! We landed in the wrong time."

The data would clear him, then, once the translated transcript was created in a day or two. Good.

One more question, but this one was the crux of his uncertainty surrounding Feinan. If Feinan were to help him, he'd have to be innocent here. Aaron leaned forward.

"You don't take the *Danan* for two more hours. But will you pass it?"

Muffled footsteps in the suite outside, and then they were gone.

Benjamin paused. "Yes, sir. I'm loyal to my country."

"You are not a follower of the Way?"

"No, sir."

Aaron studied him. "Do you have doubts, Feinan?"

Benjamin's face struggled for a moment, and then he shrugged. "How can we ever be sure about anything? I will pass the test."

Definitely some doubts. Aaron weighed the data. He thought Feinan would still pass the test although he'd have to be watched. Aaron would have to risk it.

"Good," Aaron said. "I think I now understand how things stand. And I think we can work together."

There wasn't much time to nail Gideon.

He tapped his finger a moment, organizing his thoughts. "Feinan, let me give you some information now. This is about the mole in the complex."

Benjamin nodded. "Yes, sir. I gathered he or she wasn't caught while I was in the past. Do you have any ideas who it might be?"

"Some. But no evidence that I can act on."

He paused. "We also had two deaths and a near-miss while you were gone. General Landau, you heard about. He developed flu-like symptoms yesterday, and was gone twelve hours later. Then the saboteur you caught before you went back, Seidel."

"What?"

Aaron nodded. "Shot in the lockdown. And one of my men who was guarding him is in a coma."

He clenched his fists, thinking of Dubi Hirsch in the Jerusalem hospital breathing through that ragged hole in his neck.

Benjamin shook his head. "Surely if Seidel was attacked in the lockdown, you know who did it. How did it happen?"

Aaron shook his head. "I'm not going into it right now. I need you to think about who has had access to your computer since you moved in here. I don't mean your files, but the computer itself that you keep in your quarters. Someone who might have been able to format optical discs on it."

"Optical discs? But—"

"Just think," Aaron said.

Benjamin closed his eyes for a moment.

"Not many people. Eli used it once, Gavriella, Yitzhak. Sara, of course. General Gideon over a year ago. That's all."

Aaron felt a quickening inside.

"It's interesting. General Gideon had wanted me to implement a new program for the training, but I was surprised that he came all the way over to my quarters to show it to me."

"Mmm," Aaron said.

Benjamin knit his eyebrows. "Why do you need to know this?"

Aaron shook his head. "Can you tell me about any other events that seem—unusual?"

Benjamin seemed to be turning over something in his mind. "Yes, sir," he said suddenly. "The trigger device that was used in the car bomb that killed my wife four years ago. Why was I not told when they discovered what type it was? I don't even know when the discovery took place."

"What's that?"

"The trigger device. I wasn't told about it."

Aaron felt his insides winding tight. "There's no new information. The explosion was complete. Why do you ask?"

"No," Benjamin said. "The trigger was similar to the ones that Seidel was trying to plant in the time machine."

Aaron sat up. "Where did you learn this?"

But even as he watched, Benjamin's face grew hard with resolve.

"Colonel! Your source?"

"It must be—" Benjamin looked up. "He called me while Sara and I were in the time machine that night, and told us to leave immediately. I remember thinking it was strange he knew we were there. Then he talked to me the day after, wanted to know all of the details of how we caught that spy."

Aaron was riveted. "Who?" he asked, but he already knew.

89

BENJAMIN JUMPED up in Aaron's office, energized beyond all reason by the pulse of anger that coursed through his body. Gideon had murdered his wife, Tamar.

"It was General Gideon," he said.

Aaron stood up. "Yes, I know."

Benjamin couldn't seem to get enough air, breathing heavily in the quiet room. Gideon had been like a father to him, and to realize he'd been lying for years...

"He's the mole. Why?"

"I don't care," Aaron said flatly. "I need to take him out now. He's taken over command of the complex." He paused. "Sit down, Feinan. We don't have much time."

Benjamin met his gaze, and then forced himself back down, although his legs felt as if they would spring at any moment. Aaron nodded and sat on the edge of his own chair.

"Gideon has been communicating with someone outside the complex," he said. "Your friend Mendel saw the compressed infrared flashes, although his testimony is worthless because he's a follower of the Way. Nevertheless, he saw something. I have other information that I won't go into, that corroborates this.

"The flashes came from the residential quarters and were beamed to a geosynchronous satellite. Gideon almost certainly also received return messages."

"Who is he communicating with?"

Aaron shook his head. "We're looking into it. We don't have much data at this point."

Benjamin sat back, thinking, how long has this been going on?

Aaron moved forward. "Gideon used a transmitter that probably is still in his quarters. There may be other incriminating items there as well. If I could find something during a search I could arrest him on the spot as the mole, and this whole problem would be finished. However, if I did a search and came up empty, it would be a disaster. Any accusations I made without further evidence, which frankly I'm unlikely to get, would have no credibility. Gideon is in too powerful a position, and he will protect himself.

"This is where you come in."

He thought he knew what Aaron was going to suggest. "I'm listening."

"Colonel," Aaron said. "If you were to break into Gideon's quarters and do a search, you might be able to locate the transmitter or some other evidence that I could then discover on a search. It's that simple—and that difficult."

Aaron paused for a moment, took a deep breath. "Let me make clear to you the benefits and risks of this operation. If you can get in, find evidence, and get out without a trace, then within an hour, I will guarantee you will be in the pod on the tarmac ready to transport back to rescue Sara. If you can get in and out without being detected but find nothing, then the situation will remain as it is now and we never had this conversation. But if you are discovered—"

Aaron's gaze was intent upon him, and Benjamin felt a sinking in his chest. He was a soldier. He knew.

"The security of this complex and the time machine is my top priority. I will not compromise that for anything. I'm sure you realize that right now your credibility is nonexistent. You are suspected of being a follower and of sabotaging the mission."

"Yes," Benjamin said. He found it galling.

"If security is called to Gideon's quarters because of a break-in, they will be authorized to use all force necessary to control the situation, up to and including the use of deadly force. Do you understand? You will have no standing against the commander of the complex. At the very least, you will be court-martialed and almost certainly convicted on charges that will incarcerate you for the rest of your life. I will not protect you. I will bide my time, and wait to have another opportunity to nail Gideon down the road."

"I understand, sir."

"Unfortunately, you're going to have to make a decision now." Aaron glanced at his watch. "We don't have much time. Let me say two other things that may help you make your decision. The first is that my assistant, Etan, and I were in Gideon's quarters when he was not present. We didn't have time to look around for more than a few minutes, but we're pretty good and still found nothing. If anything is hidden there, it will be difficult to find."

"Yes," Benjamin said.

"The second is this: You are not obligated to do this. If you do nothing, and what you've told me is true, then the evidence will clear you within a day or two. Your reputation and honor will be intact. If Sara is left in the past, she has already lived her life, and maybe it was a good, long life. Do you understand me?"

Yes, he did. The choice was crushing but he knew there was only one way he could decide, consequences or not. *Sara.* Benjamin drew in his breath.

Aaron paused, intent, meeting his gaze. "Do you need a moment more to ponder this?"

"No, sir," Benjamin said. "I've made my decision."

90

BENJAMIN WAS ALMOST THERE.

He paused as he turned the corner to the last hallway, the sixth floor where the VIP quarters were located. Gideon's door was halfway down the well-lit, carpeted corridor. Aaron had confirmed that Gideon was currently in another debriefing, reviewing some of the evidence from the pod, a meeting scheduled to continue another thirty minutes at least. Still, that time would evaporate all too quickly. *Hurry.*

The biometric key to the right of the door flashed its dim green light below the hand scanner. Benjamin took out the security card that Aaron had given him and swiped it along the side of the scanner. He smiled grimly as the lock opened, then pulled on latex gloves and slid inside before anyone might see him. *Clear.* The latch clicked behind him, locking him inside. He took a deep breath.

Despite the fact that it was daytime, the room was dark. Gideon must have closed the doors to the other rooms. Benjamin ran his hand along the wall next to the door to find the light switch. Still he rested his gloved hand on it for a moment before pushing it up. He felt nervous as the shadows disappeared, but speed was critical, and he could search more quickly with the lights than with a flashlight.

Gideon's quarters were well-ordered, about twice as wide as his own. Benjamin stood on plush, deep maroon carpeting in the living area. The furniture was expensive: cream sofa and two chairs, and a teak dining table. Two modern paintings were on the wall, and near the table was mounted a small case displaying a Walther P08, the tiny handgun used by the Germans during World War Two. To his left an archway opened to a small kitchen.

From Aaron's schematic, Benjamin knew Gideon had a study through the far door on the right and a bedroom to the left. Both of those rooms had windows from which Gideon could have sent a signal.

Where would Gideon hide the transmitter?

His heart was jumping in his chest. *Sara.* Less than twelve hours remained in the transport window.

Benjamin reached behind to turn off the lights, then took out his small flashlight and walked across the room to the bedroom door.

He didn't need artificial lights here, not when the sun lit the room with a bright glow. The bed was covered by a patterned quilt, and close by stood a cleared dresser and a nightstand. There was nothing else. The bathroom was also immaculate.

Benjamin shook his head. The transmitter would be small. He might also find a telescope: Gideon probably used one to collect return messages from a distance and thereby avoid a big infrared spot being painted on his window.

First, rule out the bedroom. He went through the dresser, spanning his hand along the bottom edge of each drawer, but found nothing significant. Nor was there anything in the night table, the closet, or under the mattress. He smoothed out the quilt.

He'd used fifteen minutes.

Now check the study.

Gideon's teak desk stood against the wall. The top was clear except for the computer. Nearby was another bookshelf full of optical discs and hard-copy technical printouts. There were no built-in wall safes in the apartment, Aaron had said. Benjamin shook his head, and shut the door behind him.

Opposite the desk in the study was a waist-high matching cabinet with a lock at the top; when Benjamin pulled on the handle, it opened. Inside hung folders with papers related to the time machine and FlashBack. Benjamin rifled through them but found nothing suspicious. The desk drawers opened too, and he searched them starting at the top. He found nothing.

Wait. The bottom left-hand drawer, a deep one, didn't open.

Benjamin yanked it again. It was not stuck, but locked.

Open the drawer.

As he leaned forward to examine the lock he heard a slight click behind him, and the air seemed to change. He felt another presence in the room. With a shudder he turned.

Gideon was standing in the doorway, pointing the tiny Walther P08 at his chest.

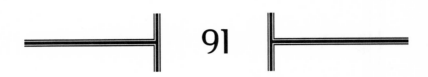

91

"COLONEL FEINAN," GIDEON SAID.

Benjamin ripped off the latex gloves and stuffed them in his pocket before Gideon saw them. His heart sank as he stood to face him, eyes on the gun's barrel that was barely visible in Gideon's hand. Benjamin didn't doubt for a moment that the gun was loaded. He knew the bullets were light caliber but exploded on impact, and at this range there would be no hope.

"I finished my meeting early, decide to come back to my room to reflect, and I find you here," Gideon said. "Is it too much to inquire what you are doing in my quarters?"

Benjamin's mouth was dry.

"I wondered why Colonel Aaron was so eager to detain me."

No, no.

Benjamin blinked. "Sir, I—don't know what you're talking about."

Gideon's mouth tightened violently. "I should kill you right now, Feinan. Make an end of it. Is there any reason I shouldn't?"

The moment tunneled down into stillness.

"Well, traitor?"

He glanced at the gun. Gideon followed his gaze, and his hand tightened.

"I'm not a traitor," Benjamin said in a low voice. "You know I'm not."

Gideon barked a laugh. "Not after I've found you here. You just ruined any chance of proving otherwise."

He felt a great weight on him; what Gideon said was true. He would not be able to recover from this.

Gideon motioned with the gun to the desk drawer. "Tell me, why are you here? What are you looking for in my desk?"

Maybe ten feet separated them. He took a step toward Gideon, who narrowed his eyes and moved his hand forward. "Don't even think about it, traitor. You stay back there, right in the line of fire. Next to the desk. Now answer my question."

Benjamin was silent.

Gideon seemed to think for a moment. Then with his other hand he reached to his neck and pulled out a string from under his shirt, then loosed it from around his neck. He tossed it to him. "Try this," he said.

On the string was a tiny key. Benjamin turned it over in his fingers.

"It fits the desk drawer. Since you've come this far, you might as well see what's in there."

He glanced again at the gun, but Gideon moved menacingly. "I know what you're thinking. You're not going to overpower me—I'm too smart for that. Now, open the drawer."

"Why?"

"Just do it!"

Benjamin nodded. If he played along, he might buy some time before Gideon shot him or turned him in. Not that it would do any good. He knelt down and inserted the key into the lock. It turned with resistance, and he pulled open the drawer.

He saw a stack of papers about an inch high, and rifled through them. "Nothing," he said. "Routine FlashBack documents."

"Interesting. Keep looking."

Benjamin scanned the training schedules and protocols again, turning each leaf to make sure nothing was hidden between.

"Not the papers. Check the drawer."

Benjamin looked up at him, then put the papers down on the floor and leaned over the drawer. The lining was grey metal, impervious. He ran his fingers over the surface, feeling for any irregularity.

"There's nothing else," Benjamin said.

Gideon laughed. "The workmanship is that good. Aaron would never have found it either. Let me suggest that you push at the back center part of the panel, and at the same time at the right front corner. Tell me what happens."

Benjamin put his hands inside and tried it.

"No! Move your right hand up a bit!"

Benjamin obeyed, and felt a small release under his fingers. The bottom panel rocked and came loose, and he slid it out of the drawer.

Now he could see a rimmed cavity underneath, about ten centimeters deep, stretching the length of the drawer. Inside was a small bundle wrapped in brown cloth.

"Pick it up," Gideon said. "Unwrap it. See what it is. That's what you're here for."

Benjamin pulled the cloth apart. "The transmitter," he whispered.

"Isn't that what you wanted to find?"

Benjamin turned it over in his hands, and then he jumped up and took a step toward Gideon.

"Careful." Gideon motioned with the gun. "Stay over there. If you approach, I will shoot you dead, and no one will question it."

"Who are you working for?"

Gideon laughed. "I'm not the mole, Feinan. You are. Why do you think you're planting that transmitter in my quarters right now?"

Benjamin gasped.

"You stole one of Aaron's security cards to get into my quarters, as well as the key that opens my desk. Deny it, and they will find your fingerprints all over it. You had planned to incriminate me to deflect suspicion from yourself."

"No."

Gideon laughed. "Do you deny you broke in here? I have you. Who will take your word over mine?"

"No." He felt a great flush of anger pass through him. He would kill him.

"Careful!" Gideon said. "Stay where you are."

"You killed Tamar. I trusted you, and you gave those terrorists the location of my car. Did they pay you even though you killed her, not me?"

Gideon shook his head. "Quiet. We'll be done here soon enough. It's finished for Tamar, and it is for Sara too. You know, once I shoot you, everyone will believe that you're the mole. Somehow, though, that seems too easy. You have no idea how much I want you to suffer."

Gideon was getting distracted. Just a little, but if it continued, Benjamin might have a chance. He took a step toward him.

Gideon cocked the weapon. "Get back. Before I kill you, don't you want to know about Tamar, how she died? It was your fault. You sent her out to the car instead of going yourself."

"No. It was supposed to be safe—"

"You call yourself a soldier? Those brave rescues in Special Forces, and yet you don't bother to protect your own wife."

"Stop it."

"And Sara. The same. You sacrifice her so you can make it back. You keep offering up the women you love to take the penalty for you."

"I had no control over what happened."

The words were hitting too close, though. He had to shut them out.

"And even now, you will have a quick and painless death compared to what Sara faces in the past. What will happen to her, do you suppose? She's a single impoverished woman in that culture. You saw it. How will she be able to support herself? Who will protect her if she runs afoul of the Romans or the Jewish authorities?"

Benjamin shook his head, trying to shake the images away.

Gideon smiled. "What is it? You can't handle the truth?"

The room grew still. It was impossible. The transmitter as evidence now meant nothing.

"I want you to suffer," Gideon said again. "In a quick kill you won't—" he motioned with the gun, "although I have no

qualms about shooting you if I need to. I could have you
arrested and then you would suffer, but maybe not enough,
and besides there might be someone foolish enough to listen
to your talk.

"So what shall I do?"

He paused.

"I may have a solution."

Gideon had spoken so quietly that Benjamin almost
didn't hear him. Still, he felt a chill run deep within.

"At this point you've sealed your guilt, no matter what
happens. Yet I think I may still be able to offer you a trade. I
want you to think about it."

"What is it?"

Gideon glanced at the clock on the wall. "The window
closes in a little more than eleven hours. There's still time for
you to go back to rescue Sara. That's what you want, isn't it?"

He studied him.

"I know it is. And I know that I'm the only one who can
give you that opportunity."

Benjamin shook his head. "Why would you ever do that?"

Gideon smiled, a thin, cruel smile. In the silence,
Benjamin could hear the tiny snaps of the wall clock's second
hand as it traversed the dial. He was weary.

"Here's the deal," Gideon said. "I want you to make a full
confession that you are the mole. If you can do this
convincingly—and I will give you the details you need to
make it real—I will get you into the time machine before the
window closes. You'll be able to go back to Sara."

This was unreal. Benjamin shook his head.

"Why am I doing this?" Gideon responded to his
unspoken question. "Two reasons. First, it will be a
permanent way to remove suspicion from me. If you go into
that machine, you won't come back out to defend yourself or
give any other uncomfortable testimony. You will remain
silent in the past."

"Sir—"

"And second, while you're trapped in the past with Sara, I
think it might torment you to know that you are considered
one of the most dangerous enemies this country has ever

known. All of your previous good works will be ashes. You would live with that for all of your days."

Benjamin stepped back, suddenly weak. Sara. He thought of her in his arms, her smile.

What did he have here? He'd lost everything when Gideon discovered him here. He would either die of a bullet wound, or he would be arrested and accused of being a traitor. There would be no defense, and no one would come to his aid. He looked forward, at best, to court-martial, conviction, and jail.

Gideon's deal wasn't so bad. He wouldn't be here to suffer the havoc his confession would cause in the country, and if Gideon wasn't stopped now, he might be later. Even if he wasn't, well, that wouldn't be his problem.

"How much is Sara worth to you?" Gideon asked slyly.

THEY WERE IN AARON'S QUARTERS, adjacent to Gideon's, and Aaron held the earpiece close. "Come on, Feinan. Just get him to confess."

Etan pointed to the screen. "They haven't moved from the doorway. It's got to reach a head soon."

"It's recording," Aaron said. "Gideon hasn't quite come out and said it yet. I just want a clear statement, one statement, and we have him. Feinan, keep him talking."

93

SARA WAS SO CLOSE he could touch her. He could go to her and protect her in the past...

Gideon was watching him.

"No," Benjamin said. "I won't do it."

He had to take control now, even if he died, even if he was dishonored in life or death. It would be a grave sin against his country to leave Gideon in power, no matter what the cost.

Take control.

Gideon's face snarled. "You're a fool, Feinan. And she will die horribly."

Benjamin threw the transmitter at his head, then he ducked and took three staggered steps to close the ten foot distance to Gideon, grabbed for his wrist, and pulled it up—

Gideon was ready for him. He was older but he was also fit and a trained soldier, and even as Benjamin pushed him back, he saw something silver in his left hand.

He smelled a sickly sweet odor, and held his breath. It was too late, though. His vision blurred, and he felt Gideon's foot sweep behind his knees.

94

"WHAT HAPPENED?" Etan asked. "Gideon got him down, that quick. Feinan's not moving."

Aaron felt a great sinking in his chest.

"He'll shoot him in cold blood. I'm going in now."

"Stop!" Aaron grimaced. "Feinan knew the risks when he went in. We don't have a confession yet. This is our only chance to expose Gideon."

"But, sir—"

Aaron motioned him to stay. "We've got to wait."

95

HE MUST HAVE LOST CONSCIOUSNESS.

Benjamin's eyes slid open. It had only been a moment but that was enough. Gideon leaned over him, breathing heavily, and Benjamin could feel the cold circle of the gun barrel pressing into his temple.

"You lose, Feinan," Gideon said. "I offered you a way out. Now you'll die, and everyone will still think you were the mole. I'll be able to carry out my plans. Everything is in place now."

"No."

Gideon shook his head. "I've wrested control from right under their noses! Aaron suspects me, but he'll never prove it before I get rid of him too."

Gideon moved the gun back to the base of Benjamin's skull. "I'll give you a clean shot, Feinan. I'll do that much for you, although you don't deserve it. Now, despair and die."

He pressed the gun further in, ready to fire—

"No!" Benjamin shouted, and at the same time swung up with his arm, turned, and pushed him off balance.

The gun went off. Benjamin slumped forward.

96

THE LOCK GAVE under the security card, and Aaron pushed the door open. Behind him was Etan, gun drawn as they ran into the room.

Gideon and Feinan were visible in the doorway to the office. Gideon startled when he saw them but had no time to do anything else before Aaron tackled him and pushed his face into the rug. Etan knelt on Gideon's neck, gun barrel resting on Gideon's cheek.

Feinan was still, no movement.

But—

Aaron looked carefully.

No blood.

97

BENJAMIN MOVED his hands and feet, determining that everything was working. He rolled over.

"You got him," he said to Aaron.

The chief of security nodded. "Let's get you ready for your transport."

Fifty minutes later Benjamin sat with Aaron in the time machine area, receiving his final briefing.

"This pod is smaller than the one you used before," Aaron said. "But it works pretty much the same. You need to go in, find Sara, and bring her back. The window closes in ten hours. I'm going to bring the pod back then, but it's unlikely you'll find her that quickly."

Benjamin nodded.

"If you stay, you'll need to get the supplies—food, tools, and clothing—out of the pod before it disappears. There's another transport window opening in sixty-two days. The machine will lose its calibration to your precise time, but when the window opens, we will transport a pod as close as we can make it. It should be bang on, within a few days of your time, not more. We'll keep the pod there exactly seventy-two hours and then pull it back. Make sure you and Sara are in that one."

Benjamin knit his eyebrows. "But, sir, the time machine was off by nine years. That's a lot of error introduced in the system."

"The time machine is quite reliable. We discovered a dropped trigger device from the spy, Seidel, that interfered with the timing of the machine. The situation has been fixed."

"So I just check every day for a pod to appear."

"Yes," Aaron said. "But there's one more thing."

Benjamin felt his heart sink.

"Sara. She may be difficult to locate because she doesn't have her transponder. I'm not sure how you'll overcome this unless you can find the crash site or you know where she might go. Remember, she may not be expecting a rescue."

"She doesn't have her transponder?"

Aaron shook his head. "She put it in with her note, in the information capsule. I don't know what she was thinking."

"You mean David's transponder?"

"No, Sara's," Aaron said.

Benjamin was confused. After he and Sara had moved the rock in the past, before Sara had gone back to the pod, she had given him her transponder for communication because his had still been lost. When Sara had taken the paraglider over the Qumran mountains, she'd had David's transponder with her, not her own. In fact, he had Sara's transponder with him right now. Yet, it had also been found in the capsule from the past. That meant—

Could it mean that he was destined to meet with Sara in the past, before she launched that capsule?

It must be.

Aaron looked at him closely. "Feinan, is there anything you want to tell me?"

Benjamin shook his head.

"All right then. Are you ready?"

"Yes, sir."

"Then let's go. I want to give you as much time as possible."

Benjamin put his hand in his pocket and touched the transponder again. Sara's transponder.

THE END

Point:

"And if Christ has not been raised, our preaching is useless and so is your faith. More than that, we are then found to be false witnesses about God, for we have testified about God that he raised Christ from the dead...If Christ has not been raised, your faith is futile; you are still in your sins."

Paul the Apostle
1 Corinthians 15: 14, 15, 17 (NIV)

Counter Point:

"We cannot use electric lights and radios, and, in the event of illness, avail ourselves of modern medical and clinical means and at the same time believe in the spirit and wonder world of the new Testament."

Rudolf Karl Bultmann
New Testament and Mythology and Other Basic Writings.
(Minneapolis, MN: Fortress Press, 1984): page 4

ACKNOWLEDGMENT

The list of historical facts on pages 324-325 was directly adapted from the writings of Dr. Gary Habermas (Habermas, Gary R. and Moreland, J.P. *Beyond Death.* Wheaton: Crossway Books, 1998, page 115. And others). Dr. Habermas has generously provided permission to allow this list to be included in *A Lever Long Enough.*

Printed in the United States
212911BV00001B/2/P

9 780981 899725